A Little Distillery in Nowgong

A Little Distillery in Nowgong

Ashok Mathur

Arsenal Pulp Press

Vancouver

THE LITTLE DISTILLERY OF NOWGONG
Copyright © 2009 by Ashok Mathur

ARSENAL PULP PRESS
Suite 200, 341 Water Street
Vancouver, BC
Canada V6B 1B8
arsenalpulp.com

The publisher gratefully acknowledges the support of the Canada Council for the Arts and the British Columbia Arts Council for its publishing program, and the Government of Canada through the Book Publishing Industry Development Program and the Government of British Columbia through the Book Publishing Tax Credit Program for its publishing activities.

This is a work of fiction. Any resemblance of characters to persons either living or deceased is purely coincidental.

Book design by Shyla Seller
Images courtesy of the author
Photograph of the author by Ray Chwartkowski

Printed and bound in Canada on FSC-certified paper

Library and Archives Canada Cataloguing in Publication

Mathur, Ashok
    A little distillery in Nowgong / Ashok Mathur.

ISBN 978-1-55152-258-6

    I. Title.

PS8576.A8286L58 2009   C813'.54   C2009-903653-3

for P.P.

Part One

Jamshed

All good stories begin with a birth

Jamshed takes a deep breath and feels the unfamiliar substance fill his nostrils, wave down his breathing pipes, and settle gaseously in his wet lungs. Not in the least bit fluid, the substance must be expelled, immediately and predictably, and Jamshed does this with a noise that surprises even him, a cry that is at once too loud for the occasion and not quite loud enough for the offence. What a few moments ago would have emerged from his mouth as a burble comes forth fully sounded now, travelling at a wavelength that surpasses that which he has become used to. Exhaling, he realizes, with or without sound effects, will be much easier this way. Not the comfortable, easy equilibrium of gentle external pressure on his chest cavity gracefully letting the breath from him, but a surprisingly light movement performed from somewhere beneath his diaphragm that can veritably shoot his breath farther from his body than he has ever experienced. Indeed, instead of his liquid exhalations cocooning around him, his gaseous expulsion is gone from his perimeter, nowhere to be felt. In its place is the feeling of death, clammy and rough, and it is as if the world itself, the world outside of the known world anyway, has breathed its worst back on Jamshed. There is no way he should have done this, no way at all. He was fine just a moment before, and he should have resisted that unfortunate impulse that led him to this ugly, cold, and unforgivingly bright space. All this Jamshed is experiencing, loathing the world, so he is genuinely surprised when his next breath, still harsh and bitter on his lungs, is not as shockingly painful as the first. Oh yes, he still expels it in short order with the best little warrior cry his lungs can muster, but this time he finds he can modulate the tone and timbre of his noises by shaping his mouth this way and that, and it is not a displeasing experience. From a world of full containment to a world of such choices, opportunities! All right, so it comes with a load of discomfort, but what the hell. By the time little Jamshed inhales his third breath of air, he has almost forgotten what it was like to breathe fluid, and he has convinced himself that it was not inevitable that he arrived at this place (for he could have resisted, fought back, put down roots, decided to stay put), but an act of will. This will go down in history as Jamshed's first conscious act. To be born instead of being not-born.

"He has a set of lungs that show his health," says the midwife, an elderly Parsi lady with flaring nostrils. "A crying baby is a healthy baby," she says to the parents, neither of whom are listening to her.

"He will be a true leader," thinks his father, "a source of purity and truth, a man among men who will lead his people from the darkness to the light. Look at his eyes, so clear, even as he wrinkles up his entire face to bellow and complain! Those eyes will see past any horizon, and the people will see his eyes, and it will be like looking onto *asha*, the very purity of his people. This boy, this man, this son of mine will be a *dastur* like me, no question about it, and the people will say the Khargat family are the spiritual centre of Surat."

"He is finally out of me," thinks his mother, "and about time." Nine months, two weeks, and three days, and this her first, which everyone said would be coming quickly, yes, that's what they said when she came to her own mother, tearily, "I am with child, and so early on in my marriage; why couldn't this wait?"

"Don't worry, Soona," her mother had said, "you are four months along and already you are showing like six (and besides, what's all this about early in married life? It's been five years, hasn't it, or is it six?) Unless you're carrying twins, this one will be a bigheaded one who will pop out in eight months, mark my words, only another four months, that's sixteen weeks, and out he comes." Soona had not appeared on her mother's doorstep to complain; rather, she had come along with her husband for her *panchmasyu* ceremony, to commemorate the end of her fourth month of pregnancy. She dutifully accepted the attention paid to her, the ritualistic placing of vermillion paste on her forehead, the sprinkling of coconut-scented rose water, and was actually feeling quite fine until she and her mother were sitting on the veranda together and Soona broke into tears. At first, her mother's dismissive comments actually gave Soona some comfort. At first. But at eight months to the day, she had gone to her mother and said, "What of this then, eight months you said, and here it is, and the baby has not dropped as you said, there is no water breaking on the ground."

"Give it time," her mother had said, "it will be a week more, maybe two, but make no doubt, this baby will be born before the month is out, and we are already midmonth, are we not? You will see—and we have not yet performed the *agharni*; that should have happened last month, or we can do that in the ninth month, but mark my words, you will not have a ninth month." Then, again, at eight months and three weeks Soona returned to her mother and said nothing, just pointed at her belly and turned the same gesturing hand palm upward, a question mark in any language. "Well," her mother had said, "a baby's natural path is almost nine months, you shouldn't complain; at nine months it will be big and healthy, just think of the scrawny boy you would have birthed three weeks ago, you should be happy to keep him inside, even it means you need assistance to go from sitting to standing. And besides, we can do the *agharni* now, and we will all be pleased." And then last week she had returned to her mother a final time. "The baby will not leave me.

You must do something. You must give me something."

"Like what?" her mother asked. "Do I look like a woman who gives medical advice? I studied maths at school, and I keep your father's accounts, but look here, as soon as he gets the slightest belly ache, off I send him to the doctor. Do I try to treat him at home? Am I a nurse that I should do this? Go home, put your feet up, breathe deeply."

Soona had looked at her mother and said simply, "The baby will not be born, and by this time you said I'd be happily nursing away. I think I should not believe you in matters involving my family." But the next week, finally, with a little funny sensation she thought was a result of the pickle she had eaten before bedtime, Soona awoke at 3:23 a.m., took a breath, and said to her husband, "Yes, now it is ready." In short order, the midwife had arrived and busied herself with midwifery things, and the labour was easy at first, but that was because, Soona was to find out later, the labour had not begun in earnest. Not in the first two hours, not the first six. Only when the morning light was well upon them did the pains start—and did they last; all through the morning, the midday, well into the evening as the light faded. And into the night. It was fully two in the morning when the midwife told her that the baby would be born soon, although she was lying to keep her from asking when the baby would be born. It was not until 3:29 a.m. (a full day and six minutes past the first warning signs) that Jamshed's crown appeared. All too late and about time.

And so Jamshed was born in the town of Surat on the west coast of India. Nine months, two weeks, and three days earlier, a midforties dastur looked fondly at his wife of five years. Although very much in love, they did not make love all that often, not for any particular reason, just that it didn't occur to them to do so, neither of them being especially needy in that area of human interaction. But at that moment, the dastur looked at his wife and reached out to touch her cheek. She looked back at him with love, although with some alarm since it was early afternoon in the middle of the summer and surely too hot to do anything but laze about in the shade until the late afternoon when it cooled ever so slightly and one could return to the work at hand—which was, of course, precisely the reason her husband was at home, waiting for the reduced heat of the evening when he could return to his duties. So it surprised even him that he reached out and stroked his wife's cheek. And, as such things go, one thing led to another, and at the end of it all they lay side by side, perspiring far more profusely than might seem warranted under the circumstances. Jamshed's mother-to-be lay on her side, her feet propped up on a pillow to keep her feet cool (who knows if that up-propping was enough to convince an overheated spermatozoa that it might as well continue on its journey since it was, after all, downhill, and without which effort an egg might not have been rudely awakened and little Jamshed never, eventually, born), and she thought of how this had been pleasant but would have been more so if it had happened when the sun wasn't so hot. But they had been married for five years without so much as a thought of pregnancy, so there was no need to entertain such thoughts right now, was there? At least that's what Soona thought at the time and continued to think for two months and then beyond that, even though by then it had become obvious that either she was pregnant or something was seriously wrong, but even then …

And then, nine months, two weeks, and three days later, Jamshed was born, and another nine months, two weeks, and three days later, after Jamshed's birth, there was much celebrating in Surat as the townsfolk bid goodbye to 1899 and welcomed in the turn of the century, the turn into the twentieth century. And all this was to make a profound difference to the Khargat family and, of course, to me, but that in itself is a story so strange that it will take some time to come around to it. So I shall just have to be patient.

After Jamshed was born, he and Soona were immediately sequestered in a tiny room toward the back of the house, a room normally reserved for having tea in the middle of a summer day's heat. In one corner of the room a *divo* was lit, and it was in that room that mother and child happily remained for six days, since it was the coolest room in the house, and finally gave Soona some privacy. On the sixth evening, of course, her mother arrived to perform the *chatthi*, purifying both Soona and the room, and bringing with her a set of new clothes that her grandson would wear to his first trip to the *agiary*.

After Soona's mother had left, Jamshed's father proudly strutted into the room, produced a piece of fine writing paper, a quill he had borrowed from his friend Rustom (a customs official and thus a fine writer), and a pot of red ink. "When Vehmai arrives," pronounced Beramshah, "he will find before him such a beautiful boy that he will write only the finest destiny for the child." Then, declaring himself a man after all, and man enough to produce a male heir, "I have decided on his name," said Beramshah Khargat.

"Whose name?" asked Soona, looking fondly at her newborn.

"Whose name? Whose name? Why, his name, the little fellow here, my son. I have decided on his name."

Soona looked up disinterestedly, smiled Mona-Lisa-ly, and said, "But he already has a name."

Beramshah sputtered. "But I have not yet named him!"

Soona smiled in response. "Fine, then let us name him. We can decide on this together, can we not?"

"But I have a name."

"Indeed you do, and it is a fine name for a leader such as you, but our son should have a name that distinguishes himself."

"That's not what I mean—I mean, I have decided on a name for my boy."

"Is it Ferozsha?"

"Ferozsha? Ferozsha! Certainly not. That is a girl's name, and my son is—he is my son and deserves a man's name."

"Fine, fine, that he shall have then. A strong man's name. Aha: Sir John Malcolm, do you remember him? Governor of Bombay, a fine man and strong supporter of us Parsis. We shall call him Malcolm."

"Malcolm? Malcolm! No, never! He should have a good Parsi name, a name that will recall his family's history, his legacy. This boy will grow to be an outstanding man, my dear, and he will follow in his father's footsteps. He will be a great dastur, mark my words, and his name should befit someone of this stature."

"Sounds a bit conceited, does it not? Yes, he will be a fine young man, whatever path he chooses, but let's not give your heir airs before his time. Let us be careful in choosing a name."

"But we are not choosing. I have chosen, is that not clear?"

"Abundantly. But life is a compromise. So I will agree to compromise as well. You had a name picked out, did you say?"

"I have a name picked out, indeed."

"And I have a name picked out too. Oh dear. With all the names around, it's unlikely that it's the same name, I suppose."

"That doesn't matter! He has a name. I am his father and I have decreed."

"Oh, decrees and degrees, I'm tired of all that. What did we just say about compromise?"

"Compromise?"

"Indeed. Let us do our son justice. You throw out your name and I shall discard mine."

"Discard a perfectly good name, one that my son was born into?"

"Yes, that's a sacrifice I, as only a mother can, will make."

"You will make?"

"Yes, I discard my name for my son; you throw out your name for my son."

"My son."

"Indeed."

"And?"

"And we shall choose an entirely new name for him."

"Which is?"

"Jamshed."

"Jamshed?"

"Yes, wonderful. See what good a compromise does a body?"

"But—but what was the name you had originally chosen?"

"Shush! It's bad luck to utter a name that was once chosen and is now no longer!"

"But—"

"But nothing. From this day forth, neither of us will utter our previously chosen names for little Jamshed ever again. Indeed, we must put those names out of mind entirely, for they can only come back to hurt him."

"Hurt him?"

"Yes, you wouldn't want to do anything to harm a little hair on little Jamshed's head, would you now?"

"No, no, of course not."

"Then it is settled."

"But—Jamshed—wasn't Jamshed your father's name?"

"Ah yes, happy coincidence. Who would have guessed? You see, compromises can bring good things to bear."

"I suppose so."
"Yes, indeed."

Postnatal cares in the world

I should say from the start that I do not know all that much about being born, leastwise not firsthand. It may be true that taxation and deceasing are the only certainties in life, but that all comes after a life begins is a given, so they say, although who it is given to is an entirely different matter. But there I go again, making things more complicated than they need be. Suffice to say, for now, this is what I know: babies gurgle, sputter, and stare, not necessarily in that order, but necessarily. And little Jamshed was no exception, gurgling when delighted or gaseous or distraught, sputtering when ecstatic or despairing or constipated. And staring when a person or object was particularly inspiring. And oh, how babies can stare. Some say it's no more than the unfocussed gaze of a new body trying to find stability. Others say light and colour catch the baby's attention. Some insist it's an act of recognition, of familiarity, or perhaps of downright determined communication. Whatever the case, little Jamshed stared. He stared at mama, he stared at papa, he stared at the various visitors and comers-and-goers during the first few weeks of his life. He stared at red objects, at blue ones and green ones, at any solid-colour object, and a few that were striped or speckled as well. He would have outstared a cat, if they'd had one. And, as his caretakers noticed, he had a different stare for each occasion.

"Look, he's looking at his mummy."

"Look, he's looking at the window."

"Look, he's looking at—what is he looking at there? Right beside him, see? He's looking at, at something."

Indeed, baby Jamshed, just two weeks old, developed a certain distinctive stare in that he appeared to focus, always to his right, and always to a distance of three feet, three inches, on some invisible entity. This was not, clearly, an unfocussed gaze, for it would come upon him with what appeared to be great urgency, the sort of glance that a baby makes when attentive to a sound, a loud sound, or a call of his name. Certainly some will say that a child this young can barely respond to a mother's voice, let alone an absent calling of his name, but this is where baby Jamshed differed. Oh, his little head would seem to say, gesturing about wildly, then fixing to the right and out to thirty-nine inches away. And there he would be transfixed, sometimes for several seconds, sometimes for minutes on end, the longest recorded time (for his mother had little else to do of interest, during those first few weeks, than watch the clock and her baby) of two and a half minutes exactly. After which Jamshed would, inevitably, either gurgle or sputter, and immediately thereafter break off his gaze.

"Whatever is he looking at?" asked his great-aunt, who everyone knew as Tata, even though her family name was also Khargat (although there had been rumours that, in her youth, this great-aunt had travelled to Bombay and taken up with a young gentleman, but that was all talk). "He is looking at somebody, that much is sure," she said one day.

"That is nonsense," said Jamshed's father. "If there was someone there, do you not think we would all see him?"

"Good nephew," said Tata, "it is a very good thing you became a dastur and not a politician, because while you are very good at guiding people on principle, you have no fantasy life, do you?"

"And why would a politician need a fantasy life?" asked Jamshed's father earnestly.

"Ah," replied Tata, "because politicians must imagine what life would be like after they are elected, and then again after they are elected out. They must think of all the options and then choose the one most pleasing, even if it is one that is not evident."

"Nor visible?"

"Nor visible."

And so it continued, little Jamshed growing into his first year with a propensity for staring off to his right, listening to imagined conversations and, on occasion, smiling in response. It became so that adults would cease talking to Jamshed once the baby's attention was fixed on the invisible source, a cessation that was the result of a realization that, when Jamshed stared right, no amount of coaxing or coddling could bring him back until he was good and ready. It became such a common occurrence, and so familiar to the community in Surat, that Parsis started using the expression "going right" to mean that someone was lost to the world, had stopped paying attention to a conversation, or was in a state of preoccupation:

"Oh, I was talking to Papa-ji yesterday and in the middle of it there he was, going right, can you imagine; it's so hard to talk to him sometimes."

Or, "That girl there, she is a nice one to look at, but you can tell she has tendency for going right; however will her family marry off one like that?"

Or, "*Arra*, I cannot concentrate now, something is terribly wrong, as if I have gone right for no good reason whatsoever."

And so it was that a pre-school Parsi boy's peculiar habit entered not just into the consciousness but the vernacular, the very vocabulary, of an entire community. And there would be little to be made of that, perhaps, had not such a combination of language and action created such a furor just a few years hence. I suppose for that I am partly to blame, but I do refuse to take full responsibility for this, truly, because choices are to be had and to be made. Ipso facto, it's not all about me, even though I may sound off so sometimes. No, the players need to take some of that on for themselves, I do believe; and for stories to be made, things have to not just happen, but happen in a certain concatenating fashion. Otherwise, well, there is no otherwise. Not one I can imagine, anyway.

Going right

By the time Jamshed was four and ready to head off to primary school, he was already well-known in the community for being the little boy who goes right. If it had been just a baby thing, the sort of inexplicable baby action that babies did for no good reason, that would have been one thing. If it had been something that toddler Jamshed did until he was terribly two or tantalizingly three, that would have been all right, too. But while this going-right thing was far less embarrassing (in some ways) than wetting the bed or nervous vomiting, it was distinctive and distracting and, whatever else it did, it gave Jamshed a name for himself. It carried forth, this going-right did, until Jamshed started school (and then far beyond, but that is yet to come), and so spectacular an action was this, that it was at once a thrill and a threat to have young Jamshed as your student, particularly if you were one Percy Khargat (no relation) and this was only your second year of teaching.

Percy was an unassuming young man, stick-like in build and sparrow-like in character, possessing that annoying habit that such people have of pushing up on the bridge of his spectacles at least once every minute and thrice that often when nervous, which was more often than not, thereby making the glasses-up-pushing rather more regular than once per minute for most of his waking life. Now, unlike most Parsis of the day, who were not exactly making an exodus from the city of Surat for Bombay, but were certainly leaving in more than just dribbles, Percy had been born and raised in Bombay but chose to return to Surat (the city where his parents, grandparents, and great-grandparents had lived) to teach. And while most young men in the Parsi community who became teachers decided to teach at the upper levels, Percy told himself early on that the most important education a Parsi child would ever have was that first year in school. Everything a child took with him through his life, Percy would tell his friends over tea, could be traced back to that first year, and not just the first year, but the first month, perhaps even the first day of school. What influence a young teacher could have over these barely sentient minds—think of it! After five years of teaching, with four classes per day, and twenty-five students in each class, that was five hundred new faces, five hundred new minds, and each and every one of them owing their entire future to what primary teacher Percy did in that first year, that first month, that first day. And so it was that Jamshed Khargat (no relation, other than being a member of the Khargat family whose numbers had obviously extended beyond Surat to Bombay and beyond) began school one fine day in 1903.

"My name," said Percy Khargat to the trembling assortment of four and five year olds, "is Percy Khargat," and he pushed his glasses up his nose with vigour and turned to write his name on the blackboard with clear and distinctive strokes. "This is how my name is spelled. By the end of your first month here with me, you too shall be able to write your name on the blackboard. Do not worry. I am here to teach you. If you listen to me well, as you do your parents, you will learn a great deal, and, what is more, you will learn to love learning! That is my job as a teacher, to teach. And your job, as young as you are, as students, is to mind me and to learn. Nothing more but, my young students, nothing less."

And then that fatal moment, for Percy looked up just as Jamshed did the unfathomable, because, as eager as he was to learn, and as much as he already liked his teacher, nothing could prevent young Jamshed, at that very moment, from going right. Percy Khargat stared at the boy in disbelief, and his classmates giggled,

23

at the incredulous sight to begin with, then at the growing awareness that this was the first moment of trouble in their young school
lives. Seconds passed with no word from anyone. Classmate giggles
subsided, but the ensuing silence gave way to more giggles of a more
urgent nature, every ten seconds or so. Yes, a full minute passed this
way, as Percy Khargat watched Jamshed Khargat with such studied
concern that the teacher forgot his own desperate need to push his
glasses farther up his nose. The giggles were now nonexistent, and
the children stared at Jamshed nervously, feeling, perhaps, that if
they emulated their teacher they were less likely to experience his
wrath.

None of this, of course, had any effect on the going-right Jamshed, who was, as per usual, lost to the world, at least to any world
outside his own making. And when it became apparent (in the third
minute) that this was to be one of Jamshed's longer going-right
moments, it was then that Percy felt he had to speak. The teacher
cleared his throat. As he swallowed, he remembered to push those
spectacles back where they belonged and felt most comfortable.
Then: "Mister ... Jamshed ... Khargat." (Pause, no reaction, then
louder.) "Young SIR!" And still not a bat of an eyelid from Jamshed.

Percy, a teacher given to raising his voice but rarely in bouts of
anger, did what any good teacher would do at that moment, which
was to reach for the blackboard and find, hanging on its own little
nail as it had for the past two years, the yard-long ruler, useful for
classroom measurements, occasional pointing to alphabets and pic-
tures, and, of course, for violence. Percy cleared his throat again,
grasped the ruler in his right hand, steadied his stance, and brought
the ruler down as hard as possible on his own desk. Jamshed's was
the fourth seat in the middle row (directly in front of the teacher's
desk), and in front of him sat three children, a boy and two girls.
One of the girls, Farah Merchant, sat in the very front seat of the

middle row (obedient to her mother's injunction to get to school early on the first day of class and go immediately to the seat that was closest to the teacher, for as important as religion was to Parsi children, so too was education, and as a respected dastur was to the Parsi's continued faith, so was the child's first teacher to her lifelong education, and this was a message not lost on little Farah, who had to squeeze by the pimply faced Wadia boy to get that prized seat). The choosing of this seat, however, was to be her undoing, little Farah would tell her younger sisters in years to come as she urged her siblings to find the classroom seat as far away from the teacher as possible, for as important as it is for Parsis to be close to god, and inasmuch as a first teacher is an emissary of a child's whole educational path, sometimes, she would tell her sisters, the light of truth is best beheld from a distance. As the ruler came down on Percy Khargat's table, Farah was doing what the rest of her classmates were doing, which was to stare incredulously at the going-right Jamshed, still lost in that odd world of his. But, because Jamshed's seat was three directly behind Farah's, requiring her to turn an entire 180 degrees to observe this childhood phenom, Farah had her back to the downswinging ruler. So when it smacked the table, other children saw this coming, directly or peripherally, depending on how they triangulated between themselves, the teacher's desk, and Jamshed. But Farah had not a clue that the loudest noise of her life was about to unleash a torrent of urine straight into her undergarments with such force that there was actually a tiny backsplash when the pee hit the seat and spurted out to the left and to the right of her, marking the trousers and dress of the young boy and girl in the seats on either side of her (they, too, having being implored by their parents to get a front-row view of the teacher).

This explosion of child's urine had a deleterious effect on Percy, particularly so since the teacher had an unnatural aversion to all bodily fluids, especially those egressing from children. At twenty-seven years of age, Percy was not yet married, and although he had yet to break the news to his parents, he had no intention of getting married, since the only logical purpose would be to have children, beings whom he deemed, in and of themselves, to be corporeal effluent, at least at the baby stage. Not that he thought children *per se* to be the work of Ahriman, but it couldn't hurt to keep himself clear, at least in a direct visceral fashion, from the contamination and defilement that go hand-in-hand with children's bodies. Perhaps that was why Percy had decided to become a teacher, to influence young minds: If he were never to have heirs of his own, why not, at the very least, become a surrogate father to a classroom of four- and five-year-olds, when they were at the most impressionable age; possessing language skills, however rudimentary, and fairly good control of involuntary bodily functions? Such was the argument in his mind up to and including the moment when, in an attempt to discipline the errant Jamshed, he had levelled his teacher's ruler on his teacher's desk; beyond that moment, however, he was forever disabused of the notion that primary school children could wilfully control their nether regions when they were shocked or scared (or, as he was to find out later, mirthful, anxious, desperate, bored, inattentive, tired, over-exercised, under-slept, or just plain and simply malicious). But perhaps the most shocking thing about this entire tableau was not that Percy's nose, wrinkling in disgust, managed to push his glasses up all by itself, nor that little Farah, after a moment of utter disbelief, erupted into a surprising variety and pitch of mournful wails (joined, chorus-like, first by the two neighbours she had pissed on, then, by algorithmic succession, pupils who were closest, middling, and farthest from the urine-splashing event), but that Jamshed Khargat might just as well have been in another classroom, school, city, or country for all that he responded to this desperate set of affairs. He was going right for nigh on three minutes and nothing, not a boom-voiced teacher, a wood-ruler-through-air whoosh culminating in a terrific smack on a wooden desk, not the displeasing squirt and splash triggering a great caterwauling of children, indeed, nothing could break him from his right-going reverie. So, with children crying and screaming, Percy Khargat brandishing his ruler high in the air again as he swallowed repeatedly and began sweating from glands he didn't know he had, Jamshed continued to go right as the door flew open and Mrs Gloria Hansen, principal of the Surat District Primary School #7, squeezed her considerable form into the room. All the children stopped crying instantaneously for three very long seconds, then renewed and redoubled their efforts before Mrs Hansen could utter her patented phrase, "Now then, what have we here?"

It was some time before Percy could calm his class down to the point where the two adults could talk without shouting (his efforts hindered by his lack of awareness that he still brandished the ruler like a Gurkha's sabre as he madly gesticulated at his young charges, renewing their fright and screaming until he dropped the ruler, which clattered to the cement floor and lay there for the rest of the morning). "We have," began Percy, "a situation here," and he bubbled and frothed a bit at the mouth as he pointed, more with his blowfish eyes than any other part of his body, toward Jamshed, who, sitting at his desk, chose this moment to break away from his precipitous going-right motion to look squarely at, first, Percy Khargat, then Gloria Hansen.

"What on earth, young man," asked Mrs Hansen sternly, "was going on here?"

"Yes, yes," added Percy, "what was going on, tell me, *tell* me, what is it?"

"Yes?" queried Jamshed, so clearly oblivious to the previous go-ings-on that he was not the slightest bit scared or ashamed.

"You were," sputtered Percy, "you were staring off in that direction, and I, the ruler, she, that is, that is, what, who, were you staring at?" And with that, he pointed at exactly the place, three feet, three inches from Jamshed's nose, where Jamshed had, until just recently, been focussed.

"Indeed, young man," broke in Mrs Hansen, "your first day at school, and already breaking the law, is that it?"

"No, ma'am," said Jamshed, shaking his head vigorously and wondering what this would mean at home. "No, I was—"

"You were what?" insisted Percy, now exercising authority that he hoped Mrs Hansen would see as responsible and very mature.

"I was," said Jamshed, "I was only listening."

"Listening? Listening! To whom, an invisible girlfriend? An imaginary brother? A fantasy fairy?" Percy Khargat was in full swing now, hoping this last wave of scorn would help drive Mrs Hansen out of his classroom.

"No, sir, Mr Khargat," said Jamshed. "No, sir, no. I was listening to my grandchild."

Go forth and intermingle

The ceiling fan is wooden with brass tips, and it rotates just fast enough so the casual observer can make out each blade, not in exact detail, but enough so that each blade is distinct from the next. Any faster and the blades would blur into each other and, indeed, the fan might then be performing up to its teleological good, for at the current speed, apart from allowing bored sets of eyes to discern its wooden detail, the fan does little more than circulate risen warm air back from whence it came, that is, toward the floor, without even close to the desirous effect of providing a cooling breeze.

This is exactly what Beramshah is thinking as he watches the blades rotate, that all the fan is succeeding in doing, miraculously, is to make the room hotter than it would be were the fan to be shut off entirely. Beramshah is sitting in a creaky wooden chair, supposedly the teacher's chair, his back straight and posture perfect except for his head, which tilts upward and wonders at the fan. Directly in front of Beramshah is a large mahogany desk that has seen better days, and were Beramshah to examine this desk closely, he would notice, along with various scratches and scars from years gone by and the occasional carved initials and dates inscribed under the lip of the desk, that the most recent abrasion was a long, faint mark running diagonally across the surface of the desk, approximately an inch wide and almost as long as a teacher's ruler. On the other side of this desk, squeezed uncomfortably into a desk used to holding the bodies of five-year-old boys and girls, sits Soona. She has been sitting awkwardly like this for five minutes, passing the time by watching her husband watch the ceiling fan and looking around the classroom to take note of all the items her son will observe over the course of his first year of school—that is, of course, if the school allows him to stay and does not expel him for the very reason that she and her husband are now in Jamshed's classroom, waiting for Jamshed's teacher to return with two chairs and the school principal. Soona squirms in the tiny seat and wonders how children Jamshed's age can possibly learn their lessons in this environment. There is one small window on the east wall, looking out on to the school compound. On the west wall are a number of maps of the region and of India and of the British Commonwealth. Above the blackboard, which is on the north wall, are two portraits, one of Zoroaster and the other of Queen Victoria. Both are realistic paintings, but the one of the prophet is done in lighter tones with more highlights and a familiar halo effect around his head, while the monarch looks stoic and is dressed in dark colours, even the crown on her head painted in sombre tones. Soona wonders why the portrait of the Queen is slightly larger than that of the prophet, wonders if there is any significance to the difference in the colour of the frames (the monarch's gold versus the prophet's black) and is thus engaged in that internal debate when Percy Khargat kicks open the door and penguin-walks in, carrying a large wooden chair under each arm, resting them on his hips. Behind him enters Gloria Hansen, looking very much the part of Queen Victoria, thinks Soona, as the principal waits for Percy to place her chair at an appropriate equidistance between Soona, Beramshah, and the mahogany desk. As he does this, Mrs Hansen sits slowly and with great grace while Percy hurriedly places his chair adjacent to Mrs Hansen's and plops himself down.

"I have summoned you, as you know," begins Mrs Hansen, "because of a concern we have with your young Jamshed."

"Yes, yes," interrupts Percy, "we have a great concern." Mrs Hansen glares over at Percy to indicate that her *we* did not really include the teacher.

"As I was saying, the concern we have with young Jamshed is one of reality versus fantasy." She fixes her gaze on Beramshah. "Mr Khargat, I am well aware that you are an extremely well-respected dastur within your Parsi community—all the more important that we address this concern now and nip it in the bud. I believe a man of your stature will be equally concerned with the actions of his son."

"Mrs Hansen," Beramshah begins, "we greatly appreciate your concern, and you must rest assured that we will talk to Jamshed about this."

"Mr Khargat, I am not sure at this stage if a parental talking-to will be sufficient. Your son's behaviour is, shall I say, disruptive and not befitting this school. Do I make myself clear, Mr Khargat?"

"What Mrs Hansen is saying," says Percy, unable to contain himself further, "is that we think it might be best if Jamshed were to be placed in a different school, entirely for his benefit, of course."

"A different school?" Soona is now unable to contain herself, and she is surprised her voice sounds so large, coming as it does from behind such a tiny desk. "Percy, you know very well that there is no other school for Jamshed in Surat. Oh, certainly there are other schools, but none where he can have a good Parsi education and—"

"And a good English education at the same time," Mrs Hansen says, finishing Soona's sentence for her. "Indeed, you are correct. When I came here, as you know, it was my intention to provide schooling for the small number of English students being raised in Surat. And, as you know, after the first year, which was only three years ago now, we decided to admit Parsi children as well. Indeed, your people are a fine people, and you have leaders such as your good husband to thank for that, Mrs Khargat. You Parsis are well-liked by us English, I think you know that, and it was for that reason I felt that Parsi and English children might be able to learn together. I must say that I still believe that is a possibility."

"Then perhaps we can talk to Jamshed and come to an arrangement," says Beramshah.

"Ah, I do not believe that is possible at this time. You see, it is one thing to have the intermingling of Parsi beliefs and Christian beliefs. We are, of course, both believers in one god, are we not? It is yet another thing, and I am sure you must agree with me, Mrs Khargat, Mr Khargat, for these eager young minds to be, ah, infected with talk of supernatural conversations with ancestors and the like."

"Descendants, actually," says Soona under her breath but loud enough for all to hear.

"Yes, technically that is correct, descendants. I believe that is the story Jamshed gave to us, talking to future offspring—but where he gets these ideas, I can only imagine. The Hindus believe in all this talking to spirits rubbish, I understand, but civilized people—and I think I can safely say that Parsis and Christians might be considered among the civilized—do no such thing. In fact, such fantasies are, I would suggest, the manifestation of a primitive mind."

"A primitive mind?" Soona glares at Mrs Hansen, then looks over at her husband. Beramshah has the unique ability to shut down his face so that no emotions can be read across his expression, and it is such a face he now shows to Mrs Hansen, Percy Khargat, and his wife.

"I believe I have said quite enough." Mrs Hansen stands to leave and gestures to both men to remain sitting, though neither shows any intention of rising until she does so. "I must take my leave of you, and I wish you all the very best for poor Jamshed. Percy, I believe you have other matters you wish to pursue with the Khargats. Good day, Mr Khargat, Mrs Khargat." And with a regal turn of her head, she is gone.

Beramshah and Soona watch her leave, then turn their attention to Percy. The young teacher clears his throat and begins to speak.

"Mr Khargat, Mrs Khargat, you have to understand that this is not just a matter of Jamshed. With respect, sir," he says looking at Beramshah, "this is quite a larger matter of concern to the Parsis in general."

Beramshah smiles at Percy, though it is not a smile that delivers any goodwill. "And how is that, Percy?"

"Uh, Dastur-ji, we Parsis are at a turning point in our relationship to the world around us. We are at once too isolated and too intermingled. I returned from Bombay specifically to teach at this school, for I believe Parsi children must have a good Parsi education, but in the context of a British school system. That is where I believe our isolation must end. But we must be equally cautious of how much and in what way we intermingle. Mrs Hansen, all she sees is that a Parsi boy, your Jamshed, may put mystic thoughts into the heads of the English pupils. But my concern is that this intermingling does not stop there."

"Now you have truly lost me," says Soona. "Who is intermingling with whom? And what does it matter?"

"Yes, well, that is my concern too. Who is intermingling with whom. In this case, we have Jamshed claiming to talk to his grandchild. Where did he learn this? I say this with great respect, Dastur-ji, for I know he did not learn this at home, but yet he learned this. From his playmates, perhaps? From the talk when he accompanies his *ayah* to the fish market? Who knows. We only know that he is influenced by someone. Parsis do not talk to their unborn grandchildren, I am sure you must agree. We do not reincarnate, now do we?"

"You mentioned the problem of intermingling, Percy," says Beramshah impatiently. "Like my wife, I do not see how this has anything to do with anything beyond a child's imagination. We should be grateful that the child has an active mind, should we not?"

"Perhaps, perhaps, Dastur-ji. But my question is, where does this stop? A Parsi boy not five years old is adopting the customs and beliefs of the polytheistic Hindus? Our community runs the risk of falling apart. You are aware of what happened in Bombay last year with Rana-ji Dhadabhoy Tata, are you not?"

Beramshah looks aghast. "What happened with Tata in Bombay and what happens with my son here in Surat are two different things. I am surprised at you, Percy, surprised and disappointed."

Percy sighs and pushes his glasses up on his nose fiercely and forcefully so that the lenses appear to almost touch his eyeballs. "I am sorry, Dastur-ji, I do not wish to disappoint you. But I have a task, as a teacher, and as a man who wants to see the Parsis flourish. What happens in Surat affects what happens in Bombay. Already my friends in Bombay, they tell me they are hearing rumours of a young boy here who talks to—well, you understand how word gets around."

"I do indeed," says Beramshah. He looks at Soona. "Perhaps it is time we say goodbye to small-minded ideas here and move to Bombay." Both Soona and Percy look at Beramshah in amazement.

"Dastur-ji, I did not mean for you to—"

"I know perfectly well what you did and did not mean. And I too mean what I say."

Soona reaches forward and, uncharacteristically, touches her husband's wrist. "Perhaps there is another way for us to resolve this."

"Yes, Dastur-ji, Mrs Khargat is right. There is no need to be hasty."

"No, this is not a decision made in haste," says Beramshah. "I have taken advice on this, to be sure."

"Advice?"

"Certainly." And Beramshah rises. "I have heard from my son that it is time to move to Bombay. And I have it on very good authority that my son has heard this from my great-grandchild, a

Parsi who will be known throughout the land!"

It is several minutes after Beramshah and Soona have left the school before either of them speaks. Finally, it is Soona who breaks the silence. "Well, that went well, I must say."

"I have had enough," says Beramshah, not looking at her.

"That's it? No argument, no fight, we will just go south to live in Bombay? What is so special in Bombay anyway that this will not happen there?"

"You heard Percy. He is worried that intermingling will be the death of the Parsis. Well, so be it then, if it's good enough for Tata-ji, then it should be good enough for us."

"So Tata can bring back a French prostitute and call her his wife and then have her *navjote* done and claim she is a fine Parsi wife— that is somehow similar to Jamshed making up stories? And what of this Tata fellow, anyway? How can what he does hundreds of miles away make us have to remove Jamshed from his first year of school?"

Beramshah stops walking. The school is only a ten-minute walk from their home, through the market, and it is there they have stopped, in front of a silk merchant who recognizes Soona and beckons to her—new material has just arrived, and it would be perfect for her, absolutely perfect. Soona ignores the merchant and looks at her husband. "Tell me then, do you decide that we should move to Bombay for this Tata fellow, or for you, or for me?"

Beramshah smiles at Soona and takes a deep breath. "More than 3,000 Parsis have signed a petition and presented this to the Panchayat, all because of what Tata-ji has done. Here, there might as well be a petition by this English teacher lady and by Percy (who does not deserve the Khargat name, I shall tell you that now), a petition signed by only two people, but that is enough to see our Jamshed ousted from his education. It is not right, Soona. If this is our history and our custom, perhaps it is time to re-examine that custom and jettison all that is holding us back."

Soona smiles back at him. "Once again, you have surprised me. For a man with no imagination, you have produced not only a son with an overactive one, but you yourself sometimes show you can see into the future! But let me ask you this one thing. If Jamshed grows up and goes to France to find himself a bride, or if he does not become a dastur like you and your father, perhaps by choosing to chase after his grandchild instead, if that happens, will you still think like you do? If that happens, if Jamshed turns his back on his faith, what then?"

"You asked me if we were moving to Bombay for Tata or you or me. The truth is, we will move to Bombay for Jamshed. And as for your last question, I can only answer that with an assurance. Jamshed will never do any of those things, for he is my son and he is your son, and he knows which way duty lies."

Going south

Beramshah has called a family meeting. He does not call it this, for the truth is the people in attendance are a hodgepodge of relatives, friends, and other acquaintances in the Parsi community. There are nine people in the room, including his brother, Adi, a learned young man who has made a name for himself as a census taker and hence a writer; his sister, Ferozha, probably the most intelligent person in the Khargat family but, in spite or perhaps because of this, perpetually bored with her life and all that occurs around her; Bhika and Dinshaw Bhownagree, a constantly bickering couple whom everyone agreed epitomized Parsi marriage, she a fiery anti-imperialist communist who lived and breathed the expulsion of the British, and he a cotton merchant who listened patiently to his wife, nodding occasionally, while calculating silently the amount of money he was making from ongoing British rule; Soona and her mother, both taking turns fussing with Jamshed's collar; a very ancient dastur named Kaikhasru Cama, known affectionately by the shorthand name of KaCa, a wizened and wise man with a penchant for falling asleep in the middle of his own sentences; and, of course, Jamshed himself. They are all drinking tea waiting for Beramshah to start, which is exactly what he does, standing, clearing his throat, and beginning his story.

"We are people who have always moved," he begins slowly, "when the need arises." KaCa nods in agreement and such nodding causes his eyelids to droop a bit, but not close. Everyone else in the room either allows for the corners of their lips to rise in slight acknowledgement or turns his or her head slightly in a similar gesture of yesness.

"We all know the *Qissa-i Sanjan*, written by the great Mobed

Bahman himself, which tells how Zoroastrians wandered Persia for a hundred years and then came to Hormuz before setting sail in seven boats, landing here in India at Diu, which became our temporary refuge."

"Temporary refuge," reasserts KaCa.

"We stayed at Diu for nineteen hard years, nineteen years in the dust and arid climate, before Dastur-ji had a dream and led us to the mainland. We suffered storms that would have destroyed us but for our faith in Ahura Mazda and Dastur-ji's promise that, should we survive, we would build an Atash Behram at our place of landing. And this brought us to Sanjan where the Gujarati king Jadi Rana allowed us to stay under five conditions."

"Five conditions," grunts KaCa.

"And those five conditions were?"

"The dasturs had to explain the beliefs of Zoroastrianism," says Adi, jumping into the participatory section of the speech.

"We were to adopt Gujarati as our new language," pipes up Dinshaw.

"And we were told, the women, that we must succumb to the Indian dress code of the sari," adds Bhika, hardly hiding her resentment at being told what to do by a foreign power, even if it was a millennium ago.

"And the weapons," Ferozha interjects as she inspects her fingernails. "Let's not forget the weapons. Jadi Rana said we should give up any warrior ways, not that we had them, I would think."

"Yes, yes," says Beramshah, "all that is true. And lastly? Jamshed?"

Jamshed knew this was coming. As a son following in his father's footsteps he was supposed to know the history, even though he was barely six.

"Marriage," says Jamshed. "We could only marry at night."

"This is true," confirms Beramshah. "Zoroastrian weddings were to happen only after sunset. And why was this?"

Jamshed looks at his father. He does not know the answer, but does not know how to tell his father this.

Beramshah lets the corners of his lips turn up ever so slightly, then turns it into a full beaming smile. "A trick question, Jamshed. We do not know. Nobody knows. It is a mystery. And from that we can learn, too. Sometimes there are actions to be taken without good reason. Sometimes there are things we must do because they are needful to do. Sometimes our good actions come from our good words, which come from our good thoughts. And sometimes good words happen without thought or action, or good actions without word or thought. Do you understand this yet, Jamshed?"

"Good thoughts, good words, good deeds," utters KaCa, having just dropped off to sleep and suddenly waking himself with this mantra.

"And sometimes rules are meant to be broken," says Bhika, unable to contain herself any longer. "We must not forget that 500 years after the imprecation by the king not to take up arms, we did, and to protect his very kingdom. We fought for what was true and just and we died for the cause. This is our lot in life."

"'Imprecation' is a curse," says Ferozha, now a bit more engaged in the conversation as it slid away from practised stories. "How did the king curse us?"

"Well, you know what I mean," says Bhika. "He ordered us, that is what I meant."

"But that is not what you said. Imprecate. Fine English word, Bhika, but made all the less fine by its misuse."

"And what do you mean by that 'fine English word' business?" asks Bhika, now spoiling for an argument about colonial rule.

"Just what I said," Ferozha says, smiling back. "No need to imprecate me."

"Ferozha, if you feel you are being funny, you are not."

"Now, now," says Beramshah. "Good thoughts and good words, no?" The two women look sullenly at him, uttering silent imprecations, no doubt, but saying nothing, since this is Beramshah's moment.

"And so now is like then for our Khargat family," pronounces Beramshah. "The time has come when we must exercise our free will and make choices, difficult choices, but they are for our future, for our son's future, and for the future of the family."

Soona's mother leans into her. "Nicely spoken, but where is he going with this?"

Soona shrugs her shoulders. "I can never tell. He starts on something, and before you know it he has made some grand decision."

Beramshah clears his throat once more, partly to emphasize what he is about to say and partly to attract the attention of his wife and mother-in-law who are clearly not taking this seriously. "And so, like our forebears, the Khargat family has decided to move to Bombay."

"Bombay?" says a startled Soona.

"Bombay?" asks her mother.

"Bombay, Bombay?" each of the other attendees utters as statement or question.

"Bombay." Beramshah places the name of the port city out there and lets it speak for itself, he thinks.

"But we talked about this," says Soona loudly, then brings her voice down to a stage whisper, "and we decided it was a decidedly bad idea!"

"Oh yes, we talked of this, indeed, and yes, my friends, my good wife did try to reason with me, to convince me to stay. But I have done a great deal of thinking on this, a great deal, and I have thought of our ancestors and what they would have done. There must be respect for the Khargat family, and that respect must come from all quarters to all Khargats. It is not enough for Soona and me to benefit from the admiration of the community; that must also shine on Jamshed, mustn't it, Jamshed?"

Jamshed, not knowing what to do, nods amiably.

"And if that is not to happen, if teachers and principals and others look askance at my son, well then, I say we will move where there will be more respect. It is the Parsi way. We will not stay and face persecution but will find, will make ourselves a new home."

Soona's mother nudges her daughter. "This may be the heat talking, making him crazy-like."

Soona points to the ceiling fan and gestures to the atmosphere in the room. "It is not hot. Only his brain is on fire."

"When will you go?" asks Adi.

"We will leave immediately," says Beramshah.

"As soon as we first take leave of our senses," says Soona to her mother, a bit louder than before so that Bikha and Dinshaw, sitting next to them, look over with a combination of sympathetic and disapproving looks.

"We will leave immediately and make a new home in Bombay. I have been in contact with my cousins there and have arranged a temporary place to live. When we arrive, I will find a permanent home, a place the Khargats will be proud to live."

"Hard to be proud with your head pushed so far up your you-know," Soona's mother says to her daughter, and this time most of the room hears this but pretends not to.

"You are our closest friends and family," Beramshah says solemnly. "We will miss you."

Soona puts her head in her hands. "He will miss his brain, which he has clearly locked up in the safe box and lost the key."

"Soona, there is no need for grief," Beramshah says consolingly, either not hearing or pretending not to hear his wife's barbs. "The Khargats will rise to prominence in Bombay. There are so many Parsis there; it is a bustling Parsi city. And we shall be part of it."

"Oh, Mummy, he will make us part of a lunatic asylum," groans Soona.

"No, no," comforts her mother, "he cannot drag you down. Come, smile; we will visit Beramshah in the crazy house every week. We will make khoresh and take it to him every Sunday. We will make the attendants untie his hands so he may eat this one good meal, and we will wipe the drool off his face as a loving family must do."

"And when he speaks, we must pretend he makes sense," agrees Soona. "We must tell him that any day now he can come home even while we know he will never see the light of day outside the asylum walls, poor dear."

"Yes, it will be difficult making ends meet, but we will persevere. We are Parsis."

"Oh, Mummy, such a great loss. Jamshed and I have such a great burden to bear."

"That is true, my daughter, you are saints, the both of you."

And so they went on, mother and daughter, but both knowing it was just their way of telling their sadness because they both knew once Beramshah had truly made up his mind, there was no turning back. He was a stubborn man with no imagination, and well-known for that in the community of Surat. The assorted family and friends expressed their sorrow that the Khargats would be leaving and wished them well. The afternoon wore on, and they slowly drifted out the door until only Adi and Soona's mother remained.

"Yaar, this is the only path, do you think?" asks Adi finally.

"Yaar, yes, of course. It is a good and spiritual path."

Soona's mother glares at Beramshah. "You will leave because of a schoolteacher and a British headmaster?"

"No," says Beramshah. "We will leave so we can make a future for ourselves, one untainted by bad words."

"Then … then I will come with you," says Soona's mother.

"Mummy?"

"It is no use, Soona. He has made up his foolish mind, and if he has his way there will be no one to look after Jamshed. Come, let us pack."

Soona looks despairingly at her mother, her husband, then over at her son and sighs.

They are moving to Bombay after all.

Moving in more ways than one

If I know nothing about being birthed, I know even less about moving, other than to acknowledge that picking up stakes and transplanting a household is a substantial task. But in the year 1905, this is just what the Khargat family does. It is a mishmash of tribulations, decisions, what to take and what to leave, who to meet with once they arrive, where to settle, all those things that are part of such an action. But the most decisive action is one of noncommission, one that Soona makes and does not share with anyone, not even her mother, a decision of terminal quality. Her husband will act this way over such a minor incident with their only child, she thinks, how might he act if there were more serious incidents with Jamshed's future brothers and sisters? Would he throw himself in front of trains to save his family from disaster, or would he encourage the trains to run through the family household? So it becomes an easy decision for Soona to make, on the journey south from Surat to Bombay, that she will not, no matter what, bear any more children. She will raise Jamshed as an only child, make sure he is set for a good life, but one that is siblingless. Soona is sitting in the carriage and comes to this decision so suddenly and forcefully that she nods strongly, once, and crosses her arms. For the rest of her life, she will adopt this custom of a sharp nod and arm-cross when she makes decisions. But on this initial occasion it is so startling that Beramshah looks up and asks Soona if everything is all right.

"Oh yes," she says, smiling broadly. "Everything is fine now." And when they arrive at Bombay, one of the first things Soona does is seek out a fine young Parsi doctor and tell him that she must prevent herself from ever having more children. At first, the Parsi doctor is concerned, even attempts to talk Soona out of this line of thinking, but then, when he sees her nod and arm-cross, he agrees to help her and gives her various concoctions and advice on how to remain without child forever more. As the years pass, Beramshah will sometimes wonder why he was unable to produce more offspring (for Soona will tell him unapologetically that his seed has gone weak), but he will not be overly concerned. His duties to the community as a dastur, and his obligations to his small family of wife and single child, are enough to fulfill him. Indeed, his first task, after they have settled into their temporary accommodation, is to conduct Jamshed's *navjote*.

He does not wait until Jamshed turns seven, but insists on this happening just after his son's sixth birthday. His son is a bright one, advanced for his years, Beramshah argues, so he can take the responsibility of *sudre* and *kusti* earlier than other boys. This he tells Soona, and she agrees wholeheartedly. It is the only navjote she will know for any child of hers, so it might as well be sooner than later. For fully two weeks, six-year-old Jamshed (for his birthday occurs during the training) is made to learn his lines: "Praised be the most righteous, the wisest, the most holy and the best Mazdayasnian Law, which is the gift of Mazda. The good, true, and perfect religion, which God has sent to this world, is that which Prophet Zoroaster has brought in here. That religion is the religion of Zoroaster, the religion of Ahura Mazda communicated to holy Zoroaster." And the bright Jamshed learns them quickly even at the age of six.

When the day comes, Jamshed speaks along with his father as the kusti is placed upon him: "The Omniscient God is the greatest Lord. Ahriman is the evil spirit, who keeps back the advancement of the world. May that Evil Spirit with all his accomplices remain fallen and dejected. O, Omniscient Lord! I repent of all my sins. I repent of all the evil thoughts that I may have entertained in my mind, of all the evil words that I may have spoken, of all the evil actions that I may have performed. May Ahura Mazda be praised. May Ahriman, the evil spirit, be condemned. The will of the righteous is the most praiseworthy." And then, finally, "O, Almighty! Come to my help. I am a worshipper of God. I am a Zoroastrian worshipper of God. I agree to praise the Zoroastrian religion, and to believe in that religion. I praise good thoughts, good words, and good actions. I praise the good Mazdayasnian religion which curtails discussions and quarrels, which brings about kinship or brotherhood, which is holy, and which, of all the religions that have yet flourished and are likely to flourish in the future, is the greatest, the best, and the most excellent, and which is the religion given by God to Zoroaster. I believe that all good things proceed from God. May the Mazdayasnian religion be thus praised." And before Jamshed knows it, his father is speaking to him: May his son enjoy long health, may his son make the Zoroastrian faith flourish, may his son be virtuous, may his son perform good deeds always. Then Jamshed looks down at himself, his sudre, his kusti, and he knows he is following the ways of his father.

But a moment, if you will, because there is much to be said at this stage. See, I have watched this all unfurl from a distance (of a kind), and it is imperative to impart some details about the wondrous process of this young mind at work. Because while Jamshed freefalls into his faith, he does not do this without question, no, not even at the age of six. He knows, for he is told, that a good Parsi does not depend on the words or work of others to grow faith. He knows that he must be self-reliant, must himself practise a good moral life, and that there is nothing else upon which to depend. This all seems easy enough, thinks Jamshed. But still. Who is to say, thinks Jamshed, just as the ceremony finishes and all around him beam proudly, who is to say what is good, what is moral? And how can he know what to choose, which choices will lead him forward and which back? This preoccupies him and his loved ones think this is the visage of a boy coming into his own, but in reality, it is the face of a perplexed six-year-old, his eyes, nose, and lips forming not a solid front to a sometimes adverse world—but a question mark.

Jamshed and free will

Jamshed sits by the ocean listening to the hawkers sell their wares. He is nine years old and in complete control of his own destiny. In his left hand he turns a silver *anna*, a coin dated 1878, the head of Queen Victoria, scratched but clearly noble, on the obverse. Jamshed sits on the beach, feels the warm wind blow off the water, occasionally lifting a spit of ocean spray to dampen his face. His knees are drawn up so his legs form an isosceles triangle with the beach. He leans back, supporting himself with his right hand, squirreled away in the sand. Jamshed looks up at the blue sky, listens to the soft sounds of the ocean, and absently plays with his anna coin. Victoria on one side, ruling the waves, forty years into a sixty-year rule. Her likeness may adorn all the coins of the British Empire, but her regal, corporeal form will never traverse the ocean to alight on Indian shores. She will profess a love for her subjects on this ungainly triangle of a subcontinent, so much so that she will severely punish any of her courtiers who dare to speak ill of the Indian. She, the queendom itself, will not be amused by such disparagement. But while brown, nine-year-old fingers will rub the raised visage of the queen on the coin, touching her silvery skin, Jamshed's brown eyes—like those of his countrymen—will never see Victoria sail across the seas. It will be up to them to visit Buckingham Palace; for if the Queen will not go to the Empire, the Empire's subjects will certainly go to the royal court. They will come in dribbles to begin with, then in spurts, and finally in waves, drowning and browning out the Island people. Would Queen V. think of this as appropriate payback for 100, 200, 400 years of rule? Would Macaulay try to retract his momentary educational minute—for if he were so intent on breeding a hybrid brown man, one who was absolutely English in spirit, should he be surprised and perhaps taken aback when those brown Englishmen claimed their due presence on the Island shores?

But none of these thoughts pass through the nine-year-old brain of Jamshed, which thinks in English but loves in Gujarati, which calculates mathematical functions in the language of the crown but indulges in the values of a good Parsi in the lyrical language of his grandparents. Right now, the boy's left hand plays the coin over index, middle, ring finger, letting it roll and slide, turning it over gently but with purpose. On one side is the Queen. On the other is the nominally Indian side. Still, it is one coin, and one would not argue otherwise nor begin to suggest that the Raj was something as simple as a coin with empire on one side, independence on the other. It might be easy to say this, to say that colonialism could only be countered by its equal and reverse side, but that would be a lie, or if not a lie, much less than half a truth. In any case, Jamshed lets the coin lilt this way and that, not even glancing down, for his practised fingers can tell when he brushes the Queen's face, when he touches the lettered reverse. In the distance, a fishwallah tries to convince a potential buyer that a particular piece of Bombay duck is so succulent it most certainly warrants the two-anna price tag, but that because the buyer is like his own sister-in-law, and although he will lose substantially on this transaction, he will lower his price exceedingly and settle on a one-anna sale, although his own wife will surely snap at him for being a particularly useless husband on this day. Bombay duck for the price of the coin that Jamshed slips between fingers. Dried fish for silver queen. This he could spend his anna on, trade all his future hopes for a taste of today. Goodbye Victoria, hello seafood. Silver you can horde but not eat, Jamshed thinks he remembers his father saying to him, or perhaps it was his grandfather. But on this day, the silver is particularly important, because, unlike the fish, which might equally be tossed into the sky to see which side lands up (but who would care if it was left eye or right eye, and how could you tell the difference?) the coin, yes, the coin was a perfect choice-maker in that one side was the Queen, the other, the not-Queen. That, thinks Jamshed, was a good thought, but could he follow with good words and good deeds if he took his task so lightly? Jamshed looks down at his left hand for the first time in several minutes. His fingers are long and slender, at least that is what he will be told when he is much older and garnering attention from various quarters who are interested in such. Right now, his fingers are nothing but normal, adequate, could be thicker and more manly, but more manly would mean more labour, and that was not going to be Jamshed's choice. Now he looks at the coin and sees the year imprinted on the reverse.

He has a choice, he knows, a choice to follow his father and his father's father, or to take the route of his favourite uncle (and more than a few of his favourite aunts). To follow the path of the Persians and to secure himself in faith, or to go the trade route of business. And only one way to decide. Jamshed holds the anna coin between thumb and forefinger, then shifts it to hold it awkwardly between index and middle finger, then shifts it again so it balances precariously on middle finger alone, an edge hanging out just enough so his thumb, when flicked, sends the coin into a head-over-tail spin, high into the beach air, high enough so that Jamshed loses sight of it in the midsummer blue sky, so high that it actually eclipses the mid-day sun for a brief spinning moment, then descends rapidly and in erratic fashion, giving Jamshed just enough time to call it in the air, to say that the Queen side will bring the prosperity of business, the dated side will bring the satisfaction of a spiritual sanctuary. Over and over it spins. A more mature Jamshed would catch the coin in one hand, slap it over onto his opposite wrist, then gingerly reveal the result by lifting the coin-flipping-catching hand ever so slightly so that just one eye can see if the Queen still rules or if the date is most important. But a nine-year-old Jamshed forgets all about that in the frenzy of calling out "heads for business" and stands there, hands clenched by his side, as the silver anna piece dive-bombs into the sand just three feet in front of Jamshed. Already he has changed his mind, wants heads to be for the spirit, but it is too late, the decision has been made. A flipped coin lands one way or the other, no questions asked. Jamshed walks to the place where the coin has disappeared, burying itself in the warm Bombay sand. He can see where tiny crystals of sand have been spit out, pointing back to where his life-changing coin has landed. Like a forensic scientist brushing back the dust covering a murder victim, or perhaps an archaeologist upon the discovery of King Tut under a millennium of aggregate deposits, Jamshed brushes away the sand. He is tender at first, not wanting to disrupt the results of his life-to-be, then he is more aggressive as it becomes clear the coin has buried itself a good bit below the surface. He even gets down to the level of the ground and blows a few futile breaths so as not to disturb the lay of the coin. Finally, finally, a glint of silver belies the presence of the coin. At first, Jamshed sees only a sliver of a bevelled surface. Surely this is the Queen, he thinks. No, perhaps it is the date, raised high enough so even the blind can read it. Finger and thumb, this time of the right hand, come together to pluck his destiny from the sand. Finger and thumb as pincers. But the coin is now much narrower than before. His finger and thumb come together so they almost touch. The ridges they close around are neither Victoria's cheek nor the year of our Lord of any such dimension. They are the hash marks around the edge of the coin. Jamshed's anna has landed on its edge, directly perpendicular, no possibility of making this heads or tails. Empire or Independence. Queen or Colony. On its edge, the anna coin grins at Jamshed. He plucks it from the sand and stares at its edge. Two out of three, he thinks, but then pockets the coin and looks for the hawker of Bombay duck.

There are signs and then there are signs, and that *is* something about which I know a thing or two. Signs can be informative and practical—this many miles to the Elephanta Caves—and signs can be significant and spiritual, as when a child is born with a birthmark on his behind shaped like a donkey's very own behind, and subsequently the village it is born to experiences seven years of drought. (Jamshed heard of this one when he was just four years old and had obsessively tried to view his own bottom just in case he was such an accursed child.) But they are both signs. Jamshed's coin toss could be both, could be either. An insignificant divot in the sand pointing to the physics of tiny granular pieces of granite separating for velocity-driven matter, or a momentous occurrence, not a both-and but a neither-nor, a sign from the above that no choices are easy and maybe choices themselves are not possible, that everything is subject to strange rules and that no one has free will. Yet whoever heard of a coin toss that results in neither heads nor tails, a coin toss that ends up with the physically impossible? A double zero on a roulette wheel negates wins for either black or red. The winnings stay with the house. But there are no zeros, no double-noughts, no split-the-differences when it came to coin tosses. It is either/or. Fifty-fifty. One way or another. With us or against us. There could be no middle ground, no what-ifs, no better-luck-next-times when it came to coin tosses. Up in the air she goes, where she lands, nobody knows—but really, everybody knows, or, mathematically speaking, half the speculators know, or half of them, knowingly or not, will be right, will guess the outcome, will be the Cassandras of the coin toss, will, from the back of their minds dredge up the image of what will surely be, a heads or not, a tails or other. And if these idle speculators squint hard enough and frown furiously enough, they might even believe that their act of willpower alone can make this happen, for if they truly wish hard enough, it will come true. Rule Britannia, Britannia rules the waves, let that thought enter in and not leave, push it forward, sing it loudly or to yourself, watch with disinterest how the coin wags through the air, twisting and optically illusioning so it looks not like a flat disk but a spinning top, a spherical celestial body, an object so entirely unlike itself that it cannot possibly retransmogrify into that copper or nickel or silver bit of pressed metal. Think Queen, and it will be Queen. Or else, not. The coin will come up with the Victorian backside (not to be rude), a turning of the other cheek, so to speak, numismatically described as the obverse (at least in mixed company), and all your dreams and aspirations dashed. You cannot predict the future, you cannot urge a possibility into being, you cannot do more than ... guess. It is a coin toss, nothing more. It will be tails or it will be heads. Unless, as Jamshed himself has found out, the landing field is an ocean shore that will not accept such binary decisions, that throws back the coin toss a direct challenge to the flippers, the flippant beings who tried to use this arbitrary act as a decision-making machine. Between heads and tails, queens and subjects, empires and conquered, obverse and reverse, between all that is another choice. That which should not happen can happen; that which does not happen does. Flat landings give way to edges. Twos out of threes are not even worth pursuing.

Born again, not yet

It will be a warm and stormy night, the type of night where the winds pick up and rain clouds gather and everyone hopes for a good, solid drenching, but none comes. The worst kind of storm; always approaching, never arriving. It will be such a night, a long way from here, a very long journey, through places you can never imagine, will never imagine, even if you conjure up the most fantastic of imaginings. The place of my birth, ah, now that's a good one. For it's a place that is as close to your heart as it is to the long-time inhabitants of that place; it's a place that is closer to your home than your home now, and yet it is a place you will never visit. It is a home that your child will make, but it will never be your child's home. In fact, it will never be my home; I will never have a home, not a real home, and I will never have a place that can even approximate a home.

And the time of my birth will be the birth of a peaceful time. Well, not really, no, that would be a lie. But given the gravity of the wars that have come before, wars that have intertwined nations and peoples and cultures, wars that have professed to end all wars before or hence, this will be a peaceful time. Prosperity will be in the air, hanging there for all to take in. Whether they do or not, that is another matter. Politics will rise and fall all around me and my parents, and we will breathe those in too, make them part of ourselves, my parent (who is your own offspring) and me (who is your offspring once removed), and your child's (my parent's) spouse, all of us, not unhappily. At least, not unhappily by then, for my birth shall be a great relief for both my parents and for all around them. My birth shall signify a time of less-than-grief, a time when grief passes and gives way to something else, something that cannot be classified as not-grief, and not at all as happiness, because once real grief is experienced there can never be such a thing as unadulterated happiness. That can only occur for those who have never tasted the way grief lives at the back of your throat. It never goes away, you see, not really. And even joyous events (let's take my birth, for example) can only cloak that taste, mask it like a chewed clove hides halitosis, so that you are always aware that there's this stink at the back of your throat, this memory of taste that will, at some not-at-all-unsurprising moment, be retasted. That is the best way to describe the moment I will be born into, not just personally for my family (your child and your child-in-law and me) but for the world I am born into.

I will be a peaceful child, happy-go-lucky as they say, growing up in a happy-go-lucky time, even as such times have that lingering back-of-the-throat taste of yesteryears. Oh, there will be music from all types of unknown quarters as I grow from babe to child, there will be wondrous events and discoveries, although even key participants will be spectacularly unaware that their existence is owed to the nefarious times before. We're talking medical marvels, Jamshed, scientific discoveries that, were you to dream and then tell someone about them today, why, they would tell you that you were as crazy as they always thought you were!

And it is into this environment that I will be born, that your grandchild will come into being. You can mark my words, although, since no one seems to pay any attention to you paying attention to me, this might mean little. But there you have it. The story of my birth. Any questions?

Jamshed thinks on this, his face pensive and his mind overwhelmed. "Questions? Of course I have questions. I have a mountain of questions, and I just don't know where to begin."

Well, begin cautiously, because I will only let you ask five!

"Five? That's a silly rule. But all right. Five it is. Question one: you talk about my child who will be your parent, but you don't say if that's a girl or a boy. Which is it?"

Ha. That, my dear Granddad, doesn't matter. I promise you, your child, my parent, is a fine person, and that is all I will say.

"You tell me I have five questions, but you haven't answered my very first one. What sort of rules are you playing by?"

Well, mine, of course. Proceed.

Jamshed sighs again. "The place of your birth: is it Paris? I think it must be Paris. Daddy was just talking about Paris today. Madame Cama arrived there, he said, only a few months ago, and he says she has started a magazine for Indian independence, *Vande Mataram*. There is talk in the gymkhana of the first copies arriving in Bombay in a few days. So I am sure you must be born in Paris where wondrous things will happen."

I was—not born in Paris.

"But then where?"

That was not your question. You asked, specifically, whether the place of my birth was Paris, and I have stated unequivocally that it is not. No snide remarks now about me not answering your questions. Next?

"All right. What city were you born in? There, you have to answer. I have you!"

Well, an interesting choice of tense. Indeed, I have not yet been born, dearest Granddaddy, so the answer to your question is, I have not been born anywhere, not yet. But I will be born, almost fifty years hence, in—a city that is just as I have described. Or this might all be an imaginative act; the city, my birth, the whole lot.

"You're answering none of my questions. You might as well have given me a hundred questions since you were not going to answer any."

Indeed. Question four?

"You will be a frustrating grandchild. Question four is: will I be alive to see your birth?"

Hm, a good question. The answer is: I don't know. I'm awfully young when I'm born, so I don't remember if you are there or not. Or alive or not. Quite an interesting dilemma, no?

"No. Not really. I have one last question, Sunny, and I hope you answer this. In many ways, this is more important than anything else. You have seen your history, which is my future, and I am in a place where I really need to know which way to go. My father is a dastur and I am training to be one. I would be happy to choose that path if I felt it was the right one. But my father's brothers and sisters and my mother's sisters and brothers, they are all business people. I have to know if I should grow up to be a dastur or a businessman. This is not a tricky question since it is something that is bound to happen, one way or another, and you can save me a great deal of time by telling me the answer. Business? Or religion?"

You are what, ten years old?

Jamshed nods, impatiently.

And it is what, the end of November?

Again, Jamshed nods, this time more vigourously.

Then you shall have your answer in the form of a regal embrace in two years plus a day or so, give or take.

Jamshed shrugs, mostly out of exasperation.

No, no, trust me. Go to the foot of the Gateway of India, first thing in the morning, December 11, 1911. But before that, look for a fellow named, oh, what was it? Cricket or Wicket or some such thing. He'll know what I'm talking about.

"The Gateway of India? Where is that? What is that?"

Oh, yes, silly me, hasn't been built yet. Look, find this Willow fellow and ask him about George. He'll know.

Sunny's voice then went silent and Jamshed was left by himself, once again with more questions than answers, as was usually the case after such a conversation with Sunny. This time, however, was a bit more enlightening, and Jamshed started heading home, etching in his mind the date two years from now that held the answers to all his future possibilities.

But it would not be two years before Jamshed would come face to face with destiny, nor even two weeks; it was only three and a half days later that Jamshed's father burst into the dining area of their modest flat and announced that he had an audience with none other than Jamset-ji Tata himself. The Tata of all Tatas. The man who had, against all odds, built what was possibly the finest hotel in the world, so fine that it could be called by no other name but the Taj Mahal, for it rivalled its Agra namesake and in many ways outmatched it.

"Jamset-ji called on me himself," crowed Beramshah.

"You are sure it was him?" asked Soona graciously.

"Am I sure? My goodness, woman, do you think I would not know the great Jamset-ji's hand?"

"I am not so sure."

"Not so sure? Not so sure! And what, good woman, would make you more sure?"

"Well, if Jamset-ji had not been dead these past seven years, I would be more sure."

This did give Beramshah pause, for he had indeed conflated the reputation of the great Jamset-ji Tata with a different, younger, no doubt related, Jamset-ji Tata who had, indeed, written to him.

"Yes, well, not *the* Jamset-ji, but a Tata of considerable import, also a Jamset-ji, well, he wants to see me."

"Ah-ha," says Soona, more graciously than before. "And to what end?"

"To what end? To what end! She wants to know to what end. To what end is what Mr Tata and I will determine, that is to what end." The truth being, of course, that Beramshah had not the slightest clue to what end this Tata fellow wanted to see him about. But that was all well and good. Seven years in Bombay, building a reputation as a good and kind dastur, seven years trying to make ends meet in the middle somewhere, and now, this felt like his big opportunity. And no one, not his wife, not his friends, no one would interfere with that.

"Then this is all well and good," says Soona. "You must go and meet him and come quickly and tell me all about it."

"Indeed!" says Beramshah, turning on his heel and then realizing he has nowhere to go really, so he slouches out of the room into the midafternoon air.

Jamset-ji Tata has summoned Beramshah to no place other than the Taj Mahal Hotel itself, to the top administrative floor no less, and it is here, in an administrative waiting room, that Beramshah waits for his audience with a member of the Tata family, arriving ten minutes before the scheduled appointment, and waiting those ten minutes, then another, and then another twenty, before a well-appointed young man pokes his head out from behind an oak door and grins and says, "Mr Tata is ready for you, Mr Khargat, this way please," and ushers Beramshah into what is possibly the largest office he has ever seen. Behind a desk of indeterminable wood, hidden behind the desk, is a young man who cannot be more than sixteen years old. He rises when Beramshah enters, knocks his knee on the side of the desk as he attempts to negotiate his way around, and utters a piteous "ow" before grabbing Beramshah's hand in both of his and shaking vigourously.

"Mr Khargat, a pleasure, a pleasure. I am Jummy Tata, but you can call me Jimmy." He lets go of Beramshah's hand and rubs his knee before settling himself back down behind the desk of indeterminable wood.

"It is—it is my pleasure, Mr Tata, to make your acquaintance—"

"Ah-ah," says the young Mr Tata, raising one finger in reprimand. "Jimmy. Call me Jimmy."

"Ah, yes, Jimmy. And you may call me—"

"Ah, I shall call you Mr Khargat as befits an elder and a dastur of your reputation," insists Jimmy. "And I shall get right to the point. First, I am sure you do not know who I am. That is all right. No one does. Not to apologize. I am an unknown on the way to making myself a known, I would say."

"Well, everyone knows the Tatas," says Beramshah.

"Indeed, and would that I were a Tata," says Jimmy woefully. "Oh, but I am of course, but in name only, I am afraid. Too many cousins many times removed am I. It was, though, I remind myself, the great Jamset-ji Tata himself who discovered me on a street corner not far from here, reading under a streetlamp. Yes, that was when I was just a little boy, and he was passing by on his way to work as he was every day, and every evening he would see me under the streetlamp. You see, Mr Khargat, I love to read, always have, and darkness put a real cramp in my reading, so I would go outside and put myself under that streetlamp and read and read and read. And that is where the great Tata saw me and he was impressed, so he told me, and he talked to me on very many occasions, and finally asked to meet my parents, of which I had only one, my father (my mother dying in childbirth so that I never knew her), and he said to my father, Cousin, he said, I will take this child under my wing and educate him and he will be a great Tata. My name, at the time, was not Jamset-ji, I must say, Mr Khargat, but with a flourish the great one said he would mould me as he had been and I would take after him, and I was so pleased and my father was so pleased, that it seemed only natural for me to take his name as my own, do you see?"

Beramshah, very confused, nods.

"And since then, it has been ten years, and I have been educated here and abroad, yes, in England no less, and now I am back here to make my fortune, but more importantly, to become a Parsi whom other Parsis can be proud of, do you see?"

Beramshah saw and said so, but was now perplexed as to why he was here himself.

"And so I began to run businesses, Mr Khargat, oh, not ones as glorious as this, the Taj, no, this isn't even my office, only a good distant cousin has taken pity on me and lent me his space for interviews such as these. Do you know what interviews such as these are about, Mr Khargat?"

"No," says Beramshah honestly, "I do not."

"I am looking out to the Parsi community, Mr Khargat, looking out and trying to do my part. And do you know why I summoned you to this interview?"

"No, Jimmy, I do not."

"Indeed. You have quite a reputation, Mr Khargat, quite a reputation indeed. As does, if I may be so bold, your son Jamshed."

"Jamshed? What has this to do with him?"

"Oh, not what you might think, not that going-right business at all, no sir, that is not it at all. But I have heard from many that Jamshed is the bright spot in his generation. A ten-year-old (he is ten, is he not?) with a potential for greatness."

"Yes, you are right. He will be great at whatever he does. He will, of course, be a dastur first and foremost."

"First and foremost, most certainly. And then some. And it is that some that I wish to talk to you about, Mr Khargat. I need protégés such as him. I am building something here, Mr Khargat, something great and vast, and for this to flourish, I need young boys and girls who are our future, do you see? Yes, a wise man like you, I am sure you do. Here, Mr Khargat, is my calling card. Take it and put it away. And when your young Jamshed turns twelve, I ask you to take it out, dust it off, and have him come to see me. Is that understood?"

Beramshah nods. He understands the request but not the rationale. But when a Tata, even a quasi-Tata, asks, you respond affirmatively. "He will call on you," says Beramshah, "the moment he turns twelve."

Gateway to something

Toward the end of October 1911, Jamshed started to get nervous. Every morning he would wake up at six in the morning and have a momentary panic until he looked over at the small Ganesh-ji calendar by his bedside that would tell him that today was, not yet, the eleventh day of December. But as November dragged on, he would get even more nervous, started to wake up in the middle of the night, stare up at the lizards on his ceiling, and wait for morning light or for sleep to overtake him again, and toward the end of the month, he was, colloquially speaking, a wreck. His mother asked him on November 23 if everything was all right, as he seemed to have lost some weight and certainly had lost his breakfast appetite, but he assured her that he was fine, just not hungry today or for the last few days, and that he would work to right himself. And from that day on he would take himself out every morning right after breakfast and, before school, wend his way down from the colony to Apollo Bundar by the sea, sometimes sit on the marble steps of the Taj Mahal Hotel, and, if a doorman shooed him away, look out at the ocean and wonder what the next weeks would bring. In the distance he could see what was referred to by passersby and workmen as "the foundation stone," but he was never sure what it founded. And then he would take himself off to school and repeat the pattern the next day, and this went on for two weeks.

On December 10, Jamshed woke up at three in the morning and could not go back to sleep. This was the Day Before Things Would Happen, according to Sunny, that dastardly grandchild who had talked to Jamshed at least twice per week for the past two years, but had given no further clues to the cryptic gateway or other such details. So at three in the morning, Jamshed awoke and stretched his arms, his legs, his feet, and was mildly surprised to find his right big toe tapping methodically.

"Sunny?"

Jamshed, you old man, good to see you.

"Where have you been?"

A metaphysical question if there ever was one. How to answer? I have not been because I am not yet? Or, the question precedes my existence?

"You did not inherit my sense of humour."

And thank the stars for that.

"Sunny? Will you tell me what will happen tomorrow?"

Grandpa, you know I can't really do that. I mean, I would like to, but it's not as if I can really know myself. Not that I have a self to speak of.

"Then why, how do you know to tell me to go there, tomorrow?"

Well, you see, it's about history, not yours but mine. You use the word tomorrow in a very literal way, but I am, quite literally, a child of tomorrow.

"You mean tomorrow, Monday?"

No, no, silly, tomorrow as in mañana, *the what-comes-after, the mercurial future.*

"Then why this push, this urgency for me to be there tomorrow? And I do mean Monday."

Well, perhaps you're right. Maybe I am a child of tomorrow (the out-there somewhere) and a child of tomorrow (Monday at Apollo Bundar).

"They have been building into the sea; that is what they tell me."

Who says?

"Everyone. The doorman at the Taj, the people in the streets, the workmen."

Doesn't seem to be the most solid of foundations, does it?

"They are making it land first. They call it reclamation. Building out into the sea."

Quite something.

"Yes. The articles in the *Bombay Samachar* say they are building this thing, this gateway you talked about, into the sea, to celebrate the arrival of the King and Queen."

You don't say. The King and Queen are coming here, to Bombay? How exciting.

"I do not know, Sunny, if you truly do not know or if you are making fun of me. In either case, no, the King and Queen are going to Delhi. There is a great *durbar* to be held there in their honour."

Ah, well then, that all makes sense.

"So I should still go to the sea to see what happens there."

Indeed. It is all about tomorrow, after all.

"All right, then."

Jamshed felt his toe stop tapping and his eyelids grow heavy again, and he was off to sleep for a solid slumber of three hours before waking, rising, and taking one last trip to the water's edge to see what was transpiring there the day before his life was supposed to be indelibly altered.

"Why do you want me to go with you?"

"Because, Nouroz, I need you there."

"But it's a school day. I will be in trouble for playing truant."

"As will I. But Sunny says this is important."

"Always this Sunny. All right, I will go with you, but only for a few moments, then I will go to school."

Jamshed and Nouroz are eating roasted peanuts at Juhu Beach. It is a lazy Sunday, and they have little else to do but study, and that is not the first thing on their minds. What is at the top of their minds, or at least Nouroz's, is what is almost always at the top.

"Yaar, do you think there will be girls there tomorrow?"

"I don't know. Probably. The Samachar says there will be a small gathering. The architect will be in attendance."

"Ha. The Samachar," says Nouroz, rolling his eyes. "Why do you read that thing? It's always so full of crazy politics."

"It's run by Parsis. And I get to practise reading my Gujarati. And it's useful information."

"Hm." Nouroz spits out a piece of woody peanut. "I would rather spend that time practising lines. I am starting to learn Shakespeare, did you know? 'Arise fair sun and kill the envious moon who is already sick with something and grief,' do you know where that's from?"

"Mm … Shakespeare?"

"Yes, yaar, I already told you that. But do you know what play? It's *Romeo and Juliet*. Someday I will play Romeo, and my Juliet will be a wide-eyed girl with skin like molasses and with great huge—"

"So you always say."

"Well, all I say now is there better be girls at this pre-durbar thing tomorrow."

"Yes. We will see."

Jamshed awakes again at three in the morning on December 11 and stares up at the lizards sleeping on the ceiling. He is acutely aware of his body and that there is no toe-tapping occurring, so he stays like this, lying on his back, thinking of todays and tomorrows and lizards and gateways and grandchildren for a very, very long time. He thinks he dozes off once or twice, but nothing deep, and after some time he grows quite bored and decides to take himself out of bed. He looks at his calendar and affirms that today is the day he has been waiting for. The first day of his life, he thinks solemnly, as if all previous days were before his current life which, indeed, in a way, they were, then shakes his head because he thinks he now sounds like Sunny. Can't have that. He dresses slowly, waits for morning light in the kitchen, and then, earlier than he had planned, sets out the front door to Nouroz's house, which is only a few minutes away. When he gets there he climbs up the gnarled trunk of a tree that grows just outside Nouroz's window, his way of getting in when he does not want to wake the family, and Nouroz's way of getting out for the same or different reasons. The window to Nouroz's room is unlocked, so Jamshed pushes it open quietly and steps in. Nouroz, of course, is still asleep, and looking so peaceful that Jamshed cannot help himself but slides up to Nouroz's head and begins whispering softly in his ear, things about lovely times in bed together and how Nouroz is such a virile man. A slight smile crosses Nouroz's face before he wakes up and sees Jamshed before him, laughing.

"That was mean-spirited," he says sleepily.

"Yes, well, at least you didn't try to kiss me," says Jamshed, still laughing.

"Oh, and if I had it would have been your first."

"And yours."

"Not to be so sure of yourself, Jum," Nouroz says, and with that he pulls himself out of bed and launches into his morning routine, one he has reduced to a mere two minutes so that in less than three, the two friends are out the window, down the tree, and on their way to the waterside.

It is still before seven when they get to the Taj Mahal Hotel and they both get themselves a good seat on the marble steps to stare across at the water. There is a very small throng of people there, and after watching the tableau for several minutes, Jamshed takes a big breath and stands up. It is just as well because the large *sudar* at the door chooses this moment to saunter over to the two boys and gesture with his palms that it is time for them to take their brown bottoms off the white marble and do something else with themselves.

Jamshed and Nouroz make their way to the water's edge and mill about with the fifty or sixty others who seem to be there with a purpose, however indirect that might be. Beside the great stone foundation that still looks wildly unkempt and in process stands a tall wiry British man with a handlebar moustache and far too much nervous energy for his own good. He is ordering workmen around and is clearly frustrated by the absolute degree to which they are ignoring him, and he is checking out the crowd, clearly frustrated again because of the lack of numbers or lacklustre appeal of those in attendance. Finally, he makes his way to a makeshift podium and stands atop it, waving his arms to garner attention, futilely it seems, until one of the workmen shouts out to the crowd in Gujarati and Hindi to quiet down and listen for a moment. This seems to work, and the audience faces the podium and the wiry British fellow who begins to speak.

"Oh, hello, hello all, so good of you all to come, so good. So. So thank you all for coming here. My name, I think most of you know, my name is George Wittet, and it is my very great pleasure to be the one commissioned to build this monument to commemorate the arrival on India's shores of King George V and his bride Queen Mary. Yes, yes, thank you," he says to imaginary applause. "It was several months ago, as you all know, all know, that this foundation stone was laid, and this stone, verily, will grow to be a tremendous monument indeed. This will be," he pauses and looks around, then raises his arms in tribute to the future, "the Gateway of India. Yes, thank you, thank you," this time to scattered applause started by two workmen smoking beedies to the rear and left of the architect.

"It will be at this great port that the gateway will welcome the British Empire to its greatest jewel, yes, yes, of course, this gateway to India that Bombay is, that is, to Bombay, which is a gateway of getting into India, I mean by that, of course, that this port city of yours, fine city, this is a gateway, no, a portal of sorts, really, oh, I should have brought my notes, shouldn't I, heh-heh. Here will be built a sort of archway that will be very, very large—big, really—out there, not right here but there in the ocean once we get some sand laid down and, well, I don't need to go into all the details, you didn't come here to hear me go over such minute details," to which the same two workmen break into stronger applause, puffing beedily away. "But thank you, thank you all for coming, for offering your support for King and country and for this project of which I am so proud and pleased as punch to be commissioned for which to do. Yes. And. And that is all."

So, thinks Jamshed, *this* is the Cricket-Wicket-Willow fellow that Sunny felt he had to have him meet? And, according to Sunny's long-ago instructions, he was supposed to ask this poor excuse for a man about the King? Very well then, he had come this far. As George Wittet steps down from the podium, then, Jamshed grabs Nouroz's hand and pulls him toward the front. Nouroz resists, muttering about how he must get to school, but Jamshed holds on tight and pushes forward until they are both directly in front of the British fellow who looks decidedly lonely and out of place there on the water's front.

"Uh, Mr Wippett?"

The architect looks down and smiles awkwardly. "Well, actually, Wittet is my name" he says. "That's with Ts, not Ps."

"Yes, Mr Wittet, sorry. My name is Jamshed Khargat, and I was wondering if you have met the King?"

"Met the King? Oh my, well, you see, I was supposed to meet

him here, indeed, in Bombay, but I believe someone got the dates wrong and forgot to inform me and well, no, no, I have not met the King. But I may well do in London. That's in England. When I return."

Jamshed nods. He cannot think of anything else to say to this strange English gentleman so, instead, he nudges his friend and says, "Mr Wittet, this is my best friend, Nouroz."

"I see," says Wittet, now extending his hand to shake manfully with both boys. "Very good to meet you both. Very good, good." Nouroz nods, then pulls away, makes a gesture to Jamshed that he's now off, that this was entirely too odd, strange, and boring an event, taps him on the shoulder and runs off.

Jamshed watches him leave and turns back, half-expecting, half-hoping that this quirky British man will be gone. But he is not for he has no place to go, and he is still standing there staring down at Jamshed as if that is his purpose in the world.

"Uh, Mr Wittet, when will you build the Gateway you talked about?"

"Oh, indeed," says Wittet, his eyes flitting out to the ocean and back again, "indeed, indeed. Well, the commission, that is, has not been finalized, but those are details, mere details, yes, and so, and—oh, there he is, Mr Khory. I have been looking for you." And with that, Wittet strides off in the direction of a slightly built Parsi man with incredibly enormous ears and thick spectacles, a man who clearly knows Wittet but is less than inclined to lean forward into a greeting with him. But Wittet is forthright and clasps this Mr Khory's hand and slaps him on the shoulder and maunders on about money and banking and building, and Khory can do no more than smile and nod and push his glasses up his nose a bit. Jamshed watches this odd transaction and is about to turn away when. When …

There are certain moments that enter into a young boy's memory through orifices he did not know could bring in such thoughts, dreams, desires. But this is what happens to Jamshed at this very moment; memories of the future and past, sweeping up his nostrils, seeping under his eyelids, infiltrating his ears, swooping into his mouth and over tongue and teeth, sucking into every pore on his clammy arms and face and tummy, indeed, although it is somewhat rude to mention, slinking in through his urethral opening and sliding in down and around all the way to his bulbo-urethral gland, and also sashaying up through the exit end of the alimentary canal, yes, all this at once, the power and force and temerity of it all, a full-on whoosh of excitement and deliberation and wonderment. This is because, when Jamshed's gaze turns from Mr Khory it falls instead on a figure standing alongside him, shorter and more lithe, perhaps only two or three inches taller than Jamshed himself, but of a much more aristocratic status (is this what Sunny meant, finding regal embrace?), and Jamshed—Jamshed is transfixed. His heart stops, then starts again to keep him alive. His eyelids refuse to do their practised blinking in case they close at the very moment this vision turns to look at him or flit away. And Jamshed, uncharacteristically, actually wills his legs to move, take him forward the six steps that separate Him from Her. She, for her part, has taken on the attitude of the audience and is practising a bored look, enhanced now that her father (if that is the case) is engaged with the very subject of her/their boredom. Her eyes are light and free and clearly hide behind them a great intelligence, but at this moment pretend to be vacant of any thought or action. And when, in their state of ennui, they finally light upon the young Jamshed who has now approached and stopped still only a stride away from her face, they narrow slightly and focus in on this boy's eyes, his cheeks, his lips. Two twelve-year-olds caught in each other's gaze.

Jamshed begins to tell her how she has captured his heart, swallowed him whole, taken him for a dance in the clouds and back again, how she in her beauty can do no more than make him her eternal servant, how he and she must be together from now on and for all time, forever and ever, amen, and this is the truth spoken by Ahura Mazda and that Jamshed will speak it loudly and fully for all Mazdayasnians and non alike to hear booming in their chests as it does in his own. He tells her all this and more, although, owing to how good words cannot sometimes catch up to good thoughts, while Jamshed has miraculously willed his legs to move, he could not do the same for his diaphragm (he has forgotten to breathe) or his saliva glands (his mouth a desert here before the ocean and an angel), and these words come out thusly: "Er, egh. Er, og."

And she, now looking somewhat distracted, looks deep into his eyes and says nothing.

And he, again miraculously, manages to spittle up spit enough to massage tongue into saying, "Jamshed. I am Jamshed."

And she, eyes dancing again, says finally, "Jamshed. My name is Parvin." And then, looking up at her father, says, imploring, "Daddy, this very ugly boy is bothering me."

Jamshed and the meaning of life

Jamshed takes all this forward, carries it with him a bit like an albatross, a bit like a talisman. This or that, left or right, up or down, heads or tails. Everything seems tied to the logic of one or the other. So now, one year later, a thirteen-year-old Jamshed is thinking about the power of god and the relative insignificance of human existence. Oh, he is not overly distressed with this philosophical condition, just curious about it. He remembers his lessons well: "Ahura Mazda created humanity as a part of the struggle between good and evil. The power of humanity lies in the free and conscious choice to follow either good or evil in life, and thereby influence both one's individual fate and the fate of all humanity." This, to Jamshed, seems like a tremendous burden on each individual. Not only are you free to choose between good and evil (and who among them would decide to pick door number two, with all that is bad in the universe; it seems like a faulty choice from the start, doesn't it?), but the perpetuation of the universe depends on that.

Of course, if it were that simple, thinks Jamshed, there would be no problem. Everyone (at least all the Parsis) would mark off "good" on their ballot and that would be the end of it. Mind you, if the ultimate path of the universe was so decided, wonders Jamshed, then there wouldn't be much purpose for humanity, would there, if its purpose was to engage in this good/evil struggle? It would be a bit like a one-sided cricket match. If your team knew the other team had not a decent bowler in its ranks and couldn't hit the ball for the life of them, then no contest, run up the score; but then again, what's the point? No, it must be more complicated than that. Perhaps, thinks Jamshed, the subtleties of good and evil are beyond human comprehension, caught up in a web of time and space and opportunity and desire? Yes, that must be it. So the choice isn't as simple as whether to disobey your mother (evil) or to comply with her orders (good), but something far more esoteric than that. Perhaps, at this very moment, if Jamshed were to notice his shoelace untied and decide to stop right there in the market and stoop down and tie it up, a choice would be made. Maybe tying that shoelace at that particular time in that particular place was an act of evil? Mind you, not to do so might also be evil, mightn't it, and where does that leave Jamshed? Suddenly it's not a matter of choosing *humata, hukhta, huvarshta*—but of deciphering the many complexities that make such words, thoughts, and deeds good in the first place. Ah, thinks Jamshed, now he's hit on something, but of course, that something is paralyzing him. If he can't determine what's good and what's evil, what's the point? The point is, sometimes it's just hard to keep quiet, hold one's counsel, and the point is, sometimes there is just a need to get involved.

The point is in the struggle.

"Sunny?"

Hiya. I said the point is in the struggle.

"They say I'm not supposed to talk to you," says Jamshed, conscious that his face has already drawn, inscrutably, to the right.

So I hear. Any idea why?

"They think I'm crazy and you don't exist. And to be truthful, maybe you don't exist. Maybe you're real only to me."

Doesn't that make me real to you?

"Yes, but that's not normal."

But what about to me? I'm real to me, too.

"Ah, but you don't exist so you can't have such thoughts. You can't have any thoughts."

Oh.

74

"What do you mean, the point is in the struggle?"

Oh, that. Certainly, maybe we can't tell the difference, ultimately, between good and evil, but perhaps that's what we should labour toward. If we practise good thoughts and all, if we truly believe we are practising them, then that in itself is good.

"Even if the deeds are bad?"

Can't be bad, ultimately, if the thoughts are good. But then, what do I know? If they're right, I'm just you dressed up in invisible grandchild clothes. My thoughts aren't my own. Or, rather, my thoughts are mine, but I am Jamshed, a Jamshed who has within him a Sunny.

"So what should we do?"

About practising good in the world?

"No. Yes, that too, but about you and me. What should we tell them?"

Tell them I'm your muse, that without me you would cease to function.

"But that would be a lie."

Hm, yes, that's true. But you wouldn't like it very much, would you, if I didn't keep visiting.

"Yes, that's true."

And things you like are things that sustain you, in effect, keep you alive?

"Uh—"

So, by extension, things you don't like are the antithesis of that which sustains you, and that which does not sustain you does not keep you alive, and that which does not keep you alive does the very exact opposite. So it's not a lie.

Jamshed sighs. It always happens this way. I somehow manage to convince him of some odd philosophical point that makes sense in the saying, but never when Jamshed tries to explain it. Which is why, in his youthful years, Jamshed has spent relatively little time relaying conversations with me to other people. If they thought he was crazy just for talking to the invisible wisp, what would they think once the nonsensical language came pouring forth?

"Maybe," says Jamshed slyly, "maybe you're evil."

Maybe. Or maybe I'm the epitome of good. And you're my evil doppelgänger. But why bring that up?

"Just a thought," says Jamshed. "After all, you make me do nasty things."

Oh? Such as?

"Um, you make me touch myself."

A) I do no such thing; you simply enjoy touching yourself, and B) who says that's such a bad thing? Remember, self-touching leads to other thoughts and desires, and those desires lead to an exchange of touches, and before you know it, poof, I'm born.

"You?"

Well, in a manner of speaking and a matter of time.

"All right, say I believe you that my touching myself means you will eventually be born. Tell me the rest of the story. If you're my grandchild, what are you, girl or boy, and who is my son? Or my daughter? Who is your parent?"

My parents are, as are yours, my mother and father. And your offspring will, in good time, spring me off in necessarily decided gendered directions.

"Those aren't answers, only riddles."

The answer is right before you, Grandfather.

"You?"

Indeed.

Jamshed abruptly adjusts his head to the left and figures out I am gone, as per usual. Jamshed is never quite sure if he makes me disappear by turning away from the right, or if my disappearance triggers such a bodily motion. Whatever the case, one causes the other or they occur simultaneously and that is that. He realizes he is supposed to meet Nouroz at his uncle's shop in just a few minutes, so Jamshed picks up his satchel and races out the door. By the time he reaches the shop, he is puffing. Nouroz looks up from the tiny table reserved in the back for serious study.

"You're late."

Jamshed, winded, nods.

"Watching girls, yaar?"

Jamshed shakes his head.

"Oh. Sunny?"

"Uh-huh."

"What'd he say? Anything new and interesting?"

"Same old things. Riddles and confusing thoughts."

"He should tell you how to talk to girls," says Nouroz. "Now that would be useful."

"What, so I would share that skill with you?"

"Ha. Not a skill I require to learn from you, Jamshed-ji, for it's one I acquired long ago!"

"Yes, so you've told me. But I haven't seen any girls spending much time with you, have I?"

"Ah, Jamshed, patience, all in good time. Besides, they spend time with me in their hearts, and that, for now, is good enough for me."

"They spend time with you in your silly imagination."

"Jealousy, jealousy,

From all the fellows-ji,

Why do you suppose,

They're so jealous of Nouroz?"

"Very good. Studying your prayers, are you?"

"I am the very answer to all the girls' prayers, yaar."

Jamshed laughs. If nothing else, Nouroz can make him laugh. "All right, all right, I submit!"

"I am the master of you, the winner of the ultimate game?"

"All right, if you want. Now, what about those prayers?"

"Memorized them all, Jum; go ahead, test me."

Jamshed picks up the book and reads several lines from the first chapter of the Yasna. He stops in the middle of the fourth line and Nouroz, without a pause, finishes it. Jamshed flips through some pages, repeats the exercise with the fifty-fourth chapter, fittingly all about truth and friendship, and Nouroz is again right on target. Finally, Jamshed finds a chapter about the body of Srosh, invulnerable to the forces of evil, and a chapter he knows Nouroz always has trouble with. He reads one line from the middle and closes the book.

"No fair, I need another line."

"That's all you get," says a smug Jamshed.

"You wouldn't know it."

Jamshed clears his throat and recites, in the low, mumbly way he has learned from his father, the rest of the prayer.

"It was a trick. You memorized that one to catch me up."

"No trick. You need to work on the prayers you are less familiar with!"

"Ah, yes, all right. Let's get back to this later. I have a better idea for right now."

Nouroz is up and heading for the back door. He leaves his prayer book on the table, and Jamshed thinks about stashing it in his satchel so they can study together wherever it is Nouroz ends up taking them, but then thinks better of it and follows his friend out the door. It has been two years since both Jamshed and Nouroz underwent their *navar* ceremonies, the first step initiating them into the priesthood. Not surprisingly, both their fathers were dasturs and, as such, while they were not required to do so, it was generally expected that, as good Parsi sons, they would follow their fathers' footsteps. Nouroz and Jamshed had frequent conversations about their future in this regard. Would they indeed grow up to be dasturs like their fathers? Would they enter into different paths of life, perhaps the same path together? Would one become a very spiritual man and the other a scoundrel? These are the types of questions that kept both boys highly entertained, energized, delighted, and scandalized by the endless possibilities. And while they took their studies seriously, they took their time together even more seriously, and that meant, mostly, that when Nouroz had what he called an "idea," Jamshed was bound to follow.

Out the back door they go, down the concrete stairs to the narrow alleyway below and out the cobbled alley to the street filled with people and bullock carts and acrid smoke. Nouroz hurries ahead, his legs slightly longer and his gait correspondingly lengthier than Jamshed's, such that they make for a funny sight, one boy looking slightly rushed in front, the other looking frightfully out of step as he tries to keep up. Jamshed wonders whether he should have brought his books after all, since nine times out of ten Nouroz takes him to some place or site where Jamshed might as well just sit back and read, for what might be an exciting revelation for Nouroz was often not so for Jamshed. But this time, it was different. After a blinding this-way-and-that run through and beyond the colony, Nouroz finally takes a swift turn down yet another alley and stops in front of an unassuming building, its front doors thrown open and shouts and songs coming from inside.

"Where are we?" asks Jamshed, panting slightly and trying not to sound out of breath or bored or excited.

"You have heard of Dadi Patel?" says Nouroz in that way that makes it sound like all the world has heard of Dadi Patel and none may deny that.

Jamshed shrugs.

Nouroz sneers. "Dadi Patel was practically the founder of the Victoria Natak Mandali," he says, as if this explains it all. "Follow me."

Nouroz slides through the open door, but rather than proceeding toward the sounds of what is obviously a great deal of exuberance, he ushers Jamshed into a tiny stairwell that leads up to a second level that is no more than a metallic ramp. Nouroz signals Jamshed to be quiet, pointing to the ramp and indicating that rushed footsteps will echo and give away their location. On his haunches, Nouroz duck-walks forward, gingerly, so as to make little noise, not that Jamshed thinks anyone will hear anything with all the caterwauling going on below. Nevertheless he follows Nouroz, in path and action, and soon they are together at a metal grille overlooking the first floor where near a dozen young men and women prance around, some humming tunes, other singing, others reciting words to themselves.

"They're actors," says Jamshed.

"Of course," says Nouroz in that way that makes Jamshed feel quite silly. "But not just any actors. They are the VNM. When Dadi Patel took them over, you know what he did?"

Jamshed, again, shrugs.

"Well, look, you fool," says Nouroz, almost losing the whisper he had adopted to keep their presence secret. He gestures to the floor, then points to first one girl, then another, then a third.

Jamshed nods but does not know why. "Oh my," says Nouroz. "Don't you see? They're girls. Girls everywhere. Before Dadi, there were no girls in theatre. Well, not many. Not young ones. But Dadi changed all that and now they are up there on stage, singing, dancing, va va, showing everything to everybody."

Jamshed thinks idly that he should have brought his books, but instead says, "But why is that so interesting?"

"Because," says Nouroz, shaking his head, "girls in the theatre are up to no good, which means they are very good for me, do you see?"

Jamshed, not seeing, nods vigorously.

"And Jamshed," says Nouroz assuredly, "I will one day be with one of these girls, no, with many of these girls, and I will be a theatre manager like Dadi Patel, and I will take them to London and Paris and New York, and we will have our way with each other; don't you see how good that will be? I will start by being an actor. You see how good I am at memorizing lines, no? Well, this will be even easier because there will be so much love for me at the same time. What do you think about that, Jamshed, about Nouroz becoming the actor of the century?"

Jamshed thinks on this for some time, looks not right but up to the blackened ceiling of the theatre. "Well," he says slowly, "does that mean you can still be a dastur?"

Nouroz glares at him. It is not a glare of upset or frustration, but a glare that reflects his inner indecision at this moment. Because he has not thought about that, about how being an actor will affect his role as his father's son. "I do not know," he says matter-of-factly. "But I know this is what I have to do."

About girls

Most of the time, talking to me was simple enough. I appeared, Jamshed went right and that was that, no fuss, no muss. It did seem curious to Jamshed that I never appeared while he was occupied in conversation. Certainly, I showed up if there was a lull in the conversation, lull enough for everyone to notice the singular effect of Jamshed suddenly going right, but never right in the middle of a dialogue or someone's sentence, no, that had never happened. Not until Nouroz and Jamshed were talking about sex. Like I said, sometimes there's an imperative, and sometimes I do get impatient.

"It's like this," Nouroz says to Jamshed matter-of-factly, using his three-month elder status and inch-and-a-half height advantage to solidify his certainty, "the father puts the thing in the mother and squirts, and then it's baby time nine months later."

"But where does he put his thing in the mother?" asks Jamshed, eager to learn from his friend.

"Oh, you know, down there."

"Yes, down there, I get it, a man has a thing, but a woman doesn't have a thing, so where does he put it?"

"Between her legs, I guess. Yes, that's it. That's why women cover up that area, not because of you know, but because their legs are very sensitive down there. And if they don't cover them up, well, anyone could become the father of their children."

"So what's down there, then?" asks Jamshed with genuine interest. "Is it something to hold the man's thing?"

"No, no," says Nouroz dismissively. "They don't have anything. It's just the down there part of the woman, which is really part of the leg. The upper thigh if you must have it. The skin there is supposed to be like velvet, you know. But it's just skin."

Oh come off it! Just skin indeed. He may as well say the same of a man's 'thing' don't you think? What else is it but skin? But really, the adolescence of it all.

"Well?" says Jamshed.

"Well?" queries Nouroz. "Well what?"

Jamshed suddenly realizes my interjection, however excitable and voluble, was not one to be heard by Nouroz. And Jamshed finds himself in a quandary, not the first of his young life. Should he, or should he not, tell Nouroz of my entrance into the conversation? Or is it one of those things, one of those many things, that just aren't worth bringing up? In a moment, Jamshed decides on omission being the wiser course of action, yet he can hardly ignore me—and a good thing too, considering the odd alleyways this conversation would otherwise go.

I mean, that has to be the stupidest thing a boy can think about a woman. Who taught you that rubbish, Nouroz? Who, hm?

"Um, who—who told you about that part of a woman, Nouroz?" asks Jamshed haltingly.

"Who what? Why, it's common knowledge, you idiot. Anyone knows that. Anyone who has an interest in girls, anyway."

Whoo boy, the bullock carts are dropping their load right in your path, aren't they, Nouroz? Tell him, Jamshed—

"Tell him what?"

"What? Who's him?"

"You," says Jamshed. "I mean, I meant, I want to tell you that—"

—that his mouth is acting as his rectum—

"—that you may not know what you're talking about—"

—but at least a rectum would know what else was down there—

"I don't know what I'm talking about, Mr Jamshed Knows-So-Much?"

"Well, what I meant was—"

—that the complement to the penis is the vagina—

"—that the complement to the penis is the vagina."

There, he had said it. He had taken my voice into a conversation. There was no doubting it; his so-called imaginary friend was now asserting a very fine presence in Jamshed's daily life to the point where I was actually engaging in conversations. So what if Jamshed had to be the oral instrument for my otherwise unheard but awfully intelligent voice? My voice was now part of the world, and the world was now up to listening to me, finally. Of course, like all revolutionary plans, this one was off to a rocky start. Nouroz was not exactly in a place of general acceptance of Jamshed through my words; as a matter of fact, quite the reverse.

"A complement to the what?"

To the vagina, you silly boy, the va–gye-na, known by other less savoury, many quite vulgar terms, but all meaning the same thing.

"Um, that's what it's called, I think. The va-gye-na."

"The voh-gye-nuh? I've never heard that before. Where'd you hear that? Who told you that?"

"Oh, I just heard."

"You just heard. And the voh-gye-nuh is something like a man's thing?"

Ha, like a glove is to a hand!

"Um, like a glove is to a hand."

"Like a glove? Are you making fun of me? What does that mean, a glove and a hand? What the hell does that mean?"

It's not that Parsi boys didn't use the language of damnation from time to time, but Nouroz was not one given to such usage. That sort of language, Nouroz once told Jamshed, should be reserved for only the most special and horrific of occasions. Apparently, this was one such time.

"I—I don't know," admits Jamshed. "I just said it is all because—"

—*because you're an uncomprehending moron.*

"—because ... I don't know why, really."

"Hmph," says Nouroz.

"Hm," says Jamshed.

Ho, says I.

Sharing friends

"But why not?" asks Nouroz.

"I don't know. It just doesn't work that way."

"Why not?"

"Well, I don't know. Sunny just can't be—summoned."

"So Sunny can't always hear you?"

"Yes, well, no, only when Sunny is here, I suppose."

"But Jamshed, I am your friend, am I not?"

"Yes."

"And you know if you ever needed anything, all you would have to do is to call me, and I'd come running."

"Yes, Nouroz, I know, but this is different."

"But I want to see him."

"I know, I know. Everyone wants to see him. But I don't even know if this grandchild is a boy or a girl. Everyone thinks I'm talking to a boy, but his voice is like a small child's, so I just don't know."

Jamshed and Nouroz are discussing the direct results of those moments when Jamshed goes right, the conversations he has with his putative grandchild or, actually, the very existence of this invisible descendant. It is a topic Jamshed tires of easily since every relative, every aunt, uncle, cousin of whatever distance, not to mention neighbourhood boys, girls, acquaintances, and friends, always manage to, at some time or other, turn the subject to Jamshed's predilection for going right. It all began, of course, in Surat, and it was only several years later that Jamshed connected that first day at school with his family's sudden shifting of belongings, furniture, and abodes to a quiet Parsi tenement in Bombay. There again, tongues flapped and clucked chicken-like throughout the building, which had many walls opaque to light but porous to rumours, so the Khargat family moved from the tenement to an unassuming Bombay colony. Jamshed had only flashes of memory from that place before they moved to an even more obscure colony, its address redolent with illusions of wealth (it being a mere kilometre from a grander, much more affluent colony), and always, always those questions from those who had heard about him: "What is it like to talk to nobody, is it really your grandson, is that what you believe? Are you sure it's not Ahriman taking you for a dance? Is this not a truly bad thought, and do you truly exchange good or bad words, and does he encourage you to do good or bad deeds? Are you a saint or a sinner, young Jamshed Khargat?"

Bombay is a city of many cultures and many colonies, and it has many places to find yourself and many places to hide, and it is where the new and the old meet, where the British man is as at-home as is the Mussulman. But, truth be told, Bombay is really the Parsi heart and is, this city by the sea, at heart Parsi, and being so, there are multiple deeds done and undone by anyone calling herself a Parsi girl or himself a Parsi boy. (Especially if this boy is Jamshed, only son and child of Beramshah, the respected dastur from Surat, whose father and father's father and father's father's father were all devoted dasturs for the communities in Surat, and aren't we lucky to have him here, shame about his son, Jamshed's his name, and he speaks to angels, or demons, and there is no ceremony, no purification ritual, no thing, indeed, that will break him of this mystical ability.)

So it is not surprising that Nouroz, also a son of a respected dastur, is Jamshed's best friend and thus entitled to ask him questions about his imaginary friend. The problem is, try as he might, Jamshed is unable to summon his grandchild, his see-through companion, even at his best friend's bidding. On this one point he is certain. At first his parents were extremely disturbed that their only offspring was so indubitably touched. As Soona said to him several years before, "It is all very well and good to do this thing you do, Jamshed, only you must tell me, now that you are all of seven years old, you do not really see this boy, do you?"

"Yes, Mummy," Jamshed had replied, "I have tried and tried not to, I really have, and I have done what you and Daddy have said, which is to see Sunny but to understand there is nobody really there. And I tell Sunny this and then Sunny laughs and then I laugh because it is silly to say to someone who is there that that someone is not there."

At first Beramshah and Soona thought their son would grow out of this nonsense. Perhaps all this was a good thing, they speculated, for they moved from the land of their forebears and came to Bombay where they would make a new and special life for themselves. All things happen for a purpose. And what of it if people talked? They might gossip idly about how this going right meant this thing or that, but what did they know? No one dared to say to the dastur's face that his son was cracked (or that such ill-fitting behaviour did a disservice to his father's faith), and after a while, incredible as it may sound, Jamshed's going right became just another of those inexplicable and yet acceptable things that eccentric members of any community experience. Not something to be alarmed by, not something to fear or laugh at, just a curiosity; in fact, something to be oddly proud of: See here, we have the oddest children and yet we accept them just as we always accept change and all things good and modern.

Still, and perhaps because of the desire for things modern and western, it was soon suggested to the Khargats that their son undergo a bit of head-doctoring, a visit to the freshly trained psychiatrist, a Parsi boy educated abroad, who had actually spent a year in Vienna studying under the notable Sigmund Freud. While all this was quite new and suspicious to some in the community, it was decided, in the summer of 1912, that Jamshed should be seen by Yezdi Doctor. Yezdi's great-grandfather, as his surname would indicate, was himself a surgeon of some repute, but neither his grandfather nor his own father had studied medicine, choosing instead the equally respected fields of law and business respectively. However, his father had encouraged young Yezdi to go abroad and study medicine, which he did at Cambridge before hearing about the goings-on in Vienna and, thanks to a home-grown scholarship, went off to learn the ways of Dr Freud. In truth, Yezdi had only met Dr Freud twice, once at a reception at the university, and then again, in a less formal environment, after a lecture at the university hospital where Yezdi was studying the new field of psychoanalysis. Nonetheless, Yezdi felt himself eminently qualified in this new field, and he had no shortage of patients at his growing clinic in Malabar, both from Parsi and non-Parsi clients who felt the urge to learn about their ailments through the discoveries of this Freud they had heard so much about, even though the language of the unconscious and the analysis of unnatural maternal relationships were still some years away.

"So when will you see him?" asks Nouroz.

"I told you, I don't know. Sunny just appears and we talk."

"No, no, silly. I don't mean this grandchild of yours; I mean Doctor Doctor."

"Oh, yes, Doctor Doctor. I see him tomorrow afternoon. Do you want to come with us? Mummy says we can go for ices after."

"Ices? Can't say no to ices on the beach. Do you think this Doctor fellow will find out about your going right?"

Jamshed shrugs. Many had tried, but none had answers.

"What is it like, Jamshed, to have someone to talk to?"

"What is it like? It's like you and me, Nouroz, we talk to each other."

"Yes, but that is different. I talk to you and you talk to me. I see you and you see me."

"And that is exactly what it's like with me and Sunny."

"But it's not the same. You can see me, but so can my parents. So can my other friends, and my sister and everyone on Colaba Beach and at the temple and everywhere."

Jamshed thought about this for a while. "Well, maybe when Sunny and I are walking on Colaba Beach, other people see him too!"

"But no one can see him."

"I don't know if that's true. When you are at Colaba with your family and you go running to the water and you pass by hundreds of people, do they all see you?"

"Well, they could."

"Well, maybe they could see Sunny too."

And so it would go, Jamshed more than willing to talk about going right but never ready to concede, even as an adolescent just recently turned thirteen, that he was subject to imaginary bodies floating in and out of his world. Anyone could be real to anyone, he would argue, and so eloquently sometimes that his father couldn't help but admire the philosophical charm of his son. But where his father and most in the Parsi community saw this as a peculiarity, to say the least, it was in May of 1912 that Yezdi Doctor would pathologize the boy's idiosyncrasy as a psychological problem, which, like any such problem, was subject to cure.

"You are a very smart boy, Jamshed, everyone says so," said Doctor Doctor at their first meeting in his office in Malabar Hills.

"Thank you," said Jamshed.

"And as a smart boy, you must realize that what you are going through is a mite unusual?"

"Yes, they tell me this is unusual, but to me it feels perfectly normal."

"Of course. To you it is normal. Do you know what sort of doctor I am, Jamshed, have they told you that?"

Jamshed shrugged. "They told me you were a mind doctor."

Yezdi laughed. "Well, not exactly, but that's the idea. You see, when people get diseases of the body, they go to a physician who might give them medicine, or if they break a bone, they will have a doctor set it in plaster. But the matters of the mind, as you put it, are quite different. There are not always medicines I can prescribe and there is no plaster to apply."

"Unless I fall on my head," offered Jamshed.

"Yes, I suppose," said Yezdi, laughing again despite his attempt to make this sound suitably serious. "But when I deal with people's minds, I deal with what's inside, not outside. And I'll be honest with you Jamshed, I have no cures."

"No cures?"

"That's right. None. And do you know why?"

"Because," started Jamshed haltingly, "because you're not a very good doctor?"

"Well, that could be, but no, it's because my patients have their own cures. And it's my job to help them see those cures, do you see?"

"Not really."

"Well, it's like this, Jamshed. Suppose I were to convince you that every time you, what do they call it, go right, it's a cry for help. You don't really need to do this going-right thing, but it's the only way you know how to cope with your life, do you see?"

Jamshed nodded, although he had no idea what Doctor Doctor was talking about.

"Good. Now, if I were to tell you that next time you were to go right, instead of going off like that for many minutes on end, instead you would, oh, tap your foot, wouldn't that be much better for all concerned?"

Jamshed nodded again, although again he saw no particular use for foot-tapping in this instance.

"That's right. Well, we will talk again in a few days, and before long, I can assure you, we'll have you toe-tapping instead of talking to invisible beings."

"Uh, Doctor Doctor?"

"Yes, Jamshed?"

"Does that mean I can no longer talk to Sunny?"

"Sunny? He has a name then does he? My guess, Jamshed, is that after a while you will have no need to talk to Sunny."

Jamshed nodded for a final time as Yezdi stood up and led him to the door. *This is a very confusing world*, thought Jamshed. Doctors whose first name and last name was Doctor but who seemed very undoctorlike indeed. Family and friends who seemed desperate to have Jamshed stop doing what seemed so perfectly natural to do. And, lest he forget, a grandchild who would not be born for another forty-some years insisting on interrupting Jamshed at the most inconvenient of moments and making his life an ongoing spectacle.

Jamshed did return to Doctor Doctor the next week and then again the week after, and then for yet another five weeks, during which time Jamshed tried very hard to please the physician as he would a teacher, and not without success. Indeed, after their seventh full session together, Yezdi Doctor emerged from his office into his waiting room, his arm draped around Jamshed in a fatherly manner and, despite his earlier deferential response to his new patient about not having cures, beamed down upon the boy and announced to the nurse and assorted clientele, "Jamshed, I have cured you," which elicited a rippling murmur of approval from all those present. As he would later explain to Jamshed's parents, Yezdi had employed that toe-tapping option, suggested through a series of hypnosis sessions, so that, instead of that annoying going-right behaviour, whenever Jamshed felt the need to absent himself from a situation (undoubtedly brought about by neuroses contributed to by low self-esteem), he would begin a rhythmic tapping of his left foot, a tapping that would cease when his need to be alone and anti-social had passed.

To Beramshah and Soona's delight and the great excitement of the community in general, Jamshed's therapy was remarkably successful. It became so talked about that mere acquaintances (and occasionally strangers who had never met him before) tried to engage Jamshed in lengthy conversations, making him far more popular than ever before (much to his consternation), conversations whose entire point seemed to be a waiting game to engage Jamshed up until the time his left foot began tapping. Of course, sometimes it would happen almost immediately, while other times people would tire themselves out trying to think of new things to say to Jamshed, and yet his foot would not start its predictable and much-awaited motion. When it did happen, however, it was to the relief of all those present as evidence that Doctor Doctor was a fine doctor indeed and had enabled young Jamshed to get on with his life. Parents, relatives, the Parsi community at large all felt this relief, but it would be a mistake to think that this relief was universal, for there was one Parsi soul to whom this was anything but a relief, and that, of course, was Jamshed himself.

You've changed.

"Hm, I have?"

Yes, you've changed. You don't look at me anymore.

"I don't? I don't think that's correct. I look at you."

No, not like you used to, direct and eye to eye. Now you just look at me out of the corner of your eye; it makes you look devious.

"I suppose that's what the doctor ordered."

Which means?

"The doctor, Doctor Doctor. He wanted me so badly to stop going right—"

And when you went right, that was when you were looking at me?

"That's when I was looking directly at you, eye-to-eye, as you would have it," Jamshed says. "Oh, I still see you as I always did, which is to say not at all, because I have never really actually *seen* you, just looked at the place where you seemed to be, but now I don't have to look at that place anymore. Does this make sense?"

I see, you avert your eyes. Interesting. I feel like I'm a burning bush.

"What?"

Judeo-Christian humour. So that's where all this new musical you comes from, too?

"Oh, you mean this?" Jamshed points to his left foot, bouncing up and down as if to an invisible beat.

Exactly.

"Yes, you see, I realized that when we enter into conversation I don't have to go right. I took Doctor Doctor's advice and, whenever you come on to the scene, my foot starts tapping."

And the good doctor was happy with that?

"Well, not exactly. I had to say I was no longer 'escaping reality,' as he put it. That is, he means talking to you."

So you told the doctor you no longer talk to me.

"No, no, not in so many words. I told him that I no longer had to disengage from conversations by going right—which is true, by the way, because now I can have my conversations with you and with others all at the same time."

And that doesn't make you sound crazy?

"No. You see, the doctor did help me out. Certainly, he wanted me to deny your existence, which is quite silly as we both know, but what he did teach me to do was to concentrate. My foot starts tapping when you walk into the room, and I don't have to drop everything I was doing just to talk to you."

But when you speak—

"That's the funny thing. Must have something to do with the foot. When I speak to you, well, I don't speak, at least not out loud."

But you're speaking now.

"Not really. I mean, I've learned to speak only to you. For that, I don't need my larynx, my tongue, my teeth, my lips!"

So, I can hear you—

"Just like I can hear you, but I've always heard you. I just figured out that since nobody else could hear you, or see you for that matter, you had to be communicating with me differently. And I think I've learned how to speak to you in, well, your own language. I'm speaking to you in just the same way you're speaking to me."

That would explain it.

"Explain what?"

Why ever since you stopped going right, your lips move in a funny way, like they're out of time with your voice.

"Actually, my lips aren't moving at all. Well, I guess they are for you."

So everyone's happy now?

"Well, I am. I think you are. And the rest of them, well, as long as my toe keeps tapping and I don't look like I've lost touch with the world, they're happy."

Wonderful. Let's celebrate.

"How?"

Let's start up a band?

"A what?"

Hm, wrong context. Let's make a business plan.

Working for a living

It was not, as Beramshah promised, promptly on his twelfth birth-day, but in the early weeks of 1912 that Jamshed was sent to Jamset-ji Tata Jr's office for a consultation. It was an uneventful meeting, one of many that Tata Junior was having with young charges from the Parsi community. Indeed, Beramshah later found out that Tata had made a series of unfortunate business decisions and was trying to rectify those past wrongs by reaching out to provide education and training for Parsi boys and girls in Bombay, particularly those from not-well-to-do families. While Beramshah was pleased that his son would gain some experience and be brought closer into the fold of the community, he admitted concern that the young Tata may not be the brightest business mind from which to receive training. However, when he found out that Jamshed had been offered a job as a stock boy in a general store, one in a chain of stores operated by the young Tata, and that he would be supervised by the owner/manager, one Mr Schroff, he was consoled. Jamshed took the job and worked at stocking shelves after school, graduated to working the front counter and assisting customers, and, after two years of this, was quite an accomplished junior proprietor.

Jamshed continued his studies and continued to work in Schroff's General Store for the next several years. He also continued to have occasional conversations with me, unknown to anyone else. In 1917 he watched Nouroz cross the stage as Hamlet, even while both of them continued their studies as dasturs. I would be there every so often to remind him of rotating anna coins and the possibilities they could produce, and even when Jamshed was a bit irritated with me, he did pay attention. It was exactly seven years after he had started working at Schroff's, seven years after he had committed himself to a life of business and spirituality, seven years after he had visited the site where now stood the Gateway of India and met the person who was to change his life forever, that that person, Parvin Khory, re-entered his life.

The young schoolteacher came into Schroff's looking for school supplies for her kindergarten class, and it was as if, for Jamshed, he had never left the water's edge. Only now he had spittle in his mouth and could speak a blue streak to anyone who listened, and with such a streak, he was upon Parvin; could he help her, what might he find for her, how should he serve this particularly fine customer? Parvin, if she did recognize him, did not let on. Certainly, she smiled that sweet effervescent smile, but that was not reserved for special people, nor were her dancing eyes and playful wit. Yet she did return, week after week, always on Fridays. Jamshed would wear special clothes on Fridays, would comb his hair so many times on Friday mornings it was a wonder he did not uproot his entire scalp, would hope against hope that when Parvin entered that it was quiet in the store, which it rarely was on a Friday afternoon, but Jamshed would do what he could to serve other customers fairly before devoting himself to his fair lady. And so it went for a full forty-two weeks until Jamshed thought he could bear it no longer, and he said to Mr Schroff, "I must find a way to get Parvin to marry me."

"Marry you?" said the elderly Schroff. "What would possess you to have her marry you?"

"What do you mean?"

"Why, she is magnificent, beautiful, intelligent, the epitome of Parsi womanhood. And you, well, yes, you are a fine boy, Jamshed. But."

"But what, what is wrong with me?"

"Well," said Schroff, "for starters, your ears. And your nose. And that strange way you have of your eyes looking like each belongs to a different person. And—"

"But those are looks, Mr Schroff. Surely Parvin can see the looks that live underneath?"

"Surely. But why settle for that alone? Look at her!"

"Mr Schroff. Let it be known to you now that I will marry Parvin Khory if it is the last thing I do."

"And indeed it might be. She lives with her brother, Rustom, a fine fellow who has raised her, since her mother died when she was very young and her father died several years ago. So, I suppose it is her brother you will have to approach. But first, young Jamshed, it is likely that you should talk to her first. If she's not interested (and I cannot for the life of me see why she would be), there's no point involving family."

"No," said Jamshed. "I will go to the family first. If they accept me, then she might too."

This is exactly what he did. One Sunday in May, he called upon Rustom Khory and his wife, Naja. They were quite pleased to have him for tea, for Jamshed had a fine reputation as a good worker and a good Parsi boy, a little touched in his youth, or so the story went, but a nice chap all in all. They thought he might be approaching them with a business venture, or perhaps a spiritual matter, for the young Jamshed was already developing a reputation as a well-respected dastur. So imagine their surprise when Jamshed cleared his throat and announced he had the intention of asking Parvin's hand in marriage. Now, Rustom and Naja thought him a very nice boy, but in their eyes, his future was, if not dim then not brightly lit, and one had only to look at Parvin to see the potential awaiting this fine young woman.

"But you cannot refuse me," argued Jamshed.

"We just have," explained Naja, sipping on an iced tea.

"But I must marry her!"

"That is impossible," said Rustom, imagining the suitors that were bound to come calling soon.

"But you haven't even asked Parvin. Should she not have a voice in this decision?"

"A good point," said Rustom. "And you are quite correct. We shall ask her." And ask her Rustom and Naja did, that very evening after Jamshed had left. "This young Jamshed came calling on us, not out of politeness, Parvin, but to see if we would honour his request to seek you out in marriage. We told him no, but what say you, do you want to marry this Jamshed?"

"Jamshed. Who is Jamshed?"

"You don't know him?"

"I know no one by that name, no."

"He said he sees you every Friday at Schroff's General Store."

"Schroff's? That shopkeeper is Jamshed?"

"Indeed, at least, that is what he says."

"Oh my. Oh. Well, in that case, definitely not!"

"And that is your final word?"

"Final word? Have you seen him? His ears, his nose, his face? Why, he's awfully ugly, wouldn't you say?"

"Quite."

So the decision was made. When Jamshed returned the following week, Rustom and Naja (Parvin hid herself away in her room) informed Jamshed that Parvin had refused him and that was that.

"Oh," said Jamshed, not in that acceptance way, but in that we-shall-see way. Now, I know this is not my place, indeed, I have no idea where my place is in this endless state of deferral, but I did pop in as Jamshed left, and I suppose I am partially at fault for saying something desultory like, *Well, this may not be the end of your life, Jamshed, old man, but this certainly takes the stuffing out of mine;*

might as well drive an ice pick through my temple, the way things are going.

That Friday, Parvin came into Schroff's to purchase some more paper supplies for her kindergarten class, and Jamshed, uncharacteristically, turned away from two customers and came directly to her.

"Parvin, what can I do for you?"

"Oh, yes, Jamshed, no? I would like some corrugated paper for my students."

"Fine fine, I will get that for you. Anything else?"

"Oh, no, I do not think so."

"Good, I will fetch that for you. And then I will commit suicide."

"I beg your pardon?"

"I said I would fetch your corrugated cardboard for your students, ring it in, and then take my own life. Excuse me." And Jamshed went into the back room, emerging a few moments later with two large sheets of corrugated cardboard and an ice pick.

"Will this be all, Miss Khory?"

Parvin stared at Jamshed, at the cardboard, at the ice pick and nodded. Jamshed ran the items through the till and accepted the small change from Parvin, nodded back, and then picked up the ice pick, holding it to his throat.

"Thank you, Miss Khory, and good day."

"What in God's name are you doing?!"

"Oh, this? I am killing myself because you will not marry me. Good day, Miss Khory." And with that Jamshed began to press the ice pick into his throat.

"Stop that!"

"Oh, I'm afraid I cannot do that."

"Please, Jamshed, this is ridiculous. Stop that behaviour."

"Oh, I will stop indeed, but you must choose your words carefully."

"Words, what words?"

"You must tell me you will marry me and never part from me, and then I will not insert this ice pick into my throat."

"I cannot do that, Jamshed, and I won't be threatened so."

"Then, good day, Miss Khory, and goodbye."

"Wait. Wait! All right, let me think about this. Will you let me think?"

"Of course. Think it over. Take all the time you want." And Jamshed put the ice pick under the counter and went to serve the customers he had so rudely abandoned earlier.

So when Parvin told her brother and his wife what had transpired (tearfully, as it had been quite traumatic), Rustom and Naja both dismissed her concerns.

"He's a lying, manipulative boy, that is all," they said, almost in unison. "He has no intent on suicide. He is just doing that to impress you. You watch. Tell him no, no marriage, not in a million years, and you'll see, he won't end up in a ditch somewhere, mark our words."

Parvin nodded. "Yes," she said. "But what if he does? I could never forgive myself. Never. I could never live with that." And at that moment, Parvin remembered standing beside her father at the place where the Gateway of India would rise and how a strange young boy had approached her, and for a moment there flitted through her consciousness a sense of history and togetherness such as she had never felt before.

"Well," said Rustom, "you certainly cannot marry such a dastardly young man, we would never permit it."

"Yes," said Parvin, her eyes now far away. "I can understand that. Rustom, Naja? I will marry Jamshed Khargat." And she turned and went to her bedroom to reflect on what her married life would bring her.

The marrying kind

An ice pick?

"Seemed like a good suggestion at the time."

But I was talking metaphorically. And about me.

"True enough. But it seemed to turn the trick."

Indeed. But now I have a grandmother who thinks you're crazy too.

"It is getting to be a large club."

Why couldn't you just pursue her like any normal boy?

"I did. What is the problem anyway? Things are working in your favour."

I suppose. I just thought there would have been a better way to get to good deeds aside from strange thoughts.

"Well, it is as you say. Maybe the strangest and oddest of thoughts, the ones that seem the worst on the surface, are the best underneath?"

Oh my. One might suppose.

"One might be right. Who is to say?"

Who is to say, indeed.

It is not as if Jamshed and Parvin were married right away. Indeed, theirs was a courtship that lasted a full ten years, from 1919 until 1929. They were not technically engaged until 1922 because Parvin's family would have none of it. "This boy is touched," they would say. "First, this business of going right, now this suicidal tendency. And to what end? To blackmail you into marriage? This is not right, Parvin, not right at all." Most of this was coming from Rustom, but Naja was also there by his shoulder, bouncing her head up and down as was her wont, repeating the last two words of each sentence, so that she could both affirm his words and have the last say.

So it was not until 1922—by which time Jamshed and Parvin had a chance to truly get to know each other, explore Bombay culture together, as courting boys and girls do, to come to terms with what Jamshed called his passion for her (and Parvin called his stupid aggression that could have backfired terribly)—that the two of them decided that marriage was truly what they would do. And later, Parvin would marvel at this decision because, as much as she liked to play Jamshed on this one, she knew that without his buffoonery with the ice pick, which even then she knew was nothing more than melodrama poorly performed, she would not have given him a second glance. And now she was going to marry this Parsi boy from a not-wealthy family, and that was her choice. Choice. Yes or no. Like flipping a coin, she once thought, never herself having had the experience of having an anna coin getting stuck in the sand on end, either heads or tails, win or lose, yes or no. Middle grounds did not exist. "Yes," she said one July evening. "Yes, I will marry you." And Jamshed clasped his hands in front of him, not in overjoyment, because by that time both he and she both knew their marriage would be inevitable, but because she had finally uttered an affirmation of what for him had always been the ineffable. But why? Because, she would tell her brother and sister-in-law just moments before the wedding, Jamshed was loving, kind, sincere, and jovial, and she grew to love him more and more each day.

The wedding itself was an incredibly large affair, pulled off on a modest budget. Not only did the entire Parsi community want to see this going-right Jamshed fellow finally wed, but Parvin was known to be one of the most beautiful girls in Bombay, and to see her tie herself to the floppy-eared, skinny-nosed Jamshed was just too much for some to pass up in their almost morbid curiosity. In fact, there was even a good turnout for the *mandav-saro*, where Rustom and Nouroz jointly planted a mango sapling just near the front door of the small tenement where Jamshed and Parvin had decided (and could afford) to live. There was quite some fuss as family and friends looped flowers over the sapling and much ado about where each petal should go and where it should not, no small feat with so many insisting on proper placement. But they all got through that, as they had the *adarni* when Parvin was brought, reluctantly some thought, to Beramshah's house.

"Welcome, my daughter-in-law!" yells Beramshah, as is his habit now that he has become a bit deafer.

"Yes," says Soona, "you come today to take a new husband and a new name, quite something."

"You make me feel welcome," says Parvin. "I do take a new husband with this *adarni*, yes." But she says nothing about a new name. To go from Khory to Khargat, such a little thing one would think, barely a syllable gone awry, from an *ee* to a *gatt*, but still, these little things troubled Parvin. Troubled her greatly. So she is silent on taking a new name. Later she will say to Jamshed, "You know, I have always liked how Khory sounds, not ending with the staccato finish in Khargat." But Jamshed does not realize what she is saying and simply agrees, and while times are such that Parvin is prohibited from actually keeping her name, and from the *namzad kardan* on, she will be known as Parvin Khargat, the truth in her heart is that she is always a Khory, and her children and, she imagines, her children's children will be Khorys too. They can be Khargats as well, she admits to herself silently, but once a Khory, no going back.

The wedding is a grand affair, and it all goes swimmingly but for the *achu michu*. After the *nahn* baths, Parvin prepares her *mathabana* on her head, and then she and Jamshed perform the kusti ceremony they have known since navjote. There is that trouble with the achu michu, but it is quickly overlooked once they proceed to the *hathevaro*, the simple white sheet that hangs between them as a dastur (not Beramshah, of course, though he would have loved to officiate) winds the thread around both their clasped hands. And then, after much winding and twisting, they are turned to face each other, the beauty and the beast as others would refer to it later, and the *ashirwad* is said, and all is done. But in the back of the minds of many, and certainly in Parvin's mind, is that achu michu. It is, she tells herself, only a ceremony, nothing more, no utter significance to be read through all of this. The seven-times rotation of the egg over Jamshed's head, the breaking of the shell at his feet and the splurting of white and yolk on the ground, all very good, and then the same with the betel and areca nuts, the date, the almond and the sugar, and finally the same with the coconut, all fine and good. But when it comes to Parvin's turn to take on the ritual that reflects the seven Amesha Spentas, then, then there is oddness, to say the least.

At the first rotation of the egg, Parvin thinks: "I should have been a better future daughter-in-law to my future mother-in-law; the taking of a name, such a small thing. I should have simply said yes, what would have been the harm in that?"

At the second rotation of the egg, Soona thinks: "Such a beautiful daughter-in-law; what a surprise! I would have thought Jamshed would end up with a toad, not that he is not a wonderful son, just that, look at him. What luck."

At the third rotation of the egg, Nouroz thinks: "You lucky dog, Jamshed, you threaten to kill yourself and get yourself a wife, and here I am, bacheloring around, not that that is such a bad thing, just a fellow has to settle down, even in the theatre."

At the fourth rotation of the egg, Beramshah thinks: "I have fulfilled my charge, raised a good honest son who will be a wonderful dastur in his own right. I am proud and happy, and it is a good thing."

At the fifth rotation of the egg, Rustom thinks: "I never thought I would see the day she actually married him, but truthfully, I am not as disappointed as I thought I would be. This Jamshed fellow is actually all right; I mean, a bit strange, but at least that nervous twitch of his seems to have disappeared."

At the sixth rotation of the egg, Naja thinks: "I am hungry, but I should not think of hunger now, not at this auspicious time, yet still, I am. Oh, how beautiful they both look. What a day. What a marriage."

At the seventh rotation of the egg, as if on cue, Jamshed's toe begins to rap out a military beat on the ground, so rapid it looks like his foot is vibrating, and Sunny thinks: *Jamshed, there you go, and you said it would never happen.,*

"Go away," thinks Jamshed in return.

Away? This is my history writ small, or early, as the case may be. I want to celebrate from the rooftops. My grandfather and grandmother—can you imagine?

"Sunny, not now, please," Jamshed says as his foot begins a dance that none have seen it perform before, as if it is on fire.

But this is my day, I mean, your day of course, but now, you see, I can see myself in both your sets of eyes. Oh, happy day!

As Jamshed's foot seems about to twist off, as suddenly as it started fibrillating it stops, and there is silence. There is a beat-beat as the seventh rotation stops, and the egg begins its descent to Jamshed's now-still feet. As the egg plummets, Jamshed does the unthinkable, the thing cured by Yezdi Doctor, the return to the child that he is no longer, the movement that was so distinctive and now is but a memory, except that right now, right at this moment, Jamshed goes right. And screams, the egg but an inch off the floor by his feet, "Sunny, leave me now!"

The eggshell shatters, but not with a satisfactory crack and sploosh but a clunk and grunt. All eyes are on Jamshed, and yet all eyes are simultaneously on what should be egg yolk spilling on to the floor but is, instead, the oddest of oddities. The eggshell is broken so neatly one would think it had been carved in two, and from its confines comes rolling a ball of what looks like fur and skin and meat and bone and wizened flesh and all the composite elements of the universe itself, rolling out as if it were alive, shimmying over to Jamshed's now-untapping foot, stilling itself on his big toe, and making apparent that this ball of everything is nothing but death itself, a ball of all, the detritus of living long and full, a ball that almost burps to a stop, is still, and rocks there for a moment before becoming forever more entrenched in the memories of every single soul at Jamshed and Parvin's wedding.

Unbirth me now

What was all the commotion about?

"You were there. I thought you would know."

Sometimes I feel like I am just a casual observer to your world, Jummy. Hey, I just came by to talk, congratulate you, and then all sorts of craziness broke loose.

"You came to me just at the time of the achu michu."

Ah, now that's a nice one, all about fertility and futures, quite symbolic, eggs and such. Yes, I like that one.

"Yes. But then there you were. And then there were the contents of the egg. Not good. Not good at all."

The contents? Not the stuff of omelettes.

"No. More like a monster birth. There were things—things sticking out. Even the dastur shook his head like only something bad could come of this, although he so nicely pretended all was fine and, while he was scooping that—mess—into a bag and getting rid of it, told all our guests that everything was fine. Oh, Sunny, it was awful. And to top matters off, all people could think about was how this happened just when you appeared, or rather, when I appeared to be having foot seizures. I had to tell Nouroz it was you, and there were others there who heard me say that, too, and now they know that the going-right thing never went away, just went into my foot. And once again, they think I'm crazy."

That old thing? Crazy because of me?

"No, crazy because of me. You remember, no one knows you exist. You are a non-you. And even you admit you have yet to be born."

Trivial matter, really. But true. So what now?

"Now? Parvin is a bit sullen, but she will be all right. I think—I

109

think the only thing I can do, to prove myself to the community, is to take up my dastur duties fulltime."

Give up the shop?

"Give it up and become a dastur round-the-clock, yes. It will show everyone how serious I am—can be—how I can provide for my wife as a good-thinking, good-speaking, good-acting dastur. That should be enough."

Enough, yes, enough for what? Will they once again tell you to stop speaking to me?

"Yes, probably. Or I will tell myself this. Sunny, will you ever stop visiting me, do you think?"

Jum, would you want me to?

"Sometimes, I think—no, I suppose not, whatever the consequences."

Do you still think I'm evil?

"I never thought that."

Oh yes, you thought about that. You wondered if I was an evil entity sent to test you, if I wasn't your grandchild but an ogre of sorts. You did think that, you told me so."

"Hm, yes, I suppose. I think at one time I did wonder, but I no longer believe you are or could be evil."

And why not?

"Why, I suppose it's because I believe you, that you are my flesh and blood—you will be my flesh and blood—and will carry the Khargat name. And that stands for goodness."

What if I am both a Khargat and a delegate of Ahriman?

"Are you trying to trick me into a philosophical debate again, Sunny? I don't like being baited."

And what if I am, though, what if I might be?

"Then you are no Khargat and are, indeed, a lying demon sent here to subvert me. So I must make a choice, but as I told you, I have already made that choice. You will be my grandchild, and can no more be evil than I can. I am confident in knowing the ways of goodness such that I can call myself good-hearted and not feel vain. At the most, I might be misguided at times, as might you, ghostly apparition or not. But not evil. Not you. Not me."

Well phrased, Grandfather, well phrased. But do you believe that? I don't mean in your words, but in your thoughts? In your heart?

"I believe them, Sunny, the words, and the thoughts."

Then all actions that follow must be sprung from these thoughts.

"Yes, all actions that follow from this will be good."

You are quite an amazing grandparent, Jum.

"And you an amazing grandchild, Sunny."

Ah, but this I know, Grandfather, this I know!

"Of course you do, Sunny. And now, I must go attend to my wife who will be wondering where I have got off to."

Jamshed's slow toe-tapping stopped. He walked toward the back of the house where he knew he would find Parvin in their bedroom saying her prayers. Standing silently at the door he was not distraught but a bit curious as he heard her mutter something about what might become of her and what had become of the egg. Jamshed soon dismissed those worries, although they would stay hidden like a burning coal in the back of his mind for years to come.

Unbirth me still

The first year after marriage seemed to be the right time for a first child. Their friends and community pointed and laughed a fair bit as poor Parvin bloated up like a carcass (so said old woman Godrej, cackling as she did) at what she and Jamshed told people was four months. "No one shows like that," people said, "at four months." It had only been six months since they wed, so speculation arose that there would be an "early" child, coming at well under nine months post-marriage. Wagging tongues are not always bound to truth, and such was the case here, for at five months Parvin looked ready to burst, and at six ("according to her, tsk tsk," shook the heads of the older women), as if she was overdue and should have given birth yesterday. But the baby wasn't yet born, and the days, then weeks, dragged on. Tongues de-wagged and tsks were un-tsked, when, true to her word, at eight months and twenty-four days beyond when Parvin had surmised her pregnancy had begun (all the excitement of a new house, a new husband, a new life giving way, one night, to almost unimaginable passion), she rose from bed one morning and felt warmth and wetness between her legs, and knew that this was it.

The birthing was a fast affair, the midwives all said, particularly for a first birth, for it was no more than four hours after they arrived in midmorning (the two of them carrying small satchels with their overnight belongings because they thought they would be there until the next afternoon) that the surprisingly effortless crowning occurred. In fact, right from the start, this boy child, Sarosh, was to prove to be an easy-going baby, and later Parvin would lament that, if only he had created more stir, more trouble, she would gladly have endured even a three-day long labour. If only.

The boy grew quickly, effortlessly, and the relatives and friends marvelled at this child, who surely would be a great leader in the world. Indeed, Naja was saying just this to Parvin when the two of them took eight-month-old Sarosh to Mall Road for some shopping. Sarosh clearly enjoyed the ride in the *tonga*, lolling his tongue about and gurgling satisfaction, so that Parvin half wanted to tell the tonga driver to take them once more around the market but decided better of it. Best be frugal when times were good, she thought.

"You wait here," Naja said, "I will be gone for only a moment, and there's no point unsettling the little prince. When we go down there for vegetables, we can all go together. Driver, wait here with mother and child." And with that she scurried into the silk shop. Parvin began playing with little Sarosh's hands, up and down, watching her son smile and drool. She was aware of, but did not acknowledge, the presence of the *sadhu* who had stopped by the carriage and was staring in intently. She kept playing with her child until the grizzled man spoke softly.

"Whose child is this?"

Parvin looked up at him and saw that his face was as gentle as could be but that his eyes were cold river stones, and that frightened her.

"Whose child is this?" he repeated.

Parvin reached into her pocket and withdrew some coins. "Here, take this, sadhu, give us your blessings and go."

"No, no, I do not want your money. Whose child is this?"

"Clearly, this is my son," said Parvin, getting frustrated and holding out her hand with the coins. "Please, take this and be on your way."

The sadhu smiled and nodded and said again, "I do not want your money." And his river stone eyes looked, to Parvin, as if they had been washed over by years of a running stream, and this too frightened her.

"If you do not want my money, then please, move on."

At this moment, Naja emerged from the silk store, clearly unsuccessful in her venture, and she approached the tonga. "Nothing there, nothing there. Let us get some vegetables and be on our way." And then, noticing the sadhu, she too reached into her pocket and looked for loose coins.

"He says he does not want our money," Parvin said matter-of-factly.

"Doesn't want our money? Well, what kind of sadhu are you?" Naja said, smiling slightly, seeing if she could cajole the man into taking a few coins for his meal.

The sadhu breathed deeply, and Parvin could swear she saw the changing directions of a river in his breath, and for a moment the river stones that were his eyes became eyes again, but only for a moment.

"I only came to tell you," he said, eyes closing to hide the river, "that this child should have been born in a Raja's palace and not in your home." Parvin felt a shiver slither down her spine. She still held the few coins in her hand and she again proffered them forth, urging with chin-nodding gestures, take the money, apply your blessings, and be done with it. But the sadhu would have none of it. "That is where he belongs," he said, bowed slightly, and moved off—flowed off, thought Parvin—into the crowd.

"Now what was that about?" wondered Naja. All Parvin could do was shake her head; she did not yet understand why there were tears running down her cheeks.

Parvin could not get the sadhu out of her head, but she did not relate the story to Jamshed, nor did she allow Naja to when, that evening, her sister-in-law began to narrate the tale. "It was nothing,"

Parvin insisted in such a strong voice that it stopped Naja's story entirely. That night, when she and Jamshed lay down together, she felt those tears running down her cheeks again. So it was perhaps not so surprising that, in the morning, Parvin could not, would not, get out of bed. She touched Jamshed ever so gently on his shoulder, so that he knew she wanted him to check on baby Sarosh. He rose, and Parvin listened as he padded to the next room and heard him lean into the crib and pick up their son, and she could hear Jamshed take in his breath unnaturally. And this was enough to bring Parvin to her feet, to move silently into the room, and again touch Jamshed on his shoulder.

"What is it?" she said, her voice the colour of river stones. "Is Sarosh sick?"

Jamshed, his face pressed to the baby's cheek, separated his skin from his son's skin and said, "He is very quiet and a bit cold."

Parvin put her hand to Jamshed's cheek where it had been touching her son; the front part of her hand touched her husband, the back side of her hand brushed her boy. Warmth on one side, cold on the other, the cold that comes with laying a warm item out overnight on cold stones. A cold that so refrigerates a living hand that it might never feel warm again. Parvin did not cry now, just continued to hold her hand there and marvelled at the way warmth did not give sustenance to the cold. "We should get a doctor, then," she said to herself, but loud enough that Jamshed knew this is what they needed to do. And then Jamshed and Parvin locked eyes, finally, and it was only then that Parvin let her tears fall, but Jamshed did not, only because he did not know what he needed to do, what he could do, here in this place, and so he held his wife with one arm, his son in the other, and felt one weep and the other lie still.

In a word

Rain falls hard, the first storm of the monsoons, and Jamshed presses his face to the window of the living room. There are no tears running down his face, but the sheer waves pouring off the pane make Jamshed feel as if he is crying, as if the world is crying, and that gives him curious comfort. It is six months since he held Sarosh's body in his hands, since Parvin's hand touched his cheek. In the six months since then, she has never again touched him with that tenderness, has, in fact, shuddered if and when she came into unintentional physical contact with him. This has been a time of great remorse, of quietness. The world will never sing or laugh again, thinks Jamshed, but he knows his thoughts are running to melodrama, and he tries to push them back into goodness. Good thoughts. How to recuperate good thoughts? He feels a soft touch by his foot and does not need to look down to know that Sunny has arrived as he has every day for the past six months, always starting with the same invocation.

Grandfather Jamshed, I am here for you.

"Hello Sunny. The rains have started in earnest."

You have been watching out that window for a good deal of time.

"You've been watching me watching?"

No. No, I just surmised.

"Well surmised. A wise grandchild. But a grandchild who may never be seen by any other than me, this is what I think sometimes."

Grandfather, it may seem like that sometimes. But I will be real, flesh and blood, and I will be of your blood. Of this I am certain, if of nothing else.

"You never did tell me if your parent, my child, would be male or female. I wonder about that, wonder if your presence had something to do with—with him. Was he the wrong child, was that it? Could he not have lived and gone on to a life that did not involve you?"

You are angry with me then?

"No, I do not know what to believe. I just do not know."

You believe in yourself, and you believe in me. That's enough. Really, that's enough.

"I wish I had your faith in me. I wish I did."

You do. You will.

"Parvin cannot come near me. We sleep beside each other like two dead people, each of us unable to move, skirting around each other. Like two dead people."

Bring her—bring her some fruit tonight, Grandfather.

"Fruit? I should bring fruit to Parvin—for what purpose?"

Because it has been six months. Because she loves you and does not know how to accept that love. Because you have love to offer.

"Fruit. All right, Sunny. Fruit."

That night, there is the usual exchange of silence between Jamshed and Parvin as they disrobe and find ways to stay out of each other's way while preparing for bed. Their mattress is small, so when they lie down to sleep it is exceedingly difficult to maintain any distance between them. At first, soon after Sarosh's death, Jamshed would cycle between reaching out to comfort Parvin (at which she would recoil and pull herself into a fetal curl) or turning away from her as far as he could, balancing himself on the very edge of the bed, teetering, waiting to fall off in his sleep. But after a few weeks, a pair of months, he relaxed into a routine between those cycles, lying on his side, taking up his space, but no more.

And this is how he finds himself tonight, on his back, Parvin a world away from him and only a hands' breadth away. He can hear her breathing, thinks how it always sounds laboured at night as if she were trying to inhale too much of everything into her lungs. And Jamshed lies there for five minutes, then ten, and finally swallows, rises to a sitting position, swings his legs off the side of the bed, and brings himself to his feet. Parvin's breathing does not change. He walks like a somnambulist to the kitchen and finds a bowl of ripe mangos upon the counter. He lifts one, sets it down, chooses another, and sets himself the task of cutting it into fine slices with a slender blade. He leaves the skin on, but the slices are so fine that it takes only a thumbnail to peel back the tip of skin from the fruit's flesh, to suck in that flavour and absorb the meat over his lips and tongue, which Jamshed does with the smallest piece he has cut, and then the largest, so that what remains are eight mango slices, all about the same size. The pit sits in between them all, and Jamshed looks at it, the way the brownness is hidden by orange and green bits, tangly, like so much hair and bone, and for a brief moment it reminds him of split-open eggs, but he puts that thought away before it causes him to remember too much. He assigns each mango slice to its own eighth of a circle on a small plate, eight sickle moons resting on their backs in the sky. He stares at this arrangement for a long time, still tasting the fresh mango in the back of his throat, feeling its stickiness on his lips. And then, still moving like the somnambulist who arrived in the kitchen, he returns to the bedroom, stands at the doorway for some very long moments, then proceeds in and stands at the foot of their bed. There is enough moonlight shining in from their window that while he can make out details clearly, he can't see colours, for everything is awash in silver, even his wife's figure, even the plate, even the sickles of fruit. He turns and steps to Parvin's side of the bed, approaches her body, bends, then kneels by her side, sets the plate down lightly on the mattress and delicately picks up one piece of mango. As he does so, Parvin, lying on her side, her legs drawn up behind her slightly so she forms a backwards S, opens her eyes and sees Jamshed before her, making the most finely cut figure she remembers seeing.

"It," says Jamshed, "is mango."

"You have brought me mango."

That is all they say. Parvin keeps her eyes focussed on Jamshed's fingers, on the fruit, and she parts her lips as if she thought of something to say. Slowly, Jamshed moves the fruit to her mouth, lets it sit between her lips, and with one deft gesture pulls back the skin with an insertion of the very tip of his thumbnail, the skin falling away from the fruit, an effortless ecdysis. The fruit inhabits Parvin's mouth, she rolls her tongue around it and pulls it in, lets it push off the roof of her mouth, feels the juices trickle down, begins the slow process of chewing softly. She smiles, and while it is not the case, Jamshed thinks to himself that this is the first time she has smiled in six months.

"It is good mango," she says.

"I am—I am glad you like it," he says.

And she opens her mouth again.

From that night on, Parvin began to smile more. It did not come easily, nor did such moments stay that long, but smile she did, and things began to change. No longer did she and Jamshed lie next to one another as if in a sepulchre, and when they chanced to touch, she did not flinch. And after some time, maybe it was a month, maybe more, she came to cherish that touch, accidental though it was, and then came the moment when she reached out for Jamshed's hand and pulled it to her. After the first anniversary of Sarosh's death had passed, she came to Jamshed and told him that she was carrying a child again, and he and she were overjoyed, and they wept and laughed and wept again as they remembered the past and thought about the future.

And so it was that almost exactly two years after Sarosh was born, Parvin gave birth to a boy they called Behram. He was smaller, much smaller than Sarosh had been, and a somewhat colicky baby, but the differences were wonderful to behold. It was all they could do, at first, not to dote on the child every waking and sleeping moment, but they soon got over that urge. When Behram was six months old, Jamshed came to Parvin and said he was going on a brief business trip on the behest of Mr Schroff. This would be an opportunity for him to branch out, he told Parvin, to prove himself as a good manager. But Jamshed had never gone away from them overnight before, and Parvin worried about being alone. "We can go together as a family," said Jamshed. "It is an overnight train ride, and then we will stay at a guest house. I can conduct my business during the day, and we can return the following." And so it was decreed.

They get to the train station early and settle into their compartment, graciously paid for by Mr Schroff. Jamshed and Parvin order dinner from the dining cart to be brought in, and feast together until it is time for lights out. Parvin gives Behram his own final feeding before sleep, then rises at four in the morning to give the baby more nursing. At dawn, Jamshed lifts himself off the berth to check on Behram, his son, their collective reason for living. His boy is lying still, slumbering peacefully, and Jamshed has no reason to think otherwise until he lifts the child. He cannot, will not, believe that memory of coldness; no, it must be that the compartment itself is chilled, not the child, and he lifts Behram and tugs gently at his arm to wake the beautiful boy. Behram's arm is cold, and his little fingers are cold and his precious little eyelids will not open. Jamshed turns to look at Parvin who is already awake and looking straight into her husband's eyes. They lock gazes and do not exchange words. Jamshed finally takes Behram over to Parvin. There is only numbness between them as they touch the boy's face, and Jamshed whispers to Parvin, "Listen, we have two hours before we reach the city. If we tell the conductor this now, he will stop the train and put us off, and we will have no way to do the necessary rites for Behram out here in the middle of nowhere." Parvin nods, holds in the grief, and allows it to ball inside her throat, a hoary mass of hair and skin and bone. She takes Behram and begins to sing to him softly. For two hours they travel, and when the train finally pulls into the station only then does Parvin look at Jamshed and hold out her baby and say words that are full of nothing.

"This is done," she says.

"I have no—" says Jamshed.

"It is done." Parvin looks out the window and then back at Behram. She wraps him in the blanket she has brought for travel and rises to collect their things and exit into the cold train station.

Their grief is insurmountable. Not that it needed to be said. No one, indeed, would ever dare enter the Khargat household and say anything of the kind, for this sort of grief permeates walls and doors and windows and it goes beyond words and language. There are no good words left in the universe when this sort of thing happens, not once, but twice. This destroys the possibility of good thoughts existing, destroys the very idea of there ever being good actions for anyone to take. Mourning takes over, mourning not just for a dead son and before him a dead brother, but for all the death in the world that is yet to come, for siblings never to be born and for families never to continue.

Inexorably, Jamshed and Parvin continue. But they cannot stay, this they know, for if they stay in Bombay they cannot stay together. And Jamshed remembers that his whole life is Parvin and he will not let that be lost; he will change the universe before that happens.

"Mr Schroff," he says one day, only a week after the funeral rites, "I must leave."

"Yes," says Mr Schroff, "this I know. Where will you go?"

"I do not know."

"Then let me help. I have a friend, one Mr Cox, a British fellow, who owns a distillery in Nowgong. Do you know where that is?"

Jamshed shakes his head.

"It is far from here, but not so far you will forget your home," says Mr Schroff. "Let me talk to Mr Cox."

Before long, Jamshed is summoned to meet this Mr Cox, and, leaving Parvin in a daze, to be comforted by her brother and his wife, he takes the journey to Nowgong on a quiet autumn day in 1932.

Part Two

A Little Distillery in Nowgong

Distillate

In the heart of Chhatarpur in the state of Vindhya Pradesh is the bustling little town of Nowgong, an agricultural centre whose major distinction in years to come would be as the place tourists might pass through, or stop in for a cup of tea, on their way to sex tours of Khajurao. As such, it became known as a town known to titillate, offering a sort of foreplay before the real frieze action, a foreword to the *Kama Sutra*, if you will. But in 1932, there was not a great deal of tourist traffic to the picturesque and statuesque and oh-my-we-thought-the-sculpture-of David-was-risqué Khajurao.

Nowgong's claim to fame at that time was a result of its having been a British cantonment for irregular cavalry and native infantry, during the heady summer days of 1857, which the then-administration recorded as a mutiny that had to be put down and has since been seen as a ninety-year harbinger of independence for a nation-state and its peoples. It was in early June of that year that word came down the pipe that the sepoys at other stations and garrisons in central India were rising up in some fierce force against their colonial rulers. JiJi Singh, one of fourteen irregular cavalry stationed at Nowgong, was cleaning his carbine when he suddenly turned to one of his comrades and said, "I say, those chaps in Jhansi may have the right idea." Those chaps were the fourteen irregular cavalry who comprised the other half of the Nowgong regiment and who had, on June 6 of that year, turned their guns on their masters, so to speak. So JiJi, always the consummate organizer (the one who arranged for celebrations in the barracks when word came in that a comrade's wife had given birth), made the rounds and talked up the whole uprising to first, his fellow cavalry, then to the infantrymen, and before you knew it, there were twenty-six of them standing shoulder to shoulder, soldier to soldier, collectively uttering the invective, "We will not serve!"

"Now what?" the twenty-five soldiers asked the twenty-sixth, JiJi, who had emerged, if not their leader, then their resistance-advisor.

"We should ... take arms against a sea of troubles," he said, meticulously repeating something he had heard one of the British majors say quite some time ago. It seemed like a good turn of phrase to use, thought JiJi, so he put that forward, although it was rather confusing for most of the twenty-five, whose command of English was spare at best. But they liked the sound of it and they all tried to repeat it, finally committing it to memory, (though memory being what it is, the lead charge sometimes came out as "taking sea arms against troubles," or "taking our troubles to sea," or "troubling our sea against our arms"), and they all knew it was a good enough phrase to strike unity amongst them and fear in the hearts of the British officers.

But the truth was there was little sense of dutiful business here in Nowgong, so JiJi suggested they march on to Delhi and really become part of the stir, and so they all began packing up their kits for the road ahead. That is where the trouble started, for one Major Hal Kirk, a cavalry man himself, got wind that the dastardly Sikhs, Hindus, and Muslims were taking themselves on unapproved leave and decided he must do something about this. Onto his steed he lifted himself and trotted off to the barracks inside the cantonment (having secured quarters in the town itself, meagre offerings, but a place where he could entertain young gentlemen of the area, so it served him well). On this particular morning of June 9, the young man he was entertaining, a swarthy fellow of the Bundelkhand region, urged the major not to ride in with such a swagger.

"This is serious business," he told Hal Kirk, "serious business indeed. There is word around that they will kill British soldiers and wave their heads about on pointy sticks. It is probably best if you just come back to bed and let your superiors in Delhi handle this."

"That," said Major Kirk, "is not the British way," and, having made this pronouncement, off he went. The young man brooded for a bit, shook his head as he thought of how badly this might turn out, then packed up his slim belongings and departed from Major Kirk's place for the last time. Major Kirk rode into the barracks area and saw JiJi ordering men about. "Get this, take that, don't forget this," and on it went.

"What's this, then?" shouted Major Kirk to JiJi in particular but to the others in general. "What's this? This mutiny has reached us at Nowgong, has it?"

"Major Kirk, sahib," said JiJi respectfully, "it is not that we do not like you. It is just that we would like you more if you minded your own business and did that from your own shores."

"Never," said Major Kirk, looking at the horizon in what he hoped was a deep and meaningful manner. "The sun shall never set on the British Empire, and that includes Nowgong. Our Nowgong. Your Nowgong and my Nowgong."

"I do understand your desires," said JiJi, hoping to interrupt Kirk before he broke into patriotic song, "but it is time you understand ours."

"And what ridiculous type of talk is that?" asked the Major, now leaning forward so that his breath tickled the ears of his horse, which twitched in response.

"It is the talk of freedom, sahib. It is the talk of men who have served you well while being disrespected by pork grease and beef grease, both insults to their religions."

"Poppycock," said Major Kirk. "Grease is grease. Religion is religion. And never the twain shall meet."

JiJi did not know what this meant, but rather suspected Kirk did not either, so he continued. "Major sahib, we must do what we must do."

"Indeed, and what you must do is put your belongings away and continue to serve the crown."

"That is not what we will do, Major, sahib, sir. No. You must leave us now."

"Leave you! Ha." And with that Major Kirk pulled out a pistol he kept in his belt for just such purposes. He pointed it rather precariously this way and that and then levelled it at JiJi. "I order you to return to your barracks under house arrest," he squealed.

"You do not want to do that, sahib," said JiJi, his arms outstretched.

"I do and I am," said the major, sticking his chin out.

"We do not want to hurt you, sahib," said JiJi in the tone of a man who is giving a last warning.

"Indeed, you shan't," said the major in the tone of a man who has not the wherewithal to heed a last warning.

JiJi slung his carbine off his shoulder and, in one motion, had it pointed at the chest of his superior officer.

"Va va, what are you doing?" shouted one of the irregular cavalry members, pulling out a saddle for his horse. "The crazy British officer will shoot you."

"Listen to him," said the major. "Crazy or not, I stand ground for the crown." And with that he tugged on the reins for effect, his horse reared, the major lost a stirrup and then his saddle, and in a moment was thrust up in the air, lost for a moment in nongravitational space, and then tossed earthward, all of which would have been quite comical had it not been punctuated by a muffled popping sound coming from underneath the major's body where his pistol-gripping hand had tucked itself as he hurtled to the ground.

JiJi shouldered his rifle and went over to the major, who was rolling this way and that, grunting and holding his belly.

"Let me see," said JiJi, turning the major over to reveal a blood-stain where his buckle should have been.

"You have shot me, you swine," cursed Major Kirk.

"You should get this seen to," said JiJi, ignoring the major's misap-prehensions.

"You are a traitor!"

"And you are going to bleed to death. Can you ride?"

"Can I ride? Ha, since before I could walk."

"Very well, then." And with that, JiJi hoisted Kirk to his feet, helped his foot into the stirrup, and, one hand steadying him by the belt, lifted him into the saddle, where the major leaned forward, breathing heavily and bleeding out.

"You are devils on earth," said the major hoarsely.

"You should see a doctor. Ride that way," said JiJi. And when Kirk appeared to ignore the suggestion, JiJi took the bridle and pointed the horse in said direction, slapped its rear and shouted horse-en-couragements, and off the pair trotted into town. The major would not stop in Nowgong, however, and would ride for a full day before finding himself in front of a number of stone friezes depicting men and women performing unspeakable acts on one another, at which point he would tip off his horse, catch a foot unceremoniously in a stirrup, and die in the sand, his eyes looking up at a tangle of legs, arms, and genitalia, his foot ensnared and pointing up at an indig-nant angle that, from a distance, looked decidedly obscene.

But that was the Nowgong of seventy-five years ago, much different than the one the bus pulls into in 1932, a Nowgong into which a hopeless Jamshed disembarks on to a dusty road near the somewhat ambitious town centre where a large sculpture memorializes lost soldiers (this one looking curiously out of place, the horseman's body at a slight tilt and an unstirrupped foot wavering eternally above the fountain). Jamshed is not the only disembarking passenger, but he is the last one standing there after all the others have been greeted and spirited off with family, friends, and business acquaintances. He is to be met by Mr Cox's associate, he has been assured, but there is no one to be seen and, as people do in situations such as this, Jamshed checks his watch. And then checks it again forty-five seconds later. And then again in a minute and a half, although at fifty seconds, he has had to make serious efforts not to glance at his pocket watch again, sniffing the air instead, smelling the wood smoke, and looking around at peeling posters on the statue-fountain's foundation before relenting to check the time. For a business trip, he thinks, this has not started well. Finally, after what seems like ages but is actually only four minutes and three pocket-watch checks later, Jamshed hears a tiny throat-clearing. He looks up. He sees no one at first and then, standing right beside and at the identical height as the wire trash pail bolted to a fragile-looking fence by the fruit stand is a very petite man—at least Jamshed thinks it is a man, but his gender is quite indeterminate—holding a very small white placard upon which something is scrawled in tiny black lettering. The petite man glares at Jamshed, points to the even more petite writing, and gestures to Jamshed to come hither. Jamshed approaches and is no more than five feet away before he can make out the tiny letters: "KHARGUT."

"Is this you?" says the man/woman in a high voice that has just enough gravel in it to maintain its gender neutrality.

"Yes. Well, yes. I am Jamshed Khargat. I think my name is spelled wrong."

"Well then, you should have told me," admonishes the man/woman.

"I didn't know—" Jamshed starts but then realizes he has no finish to this sentence.

"I've been standing here the whole time waiting for you," says the figure, now dropping the useless sign to his side. "I almost left."

"But I'm the only other person here at this bus stop," argues Jamshed, looking around tentatively, for there is no evidence any longer that this is a bus stop and, what with the bustle around him, that he is the only person so waiting.

"Hm. And the only person ignoring his own name."

"But I couldn't see my own name!"

"Well, now you have, and now you do. My name is Manam. I am Mr Cox's associate."

Jamshed holds out his hand. "Manam. I am Jamshed Khargat."

Manam ignores the outstretched hand. "That we have established, Mr Khargat, at great pains." With that, the androgynous figure turns and starts marching into the street, only inflecting slightly with a head movement to suggest to Jamshed that he should follow, kit in tow. This he does, wondering how it is the tiny Manam moves so quickly that Jamshed has to hurry his pace to keep up. They circle around the roundabout statue-fountain, Jamshed is certain, two times, and Manam has already hailed a tonga and would appear to be leaving without Jamshed were not the driver to nod lazily at the luggage-toting man following in Manam's wake.

"The distillery compound is eight miles from Nowgong," Manam says without looking at Jamshed. "Mr Cox has asked that you look at these." He hands Jamshed a sheaf of papers detailing the business revenues, expenses, and other such matters. Jamshed busies himself with reading, looking up occasionally to take in the forested scenery, of which there is little, because, as they proceed along the road that is mostly dirt, the path narrows so that the trees and foliage seem to close in on the tonga, and the light appears to be sucked up by the jungle, making the scratches and marks on the paper that much harder to discern. The journey takes them a little less than half an hour, by which time Jamshed has quite familiarized himself with the business papers and is happy he has had the chance to do so before meeting Mr Cox.

The tonga pulls into the compound, a miniature town in a jungle clearing. In the middle of the compound, Jamshed can see two large buildings, obviously the site of the whiskey-making itself. From his vantage point, he can spy enormous wooden vats, two storeys high, surrounded by catwalks from which chemists and workers and all can inspect the contents. Adjacent to the work buildings are two small bungalows and an even smaller house, and from Jamshed's recent reading, he assumes the former are for the government-appointed liquor inspectors and the latter for the on-site chemist. Further back are the six houses for the clerical staff, all equipped with servants' quarters. The entire complex is surrounded by a huge nine-foot-high brick wall and a single entry gate, through which the tonga has driven upon arrival. It is a speck of civilization in the jungle, Jamshed thinks to himself, and apart from a couple of farms and a few ramshackle huts, the only form of civilization on the way from the town of Nowgong. This might be where he makes his career, his life, thinks Jamshed. And this might be where Parvin will set up home, if such is her wish. On that thought, Jamshed steps out of the tonga and takes a breath, a full deep breath, before following along behind Manam, who is already scurrying to the main building ahead.

Mr Moonalal

Manam leads Jamshed into the main building, the aroma of whiskey permeating the air, and into a back office that seems more appropriate for custodial services than business management. Behind a small wooden desk stands a rotund, moustachioed British gentleman with the air of a military officer, his hands clasped behind his back, his face beaming a huge toothy grin.

"Ha-ha, Jamshed Khargat, Jamshed Khargat, wot? Ha-ha, I am Cox!" He puts a meaty hand over the small desk and grabs Jamshed's barely proffered hand, shaking it heartily for three good pumps, then squeezing it goodbye and letting it drop.

"Wondering, I dare say, wondering what you're doing in the big house, the main vattery, so to speak, hey? Instead of a cushy office over in the clerical building? No doubt, no doubt, yes, that's what you'll be wondering. Ha-ha. Well, you see, I believe in a hands-on approach, being right at the heart of the action, so to speak, right in the middle of the mix, no sense managing from an ivory tower, out of sight, no, must get those shirtsleeves rolled up, find yourself in the trenches, that's what the boys respect, a manager who knows the job inside out, ha-ha."

Then, as an afterthought, Mr Cox turns over his left shoulder and looks to the wall, against which there is a small, creaky chair in which sits, quite upright, a small, creaky man.

"Ha-ha, this is Mr Moonalal. Mr Moonalal, may I present Mr Khargat, ha-ha. Mr Moonalal will depend on you, my boy, will depend on you to run this place, keep it in tip-top shipshape."

Jamshed reaches out to shake Mr Moonalal's hand, and the elderly gentleman—he must be about seventy—stands slowly, nods, smiles, and shakes Jamshed's hand. That feels like a dozen butter-flies in my palm, thinks Jamshed, but says, "Good to meet you, Mr Moonalal."

"*Hanh,* pleasure," softspeaks Mr Moonalal, then sits himself down quietly but a bit creakily.

"Ha-ha, Mr Moonalal doesn't know the first thing about running a distillery, not the first thing, do you, Moonalal?" Mr Cox does not wait for an answer but looks intently at Jamshed's face. "And you, Mr Khargat, do you know the first thing about running a distillery?"

"No, no, sir, Mr Cox, I do not. But if all works to our mutual ad-vantage, I am sure I can learn a great deal from you, sir."

"Indeed you could, indeed you could, and you will, my boy, if you can absorb the running of a distillery in twenty minutes, hey wot?" And with that he gestures to the wall across from Mr Moonalal where a good deal of luggage rests. "I'm off, you see, have sold the place, vat and kaboodle, to Mr Moonalal. I'll give you a tour, not to worry, give you a tour, then you'll have the run of the place, you and Mr Moonalal, and make a damn fine show of it, I am sure."

At that moment a young, very dark-skinned boy in short pants runs into the room, runs up to Mr Cox and tugs at his shirt sleeve. Mr Cox bends down so the boy can whisper in his ear, raises an eyebrow, says "That so?" and harumphs as he stands erect again to face Jamshed. "Well, sir, I have lied, lied to you I say, for I have not twenty minutes after all. My car has arrived, and I must depart. Quitting India. Good day to you, sir, and good business."

Mr Cox comes out from behind the desk and spirits himself out the door. Within seconds, a small band of men take out the luggage, and Jamshed, Manam, and Mr Moonalal are left standing alone in the office. Jamshed waits for someone, anyone, to speak, but as all are quiet, he breaks the silence. "So, what are we to do?"

Manam grunts, yawns, and turns to leave. Over his shoulder he shouts, "Good day to you, sirs, and good business."

"Where are you going?" calls out Jamshed.

"Home," Manam shouts back without turning around. "This place does not own Manam. I do not come with the distillery. Good day and good business." And then, without Jamshed ever quite identifying this curious figure's gender, Manam seems to disappear as if he'd been no more than a sprite.

"Uh, Mr Moonalal. What should we do?"

"Hm," offers Mr Moonalal, settling into a creaky wooden chair behind the ancient office desk. "Mr Cox is quite right, you know. Sold me the business, and I do not know a thing about it. He has it on good reference that you are a fine young Parsi businessman, so I shall leave things in your capable hands." He clasps his hands behind his head and does not try to stifle a yawn.

Jamshed's first temptation is to object, but then resigns himself to what now appears to be his future.

"I will manage this distillery for you, Mr Moonalal, to the best of my ability. Perhaps we should go over some paperwork?"

But Mr Moonalal, despite the excitement of all these comings and goings, has found it all too overwhelming and seems to have fallen asleep behind his desk. Jamshed sighs, sets the papers down on to the small desktop, and then, as an afterthought and an homage to the departed Mr Cox, rolls up his sleeves and begins to pore over the paperwork once more.

In the new beginnings

Parvin sits on the veranda of the magnificent house that she cannot believe she now lives in. This house reminds her of her grandmother's description of their living quarters in Surat, before their extended family fell on hard times. As a child, Parvin heard stories of landscaped gardens and courtyard walls, multiple sitting rooms and servants; all of these seemed stories of the distant past, and yet here she is, living them out. It was not as if she and Jamshed had suddenly fallen into newfound wealth. The salary Jamshed was drawing as manager of the distillery was quite a lot better than he'd earned at Schroff's shop, but was still not near the monies made by middle managers in Bombay. Still, there were perks, and one of them, a huge one, was getting to live in the manager's house, which came with a cook and a servant.

At first the servants' presence embarrassed Parvin; what to do with someone who was there to cook for you, what to do with someone who insisted on cleaning up after you, on cleaning up before you? In her brother's house, to be sure, she had been used to a bit more luxury, not excessive, mind you, but there'd been a sweeper woman who came in, morning and evening. She'd certainly benefited from the cooking skills of her sister-in-law, Naja. But this was different. There she was, all alone during the day, not a Parsi within miles, that was for certain, and this great house to manage, but without the normal chores of cooking and cleaning. And, of course, no children. After their first son died, Parvin was inconsolable; after their second son died, Parvin could see no future for herself, everything turning black as she looked forward. So when Jamshed came to her after his return from Nowgong and said, "Listen, Parvin, there is possibility there, a possibility for a—a new life," she stared at him blankly and refused to answer him. She stared at his large brown eyes and wondered what made them stay lit, and she wondered, but did not care, if her own large green eyes were still the colour of emeralds or had turned to seaweed, just as she felt inside. Jamshed had left her alone for an hour, then returned for tea.

"Parvin? I will do your bidding. This is a chance for us, and I want you to know that. But if you cannot make this journey, if you will not be there with me, I will turn it down. I would rather kill myself than not be with you." The next day, she came to Jamshed and put a hand on his shoulder and said, "We should go," and then turned and went to sit in her chair again for the rest of the day while Jamshed slowly rose and began to make preparations for their departure.

Now, in their house at Nowgong, Parvin looks at this man, her husband, and smiles to herself, although this does not escape into her lips to be shown to him. Or anyone. Jamshed is at the distillery every morning at first light, his first act of independence being to move his office to the clerical building instead of staying situated in the Cox-inspired back room. Mr Moonalal, who had puttered about the compound for the first two weeks, realized that, as an owner who knew nothing about distilleries, and with a fine upstanding Parsi chap to run things for him, he was really doing no service by staying around, so he abandoned the site, promising to make quarterly visits. It occurred to Jamshed that he did not even know where Mr Moonalal called home, but there was a lawyer in Nowgong that had all of his relevant information, and so Moonalal could always be contacted through him.

Every morning Parvin rose just before dawn, always waiting for that first half hour after Jamshed rose and began his prayers, only signalling his readiness to greet the day by a hefty throat-clearing a half hour later. At that signal, Parvin would get out of bed and wend her way to the kitchen so she could put on his tea. The breakfast was taken care of by the cook, a slightly nervous young man with shrew-like features named Gopal, but Parvin insisted that she always make the tea. What else was there to do? She thought that she would find herself very bored in Nowgong, perhaps because others had said that to her: "Parvin, you shall be dreadfully bored. Is there a school nearby? Could you teach young children? Is there charitable work to do? Whatever shall you do?" But she was not bored at all, partly because she had an active mind and mostly because she had lowered her expectations so greatly. She would make mental notes of this or that, count to sixteen on her finger joints as she had learned as a child, idly play with the occasional mathematical formula in her head, and play the observing scientist. Parvin could sit and watch the sun move across the sky, could watch the shadows cast on walls, track the movements of lizards and spiders and centipedes over the floors and ceilings, count the revolutions of the lazy drawing room fan, think of god and what all that meant, and get by as she sat in this house that she now called her home.

This troubled Jamshed greatly—how could his wife survive in body if she could not in spirit? And he would offer her everything, would sing and dance and joke, anything to break her thin-lipped non-smile, but never successfully. One night he even rose and made his way to the kitchen, shushing the cook who'd been sleeping on the cool concrete outside and had come in to see what *Baisahib* would like made. Jamshed took out a full ripe mango, cut it into tiny slivers, sickle moons, and took it up to his beloved. She opened her eyes that time, and if a tiny movement at the ends of tight lips could be interpreted as a smile, well then, perhaps she smiled, but her words belied this action. "I will not eat mango again, Jamshed," and she rolled over and shut her eyes, though she did not return to sleep that night or the night after.

On subsequent nights, she would only fall asleep for bits and spurts, always waking up fitfully with the same dream dancing through her head, of mango sickles touching her lips and sliding down her throat and lodging themselves in her belly where they began to grow, to gestate, and become something monstrous that she could not control, something terrible that would finally be expelled from her body to die. And with these dreams, her face began to grow lined and the first grey hairs appeared on the crown of her head and her eyebrows. It became so painful to watch that Jamshed would extinguish the light before coming to bed, because what had once been such a delight—to view her sleeping face—was now a terrible sadness to gaze upon. They lived this way for six full months, Jamshed rising early, coming home midday, then departing for a late afternoon session with the distillery employees, until one day Jamshed came home all excited and bubbly, and he gripped Parvin uncharacteristically by the shoulders and said he had great news, a great idea, and he must share it.

"We will," he said, trying to control the excitement in his voice, "begin to distil a new liquor." He began to babble furiously about how he had hit upon this idea in his talks with Parsi gentlemen the country over, some of whom were distillery managers themselves, and in their talks he had realized that there was something missing in all their products. In his short time at the little distillery in Nowgong, Jamshed had learned a great deal, had sampled wares from near and beyond (but sampled only, mind you, as he never did take to drink in any serious fashion), and then it came upon him. He would produce a drink that carried within it truth and justice, that brought to the recipient only the finest senses and smells, that carried in its distilled essence memories and feelings so profound that it could only be called one thing, it could only be one thing. He would produce a rum that sweetened the world, he announced to Parvin, and he would call this elixir the only name that befit its taste, its reputation, its utter godliness. He would call this drink Asha.

Parvin looked at him, in wonder at his excitement, in awe at the diverse connections he was making—liquor with religion, the Zara-thustrian way of life with a product, and his own dasturi vision with his business acumen.

"I know, I know what you will say," Jamshed said, shaking his head and holding his hand up as if to forestall her onslaught of objection. "Is this a good thing, this taking of our faith and distilling it into drink? Well, I say this in my defence: I bring humata, hukhta, huvarshta—good thoughts and words and deeds—to everything I do, including my chosen profession, no? Look, see here." Jamshed waves a letter he has produced from his breast pocket. "It is from Nouroz, you remember, you met him at the wedding, thought his ears were too big for his face, that one? He and I, we grew up together, we studied religion and art and business. This is what he has to say: 'Dearest Jum,' he calls me Jum, 'Yes, times are indeed changing, and I must say I am so very proud of you' he is proud of me! 'and what you have become. I think your idea of a new rum is a wonderful chance to express all these things in one. And what better thoughts, what more profound words, what more delicious deeds can you bring than those we have learned so well? This is a good thing, my friend.' You see, Parvin? You see? If my dear friend Nouroz feels this so passionately then it must be a true thing!"

And so it was that the Cox Distillery began producing a fine, resin-coloured drink, a rum that was, indeed, thanks to the research and perseverance of Jamshed and his dedicated staff, the finest rum in all of India, as it was soon reported to be. Asha, truth and justice, distilled.

Another sunny day

Parvin is, on this day in early March in 1933, sitting in the compound watching the marvellous flight of a butterfly as it careens upon the spring breezes that lift off from the garden. Its red-golden wings are on fire in the sunlight and this tantalizing notion fascinates Parvin. She kneels down, right into the earth of the garden, and gazes at the insect as it climbs to the height of the house and becomes ever so small, then seems to grow larger as a downdraft pushes it closer to her eyes, almost to the ground. Frail as it is, it never appears to lose control, acts as if each puff of wind enacts its own desire. Choice made manifest, flitting and flying, living and dying, thinks Parvin. The butterfly does a half turn in the draft, catches a glint of sunlight, and then is lost amidst a wash of ochre-coloured leaves that the same breeze pulls off a nearby branch. There is a bevy of floating bodies now, flitting and flying. Living and dying. When the breeze settles and calm returns, all the leaves are on the ground, and the butterfly is nowhere to be seen.

Parvin surveys the garden for any signs of the butterfly, alive and resting on a flower, or dead amongst the leaves. When she had shown initial signs of interest in the garden's potential, Jamshed had become very excited, immediately ordered special seeds from Pocha Gardens in Poona, and soon (with the help of a local gardener, Abdul, who knew the ways of the native soil, the climate, what would work best, and where and how to lay the seeds for perfect results), the garden was springing with roses and jasmine and a very lovely purple bloom known as passion flower which grew on a creeper that climbed the iron arches in the garden. Even prize vegetables are easily nurtured and harvested from this garden, squash being the particular favourite for this soil and moisture level (assured Abdul, and he was, of course, right). At this moment, Parvin looks rather intently at the passion flower, thinking she spies that butterfly perched on the purple, but it is only a fragment of leaf, and she is a bit dejected, and then alarmed when the wind picks up and she hears her name called.

"Who's there? What's that?"

There is no response but more wind, and she stands and turns a full circle. Depression is one thing, but madness and hearing voices quite another. Just the wind perhaps, flipping through a pair of branches, putting their limbs together to cause a whistling sound that sounds like her name? But then, as she stands so still, the wind disappearing like it was never there and would never return, only her own breath and pulse in her ears, that whispered name again— but where, from where?

"Who is that?"

Silence, and then: *Hello Parvin. My name is Sunny.*

Meeting the family

Thirty-four years, this going-right thing had been going on, and for most of those thirty-four years, people thought Jamshed was a bit touched. The first year or two maybe they put it down to the peculiarities of babyhood, and the last couple of decades, well, most were of the opinion that Jamshed had given up the crazy stuff of boyhood to take on manly things, though there were an astute few who felt his going-right phase had never gone away. "Oh, his eyes do not do that right-right thing anymore, no, but have you seen his foot, Dastur-ji, how it plop-plops like that? Certainly, more of the same thing."

But in all that time, in all those years, two things had never happened. No one, no matter how superstitious or beholden to supernatural beliefs, had ever affirmed that Jamshed was actually talking to somebody; certainly there were those who had insisted that something mysterious was going on, that there were spirits at work, that Ahriman was at play, that something was out there (and perhaps in there, in Jamshed's head), but no one had ever suggested that he was ever really, positively talking to a sentient being. If anyone had had the audacity to suggest Jamshed was engaged in an actual two-way conversation, which would mean there was a second party involved, then said second person in the room had never engaged anyone else but Jamshed in conversation. Certainly, Nouroz had come close, being spoken to, if not through, but that was as close as it got.

I should say that it was not out of any lack of desire to talk to anyone else, just that there seemed to be no need. I had the audience I wanted; the rest would come later. If there was any hint that the boy-turned-dastur was talking one-on-one, then that second one (who did not exist) had never taken the opportunity to talk to any-body besides Jamshed. Until now.

"*Hai nuh*, who is that?" Parvin looks about, to and fro, looking furtively behind her, one side and then the other, looking for the origin of that voice. "Come out, *baiman*, come out you cheater of women, rascal beyond words, come out!" She looks particularly closely at the Christ flower and jumps back when the voice rematerializes, not from the bloom, but from within her head.

It is all right, Parvin. It is me, Sunny.

If Parvin had gymnastic ability she would back flip. As it is, her eyes do the same trick, floating up to the inside of her skull and back down again. "*Hai*, this is craziness, this is it."

Do you really think you are crazy?

"Oh, that is priceless, priceless; the crazy voice inside my head is asking my crazy self if I think I am crazy. To whom do I answer this, hm? To myself? Talking to myself is crazy!

Well, I do not think you are crazy, Grandmother.

"*Hai*? What, 'Grandmother'? What evil voice is inside my head? Cut out my tongue, that is what I must do."

But it is true. You are—you will be my grandmother just as surely as Jamshed will be my grandfather, all things willing.

"Willing? Willing and stupid is what this is. Oh, I am in the nuthouse."

Grandmother, I have been speaking to Grandfather for the past thirty-four years. Now I realize it is time to talk to you.

"Go, go back to the foolish man; exist inside his head. You seem to have been happy there; why leave now? Not enough that there is one lunatic in the family, now there must be two. I should have left him to kill himself, my brother was so correct. It is something I have told myself over the years, if only I had let him do it. Then he could not infect me with this headsickness. Oh, it must be the heat. Or the cold."

Grandmother! Grandmother, it is not like that. For more than three decades I have come to him because he needed me. In all that time, you have not needed me, so I did not come. Now you do, so I have arrived.

"Arrived to carry me away to the place where women drool and have their hair in tatters, that is what you have come for. No, I will not go. I banish your voice."

And with that, Parvin squints her eyes shut, pushes palms against ears, and holds her breath. Perhaps it is the breath-holding or the way her eye-squinting makes the blood pump harder through her facial arteries, but when the voice comes again it is not just clearer, but sounds not just as if it arises, but echoes from inside the walls of her skull, so clear it is.

Grandmother Parvin, you need not be like that. I have come to help you. And to help Grandpapa Jamshed, and, to tell you the absolute truth, to help myself, that is, help myself into existence. Do you understand what I am trying to say, Grandmother?

Parvin opens a single eye to see if that will make the voice change, but it does not, and it repeats the question. "Yes, yes, I see that you will not go away until I am quite crazy, so you have done your job. What is it then? What do you want?"

Remember, Grandmother, the mango slices so long ago?

Now Parvin opens her other eye, unpuckers her mouth, and unclasps her hands from her ears. She takes a deep breath and nods.

That was my idea.

Parvin's eyes widen. Then soften. Then she nods again.

You see, he was trying so hard, anything to reach you. Anything to understand what was happening in your grief. And that made him do all the wrong things. Or, more correctly, it made him not do any of the right things, because he did not do anything. Do you remember?

This time Parvin's nod is more assertive. "Yes. That I remember."

And so in what you might think is a desperate urge to be born, I gave him some ideas, some suggestions.

"But mango? Why mango? Why not a different fruit or a cup of tea or a back rub?"

Good questions. But a tea or a back rub, would that have been enough?

"Silly grandchild. It was not the fruit, nor would it have been the hot liquid or the touch. It was what was in his eyes when he did that. It could have been anything. But you made him change his eyes."

Aha. You see, even the not-yet-born have a thing or two to learn.

"Hm. But, Grandchild, if that is who you are and not a devil, why are you here, what would you have me do?"

Well, I was going to suggest slicing up some mango for him tonight, but now I am not so sure. You seem to have the wisdom I would expect of my grandmother. So I suppose the choice is yours.

"Yes," says Parvin, then waves her hand in the air. "You must go now." Parvin is still for a very long time, waiting for an internal echo to re-emerge, or for her memory to wash over that voice so it never existed. It is too much to be hearing voices. And yet, somehow, a calm comes over her, and she thinks, more than she has in quite some time, about this man she calls a husband, and what he might mean to her, what she means to him. Parvin is surrounded by silence, and in the corner of her eye she catches a flitting that could be a butterfly escaping over the corner of the roof.

Nowruz Mubarek

At the edge of the front garden was a well surrounded by a low brick wall. All the inhabitants of the distillery compound drew their water from this well. Every morning at four, Jamshed carried a small bucket to the well to draw water and would use some of that water to purify his prayer room. (The extravagance and delight of it all, a house large enough to have such dedicated rooms!) Then he would light the fire in the kitchen and put a brass bucket of water to heat on the fire. While it heated, he would walk around the garden and pick flowers for his prayer room, laying them close to the small iron stove where he kept the embers going throughout the months, covering them up at night with layers of ashes and pulling out the glowing bits the next morning to feed with sandalwood and fresh kindling. Jamshed would regularly perform this routine and then bathe and start saying his prayers, chanting loudly enough to signal to Parvin that it was time for her to rise and join him in the prayer room.

The only difference in the routine is on *Nowruz*, when they lift the entire stove out into to the yard, wash it carefully, then put it back in place to start the New Year. On this Nowruz, Parvin rises earlier than usual to help Jamshed move the stove out to the yard. They replace the stove and say their prayers, welcome the New Year, and then Jamshed begins to ready himself. This will be his first Nowruz at the distillery, and he wonders what this year will bring.

He does not have to wonder long, for when he emerges from the bathroom, he sees Parvin standing before him, holding an empty plate. He looks at the plate and then looks up at her. Most striking is that he does not, at first, notice that she immodestly wears not a thread of clothing, the large plate making partial compensation, but Jamshed does not notice her nakedness because of the light that brims in her eyes. Parvin balances the plate in one hand and reaches into its centre with the other, appears to pick something up and takes her fingers to her mouth. She takes a tentative bite of the nothingness in her fingers, smiles widely, and pushes the rest of the emptiness into her mouth, which bulges with the fullness of this imaginary food. Jamshed still stares in wonder, ignoring Parvin's gestural request for him to follow suit, so she takes another piece, imaginarily larger, and stuffs it whole into her mouth, forcing it in with her thumb and middle finger, raising her lips skyward as a bird would trying to gulp a minnow down its gullet. She smiles, beams again, and as she chews and swallows, nods her head to the plate. Slowly, tentatively, Jamshed reaches out to the centre of the plate, but Parvin shakes her head discouragingly, so he reaches to the left side and she smiles her approval. He takes a very small piece, gingerly plucks it up and throws it whole into his mouth. This time, she does not just smile, but laughs, giggles, and nods vigourously. Jamshed cannot recall the last time he heard her giggle, nor can she recall the last time she laughed, and yet here it all is, so present and pleasurable. Now Jamshed takes a larger piece and scoops up another bit at the same time, almost unable to contain the two masses in his mouth, one almost slipping out so he has to catch it with his palm. He is laughing now, too, though not as hard as Parvin. Together, they devour the contents of the empty plate, sating themselves with untold pleasures until Jamshed reaches to the plate one last time and Parvin shakes her head, no, there is none left. He looks so disappointed that she saddens her face as well. She lowers the plate and lets it hang by her side, and Jamshed, perplexed, can do nothing but look into her eyes. They burn at him wonderfully, and he does not even realize that they first order him to disrobe, then stand before her, so that, through no will of his own, he and she are standing a hair's breadth from each other's bodies, the morning light now filtering in from the balcony window on to their naked skin. Parvin slowly descends to the floor with the plate, edging it on to the surface so quietly that it seems to Jamshed that it floats to the ground. When she stands she is no more than a sliver of light from him, her breath pulsing off his neck, and they stay like this for a very, very long time. Then the tips of their fingers touch, first the left hand, then the right, then palm to palm, intertwined hands, torsos skin-touching and eyelashes brushing, cheeks smoothing over each other, fingertips on hips and palms behind knees, toes to spinal bases and lips curving over everything, hair dancing dreamily over heated breaths, and eyes that skim over bodies complete, replete. There is such fullness and tautness and lightness and sweetness that, as the sun rays burst into the room, they are together in ways they have never imagined, touches and gestures such as they have never experienced, and the sun is high in the sky, and the two of them are lying on the floor together, exhausted, comforted, before either realizes that the day has not just begun but begun to fade, and they sleep beside each other until the dusk takes over on this, their first Nowruz at the distillery compound eight miles down the road from Nowgong.

First breath, op cit

If Jamshed came into this world reluctantly, fearful of all that shift-ing from a place of liquid to one of air would bring, if his hesitancy was not an out-and-out refusal but a wait-and-see-ness, if his desire to stay within a comfort zone and womb home made him wildly un-comfortable with his new life, then it was diametrically opposite at this new birth in 1934. No reluctance, no hesitancy, no stay-put de-sire, but rather a cavalier let's-get-on-with-it approach was what this newborn had in mind. She slipped out of her mother so efficaciously that Parvin could not believe she had given birth already; her previ-ous two (pre-empted so unfairly, their sadness still made her chest heave) had felt so long and protracted by comparison, although they too had been relatively short labours. Even the midwife was startled at a delivery that finished before it had a chance to start in earnest. "My, my, already out there, why, I have not had a chance to prepare myself fully, and this little mischief has the nerve to pop into the world like she is ready to put fire to it. Ho, well, my services are not needed, then."

But her services *were* needed. No sooner had the baby laid its head down for the first time, a cry still not uttered, though she was breathing well, so there was no need to thump fluid from her lungs, than she did, to all those in attendance, look like she tried to sit up. It seemed impossible; a newborn has no muscles for that, but there was the look on her tiny face, the straining of her fists. "Yes," they all said, "my goodness, she is trying to sit up—and what next? Talk, walk, jump on her bicycle and go for a ride through the compound?"

When the midwife rushed out to tell Jamshed—it was two o'clock in the afternoon when the midwife arrived, and despite her protestations that he should go to work (since he could do a full day and then return and have his dinner and perhaps a night's sleep before the baby crowned), Jamshed said this time he would be there throughout, and good thing too, for he had barely sat down to think of their family's future then the news came rushing from the room. He was delighted. A girl, a little girl given to them to be theirs, and this time—he kept back bad emotions—this time they would watch their child grow up and become a woman, this time it would all be different and the family would grow from there. The sadness was to be banished to the past and only good thoughts and good words and good actions would lead them forward.

It is unfortunate that bad feelings have the capacity to overwhelm good feelings. This is something Jamshed always felt, and in his younger days when his interests turned to mathematics and geometry, he would take great pains to draw and graph out how this seemed to work. When they were first married, he had tried to explain this process to Parvin. A good event, say receiving a good grade on a school assignment, might be two points on the positive side of the scale, and an equivalent bad event, perhaps getting into a small argument with a friend, might be two points on the negative side. Why was it, then, he would wonder, that his mind would dwell on the argument, and not on the good grade? There were always vestiges, he thought, of the negative side. To live a life that was overall balanced on the plus side, he thought, one would have to have endless strings of good things and only a minimal of bad, and even then it would require more to achieve a balance than his graph paper told him. Why was that? Jamshed thought he might have the capacity to create a negative balance for himself—perhaps for every good thing that happened by chance or good fortune, he himself would create an evil and ugly balance, just to keep it even? Perhaps it was all about his own choices and free will, after all, except in a rather extravagant and somewhat unintentional way. But how could un-intentionality be an exercise of free will? This was why Sunny was important, for that irksome grandchild could always shed light on this mess. But Sunny had not appeared to him for months, and Jam-shed, sitting there dwelling on the midwife's good news, speculated as he had for so many months now, sometimes with good humour, sometimes with an odd sense of grief, that Sunny had not come by since before the pregnancy. Where was he, was he gone for good?

Then the voices in the compound, excited voices—"Must come in, I must see Jamshed!"—and he, still caught in a reverie, thought these people had heard already about the joyous birth and were here to congratulate him. He did not hear the tension in the one voice that was most strident, the tension that tightens vocal chords, a throat-grabbing tension that he himself had experienced recently when yelling at a rickshaw driver whom he knew had cheated him on the fare. Jamshed rose to his feet to go out and meet the well-wisher. And was somewhat surprised to see a young village man, sweating, somewhat out of breath, still insisting to the sweeper that he must see the master of the house, and no, he would not go away until he had discharged his duty even if this was not a particularly opportune time. In his hand the young man held a crinkled piece of paper, which seemed odd since Jamshed knew that this young man could not read. Still, when the boy saw Jamshed at the door, his face lit up, also in an odd way, signifying he was glad to be able to reach out to the manager of the distillery, the man of the land who made work for his entire village, reach out and say to Jamshed, who was still expecting congratulations on the birth of his daughter, "*Baisa-hib*, your mother, she is dead," and push the yellowed scrap of paper, a telegram, into Jamshed's hand.

The ledger, the plus side and the negative. In the black and in the red. Words rushed out from the boy—sudden, heart, just last night, the telegram had reached Nowgong only an hour ago and he had been charged to run to the house and tell Jamshed-sahib about this terrible, terrible news. Jamshed thanked the boy and did not look at the telegram right away, but looked out at his garden, Parvin's garden, instead, wondering idly what would grow there next year or in ten years. At that precise moment his senses were assaulted by the piercing screams of his baby girl's first cry. What a balance, first cries met with last breaths. His daughter. His mother. One for the other. Jamshed thought about the last few months, how in his prayers were those unspoken thoughts about how he would give everything for his child to come into and stay in this world safely, anything at all. And anything it was. He listened to his daughter's renewed cries, and he bent his head forward and nodded, first gently, then vigourously, then viciously so that he thought he could hear the vertebrae in his neck protesting and cracking. All that was and is, he thought, is and was. He did not notice that he was crushing the telegram in his fist and that tears were flowing down his cheeks, tributaries flowing together, though he made no sound. A mother. A daughter. Trading in the world. His choice, his will, he could not let go of that. Not a choice made freely, but one of the unspoken trades, the deals we make of *if only* or *what I would not give* or *I promise anything*—and then, what happens when that anything comes? Jamshed looks backward and forward, dastur and business, mother and daughter. Tributaries flowing together, inevitably and not, making no sound.

Piroja

Let me tell you this; from my perspective, she started life as an ambitious child and changed little as she grew up. Her marks at school were spectacular, this I monitored, and she was popular with all those who came to know her. Piroja had that unique ability to be happily alone and yet be very sociable. Perhaps it was the effect of first memories—some would say it is impossible for a child to be so aware, but I was quite convinced, as was Jamshed, who could swear that his first words to Piroja—"My sweet, what madness is this that brings you into my world and takes my mother out all in the same breath?"—were ingested by the hour-old baby, who, in response, cranked her face into a frown from a wide-eyed grin. It seemed that little Piroja (for she was a small child, small-boned, fine-featured) felt these contrasts always; the very fact that life was only death in bas-relief, that for every good moment there was going to be a bad one. I thought perhaps this knowledge was absorbed osmotically from her pensive father, always thinking of the negative side of life, although I also surmised it could be put down to genetic predilection, nature trumping nurture—or perhaps it was the two frolicking hand in hand. Whatever the case, Piroja grew into her school-age years always thinking, always exploring, and always with the capacity to see multiple sides of any event. No birthday party was a joy forever, but a cause to understand that she would never be four again, or five, or six; no sunrise was observed without recognizing that the day was that much closer to sunset; no fruit digested without acknowledging that the tree that bore it would soon be out of season. Was it macabre for such a little thing to be not morose, but so caught up in the cycles of things?

Still, Piroja was, as the saying goes, a joy to her parents, an absolutely wondrous child, and they doted on her almost fiercely. And she doted back on them (if a child can dote on parents), and I thought that together they were a marvellous trio, this Parsi family out in the middle of a distillery compound near Nowgong.

Leaves of dust

There are activities that are despised by children and activities that
are loved. Among the former, generally speaking, are adult conversations that have little relevance to the world, anything that remotely
resembles a chore that could best be left undone, business affairs no
matter how colourful or playful, and anything belonging to that do-
main that is at once anticipated and feared—the land of the grown-
ups. In the latter group are such things that can be loosely grouped
under the heading of play (although that includes nearly everything
in a child's universe, if one looks hard enough): chatter, drawing, nature, anything smelly or dirty, anything capable of provoking giggles,
and anything that keeps boredom at bay. Playing in puddles and
playing in leaves are two of little Piroja's favourite seasonal activities, and are all the more special to her because they offer the satisfaction of performing two similar actions with defiantly different
results, the splash and the crunch. After the rains, when the road,
such as it was, was awash with pools of water of questionable quality, Piroja would spend hours negotiating what would otherwise be a
twenty-minute walk through the woods to the back side of the distillery. Wearing short pants and cork *chuppels*, Piroja would explore
each and every miniature pond along the way, checking for signs
of life (larvae and related insect bodies), colours, shapes, objects
that, once wet, were entirely different than in their dried forms,
and always attentive to the particularized ripples created when cork
touched liquid, which it did with great frequency and regularity on
Piroja's post-rain walks. She would return with mud splatters up to
her short pants, sometimes as high as her shoulders, so vigourously would she cork down into those temporary lakes. Parvin would

sigh when her daughter returned, exhausted and filthy, but so absolutely unconcerned was the girl with her state of disarray that Parvin could do little but smile and acknowledge that anything her daughter would do, she would do with vim, vigour, and gusto beyond compare.

But if Piroja loved the splashing sound and muddy texture of newly collected rainwater, she was even more entranced by the music and feel of leaves underfoot. Wet leaves, dry leaves, small and large leaves; the fallen detritus from the trees that filled their front yard was utterly delicious to her toes and soles and heels. She would implore Abdul not to dispose of the collected leaves right away, but allow her the pleasure of taking leaps into and virtually burying herself in great piles of the stuff. It was like being in a different atmosphere, one composed not of nitrogen and oxygen but chlorophyll and fibre, and she could breathe it in, suck it into her pores, and delight in the scrape and scratch of the vegetation across her skin.

On one such fall day, Piroja managed to compile a particularly impressive heap of leaves and was delicately circling to determine her best angle of approach. She saw the bits and twigs already blowing off the top in the autumn breeze, forming random shapes and figures on the lawn. This one looked like a bulbous cloud and that one like an elephant trunk, and she marvelled at them all. Then, with a sidelong glance, she nodded and began her long strides—one, two, three, four, five—and then leapt and danced high into the air, coming down with bare feet into the very top and centre of the pile, making the translation from air to leaf and revelling in that density shift, the way everything slowed down and crackled beneath.

What little Piroja had no way of knowing was that, just as leaves might look like clouds and trunks, living entities might sometimes appear to be leaves. A sparrow might look deceptively like a leaf when high up in a tree's branches; a lizard might have the colour, texture, and vein structure to emulate bark; and a scorpion, scrunched up, tail back and hidden, might look exactly like a ten-days-fallen-off leaf. If it were to look so and hide beneath a very tall pile of leaves, it could remain hidden there, safe, secure, until and unless a small, sun-browned little girl's foot ferreted its way through leaf-depth and, though slowed by foliage, landed hard on the back of said creature. There, at the bottom of a pile of innocent and deadened leaves, a footfall changed the course of history.

The scorpion strikes. Piroja screams—that long, loud wail that children reserve not for anger or upset but for true and real pain. It is a scream that brings adults running from whatever quarter, whatever activity, to see how bad the damage might be. It is a scream that can mean broken bones or bloodied faces or twisted knees. It is a scream that portends poisoned serum starting a flow through epidermis and into flesh, beginning a heart-assisted chug through a lithe and now on-fire body. First on the scene is Abdul, the young gardener who was such a favourite of Parvin's for his tender care of her daughter. Abdul would always acquiesce to Piroja's requests, no matter how trivial or spurious, as if he were compelled to do her bidding. And so it is not surprising that he hurdles from the flower bed and makes it to Piroja's side in three gigantic leaps and three momentous seconds. Piroja is still buried up to her torso in leaves, and her face is a grimace, a death mask, thinks Abdul, as he gently cups her in his hands and lifts her from the now-dispersed pile. From the corner of his eye he sees a scurrying black form and, while still cradling the girl, sidesteps most efficiently to block the escaping insect, then with the other foot, comes down hard, to end the existence of this creature that has caused such pain to one he holds so dear. A black scorpion does not so much crush as crunch; and, especially if it is on a bed of grass, there is considerable foot pressure required to break its tiny body. But such pressure Abdul exerts, angrily, twisting his foot until he feels the life give way under his leather sandal, tear away into two, giving him no satisfaction but a sense of fulfilling destiny. One dies so one might live. And without checking to see the lifeless form underfoot, he looks down into the pained face of the now-shrieking girl and lowers her gently from his arms onto the grass.

Parvin appears from the kitchen, wiping her hands dry, her eyes haunted by what she is afraid she might see. The image of Abdul cradling Piroja is statuesque in quality, like the temple friezes she has seen nearby, and the stillness of the pair frightens her. She rushes to them, and Piroja's cries cease as suddenly as they had started, reduced to a canine-like whimpering.

"What has happened?" Parvin asks in Gujarati, the language of the house, the familiar.

"It was a scorpion," replies Abdul in English, the language of the formal, the precise, and the very serious. He does not look up from the child's face. "Black scorpion."

"Was it large?" asks Parvin, now kneeling by Piroja and touching her forehead.

"It was not so large," says Abdul. He is trying to make it sound better. Not so large. As they grow older, Parvin knows, black scorpions lose their potency, the lethal sting held mostly by the small, somehow innocent-looking ones. Not so large means small and therefore lethal, and she can see how Parvin's right foot is already reddening and swelling.

"You must go to get him," says Parvin. Abdul nods and rises, seems to know that there are two "hims" he must fetch, one being Jamshed, of course, and the other an elderly man in the village known for his ability to heal. As he moves from a squat to a stand, takes a step that will lead from a walk to a run, Abdul hears Piroja whimper, no words coming from this child who is usually so full of them. He will run faster than he has ever run before, he promises himself, and he is out the compound and down the dirt road.

"Mummy?"

"Yes, dear, I am here."

"The leaves, they hurt. They—"

"Yes, dear. I know. Lie still."

By the time Jamshed arrives, Parvin has moved Piroja inside and has a cool compress on the girl's burning forehead. Jamshed's face is a jumble of activity. He wants to scream to Ahriman—do it to me, not her. He wants to tear the religion from his body, first the fabric, then the skin, but he does not. He simply looks at Piroja and thinks that there is no way in the world that they can lose another child. He repeats this to himself but will not allow himself to utter this to Parvin. He looks at his wife's face only once and then cannot again, knowing he will collapse if he does. So he repeats what amounts to a vow—that he will not lose another child—as he stares into the eyes of Piroja, which rapidly flutter open and then shut. To make such a vow, what does it mean? What more does one offer? Jamshed is turning an anna coin over in his head and remembering choices made, every choice made toward is also a choice away; every opening up of opportunity closes a host more. But one element stays clear. Faith. Living actions by the words from the thoughts. If his thoughts have been lacking, then by necessity, words fail and deeds collapse inward. Has he been a good Parsi? Yes and no; in the middle in all manners of being. But not this for his daughter. For her, for her life, she must be a good Parsi, the best, and for her sake, he must enforce this with the vigour of his very life. Where once he felt he would grant her every desire, now Jamshed closes down, every choice limiting further options, and vows that she will do everything as a good Parsi should. Pure in thought and prayer, in what she does in life, in who she marries and how she raises children, all this drives through Jamshed's mind in but a moment. And if there were flames inside Jamshed that once lit up numerous options in his life, they were at that moment extinguished, and the options darkened out, leaving only one. Jamshed closes all doors and leaves but one open, one that he decrees, and the choice is his alone.

When the healer arrives from the village after what seems like hours, Piroja's fever is high and her eyes remain closed. Her skin is tinged with blue and her breathing is shallow. The healer begins his ritual of chanting mantras and waving a brush of long green grass over the little girl, but all the action is lost on Jamshed, who watches as if this were a dream writ wrong. The healer looks up at Jamshed, then at Parvin, and neither can decipher if the shake of his head is a bad sign or a signal that he simply does not know. Without speaking, without looking at each other, mother and father rise and take a step away from the bedside. Someone initiates the curling of fingers inside the palm of the other's hand, though neither knows whose fingers, whose palm. They do not cry, but they do not hope. They clench fingers in palm-turned-fist and together turn to the veranda, watch the wind blow a few more leaves off the pile. They try to breathe in unison, then they try to breathe in complement. One in, one out. Then, on the third in-breath of Parvin, Jamshed's out-breath poses words:

"She will live if we will it." In.

"We will will it then." Out.

"You must listen to me, Parvin. Listen to me. We must make a decision now." In. Out.

"Yes. A decision." Out. In.

"She is our child, and we have had children before who have been taken away." In. Out. In. Out.

"Yes, they have been taken away." Out. "She will live. But if she does, Parvin, if she does, we must send her away." In. Out.

"Away? Yes. But we must do this carefully, Jamshed. Away, but not forever." Out.

"No, not forever. To be a good Parsi, she must have knowledge." In.

"Knowledge. She can get knowledge from us." Out.

"We can keep her here and teach her well, yes. But we must also let her learn the ways of the outside world and thus make her understand the Parsi ways even more strongly." Out. In.

"Yes. Knowledge from home and away." Out. In. And when their breaths are between in and out: "Oh. I have heard from Sunny."

"Sunny? Sunny! He—you—he has spoken to you?" Out, out, out, and in.

"Sunny has spoken to me but not in words. And he has told me that to preserve the future we must prevent too much presence in the past" In. And out.

"Speaking in riddles, damn him." Out, heavily out.

"I know what he means, Jamshed. I know, too. We must send Piroja away, send her to school in a good place, a place where she can learn and grow and be the girl and then the woman she needs to be." In, rapidly and heartily, in.

"Then—then that is what we will do. But we will send her with good thoughts in her heart." Out and in, in unison.

"Mummy? Daddy? I'm thirsty."

And eyes flutter open, breathing quickens for all present, then slows, and a little girl's fever is broken and a future is written.

It was written

This is what happened. I was looking backward and forward, and this is what happened. I saw a black scorpion running away, and I saw my mother as a young girl, dying in fever. It is not as if poison alone gets pumped through the blood system; other things—foreign objects, diseases, malformed platelets, pieces of glass, thinning and thickening agents—all of these are pumped through the veins and arteries, but more than that, futures and pasts, kathump, kathump. So from the sharp prong of a black tail teems everything that was and is, and this is what I saw before visiting my grandmother. Why did I now visit her and not my usual conversational and grandpaternal partner, Jamshed? Perhaps this is a time when, as before, Jamshed cannot or will not listen to me; the choice may not have been his. And since my visit to Parvin started this whole ancestral slippery slope, it only made sense for a revisitation to matrilineals, which themselves will lead to matrimonials, which themselves will lead to me. And so I appeared, and this is what happened.

The time will come, Madama Walrus, to talk of many things.

"Who, what, Sunny? Where are you?"

Too easy and too difficult a question, Grandmother. Everywhere and nowhere. The choice is yours.

"Riddles. Let me tell you something. As soon as you are born, the very moment you are born, I will slap your bottom so hard to pay back all these riddles!"

And I will welcome that slap, Grandmother. But now, the time has come.

"Time—what is this time thing? Time for me to block my ears?"

It will be. It is not now, unwritten as it were, but it will be. Grandmother, I must speak to you about loss and loss.

"Loss? You speak of loss? Why not gain, why not good things? Good thoughts, no? Think good thoughts and, pell-mell, good things will happen."

Yes, Grandmother, on this I agree. But sometimes the way up is the way down.

"Yes, yes. Tell me, foolish grandchild who does not have the sense to keep his counsel until he has been born, tell me about this loss."

Grandmother, there will come a moment, very soon, when in order to prevent a larger loss you must facilitate a smaller one. A petit mort so to speak, except this is not ultimately about, well, that.

"Petty more? What sort of foofoo is that? Speak in Gujarati, silly boy, or do not speak at all."

Indeed. Grandmother, this is important. Soon you will be on the precipice of loss. To pull back from the brink means giving up something you love. Yes, I know that sounds trite. But in this case, it's true.

"To pull back means giving up. This is about Piroja, is it not?"

Yes. And more than about her. It is about the future. Tell me, Grandmother, what do Parsis treasure above all else?

"*Asha*, truth, of course."

And the way to such truth?

"Humata, hukhta, huvarshta. All things good—thoughts, words, deeds."

And the way to humata, to good thoughts, how do we come to good thoughts?

"Contemplation, reflection, education. What are you trying to say, strange grandchild?"

Only that, Grandmother. Tell me this: how will Piroja be educated, here, at the distillery?

"She will learn from me and from Jamshed. And she is a watchful child, so she will learn from watching the world around her."

And would you give her up so she might learn more?

"This is what this is about, my daughter's education? Yes, the answer is yes. I would give up time with my daughter so her mind might grow, but I will never give up my daughter, do you understand?"

Perfectly. But small losses to prevent larger ones.

"Riddles. Ridiculous riddles. Go back to the place of the yet-to-be-born."

And so this is what happened, this conversation with my grandmother, a schoolteacher in her unmarried life, who knew that good deeds could not come out of nowhere, that good words were good only because they had been learned, and that good thoughts must come from a spark inside, but that spark had to be fuelled. We made an unspoken covenant between grandchild and grandmother that the way up may be the way down, and to get inside you sometimes have to go outside. When scorpion tails strike, it takes a small loss to keep bigger losses at bay.

A little schoolhouse in Jhansi

The ceiling fan is wooden with metal tips, and it rotates just fast enough so the casual observer can make out each blade, not in exact detail, but enough so that each blade is distinct from the next. Any faster and the blades would blur into each other, and indeed, the fan might then be performing up to its teleological good, for at the current speed, apart from allowing bored sets of eyes to discern its fine detail, the fan does little more than circulate risen warm air back from whence it came, that is, toward the floor, without even close to the desirous effect of providing a cooling breeze.

This is exactly what Jamshed is thinking as he watches the blades rotate, that all the fan is succeeding in doing, miraculously, is to make the room stay at the same temperature as it would be were the fan to be shut off entirely. Jamshed is sitting in an old wooden chair, supposedly the teacher's chair, his back straight and posture perfect except for his head, which tilts upward and wonders at the fan. Directly in front of Jamshed is a large mahogany desk that has seen better days, and as Jamshed examines this desk closely he notices various scratches and scars from years gone by and the occasional carved initials and dates inscribed under the lip of the desk, and Jamshed has a faint sensation that all this has happened before, in another place not here, but he does not realize that a generation has passed, and what his father once experienced, he, as a father, is now experiencing.

On the other side of the desk, squeezed uncomfortably into a desk used to holding the bodies of five-year-old boys and girls, sits Parvin. She has been sitting like this, awkwardly, for five minutes, passing the time by watching her husband watch the ceiling fan and looking around the classroom to take note of all the items her daughter will observe over the course of her first year of school— that is, of course, this boarding school in a town so far, far away from their beautiful compound in Nowgong. Parvin squirms in the tiny seat and wonders how children Piroja's age can possibly learn their lessons in this environment, here, so far away from the home and love of their parents. Still, her daughter is alive, thinks Parvin, alive, and the deal has been struck, and now it is time to lose a little so she does not lose a lot.

Across from Jamshed and Parvin sits Reverend Mother Mary Something-something (Parvin did not get the entire name, rushed from the mouth of the Irish nun and with all sorts of English banter around it, to boot). That is another thing, thinks Parvin; will her daughter lose all her Gujarati in this oh-so-English schoolhouse with Irish, Anglo-Indian, and German nuns as her tutors? Parvin listens intently as the Reverend Mother speaks, noting how her thin lips curl up at the edges at the end of each incomprehensible sentence (the woman needs to learn how to smile, thinks Parvin), and how she pauses at the end of each sentence, as if she is paying respect to the effect of each full stop.

"Mr and Mrs Khargat, it must best be known that the girls of this school are of the utmost superiority in quality and educatability," says the Reverend Mother. "They are tippled notch, as the expression goes, tippled and well-bredded. Not a stray bullet among them."

Jamshed tries to translate the apparently endless and often nonsensical English into a succinct packet of Gujarati, sometimes nervously adding a few lines: "Parvin, the good Reverend Mother has gone on for quite a bit describing the efforts made by the nuns to educate the girls, but the detail she has gone into is truly uninteresting, so rather than translate it all I am just dragging this out so it seems like I have translated the uninteresting bits for you," to which

Parvin nods and smiles at the Reverend Mother, who curls the very edges of her lips up in response. And then she carries on again, Jamshed nodding agreeably at everything she says, Parvin nodding in similar fashion at an appropriately post-translative time.

"And Mrs Khargat, your mind might be settled at ease, not a worry to the wind, as upstandingness is our middle name here at St Francis, and wholesomebeingness is our other middle name." Jamshed translates this as, "She says everything will be all right."

After they finally bid their farewells to the Reverend Mother and leave the cramped office, Parvin turns to Jamshed and gestures, palm upward.

"This is where Piroja should spend the next ten years?"

"Parvin, I do not know. The Reverend Mother seems nice enough, and the nuns we have met seem both sweet and intelligent. But I do not know."

"Sixty-five miles. Jhansi is sixty-five miles from Nowgong, and it is not a trip Piroja can do every weekend. I will not be able to see my little girl for any time at all. She will grow up with these nuns. She will forget how to be a Parsi."

"That she will never do, Parvin. This much I promise you." Jamshed's hands close into fists; hands close as hearts do with vows made not to be undone. "Parvin, already our tiny girl knows so much about her faith it surprises me. She will learn the teachings of the nuns, certainly, but she will always be our little girl. I will not have it any other way."

"Then it is settled?"

"No, of course not. It is settled when you say it is, when you say we should send Piroja to this boarding school. And if you say no, we will not."

"Then I say no." And Parvin looks defiantly at Jamshed who holds her gaze and does not change the expression on his face. "Then I say no, I do not want this. And yes, she should come to boarding school here, our little girl. Our Piroja."

It is the sort of statement that should be followed by great amounts of emotional upset, by tears and wails, but having said what she had to say, Parvin only smiles, and it is Jamshed who notices that he is crying silently as they stand outside the schoolhouse in Jhansi. Choices made.

The Germans wore blue

Piroja was not at all certain why her parents were so upset, so sombre, when they told her she would soon go away to boarding school. She had been to Jhansi once before, at the age of four, and quite enjoyed the bustle of the city compared to the slowness of Nowgong. All those colours and sounds, enough to turn one's head. Jamshed had walked into shops and supply stores as if he owned them, confidently making friends and dragging little Piroja with him from stall to stall, delighting in all the attention she received from these total strangers. And now, at age five, she was being told by her teary parents that she would spend a great deal of time in Jhansi, learning from the nuns, and visiting her parents in Nowgong during school breaks and special occasions.

After they broke the news to her, Piroja ran out to the front yard, as was her ritual in the late mornings, and picked a choice guava from the tree whose branches overhung the front of the house. She wondered if they would have guava trees, or mango or lemon, at the Jhansi convent as they did here in Nowgong. But, exercising surprising maturity for a five-year-old, she decided that it did not matter if there were or were not fruit trees at her school, for she would adjust and would always find fresh fruit when she returned to Nowgong, which she vowed would be far more often than was promised. As she bit into the guava, she caught sight of Abdul working some garden utensil in the corner of the compound.

"Abdul-ji," she called out to him. "I am going away to school soon!"

The gardener straightened and nodded but did not look over

to the house, afraid to show his own tears to the girl. Everyone, it seems, is trying to be strong for everyone else.

Several weeks later a tonga pulls into the compound to take Piroja and Jamshed into Nowgong and from there along the road to Jhansi in a belching and rattling bus. A five-year-old and a thirty-nine-year-old, daughter and father, bouncing along in an old bus bound for the future (thinks Jamshed) and a new world (thinks Piroja). It is only when Nowgong is a good hour behind them that Piroja feels fatigued, her overexcitement taking over, and she puts her head down in her father's lap and pretends to mutter her prayers but is really only doing so to cover her burps of sadness. "Say your prayers," Parvin had instructed as the tonga pulled away, and Piroja promised she would. Goodbye mother, hello new world. It is a short ride to Jhansi, relatively speaking, and one that Piroja remembers well from the year before, but this time it is different, not bound for shopkeepers and sounds, but a dormitory and an educational expanse. Piroja falls asleep on her father's lap, is still drowsy when they exit the bus and hail a tonga whose driver Jamshed instructs to take them and Piroja's substantial luggage ("She will be away so long, Jamshed, we must make sure she has everything she needs") to the side entrance of the grey structure that is St Francis convent. When they arrive, Piroja is much more alert, attentive to the flurry of activity by the strangely garbed nuns as they busy themselves around her, help the driver negotiate the trunk into the dormitory, and greet Jamshed in thickly German-accented English.

As quickly as it began, the flurry subsides, and Piroja is alone with her father, saying goodbye, goodbye, clasping his leg vice-like, maybe he won't go, but then, with a final touch of hand to forehead, a blown kiss, Jamshed is out the door (instructing the Reverend Mother to take especially good care of his only child). The nuns,

Piroja notes, all dress the same, not in black, as she had been told, but in a deep, dark blue. It is a colour she will identify with photographs she sees later that year, of a different group of Germans, marching with the same conviction, but in a different part of the world. She will notice the nuns gathering and talking softly, furtively, and Piroja will not know that they worry about reprisals from the local population, for they are foreign nationals, and despite their religious separation from the ways of the world, belong to the same nation now at war with king and crown. Brave new world, indeed.

St Francis, making strange

Jamshed has no sooner walked out the front door than Sister Ida comes over to Piroja, takes her small hand, and pats it gently. Beside her is an older girl, perhaps ten or eleven, with distinct, sharp features that Piroja finds familiar and comforting.

"Piroja, this is one of our fourth standard girls, Heera. Heera is also Parsi, and I told your father I would bring her to meet you."

"Hello, Piroja, very pleased to make your acquaintance," says Heera, patting Piroja sisterly on the top of her head.

"I will leave you to get to know each other," says Sister Ida and glides out of the room.

"Another Parsi girl, this will be fun," says Heera, smiling. "There used to be one other Parsi girl here but she finished her O Levels and left two years ago. She was older than me and treated me just like a sister. An older sister. So I am very pleased to be able to act like your older sister, if you will let me. Do you have any sisters, Piroja? Or brothers? Your hair is so beautiful and long, you must let me brush it for you, one hundred strokes, every evening. Oh, what fun, what fun this will be. A little sister and a Parsi to boot. If you need anything, anything at all, or if you are lonely, or sad, you must tell me, your older sister, and I will be there for you, all right, Piroja? Is that all right?"

Piroja has tried to interject a response at least four times, but Heera's patter is magnificently swift, and she appears to take no time for breaths between words, so that by the end of her little speech, she is veritably wheezing out the last bit of air to finish the sentence. When she does stop and gulp air like a huge mackerel, Piroja manages to slip in a few words.

"Thank you, Heera. I do not have brothers or sisters. I hope I am not too lonely, but I will tell you if I am."

Heera, recovered and oxygenated, bursts in again: "Very good, very good, but one thing, Piroja, the nuns don't like it when we speak Gujarati. I mean, they are not mean or anything and you won't get beaten or punished, but they will look at you sternly and act cross. You do speak English, do you not? Yes, I am sure you do, I have been told this by Sister Ida, I am sure you do speak it, and I think you probably speak it exceedingly well. They tell me you are smart as a whip, that's what they say, which is good, because I do not want any sister of mine to be made fun of for being a dullard, but you're in no danger in that, I do not think. No, I am sure you are quite the intelligent girl, and we two shall give Parsis a very good name because, you see, I am quite smart too, top of my class, so if you can be top of your class, why, these Catholic girls will start to see that they do not rule the roost, do you see? That we Parsis can teach them a thing or two, in the classroom and on the field. Are you good at sports? I don't doubt it, though you are quite small, even for a five-year-old. I am sure you have some spirit though, do you not? Yes, I am sure." Heera wheezes again, barely getting out her last I-am-sures before running out of breath entirely.

"I do like running and playing," admits Piroja, this time carefully in English so her new big sister will see how well she can speak it. "I am fast, but the other girls are sometimes bigger and faster. But I don't give up."

"That's the style, Piroja, that's the Parsi spirit, we'll teach them all a thing or two. We didn't survive this long by being weak, did we? No matter what they throw at us, this is what my father says, no matter what they throw, we Parsis stand tall. Persecution, we can take it, isn't that right, Piroja? Why, the two of us, the two Parsis in a whole convent full of Catholics, we can take them all on if we have to, no? Not that we have to be adversarial—do you know that word, Piroja, *adversarial*? I can teach you many good English words, you know. It means, well, it means to be against somebody. But we are good communicators, too, we Parsis, we know how to talk our way out of things, don't we? Not out of things, you know, but out of trouble, because we know how to negotiate. Is that a new word for you, too, Piroja, *negotiate*? I only ask because you are so dreadfully quiet, and I am wondering if you do not understand some of what I say? Never mind, all in good time. All in good time. What do you say I take you out and introduce you to some of the girls? I have met some of the first-standard little ones. I am a bit of a den mother, I suppose! I will introduce you to them, never you worry."

With that, Heera prances out of the room, turning abruptly to gesture furtively to Piroja to follow. In a whirlwind tour, Heera introduces Piroja to Anna and Mary and Celeste and Anjou and a half dozen other first-standard girls whose names Piroja does not catch. The girls are all pleasant and happy to meet Piroja, whose mature nature and always-bright visage quickly make her one of the most popular girls in school. And, as she has promised Heera, she is quick both on and off the playing field, studying and sporting with such heart that the girl whose slight build makes her the last to be picked for teams at semester's start is the most prized pick by midsemester, for all the girls know that if Piroja is on your team, you will most likely win, or if not win, thoroughly enjoy the game with the little Parsi girl drumming up team spirit. And, I'm proud to tell you, thanks to her mother and father and home tutoring that prepared her for such learning, Piroja is also quickly identified as the smartest girl by far in first standard. Here at St Francis, Piroja is surrounded by the energy of young girls and older women, and from this she learns to be comfortable with herself. It will be these girls and women whose supportive energy will remain with her over the years, those many hands holding her aloft.

"Hello Anna, you are looking very fine this morning!"

"Piroja, you always have such nice things to say."

"Mary, I really must learn to kick a football like you do, so daring, so natural."

"Thank you, Piroja, but if I had half the skills you did, I would not have to try at all."

"Sister Ida, you look sad today, is there something the matter?"

"Why Piroja, I did not realize it showed. Yes, my brother died last week, but he was in Madras and I could not afford the time for travel. Thank you, Piroja, for asking."

"Anjou, you sometimes pretend not to be very smart, but you are quite a whip, no?"

"I suppose so, Piroja. Sometimes it's better not to draw attention to yourself, though, does that not make sense? I wish I had your confidence to be smart and show it."

This is what I observed as Piroja learned to be part of this convent, befriending all and loved by all, although such love does not come without conditions, without certain moments of tension. The bond between Heera and Piroja grew during the first few months together. Having a big sister had its advantages, Piroja had to admit, for even while the girls, for the most part, were kind and generous, there were moments when being the smallest, most outsiderly of the newcomers was challenging. One time, after jabbering in Gujarati with Heera, Piroja ran off to go find her first-standard classmates for a game of stickball. Running up to Sheila, a tall slender girl in second standard, Piroja began peppering her with questions about the activities to come—"Have we struck teams yet? How many girls from first standard will be there? Will we play all the way until study time?"—only to be met with a glare of incredulity from the dark-eyed Sheila.

"What in heaven's name are you saying?" Sheila finally said.

Piroja looked at her blankly—why was she being met with such frigidity, such apparent lack of comprehension? Was this some sort of collective joke the girls were making for, indeed, all around her, Anna, Mary, Celeste, and Anjou were likewise staring at her, open-mouthed and in some amazement.

"What sort of language is that anyway?" asked Sheila, none too graciously.

"Language? English, you silly," Piroja admonished, hoping it would be taken in good spirit. Perhaps she had just been caught up in speaking Heera-speed and no one could understand her.

"Why, that's no English any of us understand!" And Sheila laughed, and before she knew it, the other girls were laughing too, so hard that tears were forming in Piroja's eyes. Out of the corner of one of those teary eyes, Piroja saw Sister Ida approaching from her outpost a few yards from the girls. For whatever reason, the gait of the older woman, the laughter of her friends, Piroja chose this moment to burst fully into tears.

"Now, now," said Sister Ida, "what have we here?"

"They say they do not understand my English," said Piroja between blubbery sighs.

"Well, it's no wonder, dear child," said Sister Ida, now cuddling Piroja's head, pulling her into the warmth of her chest, "for from where I was standing, I could not understand it, either. You know you are not supposed to use Gujarati here, don't you, child?"

"But I was speaking in English," stammered Piroja, catching herself on the word "English" as she realized that everything she'd said in last few moments had, in fact, been in Gujarati, because of her recent chatter with Heera. Only when the word "English" emerged and her brain had to switch from Gujarati pronunciation to the differently tongued and lipped word that denotes the language itself, did Piroja realized her error.

"I—I am sorry, Sister Ida. I must have forgotten myself," she said in perfect English, one in which a stranger might detect the vaguest of German accents.

"That is all very well," replied Sister Ida, stroking the girl's head and then nodding at the other children before walking away.

Children, like predatory animals, can sense weakness, can smell blood, so when Sister Ida departed, there remained a residue of bestial attack.

"So," said Sheila, her arms crossed, a hint of a smile on her face. "That is the language of the fire-worshippers, is it?"

"We—we do not worship fire," answered Piroja, but without the confidence that was normally hers. "Fire is—purity. But we have one God, just like you Catholics do."

"One God? But He's on fire, is He?"

"No. Not on fire. I told you."

But by this time the other girls were snickering as well, and Piroja was forced to take a large gulp and silence herself. It is not worth the trouble, she told herself. But she will later tell Heera of this insult, and together they will find a way to stand tall. Not to fight back, but to stay true. That is their way.

In her first year at St Francis Convent, although Piroja was adaptable, she was sometimes quite lonely (as Heera had predicted), and she did depend on her older sister considerably during this time, retaining her assistance to write letters home, learn her maths, and understand the ways of girls so far from home. Heera and Piroja attended Sunday mass with the Catholic girls, but during the week they were excused from religious responsibilities, which meant the two Parsis had the run of the convent three times per week, which they used to natter away in the forbidden Gujarati and talk about all things Zarathustrian. In this way, Piroja managed to foil Parvin's fears that she would lose her faith. When Piroja returned home during the first holiday break at Christmas, her Gujarati was, in fact, improved, and her understanding of Parsi tenets more sophisticated—to the delight of both her parents.

Private magic lantern

This is like watching a film run through the projector at twice, thrice the normal speed, so every bit and character and moment seems both hyper-real and super-jagged. This is what it is like for me, except it is also like watching a family movie, which indeed it is, a family movie I will someday be part of.

During Piroja's first semester at school her parents come to visit her exactly twice. Actually, her father comes twice; her mother comes only the first time, as before the next visit Parvin is stricken with a mild bout of malaria and, Jamshed tells Piroja, cannot travel, as much as she wishes to see her only child. The first visit with the parents she has not seen in six weeks lasts only a weekend, and then the time is truncated because of bus schedules and weather problems. There is plenty of mirth and both Jamshed and Parvin try to show how well they are getting along, although Parvin can tell that, as much as their daughter misses them, they miss her more.

Maybe this is where the film slows to half speed and the musical score is full of dramatic violins. Midway through the evening, before dinner, Piroja says to herself (*sotto voce* or voiceover, depending if this is real or filmic) that when she has children of her own, she will never send them away, not only for their sakes but for her own as a then-parent. She is so resolute in formulating this plan, and it is one from which she shall never waver, that Jamshed asks his daughter what it was that has caused her to nod so vigourously. She knows she cannot tell her father, for it will hurt her parents in ways that would be entirely inappropriate, so she simply says she was thinking of a particular friend in the convent, a girl also in first standard, and how Piroja has just then and there resolved to buy a small red ribbon for her friend's black hair. This is all very fine, says Jamshed, and Parvin nods her agreement, but both have a lingering doubt about this story from the mouth of their five-year-old.

All three of them enjoy each other's company, and when Jamshed and Parvin leave the following afternoon, all three allow a few tears to fall.

Dreaming of a white Christmas

The following visit, some four weeks later in mid-November, Jamshed comes alone and is able to stay for three whole days. This time, the nuns find a room for him at the convent, one that is normally occupied by the building's caretaker, who has gone to visit a sick sister. This is much finer, for Piroja can introduce her father to the other boarders (the day-school girls are not there on the weekend) and together they all laugh and eat and tell stories, although Piroja is careful to remind her father privately to speak only in English lest he face the disapproval of the nuns. Yes, I'm still showing you my family home movie, or perhaps it's a slide show that never ends, but the truth—the truth is that this is really the beginning of my life, although I'm not even a seed, of course, but it is in this relationship between my grandfather and mother that I feel myself sown.

Jamshed takes her to a number of little out-of-the-way stalls, and they meet the managers and owners, all Parsi, with whom Jamshed talks freely and eloquently in Gujarati, first to the awkward embarrassment, then the delight, of little Piroja. These are the same stores, many of them, at least, to which Jamshed had taken Piroja when they first arrived in Jhansi. If then it was as if Jamshed had known the shopkeepers for years, now it was as if he had known them all his life. And now more confident, and with a half semester of school behind her, Piroja is more than willing to carry her end of the conversational responsibility, telling all who listen about her studies, her friends, her sports. All of them, men and women who remind her so much of her own parents, laugh loudly and ask her multiple questions, at first rather simple ones, as would seem to befit a five-year-old, but upon hearing her response, they ask more detailed, intricate, complex questions, all of which Piroja handles not just with ability but evident glee. This is a Saturday afternoon, and after many visits to several streets and after purchases made for the trip home, Piroja finally tugs on the sleeve of her father.

"Papa, I think it is time to return now."

"Oh, little one, you think so, do you?"

"Yes, Papa, Saturday afternoons we have a study session."

"And you cannot miss one of them?"

"Papa! The girls who are not boarders can study all the time. But we boarders have only two hours per day."

"But Piroja, look at the colours in the street. Smell the city. Surely this is better than sticking your nose in a book."

"Papa!" Piroja knows her father, always a stalwart supporter of education, is teasing her, but he does not indicate any move to take her back to the convent.

"I tell you what, Piroja. How about we make this afternoon our own study session? I have talked to Sister Ida and she thinks it is a fine idea. We will explore and then you will write your thoughts down for your English class."

"But what about the rest of my subjects?"

At this, Jamshed has to laugh. Five years old and concerned, to the point of ulceratic anxiety, about getting enough done. But no, it is not a serious compulsion, he tells himself, only a desire to learn. "The rest of your subjects you will do tomorrow. Today, we explore Jhansi."

He grabs Piroja's hand, bids farewell to one Mr Karaka from whom he has just purchased some dates, and heads into the bustling street. Before long, they are proceeding to the Jhansi Fort. They have not yet come upon it when Piroja notices the figure of a statue in the distance. It appears to be a slender young man atop a snorting, rearing horse. The rider brandishes a sabre high above his head, ready to charge, and it draws Piroja near. She tugs at her father's sleeve and points. "Who is he, that soldier, Papa?"

Jamshed looks down and smiles. "Ah, well, *he*, my little girl, *he* was the Rani of Jhansi. Do you remember me telling you the story of her before we came to bring you to St Francis?"

Piroja nods, but her memory is vague. She remembers her father beginning a story about a warrior queen, but because Piroja was preparing for her new life at the convent, she did not retain all the details.

Jamshed understands. "Tell me, Piroja. What is 'huvarshta'?"

"Those are good deeds, Papa," Piroja says proudly. "I have tried to explain that to the Catholic girls when they ask me about my sins."

"Oh, indeed? And what do you tell them?"

"I tell them that we Parsis do not sin because we believe in doing good things."

"Ah," laughs Jamshed. "So we do not sin then, not at all?"

"No, and especially not this original sin they keep going on about."

"Listen, Piroja, what you say is quite true. Well, mostly true! But different people have different beliefs and different ways, you do understand that, don't you? And so, just as you do not have to believe what they believe, you do not have to convince them either."

Piroja nods. "But the soldier?"

"Yes, of course. Good deeds, huvarshta. She is Lakshmibai, the Rani of Jhansi. A long time ago, a long time before you were born, before I was born, even before my own parents were born, this Rani ruled all of Jhansi. She cared for her people, made sure the poor had food to eat, and she was, so they say, a good leader. But then the British came and said she could not rule Jhansi because she was a woman and could not legally remain in control. So do you know what this Rani did? She appealed to them, wrote letters and sent dignitaries to change their minds. And when they did not, she must have thought to herself, huvarshta, I must make good on my thoughts and words and take them to good deeds. She may not have said this exact thing, of course, because she was not Parsi. But do you see what I mean? People of all types can have the same type of beliefs. Lakshmibai stood by her word and fought the British. That was her way of enacting huvarshta."

Piroja now remembered her father telling the story before and especially remembered the gruesome ending. "But they killed her, didn't they? Killed her and all the people?"

Jamshed stood silently, looked up at the rearing horse, and slowly nodded. "Yes, Piroja. They killed her. But she fought them so fiercely that we will never forget her. And we will fight her fight, do you understand, Piroja? Huvarshta. For Lakshmibai."

"Huvarshta. For Lakshmibai," repeats Piroja.

"Here, listen to this," says Jamshed, producing a piece of paper from his pocket on which he has scrawled notes, as is his wont, for educational purposes. "This is from a letter the brave Rani wrote to her generals from Jhansi: 'You wrote that you are engaged in the preparation of the troops. That pleased my heart. Our opinion is that there ought not to be rule of foreigners in Bhārat. And I have great confidence in you, great faith in you. It is very important to fight the English.' Do you hear the strength in her words, Piroja? That is hukhta, good words."

"Hukhta," thinks Piroja. "Hukhta and huvarshta." She will be like the Rani of Jhansi when she grows up, she thinks, a woman warrior and defender of the truth, of asha. She nods her head, vigourously and with purpose, something that does not escape her father's attention, but this time he only smiles and nods, somewhat more gingerly, in response. He gazes down at his daughter, remembers how swiftly love can become loss, how promises must remain. "Never forget who you are," he whispers to her. "Never, ever forget." Piroja looks up at her father, a man who sometimes seems so fierce, even in his love, and she nods affably.

"Now," says Jamshed, tone adjusting abruptly, "let us go visit the fort so you may write a letter to the Sisters about all you have learned about Jhansi!" They explore not just the fort but the turns and twists of the city, and by the time they return to the convent it is already dark and past dinner time. Sister Ida is concerned that they have not eaten, but Jamshed, by way of apology for their late return, assures her that father and daughter have had their supper thanks to the various street vendors. Sister Ida squinches her face at the thought of taking food from stalls on the street, but unsquinches as she sees the satisfaction on the faces of Jamshed and Piroja. To each his own, she thinks. If the Parsis are all right with eating food that is prepared heaven knows how and by whom, so be it, and it is not hers to judge. So she orders tea for Jamshed, then trots herself off to an early bedtime.

Piroja and Jamshed have the evening to chat about their day together, for Piroja to tell her father how she misses her mother and looks forward to the soon-to-come Christmas break. Night falls and Piroja's eyelids droop, so she goes to bed, leaving Jamshed to read by lamplight until he too falls asleep, his wire-rimmed glasses still perched on his nose so that in the morning there is a little welt across the bridge. The next day is one of relaxation, and Piroja is even given an extraordinary excuse from attending the Sunday mass so she can bid her father farewell.

It will be six weeks before she sees him again, and so their good-byes are not as full of sadness as they might be if their future meetings were undetermined. Still, Piroja feels that stomach-pit tightening that she knows is about loneliness, missing her family, and when Jamshed does leave, she waves at him in the tonga long after he has disappeared around the corner. She turns to the arms of childhood friends, but that is not the same thing. She counts down the days, a forty-two to zero morning routine, and lets her solitude give way to anticipation as numbers drop to thirties, twenties, teens, single digits.

When Jamshed does arrive six weeks later to take his daughter home to Nowgong for the Christmas holiday break, it is at the end of such a waiting game that Piroja thinks she will burst, but instead, she glows and beams and jubilates. It is late evening when the two tired travellers arrive at the compound. Piroja sees her mother dressed in white, standing on the veranda and thinks she is the most beautiful woman she has ever seen, even more beatific than the saints whose statues and likenesses adorn the convent. Next to her mother stands a man who reminds her of her father, and it is a moment before she recognizes him as Uncle Nouroz, whom she has not seen since his last visit two years prior. Piroja does not realize she is crying, full streams of tears rushing down her cheeks, because all she can think of is running up to and holding her mother. This she does and thinks she shall never let go. "This is what Christmas is all about," thinks Piroja.

She turns to hug her uncle now, who lifts her up and swings her around: "My what a beautiful girl you are, and growing so quickly!" Nouroz sets her down and Piroja gleefully grabs her mother's hand and leads her inside while her father and uncle remain on the veranda. She can hear them talking about homecomings, happiness, and how everything is changing for the better in this country now.

"Yes, Jum, little girls like our Piroja will be our future in this country," says Nouroz, and despite her father's caution ("But maybe things change too quickly, Nouroz?"), her uncle just laughs.

"Just you wait, my friend, just you wait and see if she doesn't surprise us all!" Over the next two days (until Nouroz leaves to meet up again with his theatre troupe), eating and walking and laughing with her family, Piroja thinks about goings and comings and what this means in her expanding world. And when it is time for her to leave for the convent in January, Piroja does not look back to the distillery compound, but keeps her eyes forward to the road ahead.

A fit profession

This, then, became the routine for Piroja. She spent weeks and months at the convent, complemented and rewarded by her days and weeks at Nowgong. It was a not altogether unpleasant pattern, though the hardest times were the one or two days before she had to leave the distillery compound for a long stretch at school. Being a resourceful child, though, once she was back in Jhansi, she gave little undue thought to her life in the compound. She missed her parents terribly, but in order to love them, she felt, she must love them fully when she was there and not pine for them awfully (for what good would that do?) when she was away. And on one of her summer visits home, Parvin told her daughter the story of the scorpion bite and how a mother sometimes had to make sacrifices for her family. She alluded to a dream that brought her to the decision to provide a strong education for Piroja, making no mention of the grandchild that would be, if all things came to pass, Piroja's child. Neither Parvin nor Jamshed mentioned the name "Sunny" when their daughter was nearby, or, for that matter, even when they were alone. Fair enough, since I had ceased my visitations. All this coming and going seemed so unnecessary when all was progressing nicely. And besides, they had enough visitors.

One of these was Azmi Davar, a customs official who was the son of another customs official, Vehmai, the close friend of Jamshed's father. Although the two had not grown up together, they had heard of each other, and when Azmi was transferred to Nowgong with his wife, both Jamshed and Parvin were quite excited. There were not a great deal of Parsis in Nowgong, and to have another family in the area would be a treat, particularly when it came to sharing the occasional meal. While Parvin enjoyed cooking for any and all guests, if she could prepare a plate of *dhansak* for someone who had grown up with that taste, all the better. Neither Parvin nor Jamshed were all that pleased, however, when they first met Azmi's wife, Freny.

At first, she would not deign to visit them at the distillery compound—"What am I, a low-class labourer's wife, that I should be subjected to motoring out to that ridiculous village just for dinner with your friends?"—she told Azmi. But after some time, and after several visits from which Azmi returned glowing and full of wondrous stories, Freny decided to accompany him on one of these ventures and she found herself remarkably drawn to Piroja and the energy that surrounded her. This was not her habit, as she was more comfortable playing the role of curmudgeon, so Freny surprised herself with her great interest in and affection for the little girl.

"What will become of Piroja?" Freny asked Parvin one day while the two of them sat on the veranda, the two men inside enjoying the latest distilled version of Asha.

"I am sorry, Freny, dear, what do you mean?"

"Her future. What will become of her? This convent education is a fine thing, but when that is done, what then? She cannot return to this—this place where liquor flows freely and minds wither." Freny was particularly pleased with this choice phrase, as it made her feel she was a guardian angel for a wayward child.

"No," said Parvin thoughtfully, wishing she had not finished her lemonade, for she had an urge to spill some on Freny's ridiculous pink dress. "No, I suppose she will not return here for any permanent settling, unless perhaps she finds a young boy who wishes to manage a distillery."

"Ha, and what's the chance in that, a respectable Parsi boy ... ?" but even ill-mannered Freny had enough sense not to finish the sentence. "That is, the community is so small here, even in Nowgong."

"True enough, true enough. I suppose, as she grows older, Piroja will tell us what direction her life will take."

"Ah, when the child tells the parent, then Ahriman rules the world, is it not? No, Parvin, dear, you should determine her aptitude and see what best befits her. It is what my parents did for me, determined my aptitude, and it has served me well."

Your aptitude, thought Parvin, *for being an ill-tempered and spoiled woman, perhaps,* but aloud she said, "I suppose so, Freny, dear, although children will have minds of their own and directions they wish to choose."

"Hm, yes, and always good to find out what is on their minds." Turning to the door, Freny began yelling Piroja's name far more loudly than was necessary to summon the child to the porch.

Piroja, meanwhile, was inside with her father and Azmi, enjoying the company of men and their talk of business and life and religion, not necessarily in that order. How much had changed for Piroja in two short years of schooling, her lust for knowledge whetted and never sated. All this talk of grown-ups now fascinated her; she often absorbed more than did the conversants, however much they pretended otherwise. This, Piroja was to learn, was often the way of grown-ups, to feign interest when it seemed politic to do so, to never telegraph boredom no matter how boring a person or idea might be. This was a lesson she would practise well, later in life, hiding her innermost thoughts and dressing them in fabrics of disguise. But, on this occasion, Azmi was telling Jamshed about how well the distillery's liquor was being received in the parts he travelled to.

"Ah yes, Jamshed-ji, good stuff travels well in good bottles! I have taken your Asha as far as Bombay, do you know? I have told all who will listen that, listen here, this Parsi chap knows what he's doing when it comes to a good glass of rum."

"Well, that is very kind of you, Azmi. Another dram for you?"

"Ha-ha, don't mind if I do, but I was not hinting!" Then, holding out his glass and lowering his voice, not to keep the conversation more private but, rather, to indicate the sombre and serious tone of what he was about to impart, "Jamshed-ji, there are rumblings all the way down to the southern tip of this amazing country, rumblings about the end of the war and where it will all lead us."

"I have heard a bit about this, but we are quite isolated here. Is it about Congress?"

"Ah, yes, Congress and beyond. It is not just those boys in Congress, but the rickshaw drivers in the street, if you can believe it, the fishmongers in the market. India for Indians, they are saying. Quit India, they mutter under their breaths. It is really quite something."

"So, independence," says Jamshed, now pouring himself another finger of Asha, "it is just around the corner? Inevitable, as they say, after the war?"

"Indeed, so say the voices in the street. I myself am somewhat distrustful."

"Of the movement?"

"Of the movement, of Congress, of the British. I distrust even the Panchayat sometimes, the way it sits so pompous and holier-than-thou. But mostly, Jamshed, I am mistrustful about the future, of the Parsis and what will become of us."

"I can understand that," says Jamshed, now recorking the bottle lest the two of them get too carried away, "but the faith is strong, and that will keep us moving forward, no?"

"Ha, true, my Dastur-ji. I find it amazing that you yourself had the tenacity to follow your faith so keenly, to mature into the dastur that you are, yet proceed into business with such acumen! Amazing. If the future of the Parsis was to follow the path of the Khargats, I would fear nothing. But ..."

"But you are too kind. I only followed my father, trained for the faith. And learned the lessons of life and business at the same time."

"Indeed," says Azmi, then, looking down at Piroja, notices her for the first time in the room. "And you, little one. You listen so carefully, like a little sponge you are. Will you be the future of the Parsis in this part of the world, do you think?"

Piroja is somewhat startled to be addressed so directly, but, unfazed, replies, "I am looking forward to growing up, Azmi Uncle, if that is what you mean."

"Ha, as if there is an alternative! Yes, you shall grow into a fine woman, I am sure. Mind your father and his religious teachings, and your mother and her strength of character, and you can do no wrong. But also mind the choices that you make, little one. Do you understand?"

Piroja is just nodding when she hears her name screeched out by Freny. She is about to leap up and respond, but Freny, a woman on a mission, is too quick and is already entering the room, Parvin just a few steps behind.

"Ah, there you are, Piroja, so glad to have found you. Your mother and I were just talking about you and what you might decide to do when you grow up. Come, you must tell me. What is in your cards?"

Piroja ponders the possibilities open to her. She thinks most specifically of the kindness offered to her last summer when a visiting physician helped soothe a cut on her knee and how he had talked to her a great deal about the various cures and medicines that helped people, old and young, recover and lead full and healthy lives. This so impressed Piroja that she began to relentlessly question the Sisters at the convent first about health, then about the body and its organs and operations. To answer her curiosity, one of the Sisters gave her a picture book all about anatomy. "Aunt Freny," answers Piroja, "I will be a doctor when I grow up."

Nouroz's return

"And then she says she wants to be a doctor. A doctor! My daughter, a doctor? And what is worse is that Freny comes to us afterward and says she does not wish to insult us, but she knows we do not have the money to send a girl child to medical school and tells us she will help us. Help us! As if I would take money from Azmi and Freny. As if Parvin and I want help to send our daughter on such a wild goose chase."

Jamshed is talking to his childhood friend Nouroz, who showed up on their distillery doorstep almost unexpectedly when his touring troupe stopped over for a two-night performance in Nowgong. Jamshed was thrilled that his friend would not only be in Nowgong, but would take an extra two days to spend with him and Parvin at the distillery.

"I see," says Nouroz. "A wild goose chase."

"You understand, of course, what I am talking about, do you not?"

"Dear Jum, you are talking to an actor."

"Yes, but still, you are still Parsi!"

"Hm, and that is, perhaps, more than any other reason, why I am an actor, but that is beside the point. If Piroja will be a doctor, well then, what's the harm?"

"Nouroz, Nouroz, Nouroz, things are just not as they were. I have—I have made promises, and I must keep them. It is different than when we were young and everything was so … possible."

"But is it, Jum, is it? … for those still young? Let me ask you, no judgement here, but when did you change into this what-you-have-become?"

"Ha, is it that evident, then? Maybe it was becoming a businessman and a father, instead of remaining an actor and a philanderer! Or maybe talk to me when your third child is the only one surviving, and that, too, is threatened so easily, so quickly."

Nouroz at first laughs at the jibe, but his smile fades when he hears the deep hurt in Jamshed's tone. "Do you remember the theatre I took you to see that one day?"

"Yes, yes, of course, you wanted to join to meet girls, as I recall!"

Nouroz laughs and nods. "I remember, yes. And I did, my fair share, but that was only because girls were then allowed on stage, and that was thanks to Dadi Patel, a Parsi. My point is, Jum, that we cannot burrow our heads in holes just because things are not as they once were. Things change. We are part of that."

"And what of you, Nouroz; you do not want things to stay the same?"

"Ji, far from it. Do you remember your father telling us of Dinshaw Wacha? President of Congress in, what was it, 1900, 1901? 'One heart and one mind,' is what he said in his presidential address; India had to act with one heart and one mind."

"And do you believe that is what we need to do?"

"Listen, it is what we have had to do for ninety years or more. Look at you. You hold on to everything from the past, but you also recreate it, you push it forward. And if not for Piroja, then for whom?"

"Oh, now I have had a glass or two of Asha ... but whatever do you mean?"

"Well, take Asha, Jum. Was it by accident you named this intoxicating liquor after a Parsi tenet? A bit of *in vinos veritas*, no? Point is, you take a notion like truth and distil it, quite literally, and disperse it, again quite literally, out to the population at large, what do you get?"

"A drunk population?"

"Funny, but half truthful. Drunk with inspiration, maybe, drunk with asha! All right, the metaphor falls flat if you think about promoting independence movements through rum, I give you that. But think of what you have done. You have translated something into something else, to spread the word. And you have always done that. Look at you, a dastur and manager of the distillery. You are the embodiment of one heart and one mind, do you not see that, Jum?"

"Well, this is all too much for me. I am, as you say, a simple distillery manager and a dastur, with a daughter who wants to be a doctor, which is where this all started before the Asha started going to your head!"

"And a doctor she should be. Home-grown talent, in the professions, in the legislature, in the civil service."

"Piroja, a doctor? It is unthinkable."

"Because she is a girl?"

"Yes, because she is a girl. No, that is not what I mean. Nouroz, you are twisting my words."

"Ha, I am twisting nothing, old man Jamshed! What has happened? What has happened to you, to hide behind a cloak of nonthinking?"

"I am only trying to protect my daughter, can you not understand this, father of no child? It is unthinkable, that she will be hurt by such promises when no one will actually let her do this thing."

"Another unthinkable thing, Jum, is the future of this country. We have been sending our young men to fight shoulder to shoulder with the British for a year now—indeed, it was last Christmas that the first of our troops arrived to support them. And what for? Because we care what the tribals are doing to each other in Europe? Not at all. We fight beside them because we are making ourselves known as their equals, their allies. And when the war is over—and it will not last forever—what then? I will tell you what. India will stand united, Congress as our guide. Already Gandhi and Nehru have written to Hitler to urge him to stand down. But even so, even while our leaders can write to world leaders, our people are not free. Still, in Delhi, Bombay, everywhere, men are being arrested in the street for talking against the European war."

"Yes, yes, all fine and good, and as an actor you make an impassioned case for—for something about the war ..."

"For freedom, Jamshed, freedom."

"Yes, then, freedom. But what has this to do with my daughter? Is it freedom to choose folly? To choose against your own history and traditions?"

"I was getting to that. The thing is, if a young girl like Piroja can choose her future, that gives us a lesson, no? If she says to you, I will be a doctor, then what prevents me or you or others from saying, I want to be free in my own country?"

"Just like when we were boys, you are losing me. I do not see the parallel. And besides, what happened to that girl-crazy Nouroz? Do you not remember? Your sole reason for going into theatre was to meet girls! Whatever happened there? No stories to tell, Nouroz?"

"Oh the stories I *could* tell ... there have been many. The theatre opened up my eyes to many different ways of doing things, many different ways of being in the world. But, my dear friend, there comes a time when what matters is before us, you see?"

"So, you no longer try to impress the girls with your memory tricks? Ha, hard to believe that you have given up your seductive ways to proceed along the straight and narrow, to have become an honest Parsi fellow."

"I can still be that honest Parsi fellow, but only if I can do what I need to do. For my people. For myself. So no—I no longer try to impress the girls with tricks of memory or anything else."

"And no settling down for you? Just a travelling actor for the rest of your life?"

"Hm, no settling down, not the way you might think, anyway. There are changes afoot, Jamshed, that is all I am saying. We are all going through changes."

"Changes, yes. We were boys growing into men, and now we are men—and what are we growing into?"

"Into ourselves. Our futures."

"I cannot say more to you now than to tell you there have been promises made, choices made for life and living, but to send a loved one away, there is a limit to that, you know? We sent Piroja away to school, yes, but I cannot see her sent farther away, not to medical school, not to places that will take her away from us here, farther still."

"Ah, and now you are starting to make nonsense, Jum. Perhaps, then, we should close our evening with another spot of Asha."

"Hm, indeed, Nouroz. Indeed."

Years of war, abridged

Jamshed and Parvin conduct their lives in the best way they know how, he in the distillery compound from first thing in the morning until late into the afternoon, she occupying herself with duties around the house and garden and with a variety of hobbies she has picked up since Piroja went off to school—watercolours, charcoal sketches, singing (to herself only), and, oddly enough, since she was never that interested in arithmetic (although Jamshed's calculations that often moved from numerical to moral grounds had quite intrigued her), memorizing complex numerical formulae and seeing what possibilities those numbers can afford. This is something she can spend hours on, never with pencil and paper, but imagining sums and quotients with no real-world connection, only abstract and ephemeral. Parvin tells no one of this hobby, so it appears to anyone who sees her in the garden or ambling along a path that she is either lost in thought or has a vacant mind, neither one of which could be further from the truth. The thing is, she tells herself, that by doing math in her head she can at once think less of her daughter and how much she misses her, and she can connect with her daughter because she imagines Piroja might be, at the same moment, performing the same mathematical calculations. It is an odd game, to be sure, like looking up at the Southern Cross and feeling a bond with distant relatives who might also be gazing up, but it is a game that gives Parvin no small amount of satisfaction.

Jamshed does not notice this preoccupation of Parvin's. In fact, there is little that he notices about her as the war (and their daughter's absence) carries on. It is as if there is a huge blanket thrown over their lives, muffling out excess thought or emotion, everything taking on a dimmer dimension, lightness only coming into their lives when Piroja visits on school breaks during the summers and at Christmas. As she gets older and can travel on her own, Piroja begins to come home for the occasional four-day break, too, which at least gives her two full days in Nowgong with home-cooked meals and family togetherness. For her part, Parvin notices little about Jamshed or the distillery. What she does notice is that his one and only concoction, his invention, the product of which he is the sole creator and therefore the proud parent of, Asha, is doing more than famously. It, on its own, keeps the distillery flourishing. There are times when Jamshed thinks he should can the whole jingbang lot of other liquors and produce only Asha. But if his thoroughness of attention is now fixed on the next batch of Asha, and on his daughter's next visit, it is also as far flung from Parvin as is hers is from him. On several occasions during the war years, one or the other will either bring out a freshly cut mango, or play that game of pretend-mango, and there are times when the game succeeds, but not in the ultimate end of further pregnancies, nor is this a point of discussion for either of them. It is as if they have given it their all to produce a single and most exceptional offspring, and, knowing what they have had to give up (her very presence), in order that she may survive and go forth into the universe, they are quite evidently spent. So Jamshed occupies himself with distilling the next batch of Asha; Parvin busies herself with running the household and her secret complex trigonometric data; and between them, they wait out the war and wait out their lives.

It is one such day, while Jamshed is in the back room of the distillery working out refinements (the product is close to but never perfect, says Jamshed, and its need for constant refinement parallels a search for asha as a concept) and Parvin is in the garden, her eyes cast up and to the right as she tries to divine the volume of earth that is in their front garden (given that, if she were to dig down several miles, the surface area occupied by their garden would be reduced because of the conical shape that would result as the dig moved toward the centre of the earth), that Freny drops by. She leaps out of the car before it has ceased motion and runs into the courtyard to greet Parvin.

"Parvin, dearest, it has been so long!"

"Aunty Freny, what a delightful surprise."

"Yes, I am sorry for coming unannounced like this, but I just felt I had to see you, and so here I am."

"I will get some tea, then."

"Tea would be wonderful. Why, Parvin, you are always such a marvellous hostess."

All this effusion is somewhat disconcerting to Parvin, who is used to a more cantankerous Freny, but she will ride this out to its logical conclusion, which, Parvin reasons, has approximately a million and a half permutations, give or take a hundred thousand. She prepares tea as Freny rushes about, offering to help but being quite useless, as she gets in the way, drops things, and cuts herself if such assistance is ever accepted. Finally, as if she is bursting, she comes out with what she has to say.

"Parvin darling, I have the most wonderful news. There is a new scholarship put in by some of the Parsi families in Jhansi. Yes, I know, we are so few, but you also know how important education is, so the families have come together to help our future generations. The idea is this: they will provide full scholarships to noteworthy children for advanced studies, provided the child's family will provide room and board. Is this not wonderful?"

"Why, yes, Aunty Freny, it is, but why do you come all this way to tell me?"

"Because, silly, of that conversation we had about Piroja and medical school, do you not remember?"

"Yes, I do, but Freny, we cannot ..."

"Oh, yes, I know, you are thinking Piroja should do something useful like become a schoolteacher and then get married," says Freny, quite unaware that her words have great power to offend, although, in this case, Parvin, suddenly caught up in determining the square root of a particularly large prime number, does not take them so. "But Piroja—our Piroja—she has such talent. And—and I have gone to the scholarship granters and told them that I will put up the money to support Piroja through her doctoring studies. Can you imagine? A doctor, a Parsi doctor, here in Nowgong, and our—your daughter, no less!"

"Yes," says Parvin, pouring tea and mentally noting that the viscosity of the pouring tea is similar to that of water but a precise calculation would undoubtedly show a distinct difference of some kind. "Yes, but I do not think that will happen."

"What then, she should become an actress like your husband's friend Nouroz? *Va*, remember the row he caused with the Panchayat with that kerfuffle in Bombay? You would want such a life for your daughter?"

"That was just a rumour, Aunt Freny. Nouroz was always one for stirring up trouble."

"Then stir it up with his own stick, I say, not go using the sticks of other actors and saying it is all very well and all right!"

Parvin has to smile at this lewdness. "But Nouroz said nothing of this, just that his choice was not be married."

"Ah, but it was the way he said it, no? And with those other actors and the talk of lovey-love and all of that!"

"Nah, nah, Aunt Freny, this is very much exaggerated. It is only Nouroz's way of talking of freedom for India, you know that."

Freny is somewhat nonplussed by this statement but will not let it curb her excitement; she throws her hands up to end the discussion, then urges Parvin to talk it over with Jamshed and see what they can see in this wondrous future for their daughter. After some more talk about this and then some gossip about trivial goings-on in Nowgong, Freny is out the door, into the car, and on her way. Parvin watches her leave and notes, with some interest, that the sun is now casting a shadow that is almost a full circle, and she begins to do some quick notes toward determining the area of the shadow as it lies on the kitchen floor when she is interrupted by a snort. She looks up.

Three point one four.

"What?" she says aloud, looking first at the shadow, which definitely does not speak, then at the air, whose volume she begins to calculate even while knowing there is no voice being produced from the empty space.

Three point one four one seven, if you want to be more precise, but you already know all this.

"Sunny? Why, Sunny. It has been years!"

Yes, years, and look at the mess here since we last talked.

"Here?" Parvin looks around at her impeccable housekeeping. "It looks fine to me."

Oh, not this *place, but the state of the world, you know, the war, the riots, all of that.*

"Oh, that, yes, terrible thing."

Enough chatter. Let us talk about school.

"Piroja? Freny and medical school? That type of school?"

Yes. What shall we do about it, do you think?

"Well, I will talk to Jamshed as Freny suggests. But I do not think he will like it."

No, I would think not. And you, Grandmother, what do you think of a doctor daughter?

"Doctor daughter … I do not think I have thought of it. But I suspect Jamshed is right. It is not possible. Is that why you are here?"

Yes, of course. And why is it not possible? A) Do you not think your daughter capable enough? B) Do Parsis not respect education above all else? And C) Whatever happened to this grandfather of mine to make him such a stick-in-the-mud?

"Well, Grandchild, A) My little Piroja is capable of anything she puts her mind to, and B) as Parsis, yes, we adore education, and C) Jamshed is only more cautious, for (A) does not mean Piroja *should* do just anything but must make decent choices, and (B) does not mean we throw our children to the wolves of education and let them study just anything. Do you see?"

In a manner of speaking. I think she would make a fine doctor, this mother of mine, but then who am I to say? I just came to put this bug in your ear. If not medical school, then what? Decisions have to be made.

"Yes, I suppose they do. If we are to welcome you into the world someday, Grandchild, decisions will have to be made."

Parvin's mind wanders off to contemplate the peculiar nature of triangles, and she does not even notice that Sunny, if he really was there, is now gone. When Jamshed comes home, Parvin forestalls some of her more complicated mathematical formulae to inform him of Freny's (but not Sunny's) visit. "What does she think," implores Jamshed, "that we are made of money? I have told them I won't take their money." Demurely, Parvin explains the scholarship.

"So does Freny think," Jamshed sighs with exasperation, "we will take alms like beggars on the street?" Quietly, Parvin notes that if they do not send their daughter to medical school, they soon will have to decide, for she is now in eighth standard and will be out of the convent in two years, what future to plan for her.

"Is the life we have provided for her," asks Jamshed rhetorically, "a decent education, is this not good enough for the Parsis of Now-gong? She should become a doctor and cease being a Parsi?" This is not what he promised his daughter when she was granted a second life.

"No," says Parvin, "but we will have to decide. And if medical school is out of the question—and is it?" she gently pushes but goes no further, "—then perhaps a related field, something more befitting a girl child."

"A doctor," whimpers Jamshed. "I could never imagine."

"Then," says Parvin almost in a whisper but with such authority that it stuns Jamshed into silence as if a golden law had been laid down, "then she shall be a nurse."

Massacre on the pitch

It is 1945, and the war in Europe is over. The Sisters of St Francis announce this to the collected assembly of girls. The German Sisters do not hide their tears of relief—now that the war is over and done with, perhaps they will not feel like enemies of the state in the streets of Jhansi. Although few thought these women of the cloth sympathized with Hitler's regime, there was that undeniable and human fallibility around ethnicity and accent that tagged itself to the nuns' very habits—call it a smell that the Jhansi natives identified. The Sisters' accents marked them as others in an other land, faux and would-be conquerors in a nation already divided and colonized by another nation, and these complications metastasized in the marketplace as sneers or gruffness or averted eyes. This aspect of the Sisters' existence in India was now over, they thanked God, and they could start to rebuild relationships around them.

The time for change had come. The nation was at a crossroads, a point of decision-making, and not just for the nation of India (which was really not one), but the nation of the British Raj, whose time had also come. "Fight for the British in the European war!" had been the rallying cry of Congress, and the lives laid down would be doubly important, first for the end of tyranny away from home, and second for the cessation of colonial rule in Bhārat. This was not something the Sisters had even thought to contend with—first castigated as members of an enemy nation, how could they so quickly be translated into representatives of colonial rule? But such was the case, and in the weeks and months post-war, as Europe rebuilt at a glacial pace, slogans appeared on the walls surrounding the convent, and then one day, painted right beside the main entrance to the school, were the words, "Quit India!"

But neither the students nor their teachers were frightened by this new nationalist pride; indeed, the nuns themselves suggested that the end of the British Empire, something they could not have begun to whisper about when they were enemies-in-residence, was not entirely a bad thing. India for Indians, sure enough, but what was to keep holy women from preserving the words of Christ and passing them on to future converts to Catholicism? The Sisters kept politics out of the classroom, but could not prevent it from invading other spaces: the dining hall, the dorm rooms, or venues still farther afield, such as the football pitch, adjacent to the convent and within view of the supervising nuns, but also accessible to students from the district schools, making this an ideal place for fraternizing with girls, and yes, boys, from the neighbourhood. And that is where we now find twelve-year-old Piroja, in the middle of this playing field, running hard to the mouth of the goal, dribbling effortlessly, and punting the ball into a far corner, past a sprawling goalkeeper's out-stretched hands, much to the delight of her teammates, as the game is now tied at one.

"Piroja, Piroja!" they all shout in something less than unison, all rushing up to their team captain for a rapturous hug and kiss to celebrate their newly won equality to the team captained by Sheila. Piroja has to admit she loves to be the one who scores important goals like this, but she also revels in the rejoicing and back-patting and tight embraces of her teammates. It always seems so endless, so full of thrill, and her lithe body is more than happy to reciprocate, smiles and toothy grins all over the pitch, eagerness personified in the bodies of the twelve-, thirteen-, and fourteen-year-olds.

"You are the best, number one!" cries Anna, and others echo the sentiment.

Jumping and laughing, Piroja responds: "Most excellent pass, Anjou, most excellent, threaded so professionally, mark my words, you will one day be a football player on the national team!" All the girls laugh, still in glee at the goal, but also at the outrageous fantasies of a girl playing a man's game for king and country. This comment, however, does not go unnoticed by young Gopal Chakrovarty, who scowls in response as he watches from the sidelines. Girls and football. Too much. Bad enough they have to play and destroy their potential womanhood (quoting a line from his father), but to even suggest they could keep playing as they go from girls to women—and the laughability of a woman playing for the country—is outrageous. Even though he knows the girls are not serious, Gopal feels violently defensive of his gender, which he associates with national pride. He is still furious when the din dies down, and as the game is about to resume, he cannot help from spitting out the rhyme his friends have taught him:

"Girls in the kitchen

Not on the pitch-in!"

He sings this loud enough so that the girls at the far side of the pitch, while they cannot make out the individual words, can discern the intent. And being twelve-, thirteen-, and fourteen-year-old girls, while they are hurt that this boy feels the need to make fun of them, they are also mature enough to try to ignore him, for the most part. And this they all do. Except for one. Piroja still carries the football triumphantly under her left arm when Gopal's not-quite-broken voice shatters her sense of sanctuary. She turns. She glares. And then she marches up to Gopal, who stands his ground in the fire of Piroja's eyes. She stands toe-to-toe with twelve-year-old Gopal, who is also small for his age, and Piroja pulls back her shoulders and raises her eye level just slightly above his, so she can look down in disdain.

"Little boy, did you just make up that awfully ridiculous rhyme, or did one of your sillyboy friends manufacture that for you to memorize?"

Gopal, mouth a tad agape now, does not respond.

"If the cat has your tongue, it is probably a very disappointed cat, as it is likely not a morsel of significant size." And then, for emphasis and support, over her shoulder, "Do you not think so, girls?"

"Ha," yells the ribald Anjou, "his tongue is probably as small as everything else on little Gopal."

"Yes, I quite agree, Anjou," says Piroja, "for it takes a small-minded boy to say such small-minded things." Then, stepping even closer into Gopal's face, "*Little* Gopal, you and your boys would never be a match for me and my girls."

And with that, she turns on her heel and marches back to centre field, leaving Gopal turning red, sputtering but unable to respond. Piroja returns to her teammates' back-patting and rib-poking, and the girls all look back to Gopal, still standing there not quite sure what to do. And then, in an inspired moment, Piroja turns on her heel and trots back to Gopal. This time, the boy takes a step or two back, mindful that this nimble, vivacious girl might just decide to try to knock his block off. Gopal realizes this is a no-win situation, for if he takes first swipe, he will be known forever as the boy who struck a girl, but if he waits to be hit, he will be known as the boy who was punched out by a girl. All this circulates through his mind, the thoughts pushing down to his legs, instructing them to back-pedal and move from harm's way, so that when Piroja reaches him, this time not going toe-to-toe, but standing a body's length away, Gopal is almost off balance. He is two yards outside of bounds, and it is almost as if Piroja refuses to cross that line—the pitch is hers and she will not leave it to confront this pathetic boy.

"It's Chakrovarty, isn't it? Gopal Chakrovarty? Your father runs the book stall in the market, isn't it? Tell you what, tomorrow we are going to play here at the same time. You show up with your boys and see if we don't trounce you. Boys against the girls. If you have the courage to show, that is. Got it, Chakrovarty? Got it?"

Gopal is stuck. He is no longer off balance physically, but he hasn't the slightest idea what to do with this challenge. He could turn and walk away, stoically, refuse to bend to the goadings of this fiery Piroja. Or he could stammer out something witty—"What would be the use? The outcome is clear; boys are faster and stronger, and we would make you see that, believe me"—but that is not the option that comes to tongue. Instead, Gopal opens and closes his mouth like a large guppy, his thoughts refusing to coincide with his voice, so every time he has something to say, he finds his mouth closed, and every time his mouth is open, there are no words to come forth. Finally, he bubbles forth a nod, yes, he will bring his boys here. (Whatever will he tell them? The Catholic girls want a football match that he could not refuse? Oh, why did he open his mouth in the first place, and who does this Parsi girl think she is to come at him so? Misery. This is all misery.)

Piroja turns and runs back to centre field, and the game resumes, with whispering and trepidation among the girls. "Are we really going to play these Hindu boys?" they ask with an excitement that is fuelled by years of single-gendered schooling. The boys against the girls. Let the games begin.

Variav redux

It was one of Piroja's favourite stories, the massacre at Variav. Jamshed told it to her when she was on summer holidays after her third year at St Francis, and it was such a favourite story that she made him tell and retell it at least a dozen times that summer, so that Jamshed almost lamented having shared it with her in the first place.

"But would you not rather hear of other stories? There are so many good stories, many with happier endings!"

"Papa, please just tell it one more time. Start with the Parsi settlers and how they angered the Raja of Ratanpur by refusing to pay unfair taxes and how they fought the tax-collecting men and sent them packing."

"But you know this story. Why don't you tell it back to me?"

"Because I like it when you tell me stories! Go on, then, the Parsis refused to pay, and then one day the men were away at a feast ..."

"The men were at a feast, yes, Piroja, and the Raja was stinging from having his troops defeated by the Parsis, who were, after all, not known as warriors. So he sent in a larger contingent, and when the general arrived he was met with stunning force. Walking arm in arm, their heads helmeted and their faces wrapped against the elements by silk veils, the Parsi fighters marched forward."

"They were the bravest of the brave!"

"And these brave Parsi warriors advanced on the Raja's men, and a great battle ensued. And for a people not known for fighting prowess, they were magnificent, beating back the invading army so they ran like scared kittens."

"But then something happened."

"Yes indeed. Something happened. Just when the Raja's men

211

were about to admit defeat, one of their number swung a lance, and it clipped the helmet off the lead Parsi warrior. Off came the helmet, and it tore off the veil, too, and the Raja's men were amazed, for uncovered was the face of a strong and noble Parsi woman. We do not know her name, but we know she was proud, and with her long hair loosed, she stood there defiantly, grasped the offending lance, and snapped it in two."

"Yes, snapped it in two!"

"For a long moment, the Raja's men were stymied. They did not know what to do, fight women or flee warriors."

"They should have fled! They should have known they were defeated, don't you think, Papa?"

"Perhaps, Piroja. But they did not. They sent word for more troops, the general did, though he did not tell of his defeat at the hands of the Parsi village women. And this is the sad part, Piroja, because more troops were dispatched and they came bearing arms and supplies and they came to fight fiercely. In only a day, the Raja's men overran the Parsi soldiers, those brave women. They killed them indiscriminately, refusing to consider surrender of any kind. And it is told that some of the women, rather than submit to a humiliating death, joined hands and walked into the Tapti River, singing triumphant songs until their heads were below water and no one could hear, no one could sing any longer."

"I do not know if I think that is a sad part or a happy part."

"I do not know either. Perhaps some moments can have sadness and happiness happening all rolled up at once."

"Papa, do you think the women, the Parsi women, were happy to walk into the river together?"

"That is something you have not asked me before, Piroja. Happy? I do not know. What do you think?"

"I think it is as you said, that there can be sadness and happiness rolled together. Yes, I am happy to think of the women singing together, but it is sad that they had to die."

For a brief flicker, Jamshed thinks of eithers and ors, of not only choosing directions in life as the result of a coin toss, but of the fickle results of that coin toss contained in every decision.

"Yes, it is sad that they had to die."

So it is with this memory from the previous summer dancing in her imagination that Piroja sits down with the Catholic girls the afternoon after issuing her challenge to Gopal. She has raced out to the market ("But Sister, it is very important I do this errand for my father") to find Mrs Desai, the friend of her father's who runs a beautiful fabric stall. She explains to Mrs Desai that she has little money for purchasing her wares, but after explaining the purpose, kindly Mrs Desai agrees to loan her the fabric. Racing back, her arms loaded down with strips of silk, Piroja is excited. She tells the girls a truncated version of the legend of Variav, leaving out the bit about the massacre, as it would only aggravate already-frayed nerves (what are we doing, playing a football match with the Hindu boys?) and enhancing the bravery of the women. The girls examine the lengths of fabric, not oohing at the magnificent colours but eyeing them up for size and possibility—what veil will be most easily worn, will not interfere with sight or movement?

And the next day, there they are, the eight of them, all with different ensembles of veilery, and recognizable to one another only by the colour and shape of their eyes. But if there was fear or anxiety about the game before donning the veils, something soothing and incredibly powerful comes over them now. It is like this that they march out on to the pitch, the boys already there. If Gopal or any of the other boys want to say something to ridicule the girls' team, they do not act on it. Instead, like Gopal the day before, the boys stand agape, no words to speak as the masked team stands opposite them. Piroja carries the ball to centre field. She stares into Gopal's eyes.

"Chakrovarty. Are you ready for us?"

Gopal leans forward, hands on knees, looks groundward then up into the eyes that stare him down. He clears his throat. "Hm, uh-huh." And the game begins.

To the outside observer (if there were one), this game would look decidedly peculiar. On one side, gangly brown boys in shorts, tearing around the field and calling out to one another in a combination of soprano and tenor voices, their energy somewhat fevered, their desire to not just win but to overwhelm fairly obvious and, as a result of such over-trying, mildly unsuccessful. Boys overrunning the ball, tripping over teammates, kicking high over crossbars on easy approaches, and above all, showing a preternatural fear of contacting members of the other team anywhere above the shins, resulting in a comedic ballet of touch-avoidance, hands resolutely carried high above shoulders so the entire boys team looks like it is playing a concerto on an invisible keyboard secured just above sightlines. On the other side, quite less sweatily and anxiously, the girls' team holds sway on the pitch. First, they have practised together more than the boys and know each other's strengths and potentials. Second, they have home-field advantage. And third, with veils secured around their faces, ends fluttering about their shoulders, they verily feel like the soldiers of Variav, whose stories of courage Piroja has regaled them with. Their leader has downplayed the Parsi angle so as not to confuse or upset the sensitivities of the Catholic girls, but she has up-played the power that girls can have when confronted with boys. "We can teach those yaars a thing or two," she tells them, never breathing a word about defeat.

But the first goal goes to the boys, led by Gopal Chakrovarty himself, charging up the middle and popping a high curling ball toward the goalkeeper, who should have made the stop but was feeling a bit uneven and so bobbled the ball and let it slide past her across the goal line. Piroja is back there to lunge and hook the ball out before it goes more than a foot across, but all acknowledge that it was in, and her valiant effort is more to show the desire not to give up. Piroja looks toward the hoarsely cheering Gopal and nods in his direction, mouths at him, "Good job, well done," bringing his revelry to a momentary stall as he nods back and mouths "Thank you," and thinks to himself that this girl defender almost made the play that would have quite embarrassed him.

A few minutes later, though, the ball is in play around midfield. Piroja spies Anjou flying up the right side and feeds her a pass that lands perfectly on her right toe, and she, without missing a beat, dribbles forward, one-two-three strides before crossing to an open Sheila, who walks in and lays a groundball, not drilled but off-speed. This so confuses the goalkeeper that he starts to move in the right direction, hesitates, stops, and is left standing as the ball whizzes by six feet to his left, as he catches the forward looking at him hard, eye-to-eye. "Whatever are you doing?" scream his teammates, but they also recognize the skill and finesse with which Sheila has tied the game. Gopal brushes by her and brings his hand down from piano-playing in the air to pat her shoulder—good shot—and suddenly there is camaraderie on the field and a glow about the game.

Thus the game goes on, no close chances until it is nearly five o'clock, the agreed-upon cessation of the match. But at three minutes to five, according to Gail, the official timekeeper, the quiet and somewhat clumsy Celeste makes an uncharacteristically good rush down the right line and is about to centre the ball when a young fellow known to all as Boy, (owing to frequent barkings of that moniker when his father came to visit), the tallest member of the squad and also the clumsiest on *his* team, slides messily to try to steal the ball. A collection of feet and bare legs and arms and faces and jerseys all intermingle as Boy's left toe catches a piece of the ball and sends it skittering to the corner, where it exits over the line to precipitate a corner kick. All the while, Celeste and Boy are a tangle of limbs and torsos, finding themselves horizontal, momentarily irritated and worried that one or the other might be injured from such a collision, followed by a none-too-subtle chuckle from Celeste and a guffaw from Boy. They lie there, spent, their faces only inches away from each other, a hand that is on a hip not its own and a knee that jostles uncomfortably close to nether regions of another. It becomes quickly apparent that neither player is injured, and just as apparent that neither truly wishes to immediately disentangle, brush off, and verticalize. This tableau lasts for perhaps seven or eight seconds (which Gail dutifully counts off on the ticking hand of the pocket watch) before a wry smile appears on Boy's face, and he moves a. knee away from its provocative pose and rises up from the pitch, offering a hand to an equally behind-veil-smiling Celeste, who takes it, although she knows she is fully capable of rising by herself. All of this titillation gives rise to enough speculation and rumour monger-ing that none are surprised when, several months later, Celeste and Boy are often seen in similar places or, as is more often the case, not seen at the same times. This ungainly couple are later to tell their offspring that they met falling down. But that is for the future.

Standing now, hand-holding with Boy longer than should be necessary, Celeste decides to release her smile to the world, and flirts the veil away from her face, letting it drop to her shoulder with remarkable grace, and it is at this moment that both teams are transfixed by what they see. Why their faces were ever covered the boys do not know, and why this moment for uncovering is right is also unclear, and only becomes more absolute when Piroja swishes past the now-not-hand-holding couple to the goal line to take, as is her right as unofficial captain, the corner kick. But as she first retrieves then places the ball, she looks at the beaming Celeste and nods a nod that is, to the boys, ever so imperceptible, but to the girls, a command of the highest order and significance. As Piroja gently looses the veil from her face and lets it fall to her shoulder, so do all the other girls, in unison, veils dropping not to ground but to suspension on shoulder. Eight girl faces exposed, not by draconian rajas, but by their own hands, and the boys, most of whom have maintained the invisible-high-keyboard position of their hands, all, again in unison, drop arms to sides in stillness and wonderment. In this moment, Piroja backs three paces from the ball and, boys still standing dumbstruck, strikes the football with all the energy and force she can muster at this late stage of the game, curling said ball high in the air so that it hovers overhead for an endless period of time (four seconds, Gail will say later) before gravitationally inclining toward the goalmouth and the waiting goalkeeper.

Unfortunately for him, hands no longer on high but stilled by his side, there is a light speck that grows large in his peripheral vision, a speck that becomes the crown in the black mass of hair that sits atop the head of Anjou, and it is a speck that, as it approaches, is clearly a head above the now-shoulder-high arms of the goalkeeper. But while outstretched arms are an invitation to the ball, a rising, daring Anjou lunges forward simultaneously for her first and only (she will tell others later, proudly) header that results in a goal. Yes, crown makes acute and acutely painful contact with the downward spiralling football with such precision and agility that it becomes the sensation of the afternoon, the week, and, in the minds of some, the entire semester. Redirections. That which would have spiralled to ground, bouncing and following through to the other end of the field, or that which would have circled downward only to be interrupted by the loving embrace of a boy goalkeeper, either or all of which would have ended in a draw, changing, if not all things then at least the immediate future, does not occur. Vectors are inverted in a new way. Leap, crown, ball, contact. Redirection and the clockwise-spinning ball counters and spins instead just inches over the surprised goalkeeper's eyeballs, actually having the audacity to glance off the tuft of *his* crown before sailing past and in, just under crossbar, for the victory.

In the distance, the Sisters appear to find an explosion of girls, limbs, and laughter and, in the midst of it, Anjou standing at first with her fists clenched and arms outstretched, then falling to her knees so that she appears to be sinking into the quicksand of her own exhilaration. Sisters running to the pitch, boys sagging shoulders but some of them still smiling in wonder, girls all over the field hugging and jumping. And then there is Piroja, trotting then running to the goalmouth, left hand clenching and pulling from her shoulder the bright blue silk that was, until moments ago, her veil to the world. She is running to Anjou, whose raised arms now spring wide to the side. Piroja slides in on her knees to meet Anjou face-to-face, the blue silk scarf arcing around Anjou's neck so that its end encircles and meets Piroja's right hand, a lasso, pulling her in close. Two girls, face-to-face in utter ecstasy of victory, one whose hand silkties the other's neck, one whose outstretched, clenched fists open up to embrace shoulders, their faces approaching through laughter and glee until sound is trapped by embracing lips and suddenly all-new terrains are explored, interior, eyes closed, and, in that probing advance, yes, even there in that moment, a choice is made and another path unchosen. All things for a reason. And if the victory kiss were to have lasted a few seconds less (a full sixteen seconds, I swear, reports Gail when asked), then all might not be subject to the changes that ensued.

But Sister Ida, the fastest to make it to the pitch, is at once alarmed that there are eight Hindu boys in all manners of inappropriate closeness to her girls, and then doubly alarmed that two of her girls are utterly unperturbed by this boyish, or anything-else-ish, presence.

Good thoughts, uncertain words, bad deeds

The ceiling fan, same as it ever was, is wooden with brass tips, and it still rotates just fast enough so each blade is discernible, not in exact detail, but enough so each is distinct from the next. Any faster and the blades would blur into each other and, indeed, given why they have been summoned, Jamshed quite wishes they would whir out of control and perhaps fly off and massacre the three of them right then and there.

This is exactly what Jamshed is thinking as he watches the blades rotate, that all the fan would have to do, miraculously, is to make the room an all-too-welcome bloodbath. Jamshed is sitting in a creaky wooden chair, supposedly the teacher's chair, his back straight and posture perfect except for his head, which tilts upward and wonders at the fan. Directly in front of Jamshed is that large rosewood desk that is even worse off than in previous years, and as Jamshed examines this desk closely, he notices additional scratches and scars and momentarily worries that the carved initials and dates inscribed under the lip of the desk might read "A + P." Jamshed has a faint sensation that all this has happened before, in another place, not here, but he does not realize that a few years have passed, and what he once experienced as a father, wilfully giving his daughter into the charge of another, he is now experiencing with renewed intensity.

On the other side of the desk, again squeezed uncomfortably into a desk used to holding the bodies of five-year-old girls, sits Parvin. She has been sitting like this, awkwardly, for five minutes, passing the time by watching her husband watch the ceiling fan and looking around the classroom to take her mind off of what she has been told, that is, that this boarding school is a den of iniquity. Parvin squirms in the tiny seat and wonders how children like Piroja can possibly be so corrupted in this environment, here in this strange place that has taken her so far away from the home and love of her parents. Still, her daughter is alive, thinks Parvin, alive, and the deal was struck years ago, and now it is time to lose a little so she does not lose a lot.

Reverend Mother Mary-Something-something walks in, looking for all the world to Parvin like the incarnation of Ahriman, and sits herself down at the rosewood desk, crossing her hands in front of her and then leaning forward to speak.

"Girls will be girls," she tells Jamshed, who translates for Parvin, who asks him back, yes, what other choice is there, and what sort of silly Catholic nonsense is that, "but we simply cannot have girls this age losing control of their sensibility. They are passionate young girls with a future ahead of them. We must ensure we direct them on the right path."

"Yes," says Parvin to Jamshed, upon hearing the translation, "and tell this Reverend Crazy Woman that if maybe these nuns did not spend all their lives unmarried they might be able to provide a decent example for young girls, at least in terms of pointing them in the direction of the right sex," a translation that Jamshed reduces to an explanation that his wife agrees with the good Reverend Mother.

"Mr and Mrs Khargat, I do not have to tell you that Piroja is a brilliant student. No, she is our most brilliant student, and she has consistantly won school and provincial honours. She has a brightliest future ahead of her. But we must act swiftliest to quash this misdirection in the bud, to stymie our losses while we can." This Jamshed is at a loss to translate, so instead tells Parvin that the good Reverend Mother is saying nice things about Piroja, albeit with reservations.

"Yes, timeliness is as timeliness does, *n'est-ce pas*? We have decided that Piroja, as fitting a fit as she is, might unduly interrupt the intentions of Catholicism and Catholic girlhoodness. And we unilateralimously agree that we want to push her out there, into the world-at-largeness with a solid historical senseness from St Francis. So the best thing for her and for the girls here at St Francis is that she be accelerated to graduation immediatemently, with our best wishes bestoned upon her."

"What does she babble on about now?" Parvin inquires. "Is she on to that thing about fishes and wine and all that messiness about blood and all? Because if she is, Jamshed, I think I will really need to get up and kick her in that place where there is a difference between boys and girls, not that she would know, which is probably part of the problem in this convent."

"My wife says this is very kind and generous of you—"

"Munificence is our middle name, Mr Khargat, and it is with great pleasurely activity that we do this. Tell your wife, poor dear, that we shall pray for her and for Piroja. Pray and bend into backwards for her. That is the Catholic way, *n'est-ce pas?*" And she beams brightly at Parvin.

"She wishes you and Piroja well," Jamshed tells Parvin after a brief pause and reflection.

"Ah, yes, of course she does. May I kick her now?" And she beams brightly back at the Reverend Mother.

"I do not think kicking her will change anything," says Jamshed.

"Change? No, of course not, but it will make me feel better and, who knows, it might make her feel better, given she lives a life without you-know." And Parvin gets up, takes a step toward the Reverend Mother, much to Jamshed's concern, but then bows her head deeply and blesses her with the most potent curses she can think of.

"And to you as well, my, my, such honorifics, I cannot portend. Good day, Mr Khargat, Mrs Khargat," says the Reverend Mother, bowing. "Good day and a good life for you and your daughter." She crosses her chest quickly, hoping the Khargats get the message that it is not too late for conversion. Parvin raises a hand to strike the Reverend Mother about her twisty lips, but Jamshed swiftly encircles her hand with his own as if that was the whole intention, smiles a goodbye, and leads Parvin from the room.

Short goodbyes

Piroja looks about the room that has been her home for the past nine years, which feels like more of a home, however absurd that might sound, than her room in Nowgong. But this is where she has grown up, she thinks, where she first learned her letters (beyond the not-so-rudimentary teachings of her mother), where she learned to make friends, where she learned the ways of the world, and where, she thinks ruefully, she learned of affections that might leap over barbed-wire fences. Her bags are packed, most of them already shipped off back to Nowgong. The room is empty except for the small cot and a small, sad-looking bureau that used to contain her clothes. She feels the hand touch her shoulder before it lands, warm and soft, and she does not feel the need or urge to turn, just lets it nestle into her like sunlight.

"Piroja?"

"Yes."

"I do not know what to say."

"Say—say that it was good. Say that you have no regrets. Say that—"

"I can say all those things, and you know they are true. When you know someone this long, Piroja, when you grow up beside them … I will miss you, Piroja, miss you so much. I wish you did not have to go."

"The Sisters have accelerated me past tenth standard," Piroja says, mild irritation in her voice. "They say it would have happened anyway, that my exams from last year were, as they say, 'remarkable,' and that another year of school would not be beneficial to me. That I should go into the world and study, maybe at a university. That is what Sister Ida said, a university. What do you think of that, Anjou?" And then Piroja turns. She looks at the shorter, darker Anjou, whose eyes always used to light up when they fell on Piroja. They light up like that now and it warms Piroja.

She knows that she will likewise miss Anjou, and she knows that she does not love this girl. Certainly, she loves her as she loves so many of her friends at St Francis, as she loved Heera for the three years before she left the convent, how she loved all those girls she met in first standard. She loves them like family, she thinks. But she has also heard of *love*, seen it in the cinema, and beyond that, she feels she knows of it deep inside, so that however much she cares for Anjou, however much she will miss her and the girls and the Sisters and the convent, Piroja is also aware that the love she has for Anjou is not one that will become an unbearable longing. This she knows. Maybe it is because of a dream she had where she was comforted by a wise sage who was but a babe in arms, or maybe it was because of the soft voice she could swear she heard just days ago, comforting her, caressing her with waves of cotton batting. Whatever it is or was, she feels strong and knows that this is her time to leave. She leans into Anjou, places one hand behind the back of her head, strokes the long black hair, and pulls her face toward her. This kiss lasts a long time, even though Gail is not there to time it, and is full of the longing and passion that is stirred by goodbyes. Piroja thinks she would rather remember this as her first kiss; its quality is so much more intentional, although admittedly less dramatic, than the fevered pitch of the one they shared on the pitch. No need to choose between kisses, thinks Piroja, kissing ever the more deeply.

"Goodbye, dear Anjou," she says, pulling away. Anjou's face is streaked with tears. Piroja wipes them away with a sleeve, leans in again to kiss her friend on the cheek. "Goodbye."

Non-nuptials in Nowgong

"I am not suggesting *now*. I am just saying, eventually Piroja will have to be married, and what does it hurt to think of it?"

"She is twelve. Let that be the end of it."

"I know she is twelve and we are in the twentieth century and what Gandhi-ji has said, and I am not at all saying a marriage next year or even the year after, or even the year after that, Parvin; just sometime, and it would be nice if it was before she is into her twenties, that is all."

"There are other things to think about, Jamshed."

"Yes, but it is not impossible to think of two things at once."

"Can I say something?" interjects Piroja.

Both parents look at her incredulously, having forgotten, because they have lived for so long without her, that she is there with them.

"What I want to say is this: the Reverend Mother has told me that I can pass my O-Levels by examination and that I must study hard for them to stay at the top of my class. That is what I want to do right now. The exams are in two months."

"Well," says Jamshed, "that is admirable. Of course, jolly good. Do that."

"There is more," says Piroja. "I will study hard and do well. And for the past three years I have been number one or number two in the province. I want you to promise me that if I do so well again that I can go to medical school."

"Well, Piroja dear, medical school is very expensive, and your father and I ..."

"Yes, Mummy, I know. And I also know what Aunt Freny has told me, that money will not be the issue. If I could be a doctor, I could make you very, very proud."

"This is something your mother and I will have to discuss," says Jamshed, mentally noting that this is beyond discussion or consideration.

"Yes," adds Parvin, mentally calculating how many ways her husband will be able to rework the question so that the answer is always no, "that is something your father and I will discuss."

"Thank you," says Piroja, smiling on the outside as she acknowledges to herself that to become a doctor might require the greatest fight of her life, and against adversaries who are also the people she cherishes the most, so what might be the point? "Thank you for listening to me."

"Of course, of course," say Parvin and Jamshed, "you are our daughter." Of course.

Piroja does exceptionally well on her exams. She is ranked number one in two subjects and number two in three subjects. When Jamshed receives the results in the mail, he proudly shows them to his daughter. But inevitably she feels dismay, sorrow, and disappointment when she asks about medical school and Jamshed frowns and says, of course not, that was never in the cards, and Piroja wonders how to frame this fight, and cannot, and it hits her suddenly, unexpectedly, a knowledge that doctoring will not be her calling, and it brings silence to her lips. Daughter and parents engage in weeks of painful, tearful discussions on subjects ranging from marriage (but she is still too young) to college training in domestic services (just another way to arrange for marriage, Parvin and Piroja argue, both of them wailing at the thought of another trip away from home), to staying at home for "a while" to help her mother around the house ("With what?" both chime in, for what is there to do at this distillery compound?), to the inevitable, which is professional training that befits the educational background of a girl such as Piroja.

Aunt Freny visits one day and with her brings a sheaf of papers that she plunks down on the counter.

"This is it," she says, first looking at Piroja, then at Jamshed. "This is what we have been looking for."

Jamshed picks up the first sheet, and peers at it carefully; Piroja sorts through the pile and pulls out several that seem relevant.

"Irwin," Jamshed reads out from the papers, looking up curiously.

"It is a medical—a nursing school," says Piroja.

"Nursing?"

"Nursing," Piroja confirms. "A nursing hospital. In Delhi."

Irwin Hospital

Piroja does not go to Irwin Hospital that year, and would not normally be eligible to go the next either (still too young, they say), but with pressure from family in high places, the going-on-fourteen Piroja will begin as a new resident nurse-in-training in just over a year. She has her intake interview with one Miss Phillips, who peruses her top-of-the-province results and smiles approvingly. Four years of training, Miss Phillips informs her, board and lodging covered, with a stipend of 100 rupees per month. A hundred rupees. At not-quite-fourteen, this amount is staggering to Piroja and somewhat staggering for a lot of workers twice her age.

The closest Piroja has come to such sums has been in helping her family with the distillery books. ("Might as well put your schooling to good use," Jamshed tells her. "Let's see how you do in maths in the real world," to which Parvin responds by uttering a complex formula that roughly corresponds to the amount of Asha the distillery could produce if it began with one vat per week beginning the year of Zoroaster's birth and increasing production by one-quarter vat every quarter-year until halfway until today, at which time production increased by one-half vat every two months, causing both Piroja and Jamshed to glaze over as they gaze over at Parvin, who only then ceases to calculate the vats that would be produced by 1946.)

Piroja does stay home for the next year, enjoying herself in Nowgong with her family. A year of still being a young girl, even though she knows she will be taking on the role of a grown-up as soon as she departs. But what is the difference, she wonders, between becoming a full-fledged nurse as opposed to a full-fledged wife; both of them different sides to the same coin of growing up, both indicating a shift from girlhood to womanhood, to responsibilities around entirely different things. She spends some time in Nowgong imagining what it will be like to be a nurse, but she still cannot imagine what it will be like to be a wife. She thinks about her mother for hours on end sometimes, wondering what other futures would have awaited Parvin had she stayed a schoolteacher, had not bent to threats of suicide and married Jamshed (the story often told in their family), had not lost child after child until Piroja's own appearance on the scene.

Jamshed occasionally brings home guests, boys he hopes will win Piroja's attention and perhaps favour. She dutifully meets and spends time with these guests, sometimes even deigning to go for a jungle walk with this or that Parsi boy from a very good or middling-to-good family. Invariably, however, the boys return in a somewhat more depressed state than when they left, while Piroja's spirits are much higher on her return. Finally, Parvin has to sit Piroja down and ask her what is happening.

"These boys," she says, "whatever are you saying to them?"

"Oh, Mummy, I am just talking to them about general things."

"But why do they come back and feel like they must run off like that?"

"These boys ... I think they are entirely too sensitive," says Piroja.

The day finally arrives when Piroja is to go to Delhi, and she feels some sense of relief. Their daughter will mature, thinks Jamshed, and who knows, in Delhi she might find a wonderful Parsi fellow, perhaps a doctor, who knows? She might come home one day, thinks Parvin, and say she has decided to choose any one of a number of suitors who have come calling, who knows? Parvin and Jamshed each think these thoughts in isolation as they stand at the bus station in Nowgong with Piroja.

"You will write to us often, now, see to it," says Jamshed.

"And Christmas is not so far off, and you will have a good visit then," says Parvin.

And with much less ceremony than any of them expected, Piroja takes the bus one more time to Jhansi where she boards the train that will take her on to Delhi, a city she has visited only once before. Brave new world, she thinks to herself.

Piroja is exhausted when she finally reaches Delhi, amazed at the size and scope of the city but impressed by the good directions she has been given to navigate her way to Irwin and Miss Phillips. Quite to her delight, and reminding her of her first years at the convent, she meets an older Parsi girl, a third-year nurse, who knocks on her dormitory door the very first evening as Piroja tries on her new and stiffly starched uniform, which, she is led to understand, she will wear from day one as a training nurse.

"Hey little girl," comes the voice from outside the door. "It's me, Hutokshy. Open up to your Parsi sister!"

This Piroja does with some enthusiasm. "Hutokshy? Yes, so good to meet you. Miss Phillips told me you might come calling."

"Yes, Phillips, she can be good for something, no? Come, let us see how that cap fits you. It's a devil to put on the first few times, makes you look like a lady of the evening if you don't get it right."

Piroja is somewhat alarmed at Hutokshy's tone and tongue, though she immediately makes a mental note to practise some of the fluid and easy slang that pours forth from her compatriot's none-too-gentle mouth. Hutokshy's eyes are absolutely piercing, black as black can be, and her typical Parsi nose is complemented by an angular and somewhat atypical chin. "Here," says Hutokshy, "do it like this.

Think of it like a brassiere for your hair, keeping all things in place but at the same time giving the boys something to look at." She casts a sharp glance at Piroja's bosom and cackles, "Oh, the boys will be looking at you, I can tell you!" Hutokshy falls into full-out laughter and throws her arm around Piroja, who begins laughing too.

"I am not so sure about the boys," Piroja says softly after the laughter has subsided. "I think boys find me a bit difficult to deal with."

"Difficult? I can imagine. But why make their lives easy? They should indeed have a difficult time considering the reward we can offer, and they know it," and Hutokshy is laughing again after none-too-subtly pointing between her legs on the word "offer."

What sort of bawdiness is this, wonders Piroja, but at the same time is caught up in the fervour of the moment. She will have to be careful, she thinks, not to take too much of this fancy Hutokshy energy back to Nowgong, no telling how her parents would respond to ribald gestures and lusty laughter, hardly appropriate for a girl. Still, as an experiment, she lets her little finger bend to point downward, almost inaudibly repeats the word "offer," and puts out the tiniest of hoarse chuckles, something that Hutokshy misses entirely although she thinks that this Piroja will be a good egg.

"Come, this evening we will take you out, the girls and I. Can't have you arriving in Delhi without seeing the sights, hearing the sounds, can we?"

So that first night they go out, a group of four girls, Piroja, Hutokshy, a Hindu girl in her second year, and a Muslim girl in her third. They go to Connaught Place, because Piroja has been instructed by Aunt Freny to look up a distant relative of hers who runs the Regal Theatre. When Piroja introduces herself and her friends, the not-by-blood uncle will have none of it, their intention to sit in the general admission area and watch the new Bombay release, no, he will set them up in box seats and with this, Piroja has made an impression on her new friends.

The year is 1947, and Independence is looming. But freedom does not come without cost, the hand-over of government does not arrive without astronomical prices being paid, Piroja finds out. In her first year as a student nurse, working in the trauma ward, she will see things a girl of fourteen should never have to see. She will never forget the time she is working a graveyard shift and must try to comfort the young Muslim man who arrives on the stretcher, but she does not know how to comfort someone who cannot look at her because his face is indiscernible in the wash of blood he wears from forehead to neck. He seems remarkably calm to Piroja, twitching only ever so slightly as she sits beside him, taking his unblemished hand, which tightens around hers ever so slightly, holding on for the hour that she sits beside him, whispering volumes of all she knows how to speak, before, ever so slightly, he coughs and then does not breathe anymore. It is this moment Piroja will forever remember, seeing a man who could not see her, talking to a man without knowing if he could hear her, and then hearing a man die without knowing if he ever registered her presence as other than a hand in the dark. During her training, she will be scolded by the older nurses for her tendency to break into tears every time she sees someone suffering ("It doesn't make it better for them, Sister Piroja, only worse, how can you be so selfish?"). But if there was death and the sadness it brings, there was also considerable gaiety amongst the student nurses, both for relief and for pleasure. The student nurses had developed a rating system for the "doctors" (the honorific bestowed upon the interns in keeping with the British system), based on their kindness, generosity, and appearance, and a young handsome intern by the name of Ali Akram rated quite high on all their measures. It became evident early on, and to the chagrin of many, that this Dr

Akram was first and foremost focussed on his work—he aspired to be a surgeon at the end of his training—and was hard to engage on any other subject. This changed, but at such a subtle level that only Ali's best friend and the ever-observant Hutokshy noticed, when Piroja began her first week of training. There was an alertness about him when Piroja was around, and it was left to Hutokshy to mention this to Piroja, who was herself attentive only to her studies and work.

"So, young one, it appears you have the first catch of the day, hook, line, and sinker, in this Akram, no?"

"Whatever do you mean?" asks Piroja, though she realizes that a small stream of blood pulsing through her facial capillaries means that she does, at some unconscious level at least, know what Hutokshy means.

"Look at the way he looks at you. Oh, he is too clever to be obvious, will look away if you catch him, but I—I have seen him."

"Really? My goodness, Hutokshy, do you really think so?"

"There is growing evidence," says Hutokshy, laughing, and Piroja realizes this is another of her bawdy references to anatomy. "Oh my, Sister Piroja, I just remembered that you are so much younger than us, you sharp-as-a-tack thing, you. And while you have smarts in some areas, perhaps not so much experience in others, yaar?"

"Do you mean, I mean, with boys?"

"Exactly, on the head, little girl. Come, we shall have to have a discussion session." Hutokshy informs their schoolmates that they must start to educate Piroja in the ways of the world. The girls, for their part, are more than willing to impart information; how kissing leads to perspiration and beyond, what actually happens between the sheets, how to flirt without seeming flirtatious beyond repair, how to make things happen, as one of the girls says, when boys are unsure about what to do, and how to increase and decrease functionality depending on desire and intrigue. This education of Piroja takes approximately four weeks of daily tea sessions, after which she feels thoroughly informed if not experienced, and it is on the urging of the others that Piroja figures she should, so to speak, take matters into her own hands.

On a May evening Piroja is again working a night shift. Ali, as has become his wont, chooses to come to her station to fill out his reports and seems less interested in report-finishing than talking to the young student nurse.

"I have patients to attend to," says Piroja by way of extricating herself from Ali's uncanny ability to keep her standing in one place as he peppers her with questions that she feels compelled to answer or statements she feels obliged to consider.

"But answer me this one question, then, before you go to comfort these lucky patients of yours. My Jinnah, who is not really mine because I do not really believe in all he says, is challenging Mr Nehru on the future of our country. The two sides, he says, shall not mix. Hindu-Muslim. So answer me this question: is that how other Indians think, that is, those who are not Hindu or Muslim? The Sikhs, the Christians, the Jains? And the Parsis?"

"The Parsis are like everyone else, Dr Akram, they do not speak with one mind."

"And do you, Piroja, speak with one mind?"

"Of course," says Piroja, laughing, "how can one person not? Now I have to attend to these patients."

"All right, all right, I shall relent and let you go. And I must return to these reports. But before you go, this one last question: do you think, as a good Parsi girl who thinks with one mind, that Indians cannot mix with one another, caste to caste, religion to religion? What Gandhi-ji says, is this true? Do you think there can be good things that come from mixing?"

"Of course, good things come from mixing. Now ..."

"Yes, of course, you must go, but first, one more last question. What about you, do you mix with others, not of your faith?"

"Yes, how could I not? The Parsis are few and far between here at Irwin! My friends ..."

"Ah, yes, your friends. And could you get closer to non-Parsi friends someday perhaps?"

"Closer?"

"As in, well, if all Indians were free to marry all other Indians ..."

"Then it would be a confusing place, our country."

"You would not marry a non-Parsi?"

Piroja laughs at this leap, and knows her answer. "I can tell you that, but only after I attend to my charges," and with that she scampers away before Ali can say any more.

"Rattanbai married Jinnah," Ali calls out after her escaping form. Then, more to himself since Piroja has disappeared down the dark corridor, "and she was a beautiful Parsi girl, too."

Swaraj

Our dearest Piroja,

How often our thoughts are upon you in the busy world you now live in. Your mother and I sit quietly in the evening and take our tea and talk about what you might be doing this evening. We know that you work hard, but we both hope you have time for your prayers and your friends—so important, both of them.

When you were but a little girl, you were such a sweet thing, saying your prayers, and I used to smile and touch your head as you did this, do you remember? But even then I was worried that you did not have any Parsi playmates in Nowgong. So it fills our hearts with joy to read your news of such friends as Hutokshy. You must mind her well and treat her like an older sister, just as you did with Heera. You do not know how fortunate you are to have someone like her to give advice or just be a willing ear for you. How lonely you must be, although we both know you put on a brave face when writing to us. You have always done that, our brave little girl. But please do not worry about us, and you must know that you may tell us anything, any concern you have, for you are our only child and we will always love you with all our hearts.

Things are moving so fast in the world today, and it is hard to keep pace. If they seem out of control here in Nowgong, I cannot imagine how they must seem for you in the heart of Delhi. It seems like Congress is at the point where

Independence is imminent, and I think of all the excitement and danger in all of this, for Hindus, Muslims, and for us. As Parsis, I do wonder what our role will be. When Uncle Nouroz last visited in January he told me of the left-handed salutes offered by Indian naval men to British officers during last year's Bombay Mutiny. As a good Parsi I would think the correct thing to do is always follow the rule of law but to change those rules when they are wrong, so I do not know if I myself would salute with a left hand or not. And my daughter? As a good Parsi, I wonder if she salutes right, left, or is among those hoisting the ship's flags flying colours of Congress, the Muslim League, and the Communist Party, as they did in the harbour as part of the Mutiny.

Wherever you go, know that we trust you, dear Piroja, and trust your deeds will always follow your good thoughts, as you know they should.

With much love,
Your father

Piroja receives this letter on May 21, rips open the envelope excitedly, and reads, rereads, and re-rereads the letter from Jamshed. She clutches the paper until it begins to wrinkle so that she has to flatten it with the palm of her hand, taking care not to press too hard lest the ink start to fade with wear. Piroja cannot bear the thought of the words disappearing, as if they would take with them the connection to her parents. She puts the letter underneath her pillow and, the next morning, begins her response.

May 22, 1947

Dearest Father,

It is always so wonderful to receive your letters. I can truly feel yours and Mummy's love, and even though I write to you, I hope you read these letters to her as well! This card to you will be very short because I want to send it off in the post before I begin my shift, but I promise you I will write again soon.

I want most of all to reassure you that I am well and that I do indeed say my prayers and spend time listening to the advice of my friends. They are very good people, and I feel like I am surrounded by older sisters and brothers who are always taking care of me. Events in Delhi are electrifying these days! It seems everywhere we turn there is talk of Independence. It makes me wonder what similar thoughts are going on in different parts of the world. I hope to see these parts someday. Who knows what the future holds? I will write in more detail soon.

In the meantime, I love you both very much.
Piroja

The May Plan

Piroja has been at Irwin Hospital now for seven months, studying not just nursing under the tutelage of the Sisters and matrons of the nursing order, but the ways of the world under the guidance of Hutokshy.

"We need a plan," Hutokshy announces to Piroja. "A Parsi plan."

"A plan to do what?" inquires Piroja as she tries to pin her cap on, a task that has quite eluded her for these past seven months.

"Let us call it a plan of honour, of consummation, if not consumption," giggles Hutokshy, much to Piroja's confusion. "Yes, we shall call it the Akram Plan, and you shall be the sole agent, although not without a bit of assistance from your espionage friends."

"Oh, so this is about Ali?"

"Dr Akram to you, little girl. How old are you again?"

Piroja is now fourteen but because she is a nurse-in-training, all assume she started at the age of sixteen and is now a year older. And what with her confidence, no one doubts her maturity.

"You know how old I am."

"Indeed, and too old to be a maiden, I say. But first, you do like this Ali Akram, no?"

"Certainly, what is not to like?"

"No, but you like-like him, no? We will not proceed with Operation Akram without your express approval."

Piroja ponders this. Yes, she likes him, maybe even likes-likes him, and she is now beyond doubting that he likes her. But there is that nagging thought behind her eyes, deep within the core of her emotional being; how she could ever bring a Muslim boy home to her parents? Yet, as Hutokshy had made abundantly clear, bringing him home was never an option, at least, not to a parental home, just perhaps to a bedroom home. Piroja cannot believe, sometimes, the directions this is taking her. She looks up at the overhead lights, which Hutokshy mistakes as Piroja looking woefully at her untidy cap, and she rushes over to help pin it properly. Piroja's gaze then falls on to Hutokshy, who busily fixes the cap as Piroja ponders.

"So, what is the plan?"

Giddily, Hutokshy explains in great detail how the girls will plan a gathering, an informal one in the students' communal kitchen, and Piroja will use her Parsi cooking talents to make *Soonami ni Tareli Sondh*. Piroja objects that she has never made or even tasted this dish in her life. "Never what?" exclaims Hutokshy, "but of course, you are not a Gujarati girl, are you?" Hutokshy offers to do the pre-preparation, but the deep-fried baby lobsters will be such a delicacy that even a stoic intern will collapse in a heap at her feet to do her bidding, Hutokshy assures her. The flavours will explode in his mouth, she explains, and from then on no wrong can be done. The boys, including one Dr Ali Akram, will arrive for dinner, but in short order there will be an exodus of sorts, and left alone will be one Muslim boy and one Parsi girl, and the twain shall most definitely meet.

"That was delicious food," says Ali, nodding affably. "They tell me you made most of it from your mother's recipes."

"They jest," admits Piroja. "It is a Gujarati dish, and to be honest, the first time I tasted it was tonight. They were just trying to be—helpful."

"I see." And Ali continues to nod affably. "Did you hear the news today? Congress and the League? Rejected the plan put in by the viceroy; looks like it is back to the bargaining table."

Piroja reaches up to address an itch on her cheek, an action that immediately alarms young Dr Akram, who thinks her hand is reaching to *his* cheek so he stops all affable nodding and rears back in a bit of fearful anticipation, all of which just causes Piroja to laugh as she scratches her face.

"Yes," continues Ali, "they say there will be another plan next month. But it is all about separate states, one for Muslims, one for the Hindus. And, I suppose, for the rest."

"The rest of us, do you mean?"

"No. Well, yes. I suppose Parsis will stay in a Hindu state, not come along to a Muslim one. I suppose. Do you think so?"

"My father thinks so. He writes to me about the state of the country, and he worries that things will get worse, especially here at Delhi."

"Separation. Never a good thing. I wonder if there is not hope at the end of the tunnel?"

Perhaps, thinks Piroja, hope and light somewhere. Not to be found in the baby lobsters tonight though. She reaches up again, this time intent on addressing an itch that she anticipates might be wishing to be scratched on the face of this anxious boy in front of her. This time, Ali thinks she is just reaching to her own face, so he is surprised and approximates an expression of death touched by birth from behind when the soft fingers contact his stubbly cheek. He does the only thing that is possible for him in this case, which is to leap to his feet and announce that he is on-call tonight and must return to Irwin. He dashes out the door, almost leaving before realizing he has forgotten his coat, so he dashes back in and semi-salutes to meet Piroja's half-wave and then is out the door, cursing and laughing at himself and floating out a good foot above the ground, wishing he could stay, the taste of those succulent baby lobsters still tingling in his mouth, but knowing good respectfulness means he should make good his exit. It is only some hours later, when Hutok-shy tentatively enters the flat to see if she is disturbing anyone and sees only Piroja quietly sipping tea that it becomes clear that Plan A was not successful.

"We must work on this," says Hutokshy.

"On what?"

"A June Plan."

The June Plan

For the next few weeks, Ali Akram is more than a little circumspect. He takes to dropping things a lot when Piroja is around, which makes her glad that they are not further along in their training, perhaps in surgical rotation, for if she were an operating room nurse, and he maintained this penchant for letting things like scalpels slip through his fingers, it would not bode well for either of them. But the most precious items dropped so far have been a pencil and sheets of paper from his clipboard that found themselves wafting to the floor upon his spying Nurse Khargat in his peripheral vision. Once, maybe twice, Piroja stopped and stooped to help the young intern pick up his fallen papers, but after that she decided it would just embarrass him, so she would proceed as if nothing happened. She was not the only one who noticed the good doctor's newfound clumsiness, either. The entire band of nurses were quite aware that Ali would lose all ability to grasp upon seeing Piroja, and it become a source of some mirth before, as Hutokshy put it, this whole thing became rather pathetic.

"We must have a June Plan," she announces to the roomful of training nurses one Saturday evening as they sit around and rub each other's sore feet. "Hutokshy, could we talk about this later?" Piroja implores.

"No, we must do it now. It is imperative, before Dr Akram drops his brain right out of his skull."

So the plan is hatched that once again there will be a special dinner, but this time they will ensure it happens when silly Dr Akram does not have a shift to return to, and this time they will fully coach Piroja in the ways and wiles of the world when it comes to boys and girls: You must reach out to him thusly; you must touch him thisly; you cannot let him do action-A before task-B; there is a trick you can do with your thumb and forefinger; there is a knack you must learn with this particular part of your tongue; when he says X he really means Y but is too afraid to ask for Y so you have to be able to provide X, unless of course, he does not really know anything about Y and wants X, and here is how you can tell the difference.

So after an enjoyable meal in the communal kitchen, one by one or pair by pair they all slip away, leaving Piroja and Ali, Nurse Khargat and Doctor Akram, a woman and a man, with naught to do but entertain themselves with each other. And entertain they do, laughing and teasing at first, then a bit of playful touching and caressing, and then they are face-to-face, and since Ali will not lean in, Piroja does, and Parsi lips meet Muslim lips in a *fait accompli,* two peoples coming together, and there is no telling how far exploring tongues and roving hands would go were there not a shout from outside the window, and then another, such that putative lovers part and hold one another by the hand as they listen to still more shouts from the street below. They hear "Mountbatten got Congress on side!" and "The League is in league with the rest!" and "It's just a matter of time, now!" and "Who would have ever thought, no India for Indians, but Indias for many Indians." The noise from the street rises to the small communal kitchen in Irwin Hospital, and Piroja notices that her hand is clasped around Ali's, but his hand is cold and damp. And then he does what he has done best lately; he drops her hand as if it were a pen or a clipboard and rushes from the room.

"He left the room?" This from Hutokshy later that night. "He just left?"

"Yes, we heard the voices from the street, heard that Mountbatten's plan was going ahead, and then he left."

"My God, whatever do we have to do with that boy? I mean, you can lead a horse to water … I give up, Nurse Khargat, totally give up."

So do I, thinks Piroja. So do I.

Partition of the ways

The next few weeks are filled with a bulbous tension at the hospital. More and more trauma cases flow in, a Hindu man's head bashed in by an angry Muslim, a Sikh grandmother pushed to the road by an irate Hindu, a Muslim boy involved in a schoolyard fight with no idea of who instigated what, but the cut over his eye as evident as anything that there is violence ahead. Partition. The word is more significant than "Independence" in anybody's lexicon. The latter a word of freedom, of freedom from and freedom to all wrapped in one; the former, a sense of utter and ultimate loss, the whole that becomes less than the sum of its parts, divided, asunder. The results of this word drift into Irwin Hospital, shocking even the most hard-edged of matrons, the most senior of surgeons—the amount of blood that can come from a single wound, from an individual body, the amount of rage that seems to generate from each of those wounds, creating more and more and more. Stories circulate of great waves of migration, to and from, Muslim and Hindu, but also all sorts in between, stories of people passing on bridges, normal traffic, then breaking into warring words, pieces of bridge being torn up and used as weaponry. It is left to the soldiers of Irwin to remove wood splinters and metal spikes from the bodies that crowd its doors.

This is the situation on August 14 when Piroja and Ali are both working the night shift. They have been working shoulder to shoulder triaging patients as young as eight and as old as ninety, every single one of them with damage to their bodies caused by someone. All of them have that same glazed look in their eyes; who could have done this, what have we become? The twins are the worst, ten years old, a boy and a girl. There was an explosion of gunpowder near the market and these two were the closest to the basket that went off like thunder, spreading wood and debris and flesh and blood all across the stalls. They are brought in on a single stretcher, making not a sound. Where the boy's left foot should be is a stump that pumps blood, the attendant valiantly trying to staunch this flow with his left hand while with his right hand and left thigh he attempts to move the stretcher forward. His companion has his own hands full, trying to keep the bones in the girl's left forearm from bursting out on to her brother, and both attendants are crying, and both the twins are staring straight ahead, facing each other, into each other's dry eyes, and they make not a sound.

Piroja beholds this scene and does not herself break down but goes to work. She notices that Ali is beside her, and he too is working, and they spend some time getting the twins comfortable before there is a call from outside; a car of police officers has been attacked by a mob, and there is suddenly much more work to do. Pieces of uniform and metal insinuate themselves into skin, and Piroja is meticulous in separating one bit from another, causing pain and flinches in what must be done, always using a caring touch, but there is always another body on another stretcher, waiting for her care. After treating the third police officer, she looks up from this detailed work and sees Ali on the other side of the emergency room administering to the more seriously wounded, his hands a frenzy of activity without the slightest hint of clumsiness. Piroja feels the slightest pressure on her chest and believes, amidst the stench of burnt clothing and antiseptic, she smells rosewater.

But then there are more patients to attend to, a bus has overturned, and the room fills up with the elderly and the young, bruised and broken, and this goes on well into the night, and it is five in the morning before Piroja and Ali, exhausted, find themselves sitting together on a second-floor stretcher above the din that is the trauma ward. Piroja looks over at Dr Akram, who has not dropped a single thing all night, but neither has he looked into Piroja's dark eyes, which usually have the effect of making him lose, quite literally, his grip. Their shift is over, and they should have returned to their dormitories long ago, the relieving team of nurses and doctors having been on the floor for two hours. But they do not move, at least, not to go home. Finally, Piroja reaches over and picks up Ali's hand. He still does not look at her but allows her to lead him down the hallway to the room where the clean linens are kept, lining the walls, ready to be pressed into service. Piroja leads Ali into the room and turns on the light—only white linens as far as their eyes can see, piled high all the way to the ceiling. Piroja pulls Ali fully into the room and twists toward him so they are face-to-face.

Outside, they can hear a renewed bout of gunfire—one group or another is upset that one group or another is being allowed entrance to the hospital to treat their wounded, and so is shooting at the hospital to make sure this does not happen.

Inside, Piroja reaches up with her free hand and touches Ali's lips. They are soft and moist.

Outside, someone starts a chant of "Quit India," but it is drowned out by another round of gunfire.

Inside, Ali raises his courage and, with his own free hand, traces the outline of Piroja's lips, her chin, her neck.

Outside, a siren blares and grows louder, then the sound of locked brakes and rubber on asphalt.

Inside, hands are suddenly freer and exploring parts of bodies that were off limits in May and June, but this is Independence, and fingers touch breasts and palms touch thighs, and knees touch groins.

Outside, a woman screams, the type of scream that is born of grief, not pain.

Inside, white uniforms are doffed to reveal brown skin, and difficult-to-pin caps are tossed aside, and hair flows freely.

Outside, a dog barks and then another and then a whole pack, and the barking turns to yelping and then howling.

Inside, hands grope down lower, feeling parts of mystery, and now lips and teeth and tongues are everywhere, consuming everything in their path, and the single bare lightbulb that casts a yellow glow on to the whiteness of sheets chooses this moment to burn out, leaving two bodies in total darkness, but by this time there is such an awareness of senses that being sightless is in no way a hindrance.

Outside, the howling ceases as quickly as it started, and for some unknown reason, someone begins banging, slowly, on a drum, and singing voices drift in.

Inside, she reaches down between her own legs and feels herself, confident, and then reaches forward to him, feeling his firmness, grasping it, pulling it toward her, bringing it up to her.

Outside, the voices and drums co-mingle and then start to fade until only one old man's voice can be heard, cracking, then crying, blurring the words.

Inside, he is inside her, so softly at first that she does not believe this is happening, and then hips shift and bodies slide, and she feels the entirety of him, the push that leaves hips pressed to hips, and she so full of him, gasping, the both of them, in the dark, and then she is crying, or rather, she feels tears on her face but realizes that they are coming from above, falling on to her cheeks from his tear ducts, and she pushes in closer to him, again and again, until finally her own tears start to emerge, and between them there is nothing but darkness and skin.

Outside, a distant din becomes even more distant, and then, as if nothing at all were wrong with the world, there is a moment of silence that leads to another and then a full minute, not a sound in the outside world.

Inside, there is culmination, caught in a frieze, and she can feel his release and holds on so closely, for the end will surely be a tearing apart that she cannot bear, not here, not now, and when he finally does pull back, there is still nothing but darkness and skin and now rushed words, I must go, I must leave, I must go.

Outside is stillness and silence.

Inside is silence and stillness.

Outside becomes inside, and the world, if only for a startling moment, disappears.

Post-Partition repression

Piroja is trying to sleep on her back, unusual for the girl who has slept in a fetal position all her life, but it is a necessary experiment, as this is now a new world, and new things must take hold.

It is six months since Independence and, try as she might, Piroja does not feel any more free. In the bustle that is Delhi, there is great change taking place, as if one entire family was moving out of the neighbourhood, except this family has thousands of members, and trunks and train carriages and lorries are all full of their belongings, in transition. Still the injured pour into Irwin, and it is with some alarm that Piroja realizes she is no longer fazed by the sight of blunt-force trauma and what it can do to a body, no longer stunned by the marked contrast of blood and linens; in fact, she has come to expect that those walking into Irwin, or being dragged or carried, are more likely victims of someone else's furor than they are diseased or in-firm. She does not like this change in her, and while it is not as if she no longer cares, it is that she has come to expect this terrible delivery of impaired bodies to her doorstep. On her last Christmas visit back to Nowgong, she stared at her parents intently, noticing every blemish and imperfection about them (and while they aged, they aged well, she thought) and was in constant amazement that their bodies were intact. She then realized how much she had come to expect encountering incomplete or damaged human forms as part of her daily routine, so much so that she was not entirely sure how to react to bodies not under physical duress.

"Piroja, dear, you seem so mature now, and yet I know you are still my little girl of fifteen," Parvin said to her one day.

"It is the city, Mummy, and the work. To be helping patients is helping me grow up."

"No, that is not it," Parvin continued thoughtfully. "There is something else."

Piroja had said nothing. She knew that her parents would conspire toward marriage. So when Jamshed once again broached the subject—a distant second cousin wanted to visit—Piroja once again brushed it off, pointing out her chronological youth as a defence.

Now, back at Irwin, Piroja tries unsuccessfully to sleep on her back. This day has been like all the others over the past few months, although in order to cope with the massive changes around her, she has spent considerably more time with the other student nurses, taking time to see the cinema or walk around the old streets, arm in arm. She spends much more time, too, with Hutokshy, and as she looks around the streets, sees the comfort people have in spending time with their own: Parsi gentlemen in the company of their brethren; young Sikh girls all playing together; elderly Muslim women chatting quietly with their kin; and she and Hutokshy, the Parsi twins, as the other student nurses call them, inseparable.

"So whatever happened, yaar, with that silly Akram?"

Piroja shrugs. "After—after that night, he stopped dropping things, all except his gaze, which always dropped off when I came into sight," she giggles.

"So he became the ultimate *baadmash*, had his cake, and now wants to move on to a different dessert?"

"No, Hutokshy, it really is not like that. After all, it was—my idea. Ali still comes to my station to fill out reports, but now he is muddled. He asked me, soon after, what I thought of mixed marriages, and I looked around and saw all the trouble not mixing was causing, and I just could not answer. And then he said, his voice dropping, that he had talked to his father and his mother about this very idea, and they had told him off severely."

"Of course they did! Wouldn't your parents do the same?"

Piroja nods. "Yes, that is what I told him, that my parents would be overcome with grief if I told them—that is, if—well, the idea of mixed marriage. And he said, yes, his parents were very clear with him, that it had to be a good Muslim girl."

"And that was it?"

"And that was it. He looked up at me with those big, dark eyes of his, and I think he tried to say he was sorry, but no words came out. And then he dropped his gaze again, and that was probably the last time he has looked in my eyes."

"We should really hire some *goondas* to have a talk with him."

Piroja laughs. "No, really, Hutokshy, I think this is for the best. Look at the mess we are in. Why complicate things further?"

The days and weeks slipped by, trips home and new friendships, and the occasional but uninspired attempt at courtships arranged by parents (both hers and Hutokshy's), and then it was two full years since Piroja had arrived at Irwin. Hutokshy was preparing to graduate and at first was forlorn that she might have to move on, so was thrilled when informed that her nursing skills were required in obstetrics, her favourite rotation, right here at Irwin. Piroja's studies continued, and a second training year filtered into a third and the midpoint of the century came and went and finally it was 1951 and Piroja was in her senior year. She had already distinguished herself as the One to Watch for her superiors as much as the One to Be With for her colleagues, and most definitely the One to See If You Can Get a Bit Closer to for the incoming interns as she reached her eighteenth year, already having accomplished so much for One So Young. The Parsi boys come and go, there being a few interns, but more often medical-equipment suppliers and hospital administrators. On more than one occasion, Piroja feels that deep-down urge to touch her fingers to one or another set of lips, but represses that, much to the chagrin and annoyance of the owners of said lips who would give a choice appendage to be One Whose Lips Are Touched by Nurse Khargat. Yet none of this is to be. Until.

Every year, a new batch of interns arrives, already looking haggard and overworked, and in Piroja's senior year, the fourth batch she has had to work with comes in. Every new group gets a series of glimpses and glances and furtive comments in the hallway and various rating systems are shared surreptitiously between those on the nursing side and the doctoring side, but never between members of these exclusive groups. The interns tend to be brasher in these early days of nation-statehood, and that is reflected by a particular type of boyish arrogance. While a couple of training nurses have had their heads turned by this confident certitude, most of them find it all charming but bemusing. Piroja has had her fun playing the same games with the interns, but when her thoughts return to Nowgong and her parents, it is difficult for her to seriously consider the consequences of bringing home anything but the nicest of Parsi boys.

When Piroja was recognized by the hospital as a nurse no-longer-in-training-but-now-practising, Jamshed and Parvin came to visit her in Delhi. Her new position made little difference to her workload and work habits, although it seemed to solidify, at least in her father's eyes, the fact that she was irretrievably lost to the nursing profession. But it was not lost on her parents how much she attracted attention from all parties in the city. "There *are* plenty of Parsi boys here," said Jamshed to his wife, more to console himself than Parvin, and yet when they thought deeply of their daughter, neither could envision her bringing a potential husband home anytime soon. If they entertained any other possibilities, however, they shared them not with each other, certainly not with Piroja, and probably not even with themselves.

So when Piroja met a Hindu intern named Pradeep Lal, she thought nothing of it at first, because, after all, what could come of it? She did admit that her head—and maybe a significant portion of her heart—had been turned, yet, she reasoned with herself, many had gone through star-crossings before and had led full and productive lives by refusing to follow such unfortunate paths. Nevertheless, initial small talk with Dr Lal grew into larger conversations, gatherings in the common kitchen led to group outings, and furtive, mischievous glances turned into much-desired Time Alone With Each Other, and before they could say "Secular State," a young Parsi girl and a young Hindu boy were making plans that would blight—or beautify, depending on your perspective—both ancestral homes. Piroja had been so turned on the inside that she began to fancy that external and familial turns might not be improbable; she manufactured philosophical conversations with her absent parents, all about measurable mixes and cauldrons bubbling over (but oh-so-happily) with Jains and Sikhs and Christians and Muslims and, yes, Hindus and Parsis. She concocted debates with Jamshed about the need to travel and take thoughts and words into international actions. In her monologic dialogues, she was always able to convince her at-first-doubtful parents of the new ways of the world, and her fantasy conversations always ended with tearful agreements and rejuvenated spirits. None of this, of course, was ever rendered by pen or enacted in person, but, at first, that seemed to matter little to Piroja as she entertained possible scenarios. It was just Pradeep and Piroja, Piroja and Pradeep, not opposing sides of the same coin, but two faces, face to face, facing uncertain futures made supremely possible by figuring out a way to land on edge.

Piroja is not privy to conversations had in and about Nowgong, for if she were, she might think long and hard, remember the complications of Ali, and make choices for different futures. But she is not there, and does not hear when Aunt Freny invites herself over for tea with Parvin and, catching up on the news and gossip of so many young Parsi girls marrying non-Parsi boys on the claim that the latter just do not have what it takes, asks Parvin what she thinks of all this mixed marriage.

"Oh," says Parvin, "I suppose it is okay. Gandhi-ji did not seem to bother much about it, and Jinnah, well, look at him, taking that nice Parsi girl! But I only have one daughter, and my Piroja would never break my heart that way, marrying out, no, no. Not at all."

No, Piroja is not there, and as the weeks turn into months, dice are cast and coins are flipped and choices made, Piroja and Pradeep talk of religion and politics, of nation building and post-partition, of new surgical procedures and hospital rotations, of this and that and this again. Always they walk and talk and, most importantly, laugh at things one or the other will say, how one moves his facial muscles while talking, how another swallows while trying to make her point, and how the world works in all its strange ways. They are, the romantics would say, hearts together. But threaded hearts and bonded minds do not mean things are easily expressed, and Pradeep is so caught in a quandary, a dilemma of not-asking, that he is unable to bring himself to actually make the commitment to ask the so-impertinent but inevitable question. Instead, walking with Piroja in Connaught Place one day in 1952, he asks her, "So, when shall we send the invitations?"

"Invitations?" There was no party planned that she knew about.

"The wedding. We are going to marry, after all, are we not?"

"Wedding?" And later, Piroja is not sure what she says after that, although she does recall having a long and meaningful conversation with her parents, exploring the intricacies if not intimacies of unarranged marriages and revitalized nations, and, once again, a mother and father reduced to tears of understanding and joy. But this, once again, does not take place in the blood and bones of daily living, but in a young girl's floating heart where anything can happen, and disputes turn to candy floss, resistances to magician-disappeared coins, and anger to the stuff that dreams are made on.

Piroja is not entirely surprised, then, when she and Pradeep sit side by side six months later in a civil ceremony that will bring them together as husband and wife. She is blissful, and that accounts for the simple, practical act of marrying one another in an unceremonious ceremony without fearing parental repercussions. Hutokshy is there, of course, and a friend of Pradeep's from work, a roguish fellow by the name of J.J. Singh, not a close enough friend to be wagging his tongue to Hindu families. There are wedding witnesses but no family, distant or otherwise. This is a marriage behind closed doors. They will stay closed for a long time.

Once Pradeep gets his accreditation, he begins looking in earnest for a respectable post at an Indian hospital. He is not tied to living in Delhi, but this is where he starts, and a few moderately interesting opportunities do arise. Piroja, for her part, becomes more and more fascinated with the world outside, so when Pradeep comes to her saying he may apply for an internist post in the south part of the city, or a similar job just on the outskirts, Piroja is less than enthusiastic. She dreams of riding camels to the pyramids, walking for miles along the Great Wall, paddling down the Thames, all these things she has read about or heard about from travellers and patients she has met in the years at Irwin. She does not mention this to Pradeep, however, as she has seen his stubborn streak, understands that, at times, ideas must be his in order to be good. In fact, she is more or less resigned to settling in or around Delhi when an Englishwoman, visiting the city from a hill station where her husband works for the census bureau, comes to the hospital to have a skin condition looked at. Piroja is assigned to administer a cream, and the two of them engage in conversations, first about marriage and work, then about politics and travel.

"You would love England," says the woman, who insists Piroja call her by her first name, Daphne.

"I imagine I would," says Piroja, smiling, "but I doubt my husband would be interested in such an adventure."

"And do you think it was my husband's idea to settle down in British India the very year the Raj was crumbling? Good gracious, no, my girl. But I told him he could make a man of himself here, poor dear, because I had always wanted to see the treasures of Agra and the lushness of this place!"

"So it was your idea?"

"Of course not. It was all his idea, and that is the story I shall stay with."

"But it would be hard to go there without a job," says Piroja, laughing at the wiles of this woman. "What would we do there?"

"Go to Buckingham Palace and see the crown jewels."

Piroja laughs. "Ah, but I do not think the Queen of England will extend us an invitation."

"Well," says Daphne, standing up, "then I will." She nods to Piroja, thanks her for her nursing attention, and, as she leaves, requests Pradeep's full name. Piroja thinks little of this until some days later when a hand-delivered letter arrives for Pradeep, sent from the census bureau in a nearby hill station from a bureaucrat stating he has heard that Pradeep might be looking for opportunities abroad and urging him to write to the following select list of administrators at various teaching hospitals in northern England.

"I do not know how this gentleman found my name," says Pradeep as he shows Piroja the letter, "but he is so willing to help and it is nice to be encouraged like this."

Piroja takes the letter and it is a long moment before she makes the connection between this quasi-invitation and her conversation with Daphne. "This is very kind," is all she says.

"Kind and kismet, isn't that what our Muslim brothers say? Perhaps this is destiny."

"Destiny?"

"Yes, I know it would be hard for you to leave India, but think of the opportunity ... Oh, Piroja, let us just think about it. Would you consider moving to England?"

"Well. As matter of fact—well, yes; it would be difficult, but if it is what you want, I know we can do it."

After some research, making contacts, and looking into possibilities, Pradeep decides to go abroad to do his exams. Only a few weeks after their marriage, Pradeep is off on a steamer. Piroja is able to obtain references and recommendations from her supervisors at Irwin and, within a couple of months, has a written offer before her to work in a small hospital in England, in the city of York, the same place where Pradeep will be. It is all a whirlwind, as Piroja goes back to Nowgong alone, looking at her father and mother, dying to tell them that she goes to meet her husband but, instead, talking of the new opportunities that await her abroad.

"This is right for you?" asks Parvin.

"Mummy, yes. It is the best choice."

"There will be an ocean between us," says Jamshed.

"A great distance, yes. But I can never be closer to you in my heart."

"Then it is done with a certainty like my father's," says Jamshed, hoping to show admiration and not sorrow.

"I hope so," says Piroja. "I hope all this comes from good thoughts."

"And so on," says Jamshed, his eyes now laughing.

Piroja travels to Bombay with her parents, who kiss and hug her goodbye on the upper deck of the ship before they have to disembark. Parvin coughs once, twice, just before she leaves, and Piroja has a moment to worry, but then, the future dancing in front of her, lets it slip her mind. She will tell them of her marriage once she reaches England, she thinks, although Hutokshy's last words of advice were to wait until the first child was on the way, for how can parents be angry at a mixed marriage when a grandchild is about to appear? All this plays in Piroja's mind as she makes the ocean passage, barely aware of the people around her, only the long days on deck (when it is not too cold) and the rise and fall of dreams at night that coincide with the ship's soothing rhythm. Each night she falls asleep thinking of her new life abroad, and each night she dreams of her parents and the laughter and love she has left behind in Nowgong, a night-time directional switch that reminds her of the crew's indecipherable language of port and starboard, looking one way and gazing the other.

When her feet touch soil and she becomes used to walking without a rolling of waves beneath her, she finds herself moving from ship to train, dizzying transitions, and then, finally, she is on a fog-filled platform, alone with her baggage, breathing in unfamiliar air that smells of nothing. In the distance, a figure appears, moving slowly, its identity and details hidden by mist. It moves closer. Closer still. Behind her she can feel the chill of the east wind on her back. Before her, Pradeep reaches out and takes her hand, and they wander slowly down to the street where Pradeep has kept a taxi waiting. The taxi whisks them to their new home, a small flat above what used to be a Viking cemetery. And this does, indeed, become their new home.

It is said no place can be home without a new birth, and so York does not yet feel like a home of any kind to Piroja. She wonders when or if they will have a family to really make it home. But the flip side, the reverse to the obverse of new lives and new births, is old lives concluding, death taking back, bodies wrapped and unwrapped and laid bare at silent towers. A telegram arrives for Piroja; it could be an announcement of a marriage or a birth, or it could be a message short and none-too-sweet that contains the words *Regret to inform you* and *passed suddenly but peacefully* and *This is to announce the death of Parvin Khargat stop.*

Parvin's ghost

Piroja is trying to sleep on her stomach. She has been unable to go to sleep on her back, on her side, or in a fetal position, so now she is trying the last possible and most uncomfortable position that might bring her to pleasant dreams. She is almost asleep, at that place where conscious thoughts begin to transmogrify into vague, open-ended images that precede dreams, when she is startled by the throaty sound of snoring. Pradeep is still at work, will be for the next four hours as he works through a hellish night shift, yet there is an unmistakeable snoring from his side of the bed. You would think Piroja would be frightened—and perhaps she would be afraid if she heard the sound of breaking glass from downstairs (*Get the cricket bat, there's a burglar!*) or the sudden, frantic barking of the neighbourhood dogs, but she has seen so much in her young years that the almost-funny sound of nighttime breathing difficulties is not about to strike the fear of any god into her heart. She clears her own throat, as much to ensure she is not hearing her own snoring as it is to presage a question, which is: "Pradeep? Is that you?"

The snoring stops abruptly and Piroja hears a sardonic "hmph." She lifts herself off her stomach, frees her right arm, and stretches out to the other side of the bed. Indeed, there is a body there, something that should terrify Piroja but, for some odd reason, does not. She feels the fleshy shoulder, the familiar wide hips, then moves her hand up to a head of thick, straw-like hair.

"All this feely-feely stuff is odd behaviour in the middle of the night, even for my dim daughter," says the voice of Parvin in her familiar, thickly accented Gujarati.

Now Piroja is more than a bit startled and she withdraws her hand quickly, lifts herself to her haunches and stares over at the figure lying next to her.

"Mummy?"

"Oh, no, not your dear departed Mummy, simple girl, how could it be me, after all, the way you did me in, my poor frail heart broken into tiny-tiny bits by a daughter who showed me no love. No, no, it could not be me, could it? Go to sleep, simple girl."

"But you died two years ago."

"Yes, so it was. Must be a bad dream. Go to sleep."

"Mummy!" Piroja now pulls the sheets back, much to the shrieking dismay of the figure lying beneath.

"Good god, you will give me my death of chill," says Parvin, now speaking in an odd-sounding English.

"You're speaking in English? You never spoke to me in English. You never *spoke* English."

"And you would chatter away like a chatterbox, so fast-fast I could never understand a word you said. Such an ungrateful child. We learn things here, you know. ESL—English as a Second Life."

Piroja is silent for a moment. Then, tentatively, she reaches out to touch her dead mother with her index finger.

"So, now I am a pincushion for your fancy? Not enough that you poked holes in my heart when I was alive?"

Piroja, having poked Parvin harder than would be necessary to ascertain her corporeality, is not sure what to say next.

"Mummy. This does not sound like you. You were always so—understanding."

"Understanding! You wanted to be a doctor. And so I said to Jamshed, poor child, let her be a doctor. If you do not let her, I will kill myself, that is what I said."

"You said that? You never told me—you never told me you stood up for me like that."

"Well, I did in my heart, the same heart that now crumbles like so much old and dried *mithai*. I did not actually say that out loud to Jamshed. And I did not actually think that at the time, but it was all there below the surface."

"Oh. Mummy? Can I get you some tea?"

"Tea? Tea! You think tea will bring my heart back to beating? You think that this tea-shmea will make up for all that you've done? You think I will squeeze my daughter's cheeks, tell her she's *cho chweet*, just like that? Tea she offers me. Tea, like I was some hungry pauper begging at her compound gates."

"But, Mummy … What are you doing here? And why are you acting this way—this is not like how you were when you were … alive."

Parvin sits upright in bed, and Piroja sees her face for the first time. Other than a quality of translucence, this is indeed her mother. Parvin glares at Piroja.

"Yes, yes, I am different. Those fancy psychologists, like the one who saw your poor father as a boy, they would say that major changes can bring on 'personality shifts.' Well, I have been through a big change, this death thing and all, one of the big ones. They say becoming a woman is a big change and getting married and having a child, oh yes, they tell you all that, but let me tell you, it is nothing compared to this not-breathing and being-very-still-forever thing. Now that is a big change. They should talk more of this one."

"Mummy, this is all so—I do not understand. What are you doing here?"

"I think we must talk about this so-called husband of yours who is never here, out at all hours doing God-knows-what carousing."

"He's at the hospital."

"Oh, you're so sure?"

"Yes. I work there too. He's a new doctor, and they work them around the clock. But, if you're such a ghostly thing, why don't you just fly over and see for yourself?"

Parvin snorts and stares at her daughter some more.

"You should eat more. You never did eat enough. And, no, the last thing I'm going to do is fly off to such-and-such hospital like a dirty errand boy. I am a ghost, remember? Maybe I can see things that you cannot. Did you not think of this?"

Piroja had not thought of this, and this recognition shows on her face.

"Oh, stop the sad face," groans Parvin, "the louse you call a husband is not out flirting about. To tell you truth, I don't think he would know how. We must really do something about him."

"What do you mean? I don't understand."

"Oh, I think he would like it on this side," says Parvin smiling. "It's really very nice once you get used to seeing through people."

Parvin lets this sink in until the realization of what she is suggesting registers across Piroja's face.

"You want to murder him?"

"Oh, heavens-to-Betsy no, we can't do that sort of thing. We are under very hush-hush orders about meddling, you know. No, I was offering to help you out with this messy matter."

"You want *me* to murder Pradeep?"

"Murder. Murder is such an impolite word. We should just call it 'travel assistance' and leave it at that."

"No. I won't let you talk to me about murdering my husband! Why are you here?"

"Now, now, dear girl, you were always one to overreact. Let's discuss how we might best do this thing. I myself like the falling off from high mountain places, very exciting, but if you prefer a rope around the neck or a head in the oven, that would be also good."

Piroja now leaps out of bed. "I want you to leave—leave right now and never come back. I love you, Mummy, but I won't have you say such things."

"See," says Parvin, slowly fading from Piroja's sight, the blankets floating down around her to fill the vacant space, "see what I mean about overreacting? Okay, I will go for now, but dear, simple girl, we will talk again soon, you and your dear mother whose heart you split in two before spitting on her bones. Yes, we shall speak again soon."

The last words spoken by Parvin come from a misty place on the bed. Piroja blinks twice and sees only rumpled sheets where her mother's voice came from. She gets up and begins the process of making herself a cup of tea.

Murder, she wrote

The first slender fingers of a late autumn Yorkshire dawn are just beginning to creep across the southeast sky when Pradeep drags himself home through the morning mist. On days like this, cold but not unbearably so, he walks leisurely rather than briskly back to their flat just off Bootham Street. It is a short distance, no more than fifteen minutes, even if he dawdles and daydreams along the way, but it gives Pradeep a chance to clear the previous twelve hours from his head and to prepare himself for his domestic life, his chance to engage his wife in conversation if she happens to be home and not asleep. These conversational exchanges are rare enough these days since Pradeep pulls the atrocious shifts handed out to new residents, and Piroja, as day matron, works long hours to bring home the money required to maintain their small, ill-equipped flat. On this particular morning, Pradeep is well aware that Piroja has the day off, which means they will breakfast together and maybe go for a walk, at least until Pradeep can no longer keep his eyes open, at which point he will make himself dead to the world and Piroja will venture out to do the week's shopping.

Piroja is making tea when he arrives. They look at each other and each tries to determine if the other is dragged-out tired or if the other's appearance is just the result of being half-asleep. Pradeep assumes the latter, believing that he is finding Piroja barely awake from a full night's sleep; Piroja knows differently, aware that her husband is already half-dozing but that she, too, can hardly keep her eyes open owing to the previous night's visitation from her deceased mother.

"Did you sleep well?" asks Pradeep, unable to think of anything else to begin their conversation.

"Yes, very," Piroja lies, having already decided that even if her mother's midnight visit was not a result of her own overworked mind, then Pradeep would certainly believe so, might even try to arrange a psychiatric consult for her, and Piroja has no time for such nonsense.

"You look well-rested," Pradeep says, now it being his turn to lie. "There might even be some sun this morning. Perhaps we should walk through St Mary's?"

"A good idea," says Piroja. "But first, let me make you some breakfast."

Pradeep slumps himself down in the corner chair of their tiny kitchen. They have a triangular table, cut so as to fit the alcove, but seemingly designed to make dinner parties impossible. Nonetheless, Pradeep and Piroja proudly acquired a tiny sewing stool when they first moved in, easily hidden away but available should they ever have a single guest over for supper. The table would be pulled away from the wall, the sewing stool produced from its hidden corner, and placed along the outer edge of the table, so that all three sides of the rough table were equipped with seating arrangements. Dinner guests, however, were fairly uncommon, owing to their erratic schedules, but Pradeep and Piroja liked to keep up appearances, just in case they were ever in the position to invite a colleague by for a meal.

Cutting toast into finger soldiers and boiling two eggs on the single gas burner, Piroja begins to talk to Pradeep, partly out of a desire to engage her life partner in meaningful conversation, and partly to ensure he does not fall asleep in the corner, as he has been known to do in the past after a midnight shift.

"Perhaps on Sunday we can go to Leeds," she says, not turning from the stove. "It would be better to go soon, before it gets too cold. Then we will never want to go out."

"Hm," says Pradeep, aware that unless he responds he will likely fall asleep. "A good idea. We could go to the cinema?"

"The cinema would be good," says Piroja, now lifting the eggs out of the pot with a teaspoon, placing them on two small plates next to the toast.

"I'll help you," says Pradeep, making the initial gestures of rising.

"No, no," says Piroja, "I'll bring this into the dining room." This is a little joke between them, since their tiny kitchen, composed of a thirty-inch-high icebox and a single gas burner on top of an oven that can barely fit a Cornish hen, is not even a step from the triangular table. The kitchen can, however, be separated from the so-called dining room by a set of poorly fitting cupboard doors, which, when closed, conceal the kitchen. The illusion allows Piroja and Pradeep to joke about the separateness of the kitchen and dining room (or hall, as they sometimes refer to it) and it permits them to imagine future homes in which one might have to take many steps between the cooking and eating areas. But, as it is, Piroja has only to turn on her heel (indeed, if she were to take a step backward before turning, she would run into the sharpest corner of their dining table, something she's done more than once and which she is determined not to repeat) and lean forward to place the breakfast plates on the table. She smiles over at the droopy-lidded Pradeep and turns to collect a fork and spoon for each of them, an action again not requiring anything more than an angling of her body.

As she turns back with the cutlery, she catches sight of the urn that sits on a shelf directly above where Pradeep is sitting. Both of them refer to the object as "her urn," referring to Piroja's mother, not because it contains Parvin's ashes or remains, that being inconceivable given ingrained Parsi beliefs, but because it is one of the few, and certainly the largest, of the objects once belonging to Parvin that now sits in their own home. It is beautiful in a rough sort of way, with mother-of-pearl set into the clay face of the oblong object, and it was made by a village artisan in Nowgong. Family history has it that when Parvin acquired the urn, Jamshed was so delighted— for it was the first household object she had bought since moving to this small town—that he christened it by pouring a few golden drops of his distillery's own famed Asha rum into the neck of the vase. Piroja could swear that when she brought the urn down to dust it, a smell of sweetness rose from the urn's neck, a smell that could only be the lasting pungency of that rum.

And now it serves as a reminder, the only reminder, of her dead mother—at least, until the most recent and surprising visitation. Piroja hadn't the money to return all the way to Nowgong for Parvin's funeral rites. She had fully intended to borrow what she needed, but Jamshed would have none of it. "If you were here," he had written to her, "then it would be a good and warm thing for us to be together. But, dear Piroja, with you an ocean away, you must commemorate your mother in your own way. Spare the expense of returning and trust that we will do the best for her here." Piroja had been heartbroken but listened to her father's words; she stayed in England and had even found a dastur in Yorkshire who was able to comfort her, to help her commemorate her mother's memory, as her father had requested.

But what catches her attention at this particular moment is not the urn itself, but its unusual positioning, how it sits much farther forward than usual on the tiny corner shelf. This is somewhat significant since, when they first moved into the tiny flat and Piroja walked into the room carrying her mother's treasured urn, she immediately spied that particular shelf and said to Pradeep, "I've found the perfect place for this." And indeed she had, for the urn looked like it was made for that shelf, the perfect size, pushed to the back so that barely a millimetre of shelf was visible in the front and on either side. All of this is playing through Piroja's mind—the moment she positioned the urn, the fact that there was no room to negotiate a different placement on the shelf, and the unfortunate detail that the urn was now closer to the shelf's edge than ever before, which could only mean—

"Pradeep!" Piroja shouts, and, if she were more given to flightiness she would probably drop the cutlery, but instead, in one motion, she slides the forks and knives on to the table and lunges forward to prevent the inevitable from transpiring. Pradeep's eyelids have been flipping closed, and in the brief moment that Piroja turned to collect the silverware, he had felt that familiar and not unpleasant sensation of comforting sleep start to take over his body. The sharp utterance of his name drives him startlingly awake, and he does what many a sleeper is bound to do when shocked, which is to express alarm by jolting upright (if the sleeper is horizontal) or hopping up (if the sleeper happens to be sitting), which is, of course, Pradeep's specific position and action.

The first time Piroja, as a training nurse, had to deal with multiple facial lacerations was when a patient appeared at Irwin Hospital. He was a wealthy man, a magistrate and a Brahmin who was well-liked by the British and Indians alike for his fair-handedness in the meting out of justice. Because of his somewhat exalted status, the year prior to showing up at the trauma unit at Irwin, he was given a car and driver, one of the first Indian judges to win such favour. It was because of this very car that the magistrate was injured when his driver (unforgivingly) depressed the accelerator instead of the brake and ploughed into a bullock cart, utterly devastating the rig but miraculously leaving the bullock uninjured and the owner irate but essentially unhurt as well. It was in the course of cleaning out the magistrate's wounds (superficial, but bloody) that Piroja learned that while time stood still for no one, it could, according to the magistrate, slow down considerably in times of duress. This was exactly what had happened to him, he told the young nurse, at the precise moment that the car began to accelerate toward the stationary bullock cart. "It was as if I had all the time in the world," he told her, grimacing as she applied yet more alcohol to a cut above his left eye, "that is, everything was happening as one might predict, but so slowly, dear girl, so slowly I felt I could have reviewed all the details for my afternoon docket, thought about what I would ask for dinner that evening, and perhaps planned my next trip to the hill station, yes, there was that much time, even though it all happened in only seconds. I am sure time can slow to a crawl," he told her, "when it needs to."

Piroja has the chance to remember this incident, complete with conversation, and begins to lunge toward Pradeep, taking care that the cutlery does not fall to the floor, all because time has indeed slowed to a crawl for her now as well. She does not bother to think of the details of her day, their upcoming potential trip to Leeds, or what they will have for dinner that evening, not because there isn't enough time, but because there are other things to consider at this moment. For, unlike the magistrate, who was demonstrably powerless as his chauffeur drove headlong into a bullock cart, Piroja knows she has the will and power to act in defence of her husband, whose head appears to be on a similar collision course with a downward-falling urn. In fact, owing to her unnaturally quick reflexes and the undeniable truth that time was now moving at barely a tenth its normal speed, Piroja is confident that she will, with outstretched right-hand fingertips, be able to divert the deadly path of the urn. Years later, in a quiet room an ocean and a continent away, Piroja will, out of the corner of her eye, catch sight of a television screen showing a very tall, very lanky black man performing a similar manoeuvre to keep a basketball from going out of bounds, and Piroja will have a glimmer of déjà vu but will not make the connection to that particular moment when she attempted to save her husband's life. Indeed, she is fast enough and accurate enough, and spatial dimensions being what they are, she is right on track to make the lifesaving gesture, but for the unfortunate startled-awake-and-rising reflex exhibited by Pradeep. If only she had not shouted his name, she would have saved the day. As it is, she does get the tip of her middle finger to touch and begin to deflect the urn, moving it left, although it still moves downward, and because Pradeep is moving right and upward, what might have been a fatal blow becomes only a glancing blow, but a considerable one nonetheless.

Into Pradeep's eyes appears a look that could be one of deep love, slight fear, or constipation. Into Piroja's outstretched right hand bounces and lands her mother's urn, now apparently quite light, having transferred much of its gravity-induced energy to Pradeep's skull. Into the room comes a soft chuckle, followed by a whispered Gujarati phrase that roughly translates into English as "close, but no cigar."

Try, try again

"It's not her fault," Pradeep says rather lamely, looking upward toward the now-bare urn shelf as Piroja tends to a cut along his hairline.

"Not her fault! Of course it is. I can't believe she would do this."

"Do this? Do what? A vase falls, my head gets in the way."

"Oh Pradeep. You don't know. You don't know what I know. She came here, she visited me, she—"

Piroja pauses and notices that Pradeep is trying hard to focus his right eye on her left. Undoubtedly he has a mild concussion, probably nothing more severe, but what most greatly concerns Piroja now is how she must sound to her injured husband.

"Are you sure the urn didn't bounce off my noggin and land on top of yours?"

"Pradeep. No. What I mean—"

"Or maybe in trying to keep the batter from going for six you clipped your own forehead on the shelf?"

"No. It's—oh, never mind. We should take you to the hospital."

"Piroja, I spend enough of my life there. It's nothing, really."

"But you're cut."

"And you're a nurse. And here I am, a doctor. I think we can handle this one without going to Trauma One."

"Are you sure?" Piroja takes a step back from Pradeep and holds up her hand, two fingers pointing up in a V. "How many fingers am I holding up?"

Pradeep frowns. "On your right hand?"

Piroja nods.

"Six."

"Funny."

"Seven?"

"I should bash you with my whole hand, you jokester. You will still need a plaster on that cut."

Pradeep smiles and nods. "Piroja?"

"Yes."

"What was all that about your mother? All that 'how could you do this to poor Pradeep,' my goodness, I thought I really did have a major concussion and was hallucinating."

"It was nothing. But we should get rid of the urn."

"Nothing doing. Move it, perhaps, to a place where it can't become a dangerous weapon, but it was your mother's, and you love it."

"It should go."

"It stays."

Piroja purses her lips, and realizes what she has to tell Pradeep will sound ridiculous and she will sound insane, but not being one given to keeping things inside, she knows she has to share this story. As she heads to the medicine cabinet to retrieve a plaster for the cut, Piroja explains how her dead mother visited her—yes, wild but true—and is probably even now hanging about the rafters dreaming up some way to have her daughter complete her homicidal mission. Piroja finds the plaster, cuts a piece of appropriate length, and explains over her shoulder that, as bizarre as this story is, she has given it a lot of thought and has determined that the best plan of action would be a move far, far away, where Parvin's ghostly form cannot reach.

"I have heard that doctors and nurses are scarce in Canada," she says, walking back slowly as she tries to gauge Pradeep's silence, "and it would be a new start for us, don't you think?" Piroja is certain she cannot convince her mother to leave them alone, remembers childhood stories of ghosts and incantations and talking to the dead, all of it nonsense, but now, somehow, dreadfully important. "I know you must think I am crazy," she says as she approaches Pradeep to apply the plaster, "but this is the only way." Pradeep, however, has heard none of this, for due to excitement or exhaustion or a combination of both, he has fallen fast asleep, his chin resting on his chest, and he has heard not a word of Piroja's strange narrative and stranger conclusion. Piroja sighs, nods, and affixes the plaster to her husband's forehead.

Crazy little thing

Tick tock, look at the clock. Piroja often replays this childhood rhyme in her head as she walks toward the hospital for her shift. One step after another, a tick following a tock, she would say to herself, and today should be no different, although it is, after the decisions she made last night, very different. She enters the nurses' change room and methodically goes about her start-up routine, *tick tock*, a pullover replaced by a nurse's habit, *tick*, a scarf unwound and cap settled in on top of her head, *tock*, "Good morning, Nurse Catherine, Good morning, Nurse Delilah," and, *tick*, "Good morning back to you, Nurse Piroja," *tick, tick, tock*. Piroja adjusts her uniform and, as is her habit, looks up at the clock and notes with satisfaction that it is two minutes before her shift begins. She walks briskly to the ward, "Good morning, Nurse Angela, I hope you have a nice day today, is there anything on the charts that you need to tell me about? No, all right then, thank you," *tick tock*.

Today is different, as if the ticking of the clock is tocking instead, and with such inverted demarcations of second hands, I wonder if Piroja wonders if I shall be born at all, what with these temporal interruptions in potential conceptions. Piroja, for her part, moves as if in a waking dream, performing all her tasks with typical ease, yet her furrowed brow indicates a distant focus. She is actually humming to herself, something she never does, a ditty she has never heard before, and reflecting on the crazy little thing she calls her life. A mother deceased returning to take the life of a very live husband. A loving husband very much unaware of ghostly acts of attempted homicide. Piroja attends to her first patient, a double hernia in the men's ward. He is experiencing post-surgical discomfort, so Piroja

278

mops his brow and suggests he try some easy exercises to calm the pain. The man grips her hand in appreciation, Piroja smiles in return, then *tick tocks* over to the next patient, a car-accident victim with multiple facial lacerations. He is more depressed than in pain, but Piroja reassures him that the shallow depth of the cuts means he will suffer only very minor scarring, and the young man smiles his appreciation and closes his eyes to try to get some sleep as Piroja checks his chart for his most recent medications.

As always, she performs her duties admirably, and greets her colleagues and doctors jovially, as if nothing at all were tick-tocking through her head, but in that quadrant of the brain reserved for philosophical activities, Piroja is speculating on what it means to be alive, what it means to die, and what happens in those spaces in between. Are thoughts still thoughts if thought by mothers passed on? Are words from child to parent, whatever their various states of liveliness, subject to rules of fair play, and do hidden lies give way to deeds undone or undoable if done by a living girl or ghostly ghost? Piroja asks Doctor Jarvis if he needs her for anything in the men's ward now that she has finished the initial round, and he tells her no, everything seems calm there, but she should check back in an hour. Piroja sits down at the nursing station to fill out the morning paperwork and to think, *tick tock,* a bit more about the nature of living, dying, and the places in between.

Parvin plans ahead

"But it was a nice touch, don't you think?"

"No, I do not! You could have killed him!"

"Oh, yes, well that was the plan, wasn't it? I meant the Asha vase, using that to do him in, what a touch! This is the same vase you continuously call my urn, is it not, even though that is quite a *baadmashi* name for it. And I use that same piece of pottery to whack your husband, who is not one, into oblivion." Parvin clasps her translucent hands together in an expression of utter delight.

Piroja is troubled, but mostly confused. This is not the mother of her memory. "Mummy. I have told you. This is the last time. You must desist from trying to kill Pradeep. This is no joking matter."

"I agree, daughter, not funny at all that you would marry such a useless piece of manflesh, and when I heard the news I could do nothing but cry and cry and cry. Two years I waited, waited for you to come to your senses and make the right decision. But a daughter whose brain is not working sometimes needs her mother, and so I do you this favour of wiping my tears and coming to do you a favour. See, I am not crying any longer. No, I have learned to laugh again. Oh, you should have seen his face when his blunt forehead met that blunt object, so funny, like a mongoose caught in Bombay traffic it was."

"Mummy! I shall never talk to you again if you don't—"

"Oh piffle, you haven't talked to me in ages. Indeed, you didn't start talking to me until I began these as-yet unsuccessful attempts on his life. And now I can't shut you up, so no more talk about no more talking, okay?"

"I started talking to you because you appeared to me after being dead for two years, isn't that obvious? And I'm only talking now to keep you from killing poor Pradeep."

"Those young doctors work with very sharp knives, you know. Why, just this morning I was over at the hospital, biding time, floating above the surgery, and this poor Pradeep of yours mishandled a scalpel and sliced his own jugular."

"What?"

"Oh, dear daughter, I'm only teasing you now. As these things go, revenge cannot be affected by one so hollow such as me."

"Then he's not hurt?"

"No, not yet. I was over at the hospital and that gorilla of a husband of yours did bungle a knife all right, but all he managed to do was to nick a finger and contaminate the blade by dropping it to the floor. Tell me, is he this clumsy even when the two of you …? Oh, I can't bear the thought."

"What do you mean you can't take revenge?"

"You see, there are rules everywhere, even where I am. And the rule here is that only the living can kill the living, silly as it sounds. We, the passed on, may lend assistance, sure enough, but we can't do the enacting, if you follow."

"But the urn—I mean, the vase?"

"Yes, and who put it back a little too close to the edge of the shelf after dusting?"

"Me? But I—?"

"Yes, you. So now you understand, my little flesh-and-bloodly one? The living can hurt the living, however unwillingly, and the dead can only assist, put the idea to the test, so to speak."

"So you didn't make the urn fall?"

"Listen, foolish girl. Pradeep sits there, morning in, morning out, right underneath it, that Asha vase. You know that, and I just observed and helped you out a teeny bit as you dusted (as any good mother would)."

"You witch! You made me place the urn so it would fall on Pradeep?"

"Oh daughter, do try to listen to your whimpering self. Think of what will happen when you take that meat cleaver and sink it between Pradeep's eyes. What will you tell the constabulary? 'My mother made me do it.' Really, will they believe that?"

"But I don't want to hurt Pradeep. He's my husband."

"If it were my idea and mine alone, don't you think I'd be powerless to make it so? As your ally, however, anything can happen."

Piroja buries her face in her hands and cries. She keeps her fingers tightly clasped so no light can enter between them, no reminder that her ghostly mother stands before her, imploring her to kill her own husband, maliciously offering to help. She does this for a full minute, her sobs lessening slightly when she feels a cool breeze rush past her. She cracks open a space between her second and third fingers on her right hand and peeks through. Parvin is nowhere to be seen, as if she were never there. Which, of course, thinks a logical Piroja, she never was, for how could she be, how could her dead mother make this horrifying appearance? No, it must be a mental illness she has, thinks Piroja. Only a sick, sick woman would conjure up her dead mother to help her kill her own husband. And clearly, that is what's happening. She can scream and rant and blame all she wants, but what the ethereal Parvin said must be true. It is Piroja herself who has caused this near catastrophe, and if all is as seems to be, this pattern will continue until Pradeep is dead. How could she be so callous, so cruel? And what deep-seated reason might she have for snuffing out her beloved Pradeep? What has he done other than offer her his love and unending support? What bitterness does she conceal that is making her act out this way? Should she see a doctor or consult a dastur?

Piroja sits in silence, her hands still covering her face, too afraid to pull them down or to do anything. She takes a deep breath, exhales. Tries another one, deeper this time, holds it for a very long time, then lets it out in a gush. That's better. Things are returning to normal. All she has to do is tell herself that she has suffered an episode, perhaps not altogether dissimilar to those suffered by her own father throughout his life, those much-talked-about incidents when he experienced visitations from another realm. Of course, that must be it. That *was* it. And still, her father led a full and productive life, didn't he? There was plenty of rumour and innuendo, but nothing came of it. He lived and prospered, and is now a respected man. This is a relief, thinks Piroja. Chip off the old block, she is. And if he could control it, so can she.

"Oh good God, girl," comes the chirping voice of Parvin, "now you must malign your most wonderful father instead of taking responsibility for yourself?" ·

Piroja looks up and sees her now-almost see-through mother looking very cross indeed, her arms folded in front of her.

"Mummy, how did you—"

"Oh, my, we haven't learned much from our little discussions, have we? It's too embarrassing to have to make a reappearance for corrective purposes. The other ghosts laugh at me because of you. 'Couldn't do it with one good speech, Parvin?' they gibe me. You see, we ghosts know how to make entrances and exits and it's poor style to have to make an encore, so to speak. But I couldn't leave you with the impression that you were following in your father's footsteps of the mind. So I'll tell you this once, then make my exit, all right? Your father wasn't crazy. The voice he heard was that of your own child, as he well knew. And you're not crazy. This is your departed mother's voice (with broken-heart noises, I should add), and all I have said is ... true. Now, I leave." And with that, Parvin lifts her chin and dissolves into a mist.

Piroja sleeps fitfully that night. She wakes at every sound, allows herself to drift off, then wakes again with the creaking of a bedpost, the drip of a drainpipe, the whine of a car engine from two streets away. At dawn, she is almost grateful that the night is over, and she rises, exhausted, and begins her morning rituals. At fifteen minutes to eight, she is in the kitchen, nervously looking up at the clock and checking to make sure there is nothing in sight that might cause an injury or accident. Pradeep will be home any moment, and Piroja has decided that she is not, after all, crazy or even a bit deluded, that everything that has happened over the past twenty-four hours is verifiable and all too real. For some unearthly reason, her mother has come back not just to haunt her but to help her kill her husband. And, following her mother's logic, it is actually Piroja who wants Pradeep dead. But since Piroja doesn't *feel* like she wants to kill her husband, those thoughts must be buried deep inside her, and she strongly believes that she has to be alert, overtly conscious of her every action, and that if she can convince Pradeep to move across the seas, the danger will pass. After all, Parvin can't assist Piroja in this murderous act if Piroja places such distance between her mother and herself, yet until that time, vigilance is of the essence. She must ensure there is no possible way she can hurt Pradeep, even by absurd accident. So when she hears Pradeep's tired steps on the stairway, she takes a deep breath and rushes to the door. She opens it (but not too quickly lest it pull itself off its hinges, lunge out of her control, and crush her husband) and greets Pradeep with a gentle kiss on the cheek and a warm embrace, carefully tendered so as to not in any way possible inflict internal organ damage.

"Good morning," says Pradeep, managing a smile through his fatigue.

"Morning to you, too," says Piroja. And she takes her husband by the hand and leads him to the kitchen.

"Where's the urn?" asks Pradeep, immediately noticing the empty shelf above his regular chair.

"Um, I put it in the living room," she says, gesturing to a spot by the radiator.

"Worried about killing me, are you?" asks Pradeep.

"What? What do you mean?"

"Nothing," laughs Pradeep. "Why, nothing! You're jumpy this morning."

Piroja smiles with difficulty and has a fleeting thought that perhaps it wouldn't be the worst thing in the world if the urn bounced off Pradeep's head again. But what is she thinking? How can she think such things, even in imaginary retribution of Pradeep's sick humour? Is it true that she secretly wishes her husband to die? She must be extra careful, today of all days. Somehow, she manages to make it through breakfast without killing Pradeep, without even any near misses. So she is quite alarmed when Pradeep, rather than toddling off to the relative safety of their bedroom, offers to walk her to work.

"But you just came from there!"

"Yes, that's true, but on days like this when I'm tired, but not dead tired, I like the idea of walking with my wife. With our cross shifts, I feel like we're strangers sometimes."

"But you must be very, very tired."

"You're right, but what's another twenty minutes going to do?"

"Oh, but it's twenty minutes there, another twenty back, a good hour before you'll get to bed."

"Fifteen there, twelve if I follow your pace, perhaps fifteen back, and I'll be in bed in thirty minutes. But why are we haggling?"

"Oh, you know," says Piroja, but she does not know, and neither does Pradeep, so he accompanies her to the hospital despite her protestations. Piroja is careful to leave the flat in front of Pradeep and to walk slowly down the stairs. There is no way she can push him from in front, and if she has left any treacheries for him on the steps, she will surely break his fall. On the sidewalk, she uncharacteristically takes the traffic side, causing a comical ballet between the two of them as Pradeep attempts to take his gentlemanly place by the road. At last he submits when it becomes obvious that Piroja will not relent, and puzzled, he walks beside his wife. Their walk to work is uneventful, but for Piroja's rather frequent and sudden gasps of alarm, mostly made under her breath so that they go unnoticed by Pradeep. A policeman walks by (has she hired a *goonda* to dress up like that and shoot to kill?), a scooter rushes past (another hit man with a loaded shotgun?), a bird flutters close by (if pigeons can be trained to carry messages, why not seagulls with poison darts, but this is getting ludicrous). At last they reach the hospital, and Piroja rushes through the doors, pausing to look back and make sure Pradeep is not stepping into traffic where a taxi driver, his brake lines cut by a sleepwalking murderous wife, is an unknowing instrument of a dastardly crime. But, of course, all is fine; the taxi driver has perfectly working brakes and graciously applies them to let Pradeep pass. Piroja walks down the corridor to her station, confident that her husband will be safe for at least another twelve hours. When he returns, Piroja will broach the subject of emigration. She will explain it to him as a wondrous opportunity, a chance to discover themselves anew. He may resist, he may complain, but she will convince him. She has to. It's a matter of life or death.

Passage to Canada

Pradeep does not usually brood, but when he does, he broods well. His face does not change that much, nor does his body posture; indeed, if Piroja were pressed to say what actually does change about Pradeep when he broods, she would find it extremely difficult to describe. "He just ... broods" is all she could say. It is almost as if Pradeep has the ability to inhabit his brood, to crawl deep down into that dark and worrisome place and, without it affecting his physical being one iota, emanate broodiness. Broodidity. Broodability. It is just such a brood that Pradeep is now in, on this, his day off, sitting in front of Piroja as they enjoy (or not) a tidy little breakfast of English muffins, marmalade, and homemade mango chutney, a breakfast permeated by a devilishly broody silence.

"What. Is. It. ?"

This is the way Piroja punches through the silence that is created when Pradeep broods. She will enunciate each word and append a full stop behind each one, and when she has finished she will throw a question mark out at Pradeep with no more than a flicker of two brow hairs above her left eye, more a quiver than a flicker, actually, but enough to fully form a question mark and dart it through the air so that it strikes Pradeep squarely between *his* eyes. And Pradeep is left with the only option open to a spouse, responding with the only possible retort to such a periodic interrogation, which is: "What is what?"

"You. Know," says Piroja, willing a third brow hair into action for the cause. "Don't. You. ?"

Pradeep knows better than to repeat his question, but he is flummoxed because he does not really know but knows he cannot say he doesn't know or Piroja might enlist a fourth eyebrow hair into action, and that will mean trouble for days to come. Instead, he attempts to make it appear that he does know exactly or at least partially what she is talking about: "Oh, is it, that is, when you were, I was just—is it me?"

"You're doing that thing again," says Piroja, this time managing to sluice her words together in a less-than-staccato fashion.

This at least opens up sound negotiating ground for Pradeep: "That thing about not talking in complete sentences?"

"Exactly."

"Oh, I'm sorry. Just that, I, there was this, I was thinking ..."

"No, there you go again. You always do that not-sentence-speaking when you're brooding."

Ah, so that was it, his brooding. "I was brooding, yes? Yes, I suppose I was. It's just that I was thinking. Thinking we should move perhaps."

"Move?" Piroja is both stunned and excited. "Where?"

"To Canada. Or some other place."

"Canada? Whatever gave you that idea?"

"My residency is almost finished, and I have heard, at the hospital, that there are many opportunities in Canada for English doctors. Even Indian doctors."

Canada. Piroja wonders if she has the ability to put thoughts into Pradeep's head as her mother does with hers. She does not know why, but she is certain that the ghostly hands of ancestors cannot reach across whole oceans, and now, instead of having to convince Pradeep, here he is trying to convince her. Destiny. Perhaps there is a limit, an international dateline of some solidity, so to speak, that will keep her mother from forcing her to commit the husbandcide that Piroja so desperately wants to avoid. Perhaps this new world on the flip side of the globe will really turn into a new life, or at least a continued life, for her and Pradeep. Perhaps starting fresh on another continent—all that land and those lakes and mountains—perhaps that's the very thing for them. For a moment, Piroja toys with the idea of protesting, just to make the discussion complete. But before she knows what she is doing, before she can keep the words from leaving her mouth, she hears her voice babbling on about how, yes, that is precisely what they should do, and so surprising is this to Piroja that she actually claps her hand over her mouth to slow if not stop these nonsensical utterances.

"I knew it," says Pradeep. "I knew there was something wrong with this place, the way you were acting, as if you had seen death itself around the corner, the way you were fussing over me. I knew it was something. And I surprise even myself that I was right, that my wife wants to become a travel adventurer! Then it is done. I finish the residency in two months, and we shall find a steamer to take us to Canada. We must buy cardigans, lots of cardigans. And mittens. I hear it is cold, as cold as Kashmir, and I would not want my wife to catch her death of cold, no?" And Pradeep smiles, self-satisfied, and Piroja thinks again perhaps she should protest for appearances, suggest that they should stand their ground in this still-new home, but instead occupies herself with thoughts about packing up their lives and booking passage to a world away.

Fire and ice, some say

Two steamer trunks. Who would have thought it? Their lives, a combined forty-eight years of existence on this planet, summed up by
two containers and two cardboard tickets upon which are printed
many words, but three important ones: Final Destination Halifax.
Piroja looks at the steamer trunks sitting in their now-empty flat.
She stretches her arms out to her sides, realizes that her extended
reach covers almost, but not quite, the breadth of the two trunks.
She has her whole world, thinks Piroja, in her hands. She bows her
head to reflect on her past, her future. It is at this moment that
Pradeep chooses (or the moment chooses him) to enter the room,
stopping starkly at the tableau in front of him.

"You're not thinking about converting to Catholicism, are you?"
he asks with a bite of irony.

Piroja looks up, her arms still stretched out to either side. She
takes a beat and then looks at her extended right arm, her extended
left, certainly a vision of crucifixion if ever she was one. She smiles
at how Pradeep can sometimes put her at ease with the same sense
of humour that can be so frustrating at other times, even at the
same time sometimes.

"Lord forgive you," she says, letting her arms fall to her sides, "for
you know not what you do."

"A—a stitch in time saves nine?"

"What in the world is that supposed to mean?"

"Oh, you know, just playing that game, I put forward a quotation,
then you do, and off we go."

"But yours didn't make sense."

"Certainly it did. If you repair something before it's fallen into utter disrepair, well, you save yourself some time."

"Yes, that's what the quotation means, silly, but it made no sense how you used it here, with me, now."

"Oh, yes, I see," says Pradeep, now pretending to be thick. "But it is a fine quotation, no?"

"Come hither and I will smite thee," laughs Piroja. And he does come hither, but not for the purpose of being struck. They embrace warmly, both recognizing that this is the final time—they are embarking on a series of finalities, they realize—that they will hold each other in their little Yorkshire flat. They hold each other for a while, reassuring each other in their holding that they are there for each other, that they will always be so. Their connection is broken by the buzzer informing them that their taxi is here along with the two young men they have hired to help with their belongings. They pull apart, look at each other, nod imperceptibly—yes, this is the right thing to do—take a breath, and then Piroja leads them out of the flat and down the stairs into the cool York morning.

Part Three

Transmigrations

Postcards home

June 20, 1956

Dear Papa,
I think of you so often. You and Abdul and the house in
the compound, all of that. I know you miss Mummy a great
deal. So do I, but I am sure it is different for you for many
different reasons. Sometimes I feel as if she is very near
to me. This is very hard to put into words, but I hope you
understand.

I have not written to you since the week we arrived, and
for that I am sorry. I cannot use the excuse that I have been
very busy, for although I have, it is no excuse at all. But
perhaps I can blame it on a desire to fill you up with all the
details at once rather than piecemeal. We will see if, at the
end of this letter, you agree with me and forgive your daughter, or rightly hold a fatherly grudge.

When I last wrote to you, we had just arrived in Halifax
harbour. It was a welcome relief after the long journey, as
I had mentioned, to see the land where we would now be
living. It was desperately cold when we landed, though
two of the sailors teased us, I don't think I told you that,
when we noted the weather. "You think this is cold, Missy,
the brisk spring wind coming off the March waters? Well,
hold on to your hat, there, and buy yourself a warmer one,
because come December, January, now then you'll see cold!"
I suppose we still have a way to go, though, and I must say
it is hard to imagine with the weather as it is now, almost

every day sunny and balmy. Nothing like Nowgong or Delhi of course, but after a while one readjusts one's thermostats, I suppose, and re-evaluates what "warm" really is. So this is warm, even though you are required to wear a cardigan, especially when you are close to the water.

We are no longer in the small flat that we rented to start out in Halifax. We have moved across the harbour to the neighbouring city of Dartmouth where we could get a slightly bigger place for the same amount of money. Although the hospital is in Halifax, it is relatively convenient to get across since they just built a bridge across the harbour last year, and there is a bus that runs close to our flat and right next to the hospital, so it is really very easy. Pradeep works long shifts as he attempts to qualify to practise here.

It is, in many ways, worse than England—I mean the hours, and I am not entirely sure I trust the people. They all seem very nice on the surface, and I suppose that is what is so disconcerting. They all seem the same—very, very nice— and I cannot believe that everyone has the same amount of niceness, no less, no more than the person standing next to them. But that might take some time for me to figure out. I work at the same hospital, of course, but just last week I started to work night shift again. I will do that through the summer to replace the night matron (they call her the shift supervisor here), and then I will be back to days. The nights pay much better, so we can save a bit of money, and I do so want to save enough so you can take a long vacation from the distillery and visit us here in our new home.

I know you may still harbour some resentment about my marriage. I suppose I should have told you much earlier, but it seemed so impossible. You and Mummy wanted so badly

for me to marry a nice Parsi boy. I had resolved to break
the news to you as soon as we settled in England. I know I
lied to you, I told you I had a chance for a much better job
in England. Well, it was not a lie really, but for what I left
out, that I was joining my husband there. And I was going
to tell you once we got to York, but then the telegram about
Mummy arrived and I couldn't then break such news to you.
Please believe me, it broke my heart to have to hold that
news inside, as much as it broke my heart to know that I
could not be there to say goodbye to Mummy. I wish I had
had the chance—

OH, I DON'T KNOW ABOUT THAT!

Piroja looks up from her letter writing. What is that odd voice
resounding through the flat, such a loud one, as if coming through
a megaphone? Piroja goes to the window to see if something is happening on this Sunday morning on the street, perhaps a parade or
a protest (although they do not seem to protest here in Canada like
they do in India, as if everything is turned down several notches
here—no raised voices in the market, no gunshots in the street, no
calls to prayer at dusk, no grinding, choking sounds of auto-rick-
shaws and blue-smoked buses—nothing untoward except now, with
this voice booming through Piroja's living room.)

SHE SEEMS TO VISIT YOU OFTEN ENOUGH.

"Who?" Piroja turns sharply, since the voice clearly comes from
behind her, from the kitchen area, except she can see clear through
to the kitchen, and there is no one there. "What, where are you?"

*HEE-HEE, FROM THE BELLY PERHAPS, A BELLY LAUGH,
HEE-HEE.*

Piroja does a quick look around the apartment, but there is no
one, no one anywhere to be seen. She thinks about darting to the

bedroom, but the voice does not emanate from down the hall. But then, she is used to supernatural goings-on, as Parvin seems to have made the leap across the *kala-pani* and occasionally inhabits her second-hand couch, though thankfully seems to have given up on her active pursuit of son-in-lawicide. They had been in Dartmouth for three months with no sign of her, until one morning when Piroja heard the unmistakeable yawn-sigh coming from the centre of the tiny living room. But whether it was weakness brought on by transoceanic ghost-travels, or the fatigue borne of temporal distance from a bodily existence, Parvin did little more than sit on the couch and stare straight ahead, tsk-tsking on occasion, but otherwise abiding in silence. But this. This was not Parvin's voice at all, booming at her from all directions.

"Well, at least stop yelling. You're bursting my eardrums and most likely disturbing our neighbours."

YELLING? Oh, yes, yelling, quite so. I do apologize. It has been a while since I have talked to anyone, and modulation was never my strong suit.

"That's better. Now, where are you?"

Your entire family seems all too concerned about my whereabouts, doesn't it? What I was saying was that Grandmother Parvin is not exactly absent now that she is dead, is she? And a quarrelsome one, she is, much more so than when she was alive, no?

"How do you know about Mummy? And who, *who* are you? And yes, *why* is she so quarrelsome in death? Oh my God, what is going on here?"

I know a lot of things—that has been the source of quite some Khargatly irritation, for certain. And who am I? Well, look down, look way down, into the future, if you will; think about a mewling, puking little babe in arms, and then you will have it.

Piroja looks down at the ground, begins to examine the patterns of the carpet before I interrupt.

My gosh, so literal. Was speaking timescapes, not physical spaces. Never mind the carpet, as you shan't find me there, at least, not now. My name, mother dearest, my name is—

And so I spill out the entire story of pasts and presents and potential futures: how a wonderful old dastur moved his family because of his son's predilection for going right; how schoolteachers and psychoanalysts and Parsi brethren and folks both far and close were enthralled by this young boy who would be a distillery manager and a dastur himself; and I go on to talk about uncles who died as toddlers and how Piroja herself might never have been born but for necessary visitations to now-dead-but-still-around mothers; and I smile (not that Piroja can see this, but she does hear the lipturn in my voice) when I tell first of the juice of ripe mangos and then the absolutely delectable nectar of the selfsame fruit existing only in the imagination, an expression of ultimate desire that can come only from a wish to bring *something* into being; and I then relate stories that Piroja had only thought she had remembered or had been told, a litany of detail, an exhaustion of familial patterns and patter. Piroja is astounded that her brain can take in so much information, and she hardly notices how the afternoon light fades to northern twilight, and the illumination in the room drops slowly, too, so that the words on her letter to her father seem to go murky. Still she listens and listens and listens and listens, until, through the voice of this child that is not one, she hears the downstairs door flapping open.

There is Pradeep in the room, and no sooner than he appears, I dis-, and she finds herself leaning against the windowsill, looking for all the world as if she had been shot through with both adrenalin and morphine, that slight smile that only the drug-addled and newborn and elderly demented ever have. She looks at Pradeep, who looks for all the world as if he had been shot through with both gauges and a nice spread of lead pellets, and when he can finally bring himself to speak, he says:

"Piroja? Whatever are you doing here in the dark?"

And Piroja smiles, brightening the room, she knows, as twilight catches her front teeth, and she chooses this exact moment to notice that her foot, her right foot, is now quite desperately tired, as it has been tapping, tapping away for a good several hours, quieting only as Pradeep entered the space. In her smile she says to her husband, come, let us sit, let us be together, let us think about our futures and our pasts, and, most of all, what we need to do to fill our presents, and somehow, all of this information replaces the lead pellets that are not filling up Pradeep's torso, and he understands, though not fully, so he lets his arms, already by his side and slinking downward, fully relax so the tips of his fingers brush the sides of his kneecaps. Pradeep moves to Piroja, moves so there is no more than a crack of twilight between them, and they simply stand there until the light finally does dip out of existence and they are left only with their own breath, and that is enough for the night.

Inside and out

There are stories we tell to comfort each other, stories to instruct, stories to remember, and then there are stories we tell to create the next steps in front of us, to develop the bas-relief of our histories, to create. In this particular instance, this mother not-yet-mine is left with the choice to tell father-sometime-to-be the most outrageous or outlandish of stories, visitations by the now-dead and the not-yet-born, or to create different figments that might be less truthful and yet that much more real, considering what Pradeep and others are bound to believe.

So she says nothing to Pradeep, but then again, in saying nothing she cannot bring herself to bring herself forth as did her grandmother before her, to bring a child into the world. She must consider this: her mother, dead of tuberculosis before the age of fifty, was on Piroja's case to rid herself of a mixed-religion marriage and a Hindu husband, while yours truly, the unborn child, is visiting her in the middle of an Atlantic summer, on Mama's case to get on the case and birth me forthwith and immediately. And there she is, Piroja, a bright, young Parsi girl who could have and should have been a doctor had not her parents and cultural roadblocks thrown nursing in her way. It's a noble profession to be sure, but perhaps my mother is not all she could be. All this a pretty Parsi girl parses through her mind, thanks but not thankful to me, as she finishes, finally, her letter to a would-be granddad:

—to say goodbye, Papa, not only to Mummy but to you. I fully expect, of course, to see you soon and do not fear that you will be leaving this world soon, never fear, that is not my worry! But I wish I had had the chance to say goodbye to Mummy. It is odd, that feeling that you might never see your mother again. I remember so clearly standing beside her on the steamer, and then again watching her walk down the platform and seeing her and you on the dock. I waved to her and she waved to me, and then, well, that was it. There is so much I would have told her—that I want to tell her now. Pradeep is a good man, Papa, and I think she would have liked him, even if she may have made those eyes, how she would roll them to the rooftops—

"*Aré*, still she maligns me!"

"Mummy! You're here?"

"My child, my child, always the brightest star in school, but often the thickest brick on the ledge when it came to the evidence, no? Yes, I am here."

"But you haven't spoken since we came here. You just sat on the couch, I mean—well, Mummy, I still don't understand how—"

"I understand, dear, talking and piecing together a cogent sentence at the same time, a daunting task."

For a moment, Piroja is doubly flummoxed, for she had been unsure that her mother would be able to fly across the ocean to haunt her, and now Parvin is back, insulting her daughter, again in an English she never spoke while alive, an English that seems to be improving quite dramatically.

"Mummy, I just don't understand."

"There is a task to be done, dearest one; a mother can never rest her head while her daughter is in such misery."

"I am not miserable!"

"Not miserable, child, look at you, all atremble, and your eyes bugging out, enough that I might think you had seen a ghost, something we can arrange, we can both hope for, the next time you see your Prattle Prutho fellow, who is so beneath you I cannot begin to allow myself to call him your husband."

"But I thought you had accepted this, the way you sat on the couch, just sitting there like—"

"Like an old woman waiting to die? Too late for such waitingliness. I only was waiting for the right moment when my daughter would be ready to listen. Now listen."

"Mummy. Listen to *me*. I love Pradeep. And nothing you can say will change that. Nothing you can do will change that. Leave him alone. Let us be together."

"Be together? I can barely leave you by yourself. Listen to me just this once, to a dying mother—"

"Dead mother."

"As you would have it. My dying wish was that you be happy with a nice Parsi boy, and it is not too late. There is admittedly a lack of definite choice out here in this wicked part of the world, but never say never, never say die. We Parsis do like to travel, so I am sure a beautiful widow—"

"Wife."

"—such as yourself, and an educated beauty, will have no trouble snagging yourself a catch, as they like to say."

"I will not find a Parsi boy. I have the husband I want. I can still be a good Parsi, just you watch. Papa has written to me, has forgiven me, and if he can do that in life, why can't you try to be happy for me in death? … What am I doing? I am trying to convince my dead mother to respect my wishes. I truly am crazy."

"Crazy, yes, a bit touched, that flying off with this Proddish fellow, but you are so close to banging some sense into his head, very deeply if you take my recommendation, and that will, in turn, make your head stop its spinning."

Piroja stomps into the kitchen and begins banging things around in the drawers. She tosses off a rolling pin—too blunt and ridiculous-looking—and puts aside a somewhat dull butcher's knife, as it seems overly theatrical, and settles on a wooden mallet, a meat tenderizer her friend Sara at the hospital gave her in order to whack some softness into tough but affordable pieces of meat. Piroja rushes back into the living room where Parvin is now, in all her translucent glory, looking at her nail polish.

"I really must redo this," she mutters to herself, "so hard to keep good colour on your fingertips, let alone your cheeks, when you are two years past due." Then, noticing her daughter blustering into the room brandishing what looks like a miniature croquet mallet, she says, "Good gracious, dear girl, what in whose name do you plan to do with that?"

"This is it, Mummy. You have forced me into this. I am banishing you from this house until you can keep a civil word for my husband. Yes, my *husband*!"

"Dearest daughter, let me reinform you that I am a ghost and very impartial to wooden blocks aimed at my non-being."

Piroja looks at the mallet, then at the shimmering outline of her mother. "We shall see," she says with resolution, and advances toward her mother's form.

Ah yes, the complications of when the still-alive confront the already-gone, witnessed and narrated by the not-yet-born; very, very tricky terrain. So I shall try to enumerate, keep things simple and above board, for there are a number of circumstances that, when they coincide, can produce a particularly nasty affair.

1) Ghosts, in most cultural contexts (Parvin is right about this), have little material substance and thus are relatively difficult to ward

off by swinging or slashing or dicing or mincing at with destructive implements. Nevertheless, wayward feelings of fear and trepidation, that is, the ingrained need to respond to physical threats, even if you have no substance, are hard to lose. Parvin realizes this, as she backs slowly away from her daughter, staying a good three inches above the carpet, as she tends to do in this ghostly form.

2) A woman on the verge of a swinging, slashing, dicing, or mincing impulse is often unaware of both the time of day (say, shift's end plus the time it takes to walk to the bus stop, catch a ride over the Angus Macdonald Bridge, and hoof it the thirty steps to the flat) and the effects of tunnel vision, particularly when she is intent on a particularly matricidal act, absurd as that might be, since the object of her attention is already dead.

3) In a small apartment, arranged ever so carefully by Piroja with a little bit of help from Pradeep, it is important to both give the illusion of space while allowing a natural flow, a walking path so to speak, so inhabitants and guests both might make their way, say, from the second-hand couch to the window (to open it and let in some sea breeze or close it to keep out the night air) or, as is currently the case, to the front door, to where the now-fading Parvin is back-pedalling, not excessively quickly but with conviction.

4) Once a particular physical action, let us say a rather substantial swing of a meat tenderizer, has begun, it is sometimes difficult to arrest said action in midswing, owing to such factors as reaction time and inertia and motherly shrieks and opening doors.

5) Unlike in theatre, where to have several people speak at once creates a type of cacophony that, if mistimed or overused, will have audiences muttering expletives if not heading for the door, in real life, such as it were, it is possible for three distinct voices to all speak simultaneously even as each voice-owner is taking a very particular and decisive action.

There. I think that sets the tone and scene sufficiently. Back to it, then, uninterrupted by me, the unborn child.

"Get *out* of my *life*," screams Piroja as she rushes her mother's ghost, stepping in with her left foot and bringing, with a surprisingly weighty swing, the meat tenderizer down toward Parvin's fading forehead.

"You are an *ungrateful* child," shrieks Parvin as she takes yet another step backward, cowering a bit, which, were she a material person would have her stepping back into the door but, being ghostly and immaterial, sees her gingerly place tip of toe to floor and have heel descend not into but through said door, which, as luck would have it, is in the process of opening.

"Piroja, is that you?" asks a mildly alarmed Pradeep, swinging open the door in an unfamiliarly alarmed fashion, stepping into what is usually a very unmenacing foyer-meets-living-room, quite literally stepping through a now-ducking Parvin, an act that would surely seem to someone of Pradeep's logic a dreadful and heart-stopping event, were he able to see her. Being a ghost, however, and subject only to ghostly rules, she is invisible to Pradeep and, at that very moment, wisping into nothingness, if only to avoid a meat tenderizer that cannot harm her nonentity-ness. But why stay around if a daughter is treating you so?

All these events so conspire to result in what might seem to be a simple matter, that is, an unwanted husband coming home to an unforgiving wife, meeting her very undulcet tones of "Get out of my life" with an understandably confused and disturbed "Piroja, is that you?" and the coincidental action being the follow-through of a mother's-forehead-intended meat tenderizer ceasing its trajectory when meeting a not exactly immoveable object but one that, after a long and tiring day at the hospital, sports a considerable headache already, such that the stippled mallet imprints with considerable force directly into the part of the forehead that is traditionally described as "right between the eyes."

There is a respectful moment of utter silence once mallet stops vibrating on skin, then a guttural chuckle and a quaint utterance of a Gujarati phrase, one that a certain Parsi mother living in the jungles near Nowgong would occasionally whisper after her very infrequent and tiniest of sips of that rum they called Asha, a hoarse little lining of words that roughly translates into English as "What a taste magnificent!"

ArCee at the VeeGee

Constable Wei Devlin pulls his patrol car into the parking lot just outside Victoria Hospital. He looks up at the multiple storeys and shakes his head. This just does not seem like Victoria Hospital, even though it's been standing there since 1948, the same year he joined the Royal Canadian Mounted Police. His father was a member and his grandfather before him (transferring over from the Dominion Police in 1920), and they regaled him with stories of Halifax County where they had both worked for "H Division," tales from the explosion on down. His grandfather told him how he could not imagine that air could actually burn until that day, how he worked rescue for twenty-four hours before going home to see his family in Dartmouth, kissed his sleeping boy, Wei's father, and swore that he would never leave this ocean and its people. And so Wei's father, Scott, a red-faced and red-haired, barrel-chested man with a temperament of roasting chestnuts (Wei's grandmother would always say it had something to do with smouldering but never exploding, certainly not like that ship in Halifax Harbour) joined the RCMP as soon as he was old enough. Scott had wanted to enlist in the army, but his father said no, that to serve the people at home was equally if not more important, and that was the legacy of the Devlin clan, "to police and protect," their unofficial family motto.

Their secondary and mostly unofficial motto was "marrying out," reflecting the fact that the Devlin boys always found mates who were vastly different than themselves or their family. Marrying out was what their grandmother, a woman who proudly called herself of "sturdy Greek ancestry," named the Devlin tradition. She had taken it upon herself to research the family tree, so curious was she at the way the Devlin name had carried forth even while the boys looked so far and wide and found wives that had the least possible connection with the original Irish O'Doibhilins, which, so said Grandmother Devlin, was the real root of their name.

"Seems to me," she told Wei on his ninth birthday, "the boys figured they would plant their feet right here in Maritime soil, yessir, one foot in the saline mud and the other in that there Halifax Harbour, but they got their flights of fancy by marrying out, that's what they did. Look at me! Fresh off the boat, arms as wide as your thighs. I was a working Greek girl, and your grandfather takes one looks at me and off he goes, telling ever'body who'd listen that I was going to be his wife. His Greek wife, the new Mrs Devlin. And so it was. And that wasn't the first time, no sir, all his brothers did that marrying out, too; one marrying an Austrian girl who spoke not a word of English, and another hitching up with this Mic Mac from down the coast, and the third boy, well sir, he stayed a bachelor for the longest time, just went fishing with the boys all the time, and that was tending enough for him, but he eventually marries this girl from South America, I think it was, odd creature, only met her the once before they moved away, she couldn't have been more than four feet tall and the bleachiest white skin you ever saw, could almost see right through it, white skin and a throaty voice and, I could swear, five o'clock shadow around the clock. So when my only boy, Scotty, was staying away from home most nights, I finally says to him, 'Who is she, Scotty? Bring her home.' And he says to me, 'But, Mother, don't know if I can,' but I keeps prodding him, and he finally relents, he does, and brings home this fine-spirited Chinese girl. Why, the neighbours were out there on the front lawn having a bird, but I knows this was coming, so I just says to Scotty, 'Well, don't stand there, son, bring this lovely creature inside so we can have a talk.' And from that moment, me and Carla—she had a Chinese name, of course, but none of us used that—me and Carla, your mamma, were inseparable. And that's how you got the name Wei; it was a name that Carla remembered from way back in her grandparents' village. But you can be proud of that Devlin tradition, son, going out so far afield you don't think you can never come back, but you do, you know, you do, 'cuz you have one foot planted there in the saline mud and the other in that there Halifax Harbour. You be proud of that."

And sure enough, when Wei got old enough to start dating, and he was a startlingly good-looking boy, he brought home girls from "all over the blessed world," as his grandmother put it, and she welcomed each and every one of them with a plate of cookies and a word of advice—"This is my grandson, and if you do right by him, he'll do right by you or my name isn't Devlin."

And so Constable Wei Devlin sits in his patrol car and looks up at Victoria General, the *new* Victoria General as his father and grandfather would put it, and wonders at a world that can change so fast that a modest three-floor building could transform into this skyscraper. Still, the word was that a lot had changed since the VG was built in the year of Confederation, and this was the place to go if you were diseased or injured—or the place to go if you got into an altercation with your husband, which is why, Wei Devlin nods to himself, he is here now. He looks down at his clipboard with the scrawled notes from his staff sergeant and the initials "KA" written down in the margin and circled. "KA" was how his staff sergeant categorized violence in the home, "kitchen assault," he would say, and inevitably throw the case to Devlin, not punitively, but because everyone in the detachment knew it was what Wei did best. He could walk into a situation in a home where there were knives out and guns drawn, and by the end of the "talking to" that he would give the bristling husband and wife, they were falling into each other's arms. That, at least, was what others saw. Wei Devlin, himself, was not so sure, because for every subdued temper, for every softened word, Devlin imagined that he could hear restlessness behind cooing tones, and he sometimes wondered if getting these happy, loving couples back together was an act of kindness or just an act of futility. Sometimes, after a husband reached to stroke a wife's neck and he saw her flinch, or when a wife smiled up at her husband and he stoked coal with his eyes back at her, Devlin would wish he wasn't considered so good at these KAs.

But there he is, inspecting his clipboard, which informs him of an angry and quite violent assault over the bridge in Dartmouth, something about a screaming woman, a swinging hammer, and a concussed husband. Wei gets out of the patrol car, pausing to glance back at a tightly wrapped package in the back seat. It should be safe there, he thinks, then grins wryly at what might confront a would-be thief should he try to pilfer that package from an RCMP cruiser. He might run all the way home, thinking he had lifted some contraband or previously stolen valuables, only to find a slightly disfigured and most certainly dead black rat. This is the product of yet another domestic squabble, the inevitable result of which is that Wei Devlin will have to head back to the detachment later to file the report and bag the very unpleasant evidence, and he hopes to make as short work of it as he can with this current case since a closed car hit by sun can cause a mummified rodent to simmer, and all he needs is an unending case that leaves him returning to an odour of cooked vermin.

Wei makes his way to the front doors of VG and half-salutes the ancient fellow who acts as security guard at the front entrance, acknowledging the obviously painful and rheumatoid half wave in return. Wei follows the red line through the foyer to Emergency, a path that is only too well worn in his memory. As he rounds the corner, Katerina, the evening reception nurse, is having an argument with an elderly woman who wants her grandson attended to.

"Wait an hour?" says the woman. "But he's only seven. An hour for him is like five hours for you or me."

"I understand," says Katerina, sympathetically. "But we have only one doctor on this evening."

"But couldn't you just look at him? Only take a stitch or two, I would think."

"I'm afraid that's not possible. But if you have a seat—" then, seeing the constable, "Hi Wei, they're expecting you back in ER Six," and she gestures over her shoulder before returning to calm down the woman.

"All right," says Wei, nodding, moving toward the doors marked Please Wait Here Until Instructed to Proceed. "Anything I should know that's not in the paperwork?"

"Oh, it's an odd one," says Katerina. "Sara's back there. She can explain it all."

Wei walks through the left-hand doors, past the ankle fracture in ER One, beyond the diabetic ketosis case in ER Three, peeks in on Dr Walters patching up a head laceration incurred by a teenager during an epileptic seizure, and then stops at the curtain on the right side, ER Six. He pulls the curtain back and sees a dark brown man lying on the stretcher, decidedly the worse for wear, a thick bandage wrapped around his forehead and a strange stare coming out from behind his eyelids. Next to him is a petite, attractive, obviously forlorn and distressed young woman, also brown, but several shades lighter in skin tone than the man, holding the injured man's hand and guppying her mouth as if she had so much and nothing to say. Standing an arm's breadth from the couple is Sara, one of the night emergency nurses. This is the first time Wei can remember the ever-bustling Sara standing still, so he gestures to her with his chin—what's up?—and she smiles, goes to touch the young woman on her shoulder, and follows Wei outside the curtain and toward the out-of-earshot nursing station.

"Hi Wei, I'm glad they sent you."

"Yes, well, you know how it is. They throw these things my way, even if Halifax local should be handling this."

"Hm, well, city police aren't the most—the most effective from what I've seen. Besides, this one is different."

"Go on," Wei says, nodding toward the curtain.

"That's Piroja," says Sara. "Great nurse, just started here a couple of months ago, knows more than the interns, more than a few of the doctors, and certainly a lot more than me!"

"Sounds like a find. That her husband?"

"Uh-huh."

"Well, looks like he had a round taken out of him. By her?"

"Seems to be. But Wei, it's all so odd. Piroja is such a gentle thing."

"So what happened? He beats her, she picks up a hammer to make it stop?"

"A meat tenderizer. *My* meat tenderizer; I gave it to her as a present. They're new to the Maritimes, you know, came here from India."

"So, you provided the weapon? This won't go well for you," Wei says, eyes laughing.

"Yeah, yeah. But, no, Wei, he's not like that either. I mean, she says he isn't, and I believe her. The husband's a doctor. But when I asked her why she hit him, maybe she thought he was an intruder, she just starts going on about her mother, and it all gets very strange."

"Okay," says Wei. "Let me have a crack." And with that, he goes behind the curtain, introduces himself to Piroja and to Pradeep, and starts to take notes about the raw details. Pradeep keeps mumbling that he must have done something wrong and that he does not want Piroja to get into trouble; Piroja keeps mumbling about her mother (Sara was right) and how she never should have followed them across the ocean.

"Your mother lives with you?" asks Wei, looking up from his notes.

"No," says Piroja. "My mother—doesn't live." Wei raises his eyebrows. "She's dead, two years ago."

"Hm, I'm sorry. But what has this to do—?"

"She—she never knew about my marriage until after ... that is, she would not have liked Pradeep. He is Hindu and I am Parsi." Piroja looks up at Wei with exasperation. How will this Canadian police officer know what she is talking about, mixed marriages, ghostly mothers, if she herself is unclear?

Wei looks at the young woman and sees that she is troubled but also sees that something has happened between her and her husband that is not what he usually sees. This is no husband stepping out and the wife finding out, or rowdy drunks going from amorous to homicidal. There is something else going on, and Wei instinctively closes his notebook and looks into Piroja's eyes, a skill he has learned can communicate a number of things, but in this case is sent and read as a simple, I believe you, don't you worry.

"How long have you been here, Halifax, I mean?"

"Not long," says Piroja.

Pradeep, struggling to push himself up with his elbows, tries to speak: "Dartmouth. We live in Dartmouth. We work here at the hospital, both of us. Are we—in trouble?"

"Well, apart from the head trauma, no, I don't think so."

"Have we—have we broken any law?"

"No, I don't think so. But for my report, I do need to write something. You seem like good people. But the meat tenderizer?"

"It is," sighs Piroja, "an incredibly long story. And I don't think you would believe me." She looks at Pradeep. "You wouldn't either."

Pradeep leans over and puts a hand on Piroja's shoulder. She looks down at her feet. Slowly, assuredly, with no hesitation and with crescending rhythm, her left foot begins to tap.

Fruit of thy loins

That was a close one.

"I cannot believe this is happening to me."

Hm, does seem a bit farfetched, doesn't it? They sent Jamshed to a head doctor to get me out of his head, or at least that was the logic. But he didn't have generations from either side of him closing in on his ears!

"I cannot believe. This. Is. Happening."

Well, might as well make the best of it. I know I would in your shoes, and believe me, I am as close as close can be to crawling into your slippers.

"You. You, I could take. I think. But Mummy, she was just too much. She almost had me kill Pradeep."

Yes, wouldn't bode well for any of us—you, father, me. Good thing he has a skull you could chop wood on.

"What am I to do? If I thought it was crazy to talk to you, it must be doubly crazy to talk to Mummy. She's dead, you're not yet born. This is too, too much."

Well, there is a way around this.

"Do tell. I am either going to prison or my husband will leave me lest he get murdered in his sleep. So nothing you can say can make things worse."

Spoken like a true Khargat. Leastwise, what I know of them. Of us. Mother dear, lean in closer, have a listen, and do as I say.

"Mrs Khargat?"

Piroja looks up to the kindly face of the constable, who is clearly concerned for some unknown reason.

"I'm sorry?"

"You seemed gone there for a few moments. Tapping your toe to beat the band, didn't seem to hear a word we said."

Piroja looks at the officer, over at Sara who has reappeared in the room, and across at Pradeep. All share that same look of dismay.

"I have something to say," says Piroja, breathing deeply. "I want you all to listen."

Wei Devlin nods and leans back on his heels. Sara and Pradeep look at her intently. Piroja begins.

"I have a story to tell. I think I was trying to keep it inside. But now it's all out with how I acted, isn't it? When I was a young girl, my mother and father made it very clear that I would grow up as a Parsi, that I would marry a nice Parsi boy, and we should have a few, not many, Parsi children. But I grew up fast and in a world that they did not understand. I was a Parsi, I am a Parsi, but I am not everything Parsi. Not all Parsis are everything Parsi, because we change, adapt, alter. I could understand this on the outside, but on the inside, I still heard my parents' voices."

Piroja looks over at Pradeep, who is looking back at her intently. She takes a deep breath and continues.

"And those voices, God bless them, told me that marrying a non-Parsi was sinful and mischievous, and, above all, sacrilegious. Oh, my parents would never have said so in so many words, not outright, just in a way that would make me feel guilty inside. And so I grew up, fast, and then I met Pradeep and we—we fell in love," and at this point she reaches to squeeze Pradeep's hand, "and we married, but in secret, and what a toll it took. It was flying in the face of everything my parents wanted for me. And so, something inside went awry. I thought, I felt ... I had to get rid of *something*, but I did not know how to do this. Remember, Pradeep, when Parvin's urn came down on your head? I think I set it intentionally on the ledge like that, so it would fall on you. And then today—only at this moment do I understand. Because, you see, earlier in the day, before you came home, I began to think about children. Yes, children. Yours, Pradeep, yours and mine." At this, Pradeep forces a smile, unsure if she is describing a possible or impossible future.

"Yours and mine. A Parsi and a Hindu. And, you see, my mind could not take that. I took my parents' wishes from heart to hand. I broke, Pradeep. I struck out at you because I could not strike back at tradition. If I had not attacked you, I would have taken you—taken you to me as soon as you arrived home, do you understand? I would have taken you, and you and me, we would have, well. Well." Piroja looks over at Sara who is now beaming broadly. She looks up at Wei Devlin who is frowning, not quite sure where all this is leading, but is fairly confident that there will be no charges and, more than likely, no future occurrences of violence with this particular couple.

"Well, that was it. Either we take this to a fully different level, Pradeep, children that are neither Hindu or Parsi or perhaps both, or we—or I—end things in the only way I could do at the moment, a meat tenderizer and a swing at the only man I have ever loved. And so—Constable Devlin, is it?—that was what I was contemplating in my toe-tapping reverie. A sea change. A momentous decision." Then, to her husband: "Pradeep, this is what I am thinking. That we can start a family, and we do not have to wait. We are young. We are strong."

"Oh, Piroja, yes, wonderful," Pradeep exclaims, trying to prop himself up but thinking better of it when his head starts to throb.

"That was so beautiful," says Sara.

The only man I have ever loved'? I told you to make up a story, Mother, but did you have to embellish it with such, well, sappy language?

"I was hard pressed," Piroja explains to Sunny, oblivious to the short-lived toe tapping that accompanies this ever-brief revisitation.

"You try making up a rationale for bonking your husband in the forehead."

Kudos to you, then, Mother. And so long for the time being.

If the others notice Piroja's brief recurrence of toe tapping, they make no mention of it. Sara is thinking about baby showers for her new friend and Pradeep is wondering if love has to hurt this way always. Wei Devlin, for his part, snaps the folding cover to his clipboard shut, half salutes, and with a gruff but sincere goodbye is through the curtain and heading out of Emergency. Stranger things have happened, he thinks, but he really cannot remember when. Still, his brow is still furrowed as he makes his way back to his car. Struggling with difference. Marrying out. What makes people seek the same, and what makes them resist it, he wonders. In the car, he remembers, is a dead rat with one foot sliced off. In his report he will write of a man so distraught at his wife's affair that he would exact revenge in the oddest of ways.

"So's I finds this dead thing," the man has told Devlin, "and I cuts off its front foots, there, and spreads its little paw, and I sticks it in me wife's birthday cake, I does. Thirty-two candles and a rat's hand, waving goodbye, it was. So's when I takes it into her, she doesn't notice at first, 'til I says each of these candles there is for a good year you've had, woman. And see these nine separated over here on this part? Them's for the nine good ones we's had together. And this last one, this black paw thing, it's for you, dear, for the rest of your life. That was what I said, and that was all, didn't lay a hand on her, officer, and she looks at me and blanches and next thing I knows, she's lying there dead on the floor. Yes, didn't lay a hand on her, not mine, not the rat's, but sure as sure, I killed her, I did. And I'm not feared of taking the penalty. The rest of the rat, you knows, was going to make appearances bit by bit on things for my wife, you see; a rat's ear in a bouquet of flowers, maybe, a cheek with whiskers intact alongside her tea. I was that mad at her for cheating. But then she goes and cheats me out of my revenge, too, dying like that. Constable Devlin, tell me what it is I's done. And if I could bring this rat back to life, maybe she'd come back to life, come back to me, too, don't you know? Take it, please, take this rat and get rid of it. Wish'd I'd never found it. Wish'd I'd never found her. All these wishes, what's a man to do with them?"

Devlin opens the car door and looks into the back seat, assuring himself the wrapped rat is still there. Feeding vermin to a wandering spouse, tenderizing a forehead to get closer. Devlin sighs, slips behind the driver's wheel, and thinks about the report he has to write back at the detachment, with a footless rat sitting on the desk beside him. He has no idea why his grandfather, his father were the marrying-out kinds, and most likely he will be, too. He looks up at the hospital, makes a silent well-wishing nod in the general direction of where he left the head-bandaged Hindu and the story-telling Parsi, starts up the patrol car, and steers it out toward the detachment.

The question

Piroja stares at the letter she began to write so much earlier, picks up a pen, and resumes where she left off.

> —and say, what has my daughter done with her life?! Papa, I am finishing this letter to you some days after I began it, and the intervening days have been very eventful.
>
> All this has led me to think of children very seriously, however complicated this might be by religion and being in a new place. But I have not made up my mind, so I seek your counsel. Shall I bring a child into this world in a way that would be good and would make you proud, or should I ponder this further? Perhaps someone like me is destined never to have children, and that is something I will have to consider, however unhappy that makes me. I await your advice, and I remain your loving daughter.
>
> Piroja

Either/or

There are some stories just impossible to tell because the tellers are in no telling condition. There is only she and me, she dead for a ripe period of time, me unborn and unlikely to be, given the choices being made, although thanks to my quick-wittedness, my mother (is she even my mother, do I dare call her that, if I cannot ensure my own birth, which raises the spectral question of, if I can't, then who am I?) has made such a narrative that could, finally, bring me into being.

"But a child, now? I said it would happen, and I think it is what I want to have happen, but not because of her."

Not just any child.

"Oh, you again. I thought you were off trying to be born."

Not just any child?

"You mean, you?"

Could be. Life is a mystery.

"Did my father ever want to swat you one across your face?"

Oh my, yes. All the time. But that impulse faded with maturity. Or with an acknowledgement that it would do little good.

"Might have made him feel better."

Perhaps. Did the meat tenderizer incident make you feel reprised?

"That was different. And mean. You are mean, I mean. And that was different because it had nothing to do with you."

Everything has everything to do with me, thank you very much.

But Piroja goes off into a long-winded explanation about how if she tries to have a child, what proof would there be that her mother would not still try to have her kill her husband, and worse. Maybe such homicidal tendencies would turn to the unborn child. I am very well aware that is, or could be, me. No, she tells me, she cannot do this; it is too difficult.

"I cannot have a child. My mother. What will she … ?"

Perplexing. Vexing. Distrexing.

"'Distrexing' is not a word."

Should be. Some words need to be brought into existence just like some people. Ha. Distrexing: vexed to distress. No?

"No. I will have to tell Pradeep I cannot bear children."

But you want me—that is, children, no?

"Maybe some day, yes, certainly. But if my mother makes me do things …"

Then we will just have to change her mind.

"Will you talk to her? God, what am I saying? Asking one wisp to talk to another."

Hm. Distrexing. But with the way things have been going, not implausible.

"There is no way around it. I will have to talk to Pradeep. Otherwise, the Lal and Khargat lines, they end here."

And what about me?

"Your choice. You seem to have a pretty strong existence. Can't you just get born to someone else?"

Impossible. Besides, you're my mother. What sort of child would I be if I abandoned you?

"At this point, I would say a very loving child. Sometimes you have to know when to leave."

I do not know if that will happen. Knowing when to leave, that is.

"Then I shall have to do it for you. I know—I know when to leave. It is clear now. Leaving is the only choice, the only chance."

Mama, I have this feeling this isn't about me anymore.

"No, I don't suppose it is. Or ever was. Now, I have to talk to Pradeep."

Neither/nor

"Aaaack! What are you? Demon, get away!"

I am no demon. I am—I will be—oh, we've been through all this before Grandmama.

"Things are going so well now, just look at her: She is not only going to refuse your nasty child-thing business, but will leave that good-for-nothingness of a husband and find a good Parsi boy. You will see. Now, be gone."

Where would I go to?

"Go to that place where waifs like you go, I do not know, how would I know, was I never born? No—born, lived, died, the whole shebang—a lot more than you will ever know, this I know, so go, go, go!"

Not until we have a nice intergenerational chat.

"Inter ... ? Listen, Sunny, there are no generations between us. You heard my daughter. The Khargat and Lal lines end here. You and I, there is no ancestral-descendant thing here, none at all. Why, if you were alive, I would have to have someone do the nasty business to you."

Grandmother? Then is Piroja right? Not only would you assassinate my father for your selfish ends, but me as well? A baby?

"You are no baby. You are not born, so you are not a baby. You have not been conceived. You are not even an idea of a conception. Listen to my daughter, she is becoming bright again, and when she finds a Parsi boy, she can have a baby of her choosing. Listen to her and go fly off to the place of unborn things."

I have a story to tell you.

"Oh, always with the stories. Why more stories? Why can't we just talk instead of all this story-schmorying? Not that I want to talk. I just want quiet. Peace of mind. Is that so much to ask?"

There is a time for everything, dear Grandmama, yes. And so I promise you this. One last story, and then I will go. Forever if you want. If you listen to my story.

And to my (putative) grandmother's credit, she rolls her eyes and flaps her translucent arms and sighs and says, "Fine, tell me the story and then go for good." So here I am, like Scheherazade trying to keep her wits and, while she's at it, her head about her, but unlike her I am not looking for a story that hangs off a cliff to keep me alive for three years of nightly tales, no, because my task is daunting and swift and present, and I have to do what no one else has ever had to do. I have to storytell myself into birth, and it is not about convincing a distillery-owning dastur or his level-but-strong-headed daughter, no, for that would be easy, and they would both have me come into the world, half-this, half-that, it would matter not. No, I need to convince the very same woman to whom I had brought the possibilizing of her own child. And the only story that might convince her of this is her own story, and though she knows it well, could it be that, like all stories of our own, they might be forgotten, and when retold, re-remembered, they take on new life, just as I hope to? Is that the role of storytelling—not to bring newness into the world, but to tell us what is already there? Yes. That is the story I must tell, this story of her life, before and afterward and forever.

So listen to me, Grandmother mine, listen to the songs of butterfly wings and algorithms and the voices of the born-and-died as well as this voice that floats on wind to you, waiting for future moments. Remember a time when monuments were built for regal approaches. Do you remember ambling by the sea in a Bombay far away, and your chance encounter with another twelve-year-old, an awkward and unseemly child who could barely string two words together so entranced he was by how your eyes, light and free, hid behind them the wisdom of the ages; do you recall how you captured his heart then and swallowed him whole?

And Grandmother, not a day went by after that not-so-chance meeting that he did not dream of you. Years later, he waited on you every Friday in Schroff's store, wished to be your everlasting servant, and did eventually become so. Do you remember? But it took time. The ice pick held close to his own head—a suicide about to happen, his life in your hands—the resistance of family ("He is touched," they told you, and while you did not disbelieve them, you felt the odd touchingness of his touchedness), followed by the ten-year courtship, your final and not-so-begrudging agreement to marry him—what power, what responsibility, and yet, what craziness!

"Yes ... yes, there were those who told me I was a fool to submit to such blackmail, and at first I was so caught up in the intensity of it all, but then ..."

But then, you began to see the entire romance as a metaphor, a story in itself. You knew he would never kill himself, that such bad deeds would only follow bad thoughts and bad words—and those he was not capable of. You knew that, but this was a story of excess, of abandon, and ultimately, of love. You knew this. You knew, and that is why you did not send him packing, tail between his knock-kneed legs. You knew that there was something there. And you see, Grandmother, I knew this too, call it a wisdom from before the grave, before the womb, and I knew that you and he would meet and grow and love, and this would be passed down to your children and their children.

"But the boys. My sons ..." Parvin begins to weep, quietly and without tears—for how does a ghost issue tears from ducts long since barren?—but a weeping that gathers force as she speaks.

"First Sarosh. After he—I could not imagine. But then when Jamshed came to me, the mango, and then there was beautiful,

beautiful Behram. When he was taken from me"—and now she sobs, words barely utterable and hardly uttered, yet flowing forth— "when he was taken, it was the end of everything, and the times I wished he had lived and I did not, if only, if only. Behram, on the train, we travelled with our dead child, oh …"

And I wept with you, Grandmother— tears at least as full, as intangible as they are for you— that through all my efforts I had brought only grief through my love for my grandparents and the love I could only know from not yet being born, the grief wrapped in love. And then, the not-yet-final chapter, the garden in the distillery, the butterflies. We spoke, and you converted our grief to a greater love, and from that, from that …

"… came Piroja. My beautiful, darling, wonderful, gracious Piroja."

From that came your beautiful, darling, wonderful, gracious Piroja, your daughter and my mother. And then she grew and matured and began to love—as is her right—and she has chosen well, just as you chose well. She has taken the best thoughts of deep affection, turned them into magnificent words of care, and let them mature into wondrous deeds of love. She has taken this from you, your love, and turned it into something her own. And yours.

"And … and … mine." And Parvin releases her weeping now so that it is one long pitch, sustained as only those who cannot breathe can sustain such a cry, and in the midst of this, the tears turn real, water gushes forth, fills the air and splatters on to courtyards and gardens and floorboards, in Surat and Bombay and Nowgong and York and Dartmouth and all places out and in-between, on ship decks and highways and bridges, dampening the wings of butterflies and tingeing the faces of the yet-unborn, soon and future, and inconsolably, at first—do not stop— then passively—do not cease— until finally, full of utter joy, tears fall and fall and fall with the ubiquity and gentleness of an autumn rain along the seacoast, warming and wetting a window on an older second-story walk-up.

In words, veritas

July 30, 1956

My dearest Piroja,

Your letter only just now arrived, and I am writing back to you immediately as I know I must. As I have written to you before, it took some time for me to understand your decisions, and it is still difficult for me to abide your marrying out of our tradition. My saddest thoughts are for the children who will not be afforded their own navjote and will not be true Parsis. I see this as a loss, and it saddens me. But in all of this, I do see you as my one and only daughter, and I hold you precious in my heart. It does me a world of good to hear you are keeping your values, and I trust you will always hold them and impart them to your children, regardless of how they will be regarded in the community.

As you might see from my words, I hope with all my heart that you do have children. There is a very specific reason for this, which I will tell you after your first is born, and despite all my reservations, I wish for you and Pradeep to have children, and I look forward to that first meeting with my grandchild in ways you can hardly imagine. Your mother, my darling wife, would understand this as well, so put her distress out of mind. It has taken me a long time to arrive at this place, but here I am, secure, and it is with love I wish you well.

Your father,
Jamshed

The retraction

Fall raindrops streak down along the window facing out to the seacoast from the second-storey walk-up that Piroja and Pradeep call home. Piroja brings out the dhansak and sets it on the table. Pradeep sits there patiently, watching his wife, watching her bring food to the table in a manner that has always intrigued him. Today, however, she is more sullen than ever, and when she sits, she does not look at him, does not meet his eye, and she begins to eat before checking with him, as she always does, about whether there is need for salt or drinking water or anything else. Although there never is such a need, always she checks, except not this time. Silently, she takes mouthful after mouthful, and in this manner finishes her entire bowl before Pradeep is half done. Then she sits there, staring at her empty bowl, her hands in her lap. When Pradeep finally, and with great pains, there being little saliva in his mouth owing to the current state of communication, finishes his dhansak, he looks at Piroja with a question mark. She does not return his gaze but begins to speak. She has something to tell him, she says, she has something that is difficult to say, especially after all they have been through. Now she has to tell him this, this very difficult thing, that he should leave her, find someone else; they can do that in this country, she will be fine on her own, but she cannot be with him because she cannot do what she and he want most, to bring new lives into the world. And then she is done, silent again.

Pradeep does not ask her how she knows she cannot have children, whether she has seen doctors, but what he does know is that he will never leave his Piroja, not for this or any reason. And then he stands and goes to her and stands behind her and puts his hands on her shoulders and looks down at her, from behind, looks down at the crest of her head. He stares into this point and it becomes a light. He cannot think of anything to say, just looks in at the light and cannot see anything else, only a brightness that shines out of a shock of black hair and becomes everything and all things, and soon he cannot even feel his hands on her shoulders or his feet on the floor, only an urging from his deepest inside to hold on to this moment. And.

Piroja does not ask why he does this, this shift over to stand behind her and touch her that way and then go still. She laments in silence that she is lying to her husband to protect him and the children they will never have. How could this happen in their lives together? Has she been so sinful that this has been brought upon her; has all her desire for producing good deeds out of good words out of good thoughts gone still? His hands are leaden on her shoulders yet somehow soft. From the corner of her eye, Piroja can see a glint of light bouncing off Parvin's urn, safely tucked away on a thigh-high hutch so as to pre-empt any further urnish accidents. A glint of light that does not so much catch her attention as drag itself into her pupil after piercing her cornea to settle and flatten brightly on the retinal wall. She does not so much as look at it as have it look at her, and it becomes a tunnel, and she cannot see anything else, only a brightness that shines off the curve of the Asha urn. This light becomes everything and all things, and soon she cannot feel hands on her shoulders or presence from behind, only an urging from her deepest inside to hold on to this moment. And.

Piroja cannot know that this moment carries with it a memory of her mother's from her first years in Nowgong, about how Parvin and Jamshed travelled to Khajurao soon after Piroja was born. Parvin did not know what there was in Khajurao on temple walls, had only heard rumours of the provocative poses, and not until she was there did she see what those giggles and shushed whispers were about.

She was transfixed before the friezes, gluttonously taking them all in, memorizing their detail, the representation of bodies, men and women, posing and reposing, this one on his knees and paying particular attention to, oh my, and that one with a knee draped over her shoulder and pleasure folding out through, my goodness, and on and on. One that held her rapt was a figure of a woman, her torso a hairpin to her legs, presenting herself as she held herself, hands held firmly about her hips, and behind her, pressed in close but not so close, the attentive viewer could not see the goings on, the pressing of flesh (those particular kinds of flesh) and the pressure of entrance and egress, of a lightness that brillianted out all other forms of vision, a position at once beyond recognition and fully compatible with how she remembered bodies—hers, Jamshed's—fostering each other, that night of the mangos that were no more than air. She always remembered that afternoon in the heat, getting hotter and looking at friezes as she protected her baby from the sun with a white cotton handkerchief.

Now, Parvin can smell dhansak, and she sees the couple in front of her, light all around them like a white cotton handkerchief, and then the subtlety of movements that disrobe with such ease and bowls that once held dhansak shifted on the table to allow a torso to lean forward and form a hairpin with accompanying legs that open apart, and from behind, the pressing in close, the pressing of flesh and the pressure of entrance and egress, and the light, now, the light so brilliant that, even as a ghostly apparition, Parvin shields her eyes. And then the light overwhelms her, and with the pleasure of skin that comes before her she sighs, for this is the way it is to be. Then, and only then, she closes her eyes (not out of fear of the light but in deference to modesty) for the final time and blows a kiss out to her daughter and her son-in-law and all that will come from them that will come back to her, and she says something in Gujarati that roughly translates to a breezy "Then this is so, and so it is fine because it is as it must be," which both Pradeep and Piroja think they hear but are so caught up in other matters that neither mentions or remembers it, a whoosh in passing. Afterward, as daylight creeps into darkness and they lie in a curl, all they will remember, if they remember anything at all, is a whisper amidst a rush of light. And.

Nurse, heal thyself

It comes as no surprise to Piroja when she finds herself a gravida (her medical training making it natural to refer to herself thus rather than as "being pregnant"). As a primigravida, she is aware she will undergo substantial bodily shifts with this first pregnancy. She does not, naturally enough, feel anything different until early December, a good six weeks after she and Pradeep shared their meal of dhansak on the kitchen table, as she liked to refer to that event euphemistically. No awareness of fallopian floating zygotes, no notions of implantations in endometrial linings until early December when she thinks to herself that, cycles being what they are, their coming late probably indicates something substantial.

Letters from Jamshed continue to arrive weekly, but it is the one all about losses, sadnesses, and encouragements, which she keeps safely tucked in her night-table drawer, that she reads and rereads as often as she can. Jamshed's other letters have been mostly full of daily routine, explaining that he thinks he might quit the distillery and go manage a small shop and guest house in Nowgong, how he will still have a part in the distillery, of course, having worked himself into a co-operative ownership of the successful liquor operation, and he would still make sure that the Asha produced was the finest, but he longed for a bit more contact in the city, plus there were many more Parsis now in Nowgong, and he was feeling more compelled to perform dasturly duties as he aged.

This had been in a letter handed to her by Nigel, the postman, an avuncular sort who met Piroja and Pradeep soon after they moved to Dartmouth. Whenever he would catch them at the door, he would stand there and talk for up to an hour, making them curious as to the efficiency of the post in their community. But Nigel would maunder on about the travelling he would do when he retired (though he already looked as though he had crossed seventy) and how he would love to take passage to India and visit Piroja's father (this he shared when he passed that letter over, its grey-blue stamps sparking his imagination). Piroja noticed he had three almost identical paper cuts on his right index finger. Yes, Nigel said, the hazards of working with such material, and she reached out to touch them lightly with the middle and index fingers of her left hand. The dull paper-cut pain turned to a tingle right away, which he thought odd but soon put out of mind, until the next day, when he returned and made a point of ringing the doorbell, hoping he was not catching Piroja asleep after a night shift. She was resting, dozing, but not asleep, and was genuinely happy to see Nigel. He held out his right index finger for her to inspect.

"Ma'am, can't explain this. I've had paper cuts almost every week of my life, and the thing is always the same. If they aren't too deep, it takes a couple days of throbbing, then they go all red, then maybe scab a bit, and then they just sit there for a week or two before starting to fade away. Well, ma'am, look here. You can't barely see where those cuts were, isn't that amazing? And you know why I'm telling you this? Because you touched them and they tingled, and now the cuts are gone. I know you're a nurse and all, but I come here to tell you, you have the healing gift, sure as shooting."

Piroja laughed this off and congratulated Nigel on having the mental ability to cure his wounds so quickly, assuring him that she had nothing to do with it.

"Mark my words, missy," Nigel said. "You have the healing touch."

Piroja thinks nothing of this until mid-January, about the time,

Piroja knows from her training, that little eyelashes and eyebrows are starting to form, when she is working in the burn ward, a tragic place at the best of times. The discomfort her patients feel seems muted compared to what she saw in Delhi, but formidable still for those who endure endless grafts, forcing them to hold themselves in sometimes grotesque positions, friezes to ease the pain. She is caring for one Mrs Dalbrent, who is better off than some because her burns are limited to a smaller area, but worse off than some in that it is her entire face that took the brunt of an exploding propane container. The shrapnel, thankfully, caught her only on one cheek and shoulder, but the fuel lit up and burned furiously before her son-in-law smothered the flames on her face. His actions were quick enough to prevent major third-degree damage, but the scorching took away all facial hair, giving her a plastic appearance. She was, when brought in, completely sightless, and the prognosis was not good. "We will have to see," the doctors kept saying, and Mrs Dalbrent appeared to take this in stride.

"Dearie," she said to Piroja one morning, "the things I've seen, it won't be so bad if I never have to see some of those things again. 'Course, there are things I never have seen yet and would like to, grandkids for one, but you know, so long's I can hear or touch them, 'twon't be so bad. Yes, the things I've seen, some of them, won't miss them 'tal."

Piroja was changing the bandages on Mrs Dalbrent's eyes when she suddenly lurched upward, and Piroja was afraid she had been too forceful in reapplying ointments.

"Oh, no, that's not it," said Mrs Dalbrent. "Just that there was such a tingle in me eyes, like they'd been touched by sparkles from the Good Lord. Strange sensation, but awfully pleasing."

"I'm sorry, Mrs Dalbrent, if I did anything to startle you. I will try to be careful."

"Dearie, you're the most careful nurse on this floor, let me tell you. So don't you worry. Just go about doing your job and telling me about your life, for it's quite a story you have, and I do enjoy listening."

The next day, when Piroja was removing the bandages, Mrs Dalbrent suddenly sighed rapturously, her arms thrown out to the sides as though she were leaning into the wind.

"What is it, Mrs Dalbrent?"

And the old woman turned her head slightly as if she were listening to a distant sound, but Piroja realized it was not listening that Mrs Dalbrent was attempting, but focussing. On her.

"Who would've thought my angel of mercy was so beautiful," she said.

"Mrs Dalbrent?"

"Oh, yes, you know, ever since yesterday when you tingled me with that soft touch of yours, I could feel light coming back in. I didn't say anything to the night nurse or to the doctor on rounds. Wanted to wait for you. And when you touched me eyes again, there was that tingle, and then there you were, my angel."

"You can see me clearly?"

"Like a vision, dearie, like a vision."

Piroja thinks little of this—Nigel's cuts were probably so superficial they healed over in a day, and the doctors *did* say that Mrs Dalbrent's sight was not necessarily gone forever. But at the end of February, bundled up warm against the winter sea breeze howling across the harbour, Piroja is riding the bus back across the Angus Macdonald when she has her first experience of quickening, a slight tumble in her belly that she at first wills into being no more than a growling stomach, but no, this is definitely a physical tumble, a somersault even, and she smiles at that. No sooner has she let lips curl up in wonder than the bus comes to a sudden halt, right there in the middle of the bridge. Piroja, sitting right at the front, peers out through the frosty window and sees a car directly in front of the bus, sitting at an odd angle. The driver, a young man in his late teens, is struggling to get out, and as Piroja stands she sees what has happened. In front of the car lies a furry form, a large dog, and it is completely still. She can see the boy still struggling to get out of the driver's seat, can see his terror and before she realizes it, she has descended from the bus door and is scurrying to his side. The boy is crying uncontrollably now, "Didn't see it, just jumped out in front, oh my God, I've killed it," and Piroja can see that the dog, a German shepherd cross of some sort, is bleeding profusely, its front paws waving futilely as if it is reaching for something, a slight whimper coming from its open mouth.

Not knowing what she is doing, she reaches down and cups the animal's head in her hands, then kneels and cradles it in her arms and lap. The dog is still whimpering as she feels the life go out of it. And then the gathering pool of blood seems to dissipate—does it freeze to the pavement perhaps?—and as Piroja searches with her hands for the wound, she can find none, and then, as the boy cries, then shouts—the bus driver now at her shoulder also shouting—the dog raises his head, licks his lips, and struggles to his feet. If he could say he felt a tingle, he probably would, but instead, he looks up at Piroja and smiles a dog smile and darts a tongue out to lick her warmly right on the nose. And with that, he shakes himself, yawns, and trots off in the direction he was originally heading as if nothing untoward had occurred. Perhaps he was only stunned, thinks Piroja, and the blood, perhaps it was only a superficial wound, a capillary that poured out but then sealed. But this time, she is also filled with a sense of curiosity as she looks at her hands and feels, for the second time, a quickening inside.

Over the next three months, similar oddities seem to abound. Sara brings her niece to Piroja and Pradeep's for tea one day; the girl has a sore throat when she arrives, but after shaking hands with Piroja, the impending cold is suddenly gone. An old soldier, veteran of World War I, where his encounters with mustard gas made him permanently incapacitated, tells Piroja one day that when she visits him in the ward he can smell her rosewater perfume, but Piroja explains that she does not, is not allowed, to wear perfume at work. Still, he says, he smells it. Two days later, and for the first time in forty years, he is off his oxygen tank and can take full breaths without coughing. A young girl comes in with a burst appendix and is rushed to the operating theatre where Piroja is filling in as surgical nurse, and, after touching the girl's forehead and looking into her eyes, she says to the doctor, "I think her fever has broken," and the doctor, puzzled, decides to wait just a while longer before cutting her open. When he orders a renewed bank of tests, he is amazed when the white blood cell count comes back fully normal. He knows, says the doctor to Piroja, of hysterical pregnancies and mob-induced psychoses that emulate serious illness, but never has he seen this, a girl with a clearly burst appendix with no sign of peritonitis, with what appears to be an intact and perfectly healthy body, inside and out. Appendices, he says thoughtfully, do not repair themselves once ruptured. The girl said only that she had been in severe pain when she arrived, but after Piroja's touch, she felt a tremendous tingling in her belly and then felt fine.

Piroja is finally convinced, in late May, that she should now take time off from work, although she looks, to all the world, like a woman who may be somewhere in the midst of her second term but certainly not near the end of her third. The due date is mid-July, but she has been told, and knows from experience, to expect an earlier call. One early morning at the very end of June, she wakens Pradeep with a slight shake of his shoulder; her water has broken. Off they head, sleepily and with no undue alarm, to the hospital, where a final and stunning healing occurs. Before going in to the hospital, where she knows she will be for days to come, Piroja sits for a moment on a bench outside in the sun, trying to determine the most comfortable (or least uncomfortable) position. A car pulls up sharply to the curb and from the passenger side rolls a burly man, about forty, his face a bright crimson and his left arm cradling his right arm and what appears to be a small package. The man stands on the curb for a moment, reeling, then stumbles to the bench where Piroja sits, as he clearly hasn't the energy to make it to Emergency.

As he crumples beside Piroja, she looks into his arms and sees that what he is cradling and weeping over is not a package but his own right hand, still attached to his wrist by only a few tendons and a ridiculously thin hook of skin. The bone, Piroja can see, is cut cleanly through, sparkling white on both ends; the blood that emanates from the flesh seems nowhere near as severe as it should be, and the cut looks very surgical, leading Nurse Piroja to surmise it was inflicted by a very powerful blade. There is no question that the man will lose this hand, she thinks.

And with that she leans over to touch his cheek—much to his surprise, for in his shock he has not even seen her sitting there. He opens his mouth wide, acknowledging the tingle on his face, and turns into Piroja as she leans down and places both her hands on his disastrous wound, one on the fingers and knuckles of the all-but-detached hand, the other on what will eventually become the stump. Touching him like this, she feels remarkably awake, and the man urghs and ugghs a statement of what he will later remember as a recognition of electricity flying through his arm. His head drops as he loses consciousness, and then there is a flurry of activity as orderlies rush about and a stretcher is brought and the man disappears into the hospital.

Three weeks later, when she remembers this, Piroja asks Sara what happened to that man who lost his hand the day she was giving birth. Sara tells her that it turned out to be a remarkable story; the man came in with his friend and they blathered on about him cutting off his hand at the mill, but were comforted by nurses and doctors alike who, after inspecting the wound, said, yes, there might be some nerve damage, but the blade must have merely bounced off the wrist, had somehow not cut through anything more than the surface skin, and though the bone was bruised, it was unbroken. After a few minor stitches and a tetanus shot, the man was sent home, as good, or pretty much, as new. And Piroja nods and smiles and wonders, since that would be the last time in her life that she would lay healing hands on another and see such spectacular results.

Mother and son reunion

"Is that you inside me?"

I don't know.

"Hurt and injury goes away with my touch. Is that you doing this?"

I don't know.

"When you are born, will you stop—I mean, will you visit, talk to me, once you are, well, born?"

I don't know.

"You have worked this hard, worked all these years, first with my father, then my mother, now with me, all for this grand task of bringing yourself into corporeality, and with a wisdom that outstrips learned sages, and you can only utter 'I don't knows' at me?"

Yes. Yes, I suppose that is true.

"I could feel you growing in me, do you know that? But I do not know if it is you growing in me. Is the you that talks to me the you inside me?"

I don't know.

"No, of course not. This is maddening, that you do know, hm?"

I am sorry, Mother. You are right, this is most unusual, and yes, I have worked and existed in nonexistence for this explicit purpose, and now here I am stymied. Am I inside you or not? Am I both, or neither? It is as if—as if a coin is still spinning in the air, and I cannot predict how it lands, heads or tails.

"Do you know what I think? That you are inside of me, and that when you are born, there will be no more 'you,' or rather, the 'you' will be in the flesh, and then we can all live normal lives: I can go back to healing people's injuries like a regular nurse instead of through these supernatural events; you can go back to being the baby you have tried for half a century to become; and we can all go forward with our lives."

You may be right. Sometimes a child has to learn from its mother.

"And sometimes, a mother from her child, as I believe I have. But things are about to be different now, aren't they?"

Yes, Mother, I think you are right. But still, I don't know.

First and again

The cry following first breath can be especially spectacular or exasperatingly quiet or normal, but it is always a cry. Breath, taken in deeply, dries the former humidity profoundly, shifts midstream from liquid to gas, from cocoon to brave new world, from amniotic sac to the harsh surrounding air. That is the way it is supposed to be.

Pradeep, for all the time he has spent in hospitals, for all his experience in watching the anxious families and friends that accompany the patients, looks just like he is one of them now, which, at this point he is. The expectant father. Not carrying a handful of cigars, not pacing frown-faced in the waiting room, but not holding hands with his birthing partner, gowned, masked, and watching his child burst into the world. Instead, Pradeep is standing fitfully in the doctors' lounge. Every time the door opens, he jumps out of his shoes—and certainly his heart jumps out of his chest—but so far the door openings have only signified the comings and goings of fellow doctors. He clutches in his left hand, holding it low and to the outside of his left knee, a delicately wrapped must-be-a-bottle gift, and with it the explicit instructions from Jamshed, who has sent the finest and latest example of Asha by air so that Pradeep can open it only upon the baby's first cry, take a capful (as should Piroja), and then wet his little finger and dampen the baby's mouth with this tiniest flavour of the rum. After that, Jamshed has instructed him in writing, he should share the Asha with all his friends, making sure to make short work of the bottle. This all presses on Pradeep's mind: how to be a good son-in-law—Jamshed, after the longest time, has not only acknowledged Pradeep's presence in Piroja's life but now seems to relish their marriage and has been wholeheartedly looking

forward to this, his first grandchild—and how to be a good father—
what he will have to learn, how he will have to be, all the things
that will change in his life. But first, a birth must happen, and to
that end, Pradeep waits nervously in the doctors' lounge, waiting.
Again the door pops open, again Pradeep leaves his shoes under a
chair and his heart stuck to the ceiling, and Sara bolts in, grinning,
"Come, doctor—new daddy, come quick, it's a—come quick, come
quick, come now!"

If Jamshed came into this world reluctantly, fearful of all that shift-
ing from a place of liquid to one of air would bring, if his hesitancy
was not an out-and-out refusal but a wait-and-see-ness, if his desire
to stay within a comfort zone, as they say, made him wildly uncomfortable with his new life, and if, in diametrical opposition, newborn
Piroja was eager and unhesitating, then this new child, new generation, born into a new time and a new continent, was a baby indiffer-
ent to time altogether. Indeed, not a sigh or a cry cracked from newborn lungs, though mother and baby were most certainly in the best
of health (*"You're doing fine, Mother,"* a disembodied voice echoed
the doctors' reassurances, and none noticed that during the labour
Piroja's foot slowly but methodically waved back and forth), and the
new baby was swaddled and umbilical severed all without a noise.

The only sounds were the rustlings of fabric on fabric and the
odd whisper of mask-breathing until said baby, as if with all the
intention and purpose in the world, stretched an arm back—with
such decisiveness the nurse dropped a clean cotton swab—with fingers extended, then slowly retracted thumb and then little finger
and subsequent fingers so that all that was left was a pointing finger,
pointing back and up, again with such absolute certainty that multiple sets of eyes looked up in the direction of the pointing finger,

looked up at the vector created and saw the object of such pointed-ness, the operating theatre wall clock, for it seemed the baby was in some dire need to point out to those in the room, the hospital, the world itself, that time was of the essence, that time was nigh, and that the time was right now exactly one minute before midnight on the last day of June in 1959.

Gender wending

"Congratulations, it's a—" is always followed by the enunciation of what will follow that child for an entire life. That question, coming from kith and kin, "Is it a—?" results in either/or possibilities for the parents, who can be proud in saying either/or, because the response is always the same, "Wow that's great," which apparently shows the relative unimportance of the question to begin with. There are, of course, historical moments that make such declarations relatively relevant, whether a concern about boy children floating down the Nile or girl children abandoned in the woods. The question and statement are not without merit, but they do have a curious amount of import when times are such that the answer should not carry such importance.

So when Sara comes to Pradeep and rushes him down the corridor and imparts the all-important news to the beaming father, he, thrilled and enthralled, rushes in to see said baby and flushed mother. Piroja is cuddling the not-sleeping child who looks up at her in such a way as to accentuate the Madonna image.

"Pradeep!"

"Piroja! You look—this is—my God, my God."

Piroja laughs. "I am *so* tired."

Pradeep laughs. "Yes, I know. This is—wonderful."

"Yes. Wonderful."

The two of them, father and mother, look at each other; this the first time they have been in the hospital together since Constable Devlin visited them with problems about reports of meat tenderizers. Pradeep opens the bottle of Asha and spills several droplets outside the intended cap-vessel, anointing the room with the sweet smell of distilled sugar. As per instructions, he throws back the cap, feeling not rum but a sense of duty slide down his throat. He refills the cap and proffers it to Piroja, who is, by this time, laughing at his clumsiness, which results in a third of the capful anointing the blanket and pillowcase. She lets him pour the golden rum into her mouth, having been previously instructed by her father what this meant to him. And then Pradeep is scouring the empty cap with his little finger, bringing it to his nose to ensure there is a scent of rum, allowing the finger to drop down purposefully to hover around the baby's head and then gently letting it touch the baby's lips.

Piroja laughs. "From your grandfather, my precious," she says. "I think he likes it."

Pradeep is smiling, happy, but responds curiously, thinks Piroja. "He? You mean Jamshed?"

"No, silly, the baby."

"Yes, *she* does seem to like it. She is gorgeous."

She? Piroja mouths the female pronoun but does not utter it. She. In the delivery room, filled and fulfilled by the voice of her unborn, Piroja had not even bothered to check when the infant was brought to her arms. She did not hear the doctor and nurses talk about the beauty of the little girl, for how could she hear that when for oh-so-long she had been visited by *him*, by Sunny? (But was Sunny a son? The voice was decidedly husky and what she would call male, but, in all that time, the child had never referred to itself as "himself," so maybe this was a huge, elaborate trick?) Yet so sure was Piroja that she was giving birth to Sunny-the-son that she had not even done the obligatory genitalia check for gender confirmation. So she now makes a mental note to check, but not right away, for that would seem too strange, and there has been too much strangeness thus far in her married life.

"Yes," says Piroja, looking down at the baby. "She is gorgeous."

When Sara rushed, beaming, into the doctors' lounge, imploring Pradeep to follow her, "It's a girl, it's a girl, it's a girl" was what she kept shouting. Pradeep is mildly alarmed that Piroja might have erred in assessing their child's sex, but he puts that down, understandably, to fatigue.

"She." Piroja says this aloud now as if she were trying out a possible name. She. Then does this mean that Sunny is yet to be born? This thought lingers and troubles Piroja because, through their conversations and sessions together, of which there were many over the term of the pregnancy, she was not altogether certain if she would bear more children or if the first would be her only child. And if this child did not emerge as Sunny, then who was it? And where was Sunny? She stretches and starts tapping her foot manually, hoping that might inspire a visitation (though it never has before), for here she is, questioning what a gendered pronoun might possibly mean, questioning as she looks down on her little one; how *she* could be *he*? Was this the child? Yes, thinks Piroja. Of course. He.

The name game, Soona or later

It is the third day after the birth, and Piroja is getting ready for discharge. In VG, they often keep mothers and babies longer, especially after premature births, but the health of the three-weeks-early baby is not considered precarious. Piroja just wants to take her new family member home, and the hospital staff knows that Piroja's nursing instincts will enable her to take good care of the infant on her own. Pradeep sits by her bedside, nodding off, as he has just finished a night shift and, as he has for the last three nights, has followed such shifts with daytime patrol by Piroja's bed. She does not need the attention, but she enjoys the company, so it is a compatible arrangement; however, both are pleased it will end soon so they can bring their baby home.

Parsi or Hindu, Hindu or Parsi. That is the dilemma running through Piroja's brain. A name for their child. Thinking of her mother, her father, what it would mean to them, what it did mean to them to raise a child with strong Parsi faith. Having a non-Parsi father will mean their daughter will be forever relegated to non-Parsi status. The Parsi Panchayat would have it no other way, would say, "Teach her the Mazdayasnian ways, but there will be no navjote for your daughter." So, at the very least, the baby should have a Parsi name, thinks Piroja. A name that bespeaks the familial and ancestral history. But then there is Pradeep. He too has married out (as Constable Devlin might put it), and what is in it for him to fight for Parsi status for his daughter? Well, thinks Piroja, their daughter can and will be well-accepted as a Hindu, no matter what they do with a first name. But for her and the Parsis? She would have chosen her mother's own name for the child, for despite the ghostly presence and murderous aspirations, she now felt a peace between them (she was convinced that her mother had blessed her on the dhansak night). Why not call the child Parvin and be done with it? But perhaps that was too close. Her grandmother's name then, Soona, a sonorous name if ever there was one, and, not to make too light of it, easy enough for these Canadians to pronounce (you did not want a Dilshad or Firoszha or some other beautiful name to be constantly sound-butchered by Anglo mouths), and besides, she thinks, there is that comforting sound that only comes from the names of grandmothers and unborn ghosts. But no, there had to be a better path. Soona, Sunny, Sunil … ah.

"Sunila," she says to her husband. And she goes on to explain to Pradeep her process of religious connections and family orienting (leaving out the part about dead mothers and unborn sons—why complicate matters?), and most of all, she says, while it may resonate her own grandmother's name, the name Sunila is a good Hindu name, after all, is it not?

"Yes," nods Pradeep. "Yes. A fine Hindu name and a fine name for our daughter."

And they both look down at the little girl, Sunila, and wonder what she will grow into. She, for her newborn part, looks up, scrolls her hand back, and points at the ward clock, which now reads just after midday on the third of July.

That first year and beyond

It is not as if Sunila never cried, just that this proved to be such an irregular occurrence that she seemed to be the Girl Who Never Cried. It was almost as if the act of crying, utilized by most new-borns as pretty much the only way to register anything from hunger to fatigue to irritation to pain, was far too generic for young Sunila.

"Why cry?" she seemed to ask, and certainly would have if speech had not been beyond her, "when there are so many more meaningful ways to attain your desire?" Closing your eyes and frowning, for in-stance, was a clear indication to any caretakers that sleep was of the essence; waving both arms, fists clenched, back and forth in front of you was about as simple as you could get to request a bit of nourish-ment; an occasional gurgle and look of displeasure should get you changed soon enough; and if what you required was just a bit of at-tention, some quality time with Mother or Father or Assortment of Friends, then all you had to do was point. Scroll out a hand, retract thumb and excess fingers, and point at the person with whom you wanted contact, or point at the ceiling to have others engage in one-way conversations with you, or point at any numbered oval face, not only because these were in and of themselves engaging, but because you became quite a conversation piece, an article of amusement, and a joy to behold as the Girl Who Points at Clocks.

Crying was reserved for special occasions, and her parents cer-tainly heard her little whimpery wails every night as she dreamt of tetrahedrons crushing trapezoids, ellipsoids devouring parallelo-grams. Crying was also a tool for referencing pain, as it is in most of the mammalian kingdom, so the occasional tummy ache or un-comfortable position might be announced by Sunila's high-pitched banshee cry. Other than that, she not only maintained but nurtured her reputation as the Girl Who Never Cried, alternately known as the Such a Good Baby.

For Sunila, however, goodness had nothing to do with it, for while, even as an infant, she was having her own variety of good thoughts (that would later become good words and eventually good deeds, even if the Panchayat might say she was reciting only by rote, unable to fulfill true religious duties without being initiated into the faith), her intention for being was simply hedonism. In that she was just like any other baby, except little Sunila was going to maintain an element of this as a toddler, a child, and while growing up, for what would be the point of this existence, she would later explain to her closest friend, if it wasn't a ball of fun; the unfun life was not worth living.

She was never to meet her maternal grandmother or paternal grandfather, of course, as both shuffled off mortal coils well before her birth, but she was, through a variety of circumstances, to lock eyes with both Pradeep's mother, Nina, and Piroja's father, Jamshed. It was just days before her first birthday that grandmother Nina arrived on warming Atlantic shores to see the child she had always waited for.

"Parsi girls can be quite handsome," Nina had told her best friends in Delhi just before departing. "And so what if it came to this? I met this young Piroja, and I said then, what a handsome girl, and I am sure my granddaughter will be just the same." And when Nina arrives, dazed and sleep-deprived, she refuses Pradeep's suggestion that she sleep a few hours before meeting Sunila, who was herself taking an afternoon nap. "I have come this all this way, all this way," she says, her eyes involuntarily snapping shut, "the least I can do is stay awake for my darling granddaughter. Look at her, sleeping so sweetly." When Sunila does wake in half an hour, Nina, propped up in a chair beside her, bolts awake with such violent motions it would have frightened a less relaxed child. As it is, Sunila barely registers the intruding relative, appears to nod, and blinks twice to the smiling woman.

"She has my eyes," says grandmother Nina, looking proudly at Pradeep as if he had single-handedly crafted those orbs as a testament to a son's love for his mother. Sunila's eyes were large and round and had a hint of green and burnt orange when the sun hit them just right; Nina had small bulging oval eyes (that made her look a bit like a shivering toy poodle, Piroja thought but never said), both jet black, although one had an omnipresent blood blister, which gave her a bit of an Evil-Stepmother-from-Children's-Storybooks look (said Piroja to Pradeep one time, but one time only, for he shot her a look that was stern in both its agreement and its reprobation), but both son and daughter-in-law nodded agreeably, yes, she has your eyes, they are very similar (if only because you both have two each, thought Piroja, which made her smile, which made grandmother Nina smile because she thought, what lovely daughter-in-laws these Parsis can make, after all). Nina giggles a high-pitched, whinnying type of giggle that is both ingratiating and grating.

Nina's visit lasts only ten days, but during this time she dotes and fawns over Sunila, who, in turn, smiles, gurgles, and points a great deal of the time. "I will die a happy, happy woman," says Nina triumphantly as she buys a pair of ridiculous pink socks for her granddaughter. Together, as an extended family, they see the sights, enjoy meals together, play with little Sunila, and at the end of the visit, Nina again says, hugging and kissing both son and daughter-in-law at the airport, "I will die a happy, happy woman!" She leaves exactly one week after Sunila's first birthday (a low-key affair, marked by grandmotherly cooing and spoiling) and returns to tell her friends how she was right, that her son's daughter is to die for. All this death talk, however, proves a bit too foreboding, and within three months, Nina begins to feel a pain in her legs, and six months later she sees a doctor who tells her the pain is not all in her head, and in nine months, she makes a trunk call to Dartmouth to tell her son not to worry about her and that, yes, she will die a happy woman but not to worry because that will not happen for some time, and twelve months after her visit she falls asleep and cannot be woken, which is when the family calls Pradeep and says there is nothing more to do. He asks if he should come, and they say come soon, and then call to say it is over, and if he can come home, that would be a good thing.

It is July 1961. Sunila has just turned two, and the young family packs a single large suitcase to travel to India for Nina's funeral and a chance for Sunila to see the land of her parents' births, and many more things, besides.

A little distillery, re-instilled

"Perhaps we should not have come together. Perhaps I should have come on my own. She was my mother." Pradeep is talking more to himself than to Piroja, soliciting her support which, of course, he receives.

"Nonsense. It is good that we can be here together as a family. It was important for Sunila to meet her grandmother and to see her off, even if she might not remember it. And it is important for me." Piroja leans into Pradeep, not so much with affection but the type of gesture that accompanies simple familial bond.

"Thank you, Piroja. And everybody in my family loved you. Could you tell? Even my mother's best friend Lakshmi-no-like! My mother gave her that name. She said, 'That Lakshmi—I don't like this, I don't like that, she's a real Lakshmi-no-like.' And yet, there she was, fawning over you, inviting you back."

"It was—it was a bit strange. As if she thought I was somebody—"

"Somebody she liked!" Pradeep laughs at this, Piroja joins in, and Sunila, quiet until now, chortles as well.

The three of them had spent the night in Jhansi where Piroja took her husband and child to see St Francis. She had not planned to take them inside the convent, just walk them around the perimeter, but who should they run across but Sister Ida. Piroja momentarily considered the idea of hiding her head and hoping to go by unrecognized, but it all happened so fast, and Sister Ida let out such an audible gasp, and then grinned broadly and ushered Piroja into the compound while chattering, "Married, such a gorgeous child, star pupil, always my favourite," and under her breath, directed just at Piroja, "Never did understand that business of rushing you out like that, girls will be girls, after all, and it worked out in the end, what a fine husband, and what a fine child." Piroja just smiled through it all, explained to Pradeep that Sister Ida had always been quite excitable, without going into details of girl versus boy football matches and bodies and lips and her own considerable excitement such a long time ago. Their visit at the convent lasted an hour, culminating with tea with the Reverend Mother who, if she remembered anything about the acceleration-cum-expulsion of Piroja, clearly did not let on, plying them instead with tales of how the convent had hit hard times, lacked funds to support the school, but they were making a go of it as they had always done.

And now they are on the same bus from Jhansi to Nowgong that Piroja had ridden so many times at Christmas and summer vacations, on the long road home. This time she has two others in tow, company she could not have imagined all those years ago.

"Your father," Pradeep says after some half hour of silence, "what will he think of me?"

Piroja shrugs.

"I mean, will he like me? Or do you think … ?"

Piroja shrugs again, but this time with a smile. Pradeep's discomfort is palpable, but it is actually good to see him distracted with something other than the recent ceremonies around his mother. And this is part of the game they play sometimes, Pradeep seeking words of support, she forthcoming, eventually, but always with play. It is, among so many other things, what Pradeep loves about Piroja and always has.

"Will he be angry with me, do you think? A Hindu boy, taking you away? Oh, I know he has written to you with his blessings, but meeting in person, it can mean something else."

Now Piroja laughs and touches Pradeep's shoulder gently. "It will be fine, my little Hindu boy," she says, and leans into him, this time with affection, and he leans back into her. They rest like this for the remainder of the journey, Sunila happily snoozing between them, and when they pull into the centre of Nowgong, the dust rising around the wheels of the bus as it settles to a stop, they can see a lone figure, slightly hunched, appearing and disappearing in the misty swirl of dust. It is Jamshed. They disembark and the slight figure of Jamshed moves toward them, dream-like. Then he stands before them, the dust fully settled, and he smiles, slowly, broadly. Piroja throws herself into his chest, laughing, weeping, and with his right arm he embraces her warmly.

"My daughter," he says, laughing now. "My daughter." Then he looks over at the nervous-looking Pradeep and his smile broadens further. "And my son."

"She has my nose," says Grandfather Jamshed, staring at the tiny thing that was carrying on a bloodline of sorts. They have returned to the distillery compound and are all becoming acquainted and reacquainted. Pradeep's insecurities about this meeting have vanished, and he and Jamshed talk and joke as if old friends. Jamshed, of course, is besotted with Sunila.

"Good to know the Parsi nose will find its way into Canada as well!" That little joke makes Pradeep laugh and makes Piroja laugh and it even makes Sunila laugh in a snorting high-pitched sort of way, and Jamshed follows with a roaring and dominating laugh that fills the room and is punctuated by his subsequent coughing, which, he tells Piroja later that evening, he has been doing a great deal of the past two weeks, but it is nothing serious. This still worries Piroja, reminding her of the last time she saw her mother, but Jamshed assures her he is okay, though he plans to soon retire from the distillery and move into Nowgong to rejuvenate his career as a well-respected dastur.

"I have been doing more and more work for the Parsis here," he explains, "as there has been an influx over the past two years. Not many, just a dozen families, but that is substantial, and I need so little to get by, now that …"

Piroja's eyes fill at this, thinking of the last time she saw her mother (alive) and what that break from her meant.

"It's all right, Piroja, I understand. I miss her, too, of course."

Piroja cannot begin to explain to her father about the events of the past several years, about Parvin's cantankerous post-mortem appearances, the homicidal encouragements, and the now-sanctified love she feels from her departed mother. None of it she can tell Jamshed, none of it. So her tears have to speak for this, and however he interprets it, that will have to suffice.

"She was a marvellous woman, your mother," Jamshed goes on, his eyes now also a little watery. "She put up with a great deal in her life. First," and here he laughs at the ridiculousness of the memory, "a suitor like me who threatens to kill himself if she does not marry him! Then Sarosh. Then Behram. And then you came to us …"

"But then I went away, didn't I, Papa? I was strong willed. Too strong willed. I had to have a career and a life of my own. I wake up at night sometimes and think that was a mistake, my bull-headedness. But, Papa—?"

"Ha. I think I know what you will say. That had you to do it over again, you would do it over again."

Piroja laughs. "Yes. That is what I was going to say."

"A Khargat through and through! Piroja—I too am sorry."

"For what, Papa?"

"For trying to coerce you. For enforcing my authority over you. It was as if I tried to beat the will out of you. Did you know that is how it felt, that I was beating you?"

"You never laid a hand on me."

"Did I need to? I tried to impose *my* will on you and *your* future, your marriage, all of that. "

"Papa, that was so long ago ..."

And the two of them say nothing more, for there is nothing more to say, but slowly their presence turns to smiles, and smiles turn to laughter, so much and with such gaiety that Pradeep wakes himself from his nap on the veranda and wanders in to comprehend the commotion.

"Oh Pradeep!" shout Jamshed and Piroja in unison.

"I just had to see what was so funny," says Pradeep, smiling, wanting to join the humour with his own.

"Well, let's see," says Piroja. "We were talking about strong will—"

"Free will," Jamshed says in a corrective tone.

"Strong will *and* free will," says Piroja, her eyes dancing. "And how to nurture it."

"And how to prevent it," says Jamshed, his eyes now joining the dance.

"So tell me, Pradeep," says Piroja quietly. "To change my mind, would you ever threaten to take your own life?"

"Or raise a hand to her?" asks Jamshed.

Pradeep stares at both of them, for although their words speak of unspeakable things, the two of them, father and daughter, are now beside themselves with laughter, and in the breeze from the compound, he thinks he can hear a child's voice saying it needs, wants, desires someone to love.

Voice of unreason

It can be a bloody struggle to be born. Not just the trauma of rollercoasting through a birth canal, no, that's bad enough, but the preplanning of this can be beyond belief. So my question to myself, here and now, is: am I born or am I still waiting? I float over a flow of passion flowers in the garden compound of a little distillery in Nowgong, and I float between corporeal entities I have come to know as my grandfather, my mother, my father. And then there is this young girlchild, the only child of my mother and father, and so, riddle-like, this must mean this daughter is yours truly, but if that is me, then who am I to speak outside like this, floatily, freely, in a space outside of reason? I listen in, but who is it that listens? I speak to mothers, fathers, grandmothers, grandfathers, but I am heard as an internal monologue, and a crazed one. I have no self, or if I have one, it is a high-cycling bipolarized one, or so those who hear me are called. All I want is someone to love, a truism, however trite. Yet which mother, what father, who indeed, can love a waifish wisp that exists as no more than a disembodied voice in a mental vacuum? Sometimes, I wish I would never be born at all. And that may be closer to the truth than I realize.

Can we talk?

The four of them, moving around the compound as if I don't exist.

Hello? Is there anybody out there? In there?

A mother. A father. A grandfather. Family. Not mine, perhaps, but family. Familial. Familiar. Not with me, but each other.

It would be nice just to say hello. Or goodbye.

They are familial with the apple of everybody's eye, strange fruit, the darling little girl who is not me, the babychild who is her own being, the toddler who wants to break free, become somebody else.

"What was that?"

That was the oddest of sensations, as if someone spoke ...

"Hello, who said that?"

As if someone poked—

"Is there someone here? Someone trying to say something?"

There it is again, not a voice, no, not a sound, but as if someone—how can this be? How can I feel this, me, this entity who sees and hears and speaks but is otherwise quite vaporous; how can it be that I feel this—this finger, that's what it is, a finger pointing at me, touching me, pressing into what I imagine must be my cheek, poking and pressing in, fingertip to cheek?

"What is this?"

Hello, it's Sunny. And it's about time.

Khajurao

Four of them and a driver in a car hired to take them to Khajurao, a place to visit and view and sight the sites and understand passion in a handful of stone. The trip takes only two hours, but by the time they have edged out of Nowgong and toward Chhatarpur, both Pradeep and Sunila have fallen fast asleep in the passenger seat, clinging to each other in father-daughter ways that are both endearing and enduring, thinks Piroja, as she watches them snore the road trip away. She looks over at Jamshed, sitting beside her in the back seat, who is keenly awake, looking out the window at the scores of workers by the roadside and then, assured that Pradeep is out of earshot both because of somnolent and front-seat car-noise reasons, begins to speak.

"Papa?"

"Hm?"

"Papa ... I have to tell you something."

"Yes?"

"Oh, this is so hard to explain. It makes me sound crazy, really it does. I sometimes hear ... voices. Well, not voices, but *a* voice. I thought—I thought for a long time that this was the voice of my, uh, unborn child. Oh, this does not make sense, I am sorry."

Jamshed laughs and then looks over at his daughter, pulls her hand into his. "Sunny?"

Piroja recoils, withdraws her hand, and stares at her father. "He—he told me he talked to you."

"Voices can be heard by more than one, I suppose."

"When did you hear Sunny?"

"Piroja, he has spoken to me for more than sixty years. Although not for some years. Not the last two years, at least."

"You're taking this very well. I'm still—so confused."

"Well, Sunny hasn't been with you all your life, has he?"

"He said—Sunny said—that he wanted to be born. I was so sure when I was pregnant that I must be—carrying him. So sure that when Sunila was born, I just could not believe it."

"Piroja? Have you—have you talked to Sunny since?"

Piroja shakes her head. "No. I tried, Papa, I tried! But it never works that way ..."

"No, no it doesn't. Sunny was never one to be summoned. He always just—appeared."

"Did you ever see him?"

"Oh no, not like that. I mean, I *felt* him, and most certainly heard him, talked to him, but never an image, no. Just the toe tapping and there he was."

"Toe tapping? Really? That's what happened to me, too. With Mummy it was different—" and suddenly Piroja catches herself; it's bad enough sharing conversations with your father about mutual discourses with unborn children, but not worth treading into the terrain of the talk one has with the already-gone. But Jamshed misunderstands, to Piroja's good fortune.

"Yes, your mother—your mother never exactly said this to me, but I had a feeling that Sunny came to her too. Before you were born, Piroja. And—and it feels almost that he came to her so that you *could* be born. When she was dying, she said something to me about butterflies and gardens and voices that calmed and reassured her, but I could not be sure if that was delirium speaking, or something else."

"She never—Mummy would have felt angry about me marrying a non-Parsi. She must have been, would have been, very angry."

"Angry? Oh, yes, indeed! As was I when I received that first letter from England. I think I would probably have been the angrier of us two, had Parvin been alive. I kept thinking of choices, of deeds, and how I felt, I am sorry to say, I felt you had turned your back on us, your history."

"Then what softened your heart, Papa?"

"I told you that I had not talked to Sunny for some time? Well, he did come to me soon after I received your letter informing me of your marriage. I was furious, fuming all the time. I took it out on the servants, the employees, anyone who crossed me, or even if they did not. And then Sunny came to me, and I was furious with him—if not for him, I would not have produced such bloody-minded progeny, I told him! And do you know what he said? He agreed. He said the choices I had made, with Parvin, with the distillery, with the perseverance after the loss of two sons, that was bloody-minded incarnate, and he was right! What choice did I have but to expect that a daughter of mine would refuse to have her life run by anyone else, that's what he told me. I was still furious, yelling at him, must have looked quite mad, but even in that anger, I knew he was ... spot on. The anger—it did not fade for months, but it did fade, as I thought about you, your new life, your choices. And that is what softened my heart, dear one. I realized I would rather have in my heart a daughter whom I loved than one whom I dismissed because her choices were, well, not my own."

Piroja looks over at her father, reaches across to touch his wrist. In the front seat Pradeep stirs and yawns. Sunila utters a small sound of awakening too. "Thank you," says Piroja.

When they arrive at Khajurao, the driver takes them to the west temples and leaves them to find a guide to walk them through the area. This they do and spend a good part of the afternoon climbing up steep steps and revelling in the friezes of bodies quite beautiful, striking all kinds of natural and unnatural poses. The torsos of svelte women, the limbs of supple men, the intertwining of bodies and gods, and the delight of it all. They have been touring the temples for more than two hours when, upon climbing a particularly large set of steps, they decide to rest for a moment before entering the cool darkness of the interior space yet again.

"Do you remember us coming here?" laughs Jamshed. "You, me, your mother?"

"Of course not," says Piroja. "I was just a baby, wasn't I?"

"Yes, still, I thought the profound nature of the experience might have left an impression!"

"They are quite profound, aren't they?" interjects Pradeep. "So stunning."

"Yes, that is so," agrees Jamshed.

"Yes," says Piroja, nodding.

"Mamapapa," says Sunila, without warning or insistence, her quietness during the afternoon making the utterance seem all the more pronounced. But it is not the words, which, as a precocious two-year-old, she has spoken earlier and often, but that accompanying them is her patented gesture of making a trigger and barrel of her thumb and forefinger, swinging her arm back so it cocks and points, deliberately, and with certainty, at a very specific space, a place on a temple wall, a frieze that depicts the figure of a woman, her torso a hairpin to her legs, presenting herself as she holds herself, hands held firmly about her hips, and behind her, pressed in close but not so close, the pressing of flesh (those particular kinds of flesh) and the pressure of entrance and egress, of a lightness that brilliants out all other forms of vision, a position at once beyond recognition and fully compatible with how Piroja and Pradeep, their attention drawn to this magnificent scene by their toddling daughter, remember bodies, theirs, working, fostering each other, that night of the dhansak, and both simultaneously imagine they can remember, too, the scent of mangos that were no more than air.

Sibling ribaldry

"Mamapapa," says Sunila, pointing, though her own eyes do not follow the vector formed by this gesture, but instead are drawn down to her own feet, specifically her left foot, and more specifically her left big toe, which has, without her volition, begun to tap-tap-tap a tiny beat upon the warm stone of the temple.

Sister mine?

"I am Sunila. Who are you?"

I am not sure. But I think I am your brother. Maybe.

"Hello, brother. Where are you?"

A very good question, sister mine.

"Sunila. My name is Sunila!"

A very good question, Sunila. The truth is, I do not know where I am, let alone who ...

"You are funny, brother. What is your name?"

Sunny. They call me Sunny.

"Who calls you 'Sunny'? Your parents?"

Well, yes, I suppose they do, if they are my parents. But this is too difficult to explain. Sunila? How would you feel about having a baby brother?

"I do not want one."

No? But why not?

"Because. Because I do not want one."

What if—what if I were your baby brother?

"I do not *want* a brother. Or a sister."

Would you—would you like me to leave?

"No. You can stay ... You can be my brother."

I can?

"Not real. Just pretend. You can be my pretend brother."

Then—then I will exist for you? Am I—am I part of you?

"No. You are my pretend brother. That's all."

All right then, sister mine. I will be your pretend brother. And I will visit you whenever you want to talk to me or play with someone or just have somebody near. Will that be all right?

"Perfect!" And Sunila laughs out loud, loud enough that her parents and grandparent break their gazes to look down at the little girl whose toe has just ceased tapping on a warm stone at a temple at Khajurao.

Indeterminacy

Sunila meets her grandparent with elation, using the opportunity to do a lot of staring and pointing when they visit. But all visits come to an end, and two weeks after their arrival, they bid farewell to Jamshed, and with lots of tears and choked responses of things said and unsaid, they depart for Atlantic Canadian shores.

For their part, Pradeep and Piroja settle into a pretty reasonable facsimile of domestic bliss, he now working more select hours and she on leave (but with the hospital begging her to return to work as soon as she is able). There is never any mention of other grandparents, particularly dead ones, or of future children, particularly male ones, and certainly no mention of falling urns or swinging tenderizers. But when she is alone, Piroja occasionally tries to summon up this Sunny, sitting there tapping her toe expectantly, looking around as if he might appear (as he never has) out of thin air. Sometimes, she stands at Sunila's crib, looking down and tapping a toe encouragingly, hoping Sunila might look up and point, a clear gesture that Sunila and Sunny were one, or maybe she would laugh and deign to speak in the articulate verbiage of the now-absent-Sunny voice. But this was not to occur, and Piroja became more withdrawn as the days went by, and she seemed decidedly unable to fix the gender of her toddler, particularly when strangers came calling.

"Oh, what a lovely child," people would say as she pushed a stroller by the harbour, "is it a ... ?" and Piroja, on her good days, would simply pretend not to hear the question and would say something neutral about the beautiful weather or the baby's temperament, always and judiciously avoiding pronouns.

"Yes, a warm September we are having, and this one, this one quite likes these afternoon strolls." Or, "Why, thank you for the compliment! Yes, I hear some babies are quite difficult, but not so the case here." Or, "The baby's name? Sunil," and sometimes she would let an "a" drift in and sometimes not, but for the most part it did not matter because the name itself was unfamiliar enough not to raise immediate boy/girl identifications.

In the late fall, even though it was not the best time for beaches, the young family decided to take a ferry trip to Prince Edward Island to see the red sands they had heard so much about. They found through friends at the hospital a wonderful beach cottage where they could spend five days, all of Pradeep's time off combined and earned from various shifts and favours he had performed, and, after a mildly rough crossing, they found themselves driving down the coast in the second-hand Chrysler they had bought soon after Sunila was born, following the directions pencilled in on the map from their friends. It was an isolated cabin—on the left of the highway was the owner's house, and on the other side, down a cattle road, was the sweet little cottage right at the water's edge.

They made the transaction with the wife of Mr O'Reilly, the owner. (She called her husband "Mr O'Reilly" and never by a first name; it was, "Yez, Mr O'Reilly's out there looking for fish with his cronies, so's he says to me, 'These nice people from Dartmouth are coming in, so treat them fair and I'll see you Thursday!' So welcome, no key to give you as the place is unlocked, but not ta worry, nobody will bother you there.") They settled into their cottage by the sea with all the food and warm clothes they had packed and enjoyed the feeling of not working and having an irregular existence for a change. Two days after their arrival, Mr O'Reilly himself traipsed down to the cottage to welcome them personally and introduce himself. He was a tall, balding man with a face much like an eagle, very few teeth to speak of, but a disposition that was as charming as his wife's. Pradeep and Piroja felt quite comfortable greeting him when he sauntered onto what they already considered their deck to greet them right proper.

"Say," says Mr O'Reilly, "that's some good-looking lad you have there." Perhaps it was the blue woollen blanket that Piroja had protectively placed on top of the stroller as they sat in the cool fall afternoon, or maybe it was the way Sunila was looking up at the strange man, full of a vigour that might, to him, indicate the more insistent gender, or maybe it was the exuding confidence of that index finger, pointing up and trigger-pulling at the grizzled man. But Pradeep had just popped inside to get a cup of tea for Mr O'Reilly so was not there to hear the faux pas, and when Piroja heard that assumption, rather than doing nothing, as was her wont when such a mistake was aired, or correcting him, as was her habit when Pradeep or friends were within earshot, she only hesitated for a moment before nodding affably.

"Thank you, Mr O'Reilly. He really is quite a wonderful child. I know, all mothers must say that about their own, but Sunil, he's a charmer."

"That he is, that he is."

"He—he really is quiet, which I have heard is—unusual. For a boy, I mean."

"Well, Mrs Lal, we raised three of them, not a girl in the bunch, so me and Mrs O'Reilly wouldn't know any different. But ours were a handful, let me tell you. And wait 'til the girls come of age, then you'll see how you lose control of these fellas."

"Yes, uh, yes."

"And look at those eyes. He's gonna be a ladykiller."

"Oh, yes, do you think?"

"Let me tell ya, when they're teenagers, those boys have only one thing on their minds!"

At this point Pradeep pushes through the storm door with a tea-cup. He hands it to Mr O'Reilly. "What's this about boys?"

"Ah, was just telling your missus here that boys growing up are a handful is all!"

"Really? Well, I suppose we wouldn't know."

"No, not right now, no, they're charming when they're babes. But you wait a few years, mark my words!"

"Yes," says Pradeep a bit distractedly, "I suppose."

"Hm, wish we had had girls to be truthful. Seemed like Mrs O'Reilly couldn't put out nothing but boy children."

Piroja bites her tongue, refusing to get into a discussion of sper-matozoa and eggs and chromosomes. Besides, she has already sur-prised herself by crossing Sunila's gender divide, and she is still try-ing to figure this out.

"Your place," says Pradeep in learned Canadian politeness, "is so wonderful."

Mr O'Reilly nods, proudly. "Me and my sons, built this from the ground up. See, having sons has its good sides, to be true! Yes, you're a lucky couple, a lucky couple, and that boy of yours, he's gonna grow up to—"

"Would you like to try some Indian dishes, Mr O'Reilly?" Piroja interjects, a bit too jarringly.

"What? Oh, I would love that, truly, but I just popped down to say hello, don't want to be disturbing, and it's almost dinner time so I'll be heading back up now. Thank you for the tea, for certain." And he takes a big draught of his remaining tea, sets the cup down on the porch railing, and is off with a wave.

"That was a bit odd," says Pradeep after a while.

"Hm," says Piroja. "And speaking of dinner, I think I'll go inside and make some."

It was like what they say, thinks Piroja, about drug addiction.

At first, it's risky and risqué, living a bit on the edge; then it becomes part of a routine, normalized to such an extent that without the addictive choice, nothing seems normal, and then you can't live without it; the addiction becomes your reason for being. Whenever anyone made a gesture or suggestion or reference to a male identity inhabiting the infant, Piroja was happy. Before long, she made a habit of creating scenarios where this was bound to play out, idly asking other mothers in the park what they did with their boys when they were older and wanted to play sports, checking out how the parents of boy infants decorated their sons' rooms, dressed them, made them out to be boys, all those hidden and not so hidden, subtle and not so subtle acts that made boys be boys and girls be girls.

When Pradeep wasn't around, she would take this one step further, talking about the child and what "he" had done. One day, Piroja finally crossed the line when talking about her "son" and his birth with the Cliffords, who had moved in across the street. This was a lie she was bound to be caught in, and it wasn't long before that happened. At first, she could shrug it off, tell Pradeep people were mistaken, but it all caught up with her when Pradeep insisted they invite the Cliffords across for dinner. Piroja resisted at first, but Pradeep noted that they were the first Negro family to move on to their street. As the only other brown family on their street, the invitation was an act of solidarity. Still, Piroja managed to put it off until one day Pradeep came home and said he had seen Nelson Clifford on the way home from work and had invited him and Jennifer over for dinner for the following Saturday. Piroja toyed with the idea of falling ill that day, but then thought better of it, dressed Sunila in her best blue jumper with hockey players emblazoned on the front, and set to making a fine Parsi feast for the guests.

When the Cliffords arrived there was plenty of joviality and conviviality, and everyone enjoyed the food and praised the cook, and just when Piroja thought she might actually get away with her subterfuge, Jennifer leaned into the table and said, "Guess what? Nelson and me, we're going to have a baby!" This brought on congratulations and excited exclamations and then talk, as it did when such an announcement was made, about other new families, most particularly the one composed of Pradeep and Piroja and Sunila.

"Did you plan when to have your baby?" asks Jennifer with genuine interest.

"Oh," says Piroja, "in a manner of speaking, but not down to the details, I suppose."

"It must have been so exciting," says Nelson, "since you had only just come here from India, wasn't it?"

"England," says Pradeep, "but yes, from India to England and then here, quite a journey, and then having a baby on top of that."

"Let me ask you," says Jennifer, again very earnestly. "Did you wish for a boy or a girl? I know that might be hard to answer because, once you have a baby, I'm sure it doesn't matter. But I'm hoping for a boy, and Nelson says he wanted a girl, and I'm just wondering if you had had a preference?"

"Oh, well, no," admits Pradeep. "At least not for me. I didn't really think of it."

"Neither did I," says Piroja, finishing her tea purposefully. "More tea anyone?"

"I'm fine," says Nelson, but not picking up Piroja's hint to move on. "So having the boy, that pleased you?"

There is a pause in the room, the type of pause that happens in the movies when the bad guy directs a gun point-blank at the good guy and pulls the trigger to kill the good guy dead, but the gun misfires, that pause that happens right after the misfire when the bad guy has to decide whether to pull the trigger again or throw the gun at the good guy, and that moment of indecision is when the good guy heroically wrests the gun from the bad guy and punches his lights out. Pradeep downs the last of his tea.

"I'm sorry?"

"Your son. You must have been pleased to have a boy?"

"Sunila?" Pradeep looks over at Piroja, who busies herself with straightening her dress. "Our daughter?"

There is another moment here of misfiring and gun-wresting.

"Your *daughter*?" asks Jennifer. Then, to Piroja, "I thought you said Sunil was a boy."

"Oh," says Piroja, wracking her brain unsuccessfully for an intelligent defence. "No."

After yet another filmic pause, when good friends might just let things go, these two Couples on the Way to Acquainting Themselves with One Another are still not sure of such signs and signals, so Nelson adds: "Yes, that's right, Piroja, I distinctly remember you telling us that most boys were not as quiet as your Sunil."

"Uh, Sunila," corrects Piroja, trying to remember exactly what she might have said. "And I'm sure you just misunderstood. I probably did say Sunila was quieter than boy infants, that must be it."

"But," says Jennifer, now leaning in more than ever, "you also said that since you and Pradeep only planned on having one child, you were glad, I remember you saying that, you were glad you'd had a boy."

At this, Jennifer leans back, perhaps suddenly aware that she has spoken truthfully in that way she has where the truth is too much. Film noir pauses interject themselves all over the room. Finally, from Piroja comes the embattled admission.

"If I said that, I was … clearly mistaken. I don't really remember … She … Sunila … is … yes, I don't remember."

After that, someone, maybe Pradeep, maybe Nelson, maybe Jennifer, says something to veer the conversation in a radically different direction, but the evening ends soon after. The Cliffords do not come to the Lals' for dinner again, nor do they extend a reciprocal invitation to Piroja and Pradeep, though they do occasionally have parties where an assortment of acquaintances are invited for drinks, and to these their Next Door Neighbours With a Child of Indeterminate Gender are invited, though they show up only once. When the Cliffords finally make their graceful exit on this night, there is not much to be said between Pradeep and Piroja. She looks at him guiltily and he does the dishes sulkily, but no words are exchanged about this not-exactly a misunderstanding. But it is far from the end of the story of girlhood, boyhood, and Sunila.

Tug of wear

Although Pradeep said nothing of Piroja's now-more-evident predilection to boyify Sunila, he took it upon himself to enforce what little he could about what he felt was appropriate gender assignment. Never the most boisterous of boys himself, he now began to fashion himself as a man's man, and what better way than to create an ideal model of femininity, particularly through his daughter. As weeks wore on into months, Pradeep would appear back from work with various un-Piroja-solicited items that were some variation on pretty pink frilly things, girly girl toys, or otherwise female-inspiring paraphernalia.

"Look here," he would say, waltzing in with a frock embroidered with little hearts. "This will look grand on Her, don't you think?" (It could have been Piroja's imagination, but it seemed any female pronoun uttered by Pradeep these days had that emphatic upper-cased sensibility to it.)

"It's very pretty," Piroja would admit. "But she won't fit into it until she's seven."

"Ah, well then, She will have to wait to wear it."

Pradeep's most excessive purchase was an Easy-Bake Oven. Other doctors at work were talking about getting one for their daughters, lamenting that it was only available in the States. By this time, Sunila was nearly four, and Pradeep had driven their new-ish Ford (having traded in the Chrysler the previous year) across the border to find a turquoise-coloured Every Girl's Dream Toy for his own little daughter.

"Whatever is that for?" Piroja would ask, confused at the sight of the light-bulb-powered oven.

"It's the newest thing," Pradeep would say. "All the girls want one."

Piroja, for her part, bought Sunila boats and cars and footballs and heavy machinery (the toy variety). For every girly article of clothing Pradeep would bring home, Piroja would produce a boyish equivalent. For each giggly girl toy or doll gifted by father, a boy-like hands-on practice-based toy would be delivered by mother. And so it was that mother and father pushed and pulled along boy/girl lines until their only child was about to enter primary school. Since the names Sunil and Sunila were being used so interweavingly and confusingly, both parents more or less hit on the abridged version of "Sunny" by the time a fifth birthday arrived. This worked well for Pradeep, who thought such a moniker showed the sensitive and bright-sweet side of their daughter, this name that reflected disposition. And it worked exceedingly well for Piroja who, since the moment of birth had not been visited by the entity Sunny, and who heard a certain masculine sensibility about the name, a colloquial extension of his existence as a son.

For the remarkably intelligent and still gentle child, this was the best possible solution because it did sometimes feel as though mother and father were speaking to two separate children, and even for a five-year-old, this was disconcerting. Sunny, then, developed her own pidgin pronouns, referring to "meself." Sunny remained decidedly confused when it came to gendered names, people, or things. When referring to something Pradeep had said, Sunny would more often than not look up at Piroja, point at her father, and say, "But she said we could go to the park today." Or she would point at Piroja and tell Pradeep, "He's a funny mummy." Or, almost mockingly, if a child at that age can mock, repeated almost perfectly the admiration adults bestowed upon the Provincial pride with a "he's a fine ship, that Bluenose," much to the mirth of those who heard these

379

pronouncements from one so young. Dogs were called "her" and cats were called "him." The kid in the sandlot playing with dumptrucks and bulldozers was invariably called "she," and the Goldilocked, dimpled, party-dressed child was, to Sunny, a most definite "he." Even the songs on the radio—a bright new silver transistor model that Piroja had bought to keep her company by playing the day's top tunes—were not immune to the fluxing gender. In the Piroja-Pradeep-Sunny household, "he" wore blue velvet, the Chiffons crooned about how "she" was so fine, and even the Angels weren't safe from boyfriends turning to girlfriends who were suddenly back, meaning the onset of trouble. Indeed, the household was in such a twist that pretty much every boy became a girl and many pronouns either gained or lost an "s." When one of Pradeep's friends visited from London, toting 45s of the very best of the charts, songs that hadn't even graced the stations in New York or Toronto let alone Halifax's CJCH, they played the records nonstop, but "He loves you, yeah, yeah, yeah" became the anthem of the house.

In fact, Sunny's refusal to differentiate boys from girls so concerned her primary school teacher that it was in late September 1963, a scant few weeks into the first year of Sunny's schooling, that Pradeep and Piroja were summarily summoned to Crichton Park Elementary by Mrs Heather T. Snellgrove.

A little schoolhouse in Dartmouth

The ceiling fan is metallic grey and it rotates just fast enough so the casual observer can make out each blade, not in exact detail, but enough so that each blade is distinct from the next. Any faster and the blades would blur into each other and, indeed, the fan might then be performing up to its teleological good, for at the current speed, apart from allowing bored sets of eyes to discern its metallic detail, the fan does little more than circulate dust and salt air back from whence they came, that is, toward the floor, without even close to the desirous effect of providing a cooling breeze.

This is exactly what Piroja is thinking as she watches the blades rotate, that all the fan is succeeding in doing, miraculously, is to make the room stuffier than it would be were the fan to be shut off entirely. Piroja is sitting in a creaky wooden chair, supposedly the teacher's chair, her back straight and posture perfect except for her head, which tilts upward and wonders at the fan. Directly in front of Piroja is a large maple desk that has seen better days, and as Piroja examines this desk closely she notices various scratches and scars from years gone by and the occasional carved initials and dates inscribed under the lip of the desk, and Piroja has a faint sensation of déjà vu, but she does not realize that two generations have passed, and what her grandfather once experienced, what her father once experienced, she, as a mother, is now experiencing.

On the other side of the desk, squeezed uncomfortably into a desk used to holding the bodies of four-year-old boys and girls, sits Pradeep. He has been sitting like this, awkwardly, for five minutes, passing the time by watching his wife watch the ceiling fan and looking around the classroom to take note of all the items his daughter will observe over the course of her first year of primary school—in this town so far away from where they grew up, so utterly different and uncomfortably pristine. Pradeep squirms in the tiny seat and wonders how children Sunny's age can possibly learn their lessons in this environment, here, so far away (even if only two blocks) from the home and love of her parents. Still, their daughter has come to them despite all obstacles, thinks Pradeep, and now it is time to make whatever deals they need to make so she does not lose her lot in life.

Across from Piroja and Pradeep sits Mrs Heather T. Snellgrove, assistant and acting principal for Crichton Park Elementary School. Mrs Snellgrove licks her lips obsessively as she begins to explain to these parents in extremely slow, methodical, and monosyllabic language (who knows if these immigrants understand?) about the English-language problems that Sunny appears to be having. Piroja listens intently as the acting principal speaks, noting how her tongue must dry up at the end of the day, and how she pauses at the end of each word as well, as if she is paying respect to the full effect of the full stop at each thought, making Piroja want to reach over and pull the words out of her throat.

"Mr and Mrs Lal. It must. Be known. That your daughter. Is a bit behind. In her language. Skills. Do you. Understand?"

Piroja, realizing what is going on, pretends to translate the principal's halting speech with succinct packet of Hindi curses for Pradeep's benefit, to which he is forced to smile before raising his hand and explaining to the good acting principal that they both have remarkable control over the English language, and she should proceed.

"Oh, my, that is a relief," says Mrs Snellgrove, and licks her lips before snorting exactly three times like a wildebeest and continuing on the same trajectory.

"It seems like our Sun Ayela—"

"You can call her Sunny," says Pradeep.

"Oh, that's right, yes, what a sweet name, Sunny. Well, Sunny seems to have some difficulty in making out boys from girls. Now this is perfectly understandable for many young children, but particularly so, if I may be so bold, for children from your culture, where I understand you do not have words for boy and girl, is that not right?" Mrs Snellgrove is very proud of herself, for she has studied foreign languages as part of her education degree, and she knows that the Indian language does not have pronouns like regular languages.

"Which culture?" asks Piroja, innocently.

"And which language?" mutters Pradeep.

"Oh, yours. Indian. Culture." Mrs Snellgrove is back to articulating each word for the foreigners' benefit.

"We come from different cultures," Piroja explains sweetly. "I am Zoroastrian. He is Hindu. Which one doesn't have pronouns again?"

"Oh, I see. Well. Yes, yes, it is pronouns. And you are Zeus-trian, not Hin-doo?"

"Something like that," Piroja admits.

"The thing is," adds Pradeep, "is this all that serious? It is only the first few weeks. Maybe Sunny just needs to adjust."

"Adjust. Yes, that is it. I just wanted to be sure, you know, that you were aware that Sunny is a little, you know, backward in her language skills."

"I. Don't. Think. So," says Piroja.

"No. She. Will. Do. Just fine," says Pradeep. Neither of them smile. But Piroja then starts humming the tune to their family anthem, *he loves you, yeah, yeah, yeah*, and they both break out into a laugh that Mrs Snellgrove interprets as Indian friendliness and she joins their laughter with hostly camaraderie.

Chameleon

"At least she's only *acting* principal."

"Yes," says Pradeep, nodding, "but she does have a point."

"What does that mean?'

"Piroja … this thing with Sunila. It has to stop. She's getting confused, and it will only hurt her in her education."

"Sunny will do just fine."

"Yes, yes, I'm sure: But still. This boy/girl thing."

"Agh. Everyone here tries to fit the bill, Pradeep, it's really ridiculous. Boys in short pants, girls in summer dresses. Did you grow up like that? Did I?"

"Well, in a way …"

"But really, Pradeep, I'm not talking about boys and girls when they grow up, but when they're children."

"I know, I know. But that's the way it is here."

"So that means we should be that way too?"

Pradeep thinks on this for a moment and then nods. "When in Rome."

"Oh, what? Speak Latin? That foolish woman, her whole concern was that Sunny couldn't speak English. Pradeep, I've been reading with Sunny every day for the last three years! In English. And we speak better English than Mrs Snellgrove, by far."

"Yes, yes, I know. But it's not about that. It's about—her."

Piroja and Pradeep are at their kitchen table getting ready to start their day. It has been three weeks since they were summoned to the acting principal's office, and since that time they have had at least one discussion every day about how they should proceed. Sometimes they decide to pull Sunny out and find another school.

Sometimes they think they should make a concerted effort to speak Hindi at home (or Gujarati, thinks Piroja, but since Pradeep does not share that language, that would make it rather difficult and solitary). Sometimes they think they should buy more school textbooks and give Sunny a real education at home, but that would mean Piroja would not be able to go back to work. Sometimes they think they should move away from Nova Scotia to a place where Pradeep can work as a researcher at a teaching hospital instead of as an internist in rotating rounds. Sometimes, though rarely and never seriously, they think they should return to England or, even more rarely, move back to India.

And sometimes, they think they should have another child. This notion first came up the very day after their encounter with the acting principal. Piroja had been muttering about crazy schoolteachers and had, not for the first time in recent memory, made a passing allusion to how this must affect a small child like "him." Pradeep had looked at her, not with incredulity, but with a quiet resolve.

"Piroja," he had asked finally, "did you want a son?" And she, looking blankly back at him, had said something noncommittal like, "Whatever do you mean?" but then felt concern because there were tears coming from Pradeep's eyes, and before she could comfort him she felt tears coming from her own.

"No", she had said, "no, you do not understand. It was not what I wished for. It is what I expected. It is what I knew." They held each other, no words, no further explanations necessary. How could she begin to talk of this strange invisible voice that had entered her head so long ago, had told her he had entered the heads of her father and mother before her, and that this voice belonged to the boy who would be her son? She could not say this, any more than she could tell Pradeep of ghostly mothers, so she just followed his lead and helped him cry.

What neither Pradeep nor Piroja knew was that their conversations, always in the early morning or late at night and always at the kitchen table, were not shared by them alone. Carried along with the hum of the refrigerator and the slight buzz of the baseboard heater, their voices floated through the thin plaster walls to the tiny cubbyhole they had always referred to as "the baby's room" (partially because that's how it started out and partially because, shrunken as it was, neither could bring themselves to call it Sunny's room). Little did they know that, although their voices were always low and subsequently further muzzled and muffled by the density of plaster, Sunny had an acute sense of hearing and could determine and decipher every word spoken by her parents. This had been going on since Sunny was an infant, of course, the natural backdrop of her dreams being parental conversations, voices heard as if through cotton batting. As she learned language, she discerned a certain logic to the sounds, and by the time she turned four, Sunny could hear and understand pretty much everything that was being said. As a good child, Sunny would try to live up to parental expectations, so if there was kitchen-table concern about Sunny not getting out in the sun enough, the next day she would beg her parents to let her stay out at the playground all day. Or if there was next-room talk about how to interest her in reading more (for Sunny was an avid reader, but only when the mood struck her), within the week she would be imploring Piroja for daily library visits. And when she heard her parents mutter quietly, "What about another baby, perhaps a brother for Sunny?" she steeled her tiny self and began squeezing her mother's hand over breakfast, or smiling sweetly at her father over dinner, and when they would ask her what had come over her, she would coyly say, "Oh nothing."

But when Sunny heard her parents' quiet sobs that morning, preceded by her mother's soft utterance, "No, you do not understand. It was not what I wished for. It is what I expected. It is what I knew," Sunny closed her eyes and wished and prayed. She wished as she had been taught by her friends, pretending she was throwing coins in a fountain; she prayed as she had learned from watching her father in front of the corner altar with all its silver figurines; and she prayed as she had learned from watching her mother sitting softly mouthing a seemingly endless series of memorized prayers. She prayed and wished and wished and prayed. Sunny did not know to whom she was praying or wishing, just that she needed to do this. Her mother had wanted, expected, desired a boy. Perhaps if she tried hard enough, prayed and wished hard enough, she could *be* that boy.

In the playground at recess, Sunny and her friends are standing in the sandlot talking about what they will be when they grow up. In the swath of possibilities, firemen and secretaries and astronauts and mothers, Sunny mentions that her father and mother are both doctors (which she doesn't see as a lie, for she has seen them both talk of the hospital as their workplace and share details about their patients), and that she will be a doctor when she grows up.

"You can't be a doctor," says freckly Jonathon Mosely, "and neither can your mum, because you're girls." Sunny looks sullenly at him and retorts with all the invective that is hers, "Can too," and Jonathon rebukes her with a "Can't."

And then it is up to Brenda Clarke, the only black girl in the class, to offer up her question, "What's the difference, anyway, between boys and girls?" Jonathon laughs at this because he thinks it is a silly question, but then stops laughing abruptly when he realizes he does not know the answer for, like Sunny, he's an only child, and he is not entirely sure.

Anne Smithers, a cherubic blonde girl with the personality of a bully, rolls her eyes. The middle child and only girl of three siblings, she is well aware of the anatomical differences, so she drops her pants and says, "See, this is what a girl is like," much to the nodding of Sunny and Brenda, yes, that is pretty much what they're familiar with.

"Jonny," says Anne, "show them what a boy is like," to which Jonathon, perplexed, lifts an arm and flexes a nonexistent bicep. Anne rolls her eyes again and steps toward Jonathon, her moves made awkward by the fact that her pants are around her ankles, but she still manages to land a good cuff on the boy's left ear. "Not like that, stupid," she admonishes. "Drop your pants."

Jonathon looks suddenly frightened, a fright accentuated by a burning left ear, and he shakes his head vigourously. Anne sighs again and looks to the left at Sunny and to the right at Brenda, nods in that bully-leader kind of way, and the three girls descend on the hapless boy, two of them (Anne and Brenda) grabbing his now-flailing arms. Anne, still ankle-panted and careful not to trip, nods to Sunny and gestures with her forehead at Jonathon's beltline. Sunny tugs on Jonathon's shorts so that they, too, fall to his ankles. Anne, pointing triumphantly, says, "There, see, now that's a boy."

It is at precisely the moment that Anne and Brenda pin Jonathon's arms that Mrs Heather T. Snellgrove, on recess supervisory duty, turns the corner of the building to check in on the pupils in the playground. There are no children on the carousel, and none on the see-saw. One adventurous thing is making her way up the monkey bars but is only two feet off the ground so presents no danger to others or to herself. There are four children playing by the sandlot, and she sees some sort of grappling going on, and, oh my. Mrs Snellgrove sees that that large black troublemaker, Brenda, has a fierce full-nelson hold on poor little Jonny. And, oh my, clearly

Brenda has also threatened little Anne into helping her; look how Brenda has already shamed the poor little blonde girl by stripping her of her dignity. But the worst is yet to come, and it is from the ringleader, that curiously quiet brown girl, Sunny, stepping in to, oh my. Look how little Anne is shaking her blonde head, urging Sunny not to do that. Look how Brenda is grinning, leering. Look at how terrified little Jonny is. And look at how that nasty girl goes in with such terrorizing purpose, two brown hands undignifiyng poor Jonny, exposing him for all the world to see. See how Anne, innocent thing, is shouting out her displeasure at the scene, averting her eyes as a modest and decent girl would, and see how Brenda and Sunny are staring lasciviously, really, people of their kind should never ...

"*Children!*" With that siren call, four sets of eyes turn to Mrs Snellgrove fearfully. Jonathon, pinned, pantless, and embarrassed, breaks into tears. Anne, also pantless in front of the principal and seeing trouble on the way, complements Jonathon's sobs. Brenda, confused, stares up at Mrs Snellgrove, her loss of words (and inability to cry on demand) read as obstinacy. And Sunny, now kneeling in front of Jonny, her hands still clinging to the sides of his shorts (now pulled to the ground), is transfixed by the difference between boys and girls and so does not respond at all until Mrs Snellgrove marches across to the sandlot and slaps her on the head.

But at that moment, reverie broken (and even on the long subsequent walk in to the principal's office), Sunny realizes what she has to do. She is not a boy, and she cannot be a boy. But now that she has seen what the difference is, she can do what she has always done, which is to scroll out a hand, retract thumb and excess fingers, and point at Jonathon Moseley's boyness. "That," she says to herself as the four of them are rounded up, Sunny still pointing, "that is what I have to do."

A little schoolhouse in Dartmouth, redux

The metallic grey ceiling fan is turned off today so that each dust-gathering blade is distinct from the next. Turned on, the blades would blur into each other and distribute that dust into the eyes and ears and throats of the pupils. This is exactly what Piroja is thinking as she watches the blades not rotate, that all the fan can ever succeed in doing is to make the room fill with dust and to choke all who remain in its midst. Piroja is sitting in a creaky teacher's wooden chair, her back bent and posture imperfect. Directly in front of Piroja is a large maple desk that has seen better days, and Piroja does not bother to re-examine this desk but is taken with the desire to add to the various scratches and scars from years gone by with carved initials and dates inscribed under the lip of the desk, and Piroja has a renewed sense of déjà vu, but decides not to worry about figuring out where it comes from or why it is there, as this is all getting far too strange for her to become rational.

On the other side of the desk, squeezed uncomfortably into a desk used to holding the bodies of five-year-old boys and girls, sits Pradeep. He has been sitting like this, awkwardly, for five minutes, passing the time by watching his wife watch the ceiling fan and looking around the classroom to take note of all the items his daughter will likely no longer observe beyond today, halfway through her first year of primary school—this was the subject of the reproving letter they received from the acting principal. Pradeep squirms in the tiny seat and wonders how children Sunny's age do not revolt earlier in this environment, here, so far away (even if only a few blocks, generally) from the home and love of their parents. Still, his daughter has made some egregious errors, thinks Pradeep, and now it is time to make whatever deals they need to make.

Across from Piroja and Pradeep sits Mrs Heather T. Snellgrove, soon-to-be-promoted-from-acting-to-full principal, owing to her tenaciousness in the face of adversity at Crichton Park Elementary School. Mrs Snellgrove licks her lips more obsessively than usual as she begins to explain to these parents in extremely fast, complex, and irritatingly glib language (who cares what these immigrants might not understand?) about the deviancy problems that Sunny appears to be having. Piroja listens intently as the acting principal speaks, noting how her tongue is flickering more viper-like than last time, and how she pauses at the end of each sentence as if she has made a particularly fine debating point, making Piroja want to reach over and wrench the tongue out of her gaping maw and throw it, slithering, into the corner with the dust balls.

"Mr and Mrs Lal. There comes a point in time where incorrigibility goes too far, and we cannot have innocent young children being so corrupted by ... by outside influences."

"Outside influences?"

"Mr and Mrs Lal, some children—some people—are just not as easily assimilated into the culture, is what I am trying to say."

"Culture?" says Piroja.

"Assimilated?" says Pradeep.

"Exactly," says Mrs Snellgrove. "Exactly. And there are some things that cannot be tolerated, and sexual deviancy is one of them." The word "sexual" is so muted by Mrs Snellgrove that it seems to Pradeep and Piroja that she has barely stuttered and left a blank adjectival space in front of "deviancy" before they both clue in to what she is trying to address.

"Mrs Snellgrove," begins Pradeep. "I am a bit astounded. I am a doctor. It seems to me the children were only playing doctor, something we have all done as children."

Piroja nods.

Mrs Snellgrove shakes her head vigourously. If at some point in her misspent youth she ever did play doctor, she has so deeply repressed the memory it is buried forever.

"I am afraid that this is the final word," says Mrs Snellgrove, rising up from the table like a circuit judge. "Sunny is expelled from Crichton Park Elementary School."

Dopplers, blueshifts, and other gangs

Sunny sits at the kitchen table, Piroja on one side of her, Pradeep on the other, so that whichever of her parents speaks she has to turn her head this way or that to pay full attention, a tennis match of parental dimension.

"Sunny, we need to tell you something, dear," says Piroja.

Sunny looks to her right at her mother and nods agreeably.

"We want to make it clear that we don't think you have done anything wrong," says Pradeep.

Sunny looks to her left at her father and smiles thankfully.

"But there are certain things that children do that are—misunderstood," says Piroja.

Sunny bats her eyelashes at her mother and nods again.

"Misunderstood," says Pradeep, "because maybe the children do not understand what they are doing."

Sunny turns to her father, eyelashes still batting.

"Do you understand what we're talking about?" asks Piroja.

"Do you understand what we mean?" asks Pradeep.

"Do you have any questions that you would like to ask us?" asks Piroja.

Sunny tennis-matches from mother to father and back to mother, nod-yes, smile-yes, shake-no.

"Then we have something to ask you," says Pradeep.

Sunny flips her eyes over to her father and raises her eyebrows.

"Can you tell Mummy and Daddy what happened with Jonathon and the others?"

Sunny looks up at both parents and ponders this for a moment. "Well, Anne, he said that boys and girls were different, and then

Brenda, he said he didn't know, and then, well, Brenda and meself pulled Jonny's pants down, but first Anne took his own pants off, and then Jonny, she was crying. So Mrs Snellgrove comes over, and he hits me on the head! But, Mummy, Daddy, are you going to bring me a baby brother?"

Piroja and Pradeep look at each other. Then they look at their daughter.

"Why do you ask us that, Sunny?" asks Piroja.

"Because I think I would like to be a boy or have a brother," says Sunny matter-of-factly, "because, Mummy, I think you would like that."

There is a quietness around the kitchen table.

"Well," says Pradeep finally. "Mummy and I have talked about that."

"But we don't think it's a good idea just now, Sunny," says Piroja. What she does not say to either daughter or husband is that she has decided, unilaterally, that she will not have another child. She had waited so long, having those strange conversations with the invisible Sunny, waited for him to be born, and when the child finally did come, this girl, Sunila, at first Piroja thought there had been some form of mistake, then, that the boychild Sunny would come to talk to her and explain. But when he failed to visit her in ethereal form after Sunila was born, and after she and Pradeep made their peace and began thinking of their daughter as Sunny, it was then that Piroja finally realized that if there ever was to be a "Sunny" then it was in this form of Sunny, and she must not push herself in other wishful directions, for they would only hurt. She had made her choice, alone, but it was one she would abide by.

Piroja managed to broach this topic with Pradeep, first on economic grounds—raising two children would place a great financial burden on us, and we do not need to do that right now—and then in terms of career sensibilities—if we could both work, it would be a tremendous boon to us—and finally as a health argument—Pradeep, I have spoken to my gynecologist, and she feels that if I conceived again it would not be without risks, so let us just be happy as we are. And while she was occasionally given to trying to summon the strange creature from her past, she was beyond that pathetic impulse to create him. No, she had Pradeep. She had Sunny. She had a new life in a new country. What more could they want?

"But we do have to tell you," says Pradeep, "that we are about to go on a huge adventure."

Sunny's eyes open wide. She likes adventures and is sure this one, one that excites her parents, will be the best ever.

"Yes," says Pradeep. "We are going to move to a big city where you can make lots of new friends and do lots of fun things."

"Daddy has a job in Toronto," Piroja says to Sunny. "And it is in a huge hospital ten times as big as the one he works in now. And I will be able to work there, too, when you are in school."

"When do we go?" asks Sunny excitedly.

"Very, very soon," says Pradeep, conscious that as precipitated as this move is by Sunny's expulsion, they will never reveal it as the primary reason. They would have made the move sooner or later, he and Piroja have reasoned, there is no need to lay this on their five-year-old's shoulders, no matter how adaptable she seemed to be.

"Da doo ron ron," shouts Sunny, jumping up from the table and exhibiting her excitement through a series of rapid-fire fingerpointings from both hands, toward clocks, doors, stoves, parents. She runs into her bedroom and begins chatting excitedly as if to a friend. Piroja and Pradeep sit there, bemused, then a tad alarmed when it seems Sunny is humming and hemming as if agreeing with the voice of an imaginary friend. So when she runs back out and starts babbling about their move and what they will do and where they will go, her parents are only slightly confused when Sunny starts talking about travelling with her new friend.

"Your new friend?" asks Piroja. "Who might that be?"

"Oh, you know. He says he has talked to you."

"Talked to me?"

"Yes," says her daughter, staring up with wide eyes and obvious delight. "His name is Sunny, too."

Seeing things

"First this him/her-he/she thing and now this. What are we going to do, Piroja?"

Piroja is silent, one finger to her lips.

"Should she see someone here, before I take the post at the University Hospital? That's still a month away, and I don't know if we should wait. Piroja? Should we even move to Toronto? We have to move, it's the best for everyone. And this him/her thing and now an imaginary friend, well, I suppose I should just calm down, after all, it's a normal part of growing up. Isn't it? I mean, I had an imaginary friend. I even remember his name, Raju. I used to pretend he was a very tiny fellow and that I could keep him in my pocket. I would pretend to take him out when I was bored, and I would set him down and we would talk. Oh my God, do you suppose this is hereditary? Piroja?"

Pradeep is talking a mile a minute in his distracted state. He gets up from the kitchen table to start pacing, his arms clasped behind his back in anxiety mode. For her part, after making her pronouncement, Sunny has run off to her bedroom, presumably to play with her imaginary friend. Pradeep and Piroja can hear her talking, but guardedly and slowly, as if she is explaining the situation now that she has cleared the initial overexcitement. And Piroja remains sitting at the kitchen table, one finger to her pursed lips.

"Well, what do you think, Piroja? Is it hereditary? Have I infected our sweet little daughter with my madness? But is it crazy to have an imaginary friend? You never answered me—did you have someone you used to talk to like that, as a child?"

Piroja slowly removes the finger from her lips and looks up at the pacing Pradeep.

"I had someone I talked to like that," says Piroja, "only not as a child. It was much more recent than that."

And with that, she rises from the table, touches the stunned Pradeep on his shoulder, and heads into the bedroom to talk to her daughter. She sees Sunny sitting there on her bed, facing the wall. For a change, the little girl is still, so still that Piroja, just for a moment, checks to see if her daughter's right foot is tapping. It is not.

"Sweetheart," she says. "Tell me—tell me about your friend."

Sunny turns around and smiles brightly.

"Oh, he's very nice to me. He says he used to talk to you a lot and that you were nice to him too."

"What do you talk about?"

"School, friends, you and Daddy. We talk about how I feel a lot. He seems to know a lot about me."

"Yes," says Piroja, "I am sure he does."

"He can come with us to Toronto, can't he?"

"Hm, I don't see why not."

"Good. He will be happy."

"Sunny, have you told anyone else about your friend?"

Sunny squints, fingerpoints with some attitude up at the ceiling, thinking.

"No. No, I haven't. He hasn't met any of my other friends yet. But, Mummy?"

"Yes, dear?"

"He says he's my brother."

Metropolitan life

It is early January 1964, and Pradeep, Piroja, and Sunila are standing at the entrance to a two-bedroom walk-up on College. It is a bright, breezy flat and close enough to the hospital so that Pradeep will be able to walk there—it is reminiscent, in many ways, of their place in York, thinks Piroja, except this city is so strangely large and comforting at the same time. And cold. Sunila is singing the chorus from "Twist and Shout," much to the amusement of the landlady, a Mrs Olivieri who is showing them their new place.

"A catchy tune, no? What is it?"

Sunila shrugs. Piroja laughs and tells her it is the Beatles and, seeing the blank look on Mrs Olivieri's face, explains that it is a British band that is about to make its first visit to North America in a month.

"Ah," says the landlady, and starts wagging her head from side to side, "she loves you, yeah, yeah, yeah."

Piroja laughs. "That's right. We have some friends from England, and they brought us some of the records that just came out. I suppose they will be on radio soon enough here in Toronto."

"Already!" says the excited Mrs Olivieri. "My daughter, she goes crazy for them. I told her, if she keeps her grades up, I will buy her concert tickets."

"Who knows," says Piroja. "Maybe I'll even take Sunila."

"And Sunny?" asks Sunila.

Piroja smiles. Yes. And Sunny.

And so the young family moves into their College Street flat and settles into a cold Toronto winter. Pradeep quickly makes friends at the hospital.

"You wouldn't believe how many Indians work there," he tells Piroja with some excitement. "Hey, I met a fellow, Homi something-or-other, a Parsi, works in the lab. I told him we would have him and his wife over for dinner. He was surprised, let me tell you, when I said my wife was a Parsi."

"I'm sure he was," says Piroja.

Pradeep moves over to Piroja, who is busy clearing the dinner table. "We'll be all right here," he says. Yes, she nods, we'll be all right.

But Piroja is not so sure. There are stares on the street sometimes, piercing through winter clothes and scarves, stares she did not remember from York or Halifax. But along with the stares, there are also many different faces, colours, and cultures cutting through the woollen apparel. And there are foods and spices the likes of which she has not seen since shopping in London. It is not quite Delhi—far from it—but it has its charm, she thinks, and it has its opportunities. But her greatest concern is not the people, not the food, not the city itself, but her daughter. In a demonstration of will, Piroja has ceased calling her "Sunny" in favour of her birth name, "Sunila." This is not, as Pradeep would have it, a reversion to a name that seems much more fitting for a girl, but to avoid confusion, for she and her daughter have frequent conversations now about little brother Sunny, and it is just all too headswimming to have both daughter and imaginary sibling share the same name. It is not as if the confusions around name and gender evaporate, however; it is almost as if, Piroja tells herself, Sunny and Sunila exist in the same body, as if her son and her daughter—no—that her son *is* her daughter, and then it gets all too confused, so she stops trying to explain things to herself.

"Tell me, Sunila," she asks on the way to school one day in March, the weather just starting to break a bit, "what does Sunny look like?"

At this her daughter laughs. "Mummy, you're being funny."

Piroja smiles but is confused. "No, I'm just asking."

Sunila lets go of her mother's hand at the entrance of the school.

"I can't see him, Mummy, that's the funny part." Then she stops and turns, extends her index finger out toward her mother and then rotates it in a semicircle so it points to her own heart. "But he's my brother; I think he would look a whole lot like me."

Piroja watches her daughter skip into the brownstone school-house. Sunny and Sunila. Sunny as Sunila. She can see Sunila now joining a group of her Grade-One friends—when they came here from Halifax the school placed five-year-old Sunila in Grade One, since she clearly had the ability and the maturity for that level—and they all now wave to Piroja at the door, wave their goodbyes and, as a group, quickly disappear into the hallways of the school.

Dopplers, redshifts, and other gangs

Piroja stands by the lake listening to the wind howl in over choppy waters. She is thirty-one years old, and an observer might imagine her to be in complete control of her own destiny. In her left hand she turns a silver anna piece, a coin dated 1878, the head of Queen Victoria, scratched but clearly noble, on the obverse. This was a gift from her father, which he gave to her when they visited him in Nowgong. "This will be good for you," he had said, placing the worn coin in her palm and pressing her fingers around it. "We make choices, sometimes on whims, but these choices are important in the moment and for the rest of our lives," he had said, and Piroja imagined he was getting a bit teary-eyed. It had been a good visit, somewhat odd, and far too short.

The oddness had been most evident when father and daughter were in the presence of ever-sweet Sunila. Grandfather Jamshed could not keep his eyes off her, always fiddling with her garments in that way that men who have had children of their own but have never been primary caretakers often have. But with Jamshed it was something more, as if by looking and touching, he was trying to convince himself that this child was real. After their Khajurao tour, Piroja was in the kitchen one day while Jamshed sat with the sleeping girl in the living room, and she swore she heard her father say, "Sunny, is that you?" but when she asked what he had said, he denied having done anything but coo. But from that time on, whenever she looked at the lined face of her father, she wondered at the conversations he might have had as a young boy, as a young man, with the mysterious Sunny. Although Jamshed had never breathed a word of this to her until that Khajurao visit, she felt now an incredible bond—one not shared by most fathers and daughters—the bond of having conversed with putatively unborn descendants. But the speaking-with-Sunny moments remained unspoken between father and daughter.

Piroja stands on the shore of Lake Ontario, feels the stiff, cold wind blow off the water that occasionally lifts a spit of ice spray to bristle her face. Her arms are drawn up close around her and shoulders scrunch against the cold to form an isosceles triangle, arm-shoulder-head. She leans into the wind, supporting herself by planting her feet in the snow and sand. Piroja looks up at the grey sky, listens to the hard sounds of the lake, and absently plays with the anna coin. She sometimes comes out here to be alone—not a luxury she could enjoy when she worked in Delhi or York—for she misses the isolation she remembered from Nowgong. When Sunila came along, she had no privacy whatsoever. But now her daughter is at school, and Piroja works only part- time, so she can take time for herself. She rides the subway, sometimes for a couple of hours; it gives her an odd sense of being alone in a maze of others. Or she walks around, usually ending up at the Beaches, the closest thing she can imagine to standing at the ocean and looking back to wherever home might have been on the other side. She often wonders if she is she getting closer to her home or further away. Songs play through her head, light and dancey or serious and political, whenever she comes to the Beaches. This day, the lyrics of surmounting obstacles, we shall overcome, but who were the "we" and what were we battling against?

Piroja looks at the anna coin, flips the cold metal over in her hand, thinks of the difference a coin can make. On the one side, her daughter, beautiful and sunny Sunila, a joy to behold and a gift to their lives. On the other, more well-worn and harder to read, this boy, articulate and unborn Sunny, an artifice that has haunted her father's and now her own imagination. He isn't Pinocchio, jumped off the screen (she and Sunila had seen this film the previous Christmas) to become a real boy, but a spirit who inhabits her mind and her daughter's, becoming real by being known, was that it? She could not help but draw parallels between the stories of Pinocchio and Sunny. When Mrs Olivieri saw the English translation of the book in their apartment, she smiled and pointed, saying, "*un vero e proprio bambino,*" a real little boy. Then Mrs Olivieri wagged her finger disparagingly, telling Piroja, "But not like that Mr Walter Disney does it, all cartoons and fun, no, Carlo Collodi, he wanted to teach about becoming true. Anyone can be real! But to be good, ah, that's another thing." Sunny, an imaginary brother writ real. Sunny and Sunila, now so inseparable in Piroja's mind that, at times, she really did feel that she had birthed twins, or perhaps a conjoined twin, where one has totally consumed the other—but, if so, who had consumed whom? Was this Sunny in daughterly form or Sunila with a sonly soul? They may as well be twins, thinks Piroja. Brother and sister. Two sides of the same.

May I introduce to you, the boy you've known for all these years?

If Piroja had a slightly difficult time articulating this twinness in their lives, Pradeep was completely, fully, and absolutely gobsmacked. This was a term he had picked up while in York, and it suited his purposes and personality perfectly. He was gobsmacked when someone shouted a racist epithet from a stretcher, gobsmacked when he missed the train to work, gobsmacked when a meal was particularly tasty. His friends had taken him aside and explained to him that the term had a very particular usage and that to bandy it about as a generic expression for surprise, from mild to extreme, was to do disservice to the word. But that did not keep Pradeep from using it, only convinced him to change its emphasis depending on extremes, and while this amended usage satisfied neither his friends nor Piroja ("You could expand your vocabulary"), it at least telegraphed a purpose of a kind.

But when Piroja sat him down one day on his return from work and told him that she felt firmly now that this Sunny boy did exist, had found an existence real enough to taste by living inside Sunila and was becoming a corporeal being through a rather complicated history of births, rebirths, visitations, grandfathers, mothers, daughters, and acts of absolute will, well, Pradeep sat there, an expression on his face much as the one he wore after Piroja had unintentionally tenderized his forehead. He did not, for once, say he was gobsmacked, but if ever there was an appropriate use of the term, this would have been it. Indeed, to break the silence, Piroja asked him, in the matter-of-fact tone one might use when asking a small child if her skinned knee hurt very much, "Pradeep, are you gobsmacked?" At this, he nodded assuredly before returning to his statuesque pose which, thereafter, seemed to be a type of reserve he built into his body that said, "I am ready for anything, but I don't quite believe what I have got myself into."

Sunila, meanwhile, was nothing if not blasé about the whole thing. I was as real to her as anyone could be, and while I may not have walked alongside her in corporeality, that did not mean I did not walk alongside her.

Will they be all right, do you think?

Pradeep stares off at a wall, eyes glazed over and a slight saliva bubble forming through barely parted lips.

"Oh, I think so. These things take time," responds Sunila.

Hm, yes, I suppose.

If I were, at this moment, fleshlyblood, I would try to catch Pradeep's attention by making blowfish faces or whistling in a way normally reserved for communicating with caged birds. But if I seemed mercurial as a disembodied voice to Jamshed and Piroja, I am even more so as an imaginary friend to Sunila. For her part, Sunila is entirely nonplussed, unfamiliar as she is with my interplay in the lives of the generations that preceded her.

"Mummy gets a strange look on her face when I talk about you," she tells me, pointing to where I might be, were I a bodily brother standing by her side, her thick eyebrows furrowing in a manner that will later make admirers swoon.

We make choices, and in this case, Sunila, you made a pretty strong one, to bring a brother into being. Good job, I say, good thoughts can sometimes leap over good words and go straight to good deeds.

No escape from reality

Being a rather resourceful young woman, Piroja was able to make the reiteration of Sunny a fairly normal and low-key affair. But in order to do so, and in order to make sense of it all, she began a strange form of monologic muttering. This gave her the appearance of a person so busy that she had to coordinate her life by uttering aloud her day-to-day activities and tasks, though Piroja was instead fabricating a backstory for Sunny. "He is an orphan whose parents were unknown," or "He is a distant cousin born in Zanzibar," or "He is a fraternal twin to Sunila who was lost during childbirth," she would mutter indecipherably. Sometimes Piroja wondered what would happen if their small family was reported as harbouring a child illegally residing in the country, as Sunila had taken it upon herself to talk about her brother as if he were flesh and blood. She realized that she could not throw herself on the mercy of any conceivable court, explain that the undocumented child was a son of hers, per se if not per utero, that figments of imagination could become figures if you only let your conscience be your guide.

Still, this did not deter her from her daily duties and functions, and soon enough it all seemed normal. It was only when she was writing to her father that it seemed unusual, for I was clearly real to Sunila, but to Jamshed, I was still that marvellous character who had done everything from introduce him to his wife to set him up on the straight and narrow as far as his career and religious service was concerned, and for Piroja, I was a curious wisp who had somehow deliberated with her own dead mother to transform her from despising to loving a Hindu son-in-law.

But what Piroja could not know was that since Sunila had become my sister, and, oh yes, she was most certainly that, I had come into being in a way none of us could have expected. Lacking a body, I could not attend school, but now I felt a desire to do *something* between the hours of nine to three, whereas before I simply came and went. Where did I go when I wasn't talking to Jamshed or Parvin or Piroja? That I could not say, call it a deep sleep, but after talking to Sunila, it was all different, vastly different, and here I was, still. No escape from reality now. I decided to spend her school hours listening to and memorizing all the songs on the radio that played all day, to keep the burglars away, in their apartment. I could then inform Sunila of the latest in music. I took it upon myself to take up music in more than a humming-along way; too, or rather, through me, Sunila did, creating drumsticks out of ladles and stringed instruments out of surgical sutures, anything she could get her hands on to make a note, a chord, or simple melody.

Most traumatized by my presence was Pradeep, since he had never entertained thoughts of unborn children enunciating themselves in everything but corporeality before, and from his discussions with the very calm Piroja and the equally relaxed Sunila, he was convinced there was some sort of recessive Zoroastrian gene that allowed for the influx of the utterly unreal into their lives. Piroja helped feed into this, partly in jest, but partly to help Pradeep maintain that illusion.

"You try bouncing along from Persia to Diu to Surat to Bombay. This kind of migration can be hard on a culture. You Hindus have it easy. A big land mass, a pantheon of gods, and, *voilà*, a pick-and-choose reality. As Zarathustris, we have learned to be more circumspect. That silver lining on a cloud may be the glint from a machine-gun nest."

"I mean, as Hindus, yes, children might look to different gods and all. But most of them are born first."

"Oh, but look at history. Was Ganesh born? Not even the first time around; built up by Parvati, and not the second time around either, a revived model made by Shiva. I grew up with these stories too, you know."

"But that's mythology. This is—our lives."

"And a good thing it is, too."

"Besides, you're just trying to justify this crazy—"

"Family?"

"I was going to say 'situation.'"

"Maybe, true enough," Piroja would say. And that was the way their conversations would usually go before (and it did not take long) Pradeep stopped trying to make this sound logical or explain things, even to himself. He still could not bring himself to enter into lengthy conversations with Sunila about her absent-present brother and sometimes felt guilty for ignoring her, but how, after all, could he in good conscience talk to his daughter about this figment? One time only, Pradeep sat down with Sunila to talk about family matters.

"Look here, uh, Sunila, the thing is this. This Sunny fellow, well, I must say, I am gobsmacked beyond belief, and do you think it might be time, that is, I think it might be time for you to see somebody, a friend of mine at the hospital, she is very good at helping with issues such as this."

Sunila, wrapping a surgical glove around a cluster of bound eggcups, her latest musical invention that played like a wobbly castanet, nodded seriously.

"It is as if—Sunila, uh, how long do you think Sunny will be around?"

Sunila shrugged.

"I guess I am saying I am not sure if it isn't time for us to deal with this, well, professionally?"

Sunila said nothing but looked up at Pradeep and smiled.

"Tea?" she inquired, quite sweetly, and without waiting for an answer proceeded to pour for Pradeep a cup of the strong Darjeeling brew he was fond of.

"Uh, thank you," said Pradeep, watching as Sunila filled the cup to within a shade of the brim, then poured in enough milk to take it to near overflowing.

"Sugar?" she asked.

Pradeep shook his head but did not stop her when she proceeded to put spoonful after spoonful into the full cup.

"You see?" said Sunila. "This tea is your family, full to the brim. No room for any more, you say? Ah, but Sunny is the sugar. What did I put in, three, four spoonfuls? But look, no overflowing, no spilling on to tables, no wastage, no crowding."

Pradeep nodded. He had heard this metaphor many times, but had never had it demonstrated by a five-year-old, and despite her limited years, Sunila's vocabulary had advanced to such a stage that it was no longer surprising to hear her engage in almost philosophical discourses, though she had learned to speak in simpler sentences at school, just as a matter of convenience.

"And on top of that—"

"Yes," said Pradeep, "on top of that, he sweetens the family. Sugar and milk. The story of how the Parsis came to stay in India."

"Ah, you've heard this? Who told you?"

"Who didn't? Your mother, Jamshed, and pretty much any Parsi I've ever met. Okay, Sunila, your point is well made. Okay."

"Okay back at you, daddy-oh," said Sunila with a wink and a grin, throwing an approving fingerpoint in her father's direction.

When Sunila and I were together, it was as if the world ceased outside our own creative space. To the outside world, Sunila appeared to be looking into a mirror, as if she were being mimicked or was mimicking. If we were walking side by side, she ambled as if comfortably connected alongside somebody, taking care to avoid objects as if she wore a conjoined twin on her hip. When we spoke, though we did not do that irritating best-friend thing of finishing each other's sentences, we did have a way of reading each other's thoughts so that we could carry on complex arguments between the two of us. This caused more than a few raised eyebrows when Sunila was, at five and six, speaking in what seemed to be half-conversations, listening attentively to the other side of an unheard conversation.

By the time she was seven (and, back in the old country, Prime Minister Shastri experienced a life-ending coronary, and Mrs Gandhi succeeded him and began a dynasty of sorts—her sons would both be half-Parsis—and here in the new country a relatively unknown Shakespearean actor from Montreal suddenly graced the screens in a television sci-fi drama), it was less than odd that Sunila would start talking to Sunny of a Congress party investment in Russia and then skip over to the physical possibilities and impossibilities of teleporters. When she turned eight (and, in the old country, a Gujarati girl was born who grew up to be a Miss India and have Parsi children, and here, in the new country, a centenary was celebrated), Sunny and Sunila discussed the particularities of nationhood and citizenship and religious histories. And when she turned nine (and there was revolution in the air and, in India, more grumblings over borders and nations and, in the new country, a most eligible bachelor led the country out of bedrooms and into socialized medicine), Sunny and Sunila discussed military suppression and at what point do good Parsis take up arms against a sea of troubles. When she was ten (and, in the old country, a Congress bifurcated and, if hydras can have only two heads then this one did, and, in the new country, a stock exchange went up in smoke and a time of tumult and revolt and actions directly taken and *propagande par le fait* began), Sunila talked to Sunny about what they needed to do to make things happen, not just in their lives but in the lives around them, the lives of their parents, their friends, their city, their province.

This is the path that Sunila and Sunny are on, spinning ever forward, listening to the heartbeats around them, the slow inbreathing and outbreathing in the city around them and the complexities of the world that shatters and recreates around them. In 1969, Sunny and Sunila, aged ten, sit down and make a plan.

Sometimes I wish I'd never been born at all

About a year after Sunila shared with her parents my brotherly appearance, no sooner, Sunila had begun to wear a marvellously long, woollen red scarf. It was winter, and to brace against the cold on Toronto streets, such a garment was necessary. The scarf was replaced with a silken variation when the weather warmed, and Sunila often used the scarf to cover her lips, which enhanced her mystery, focussing all attention on her furrowing brow. Although, for most, this was ascribed to childish acting out, the occasional prim and proper adult demanded to "see your mouth" when she was speaking—the same type of adult who became a schoolteacher and consistently insisted on gum-spitting-out from students, no matter how unobtrusive they were being—but few made mention of the scarf, silken or woollen, believing, as proved the case, that its novelty would wear off as do most childish things.

So, when Sunila did doff this facial curtain at the age of ten in 1969, it became clear to all that, far from being misshapen, a peculiarly beautiful mouth and chin was what Sunila had kept all covered up and hidden for all that time. Her lips were veritably serpentine, able to perform the most masterful tricks, such that a smile was a godly anointment, a sight to behold, and her speech transfixed the recipient as much for what was said as for how those lips moved lyrically in the telling of the story. And that chin, with a life of its own, soft and supple and yet so eager to lean into a conversation, take part, facilitate. Sunila had a wonderfully engaging lower face, matching and perhaps exceeding the qualities of its upper half; the nose (Parsi *in extremis*), the cheeks, the eyes and lashes, and, of course, those swoon-inducing eyebrows.

It may be taking liberties to say that I resembled Sunila, that we could have passed as twins easily enough, what with facial features, body type, and temperament—for how can twins resemble each other if there is only one of them? Yet there was always that twinness so apparent in Sunila, still walking alongside me, that it is not really that far-fetched to surmise so. And then there was the music. It could be summed up by saying if Sunila was the musician, I was her number-one fan. I waited for her lead, sometimes to excess; an unfamiliar gender dynamic was being played out between us— the aggressive and assertive sister to the demure and second-place brother. But of course, none of this was apparent because I did not exist, outside of my sister's vivid imagination. Yet in that imagination, I was always listening for the newest sound, the freshest music vibe to ride, and she was listening with me.

I was as much a creation of Sunila as could be, though even with her wilful assertion, I remained a noncorporeal being, a bodyless voice. I lived *for* her because I did not have a self to live for. I was not her alter ego but a manifestation of her, pure and simple. The only difference between Sunila and her grandfather was that she did not have to go right or toe tap and be labelled "the quirky child," for her imagination was made manifest, in a manner of speaking, beside her for all to see. The significant shift between Sunila and her mother was that while Piroja waited for her son to appear, Sunila took action and conjured me up. As we grew older, Sunila knew it, though it did sometimes take some reminding.

What should we do for our tenth birthday?

"My tenth birthday."

Have it your way. I can be as ten as you can.

"You've never been ten …. What would you like to do?"

I think we should start a band.

"You have a band. You are a band."

No. I mean you and me. Like Peter and Mary without the Paul.

"Or John and Paul without Ringo and George."

No, I think we should be Ringo and George, without John and Paul.

"And what would we call this band?"

Funny you should ask. Was just thinking that. A good Parsi name.

"Sunny and Sunil?"

Those aren't Parsi names. Either of them.

"Aren't we Parsis?"

Not according to the Panchayat. Besides, the names aren't even remotely Parsi.

"How about 'A Boy Named Sunny'?"

Funny. That's more like a song than a group.

"'I Started a Band that Had the Whole World Laughing'?"

Even funnier. Why not, 'I'll Never Start a Band Again'? Or, 'Give Band a Chance'?

"So if we start a band … I'm the only one who can play. What do you do? Backup singing, silent choir?"

Ah, me. I will be the writer.

"I've had enough of this. I'm leaving."

On a jet plane?

"You know what they say. One is the loneliest number."

Ha, touché! Good one.

At that we both crack up, laughing at the play, at our lyrical witticisms. But within the humour, behind the laughter, there is a kernel of dedicated seriousness. And Sunila knew that, although she may have created me, breathed life into me so that a boy could be part of her family, I was the one who led her on, who drove her forward and made things happen. If I said we should stand out in the rain and get drenched, though Sunila might protest, we (or she) would be bone-wet by the end of it. And if I said we should mark our birthday—we always celebrated on July 1 even though Sunila was born several strokes shy of midnight, but because of her clock-pointing, her parents decided to shift things to the future—by starting a band, then that is precisely what we would do. Whether, in this complex dynamic, I was generating ideas or merely reflecting Sunila's wishes, was no one else's concern. On July 1, 1969, we two, Sunny and Sunila, started a band.

Nothing really matters

It is a few days after Sunila's birthday and the family is sitting down to a Saturday evening news show. Although we have a black-and-white television, and an older model at that, Sunila always points excitedly when the grey-toned butterfly expands its wings on the screen, thinking this time, *this* time, the ensuing show will be in colour. She has told no one but me about this fixation she has, and although she knows enough about mechanics and how black-and-white televisions do not suddenly produce colour, this is not enough to quell her excitement every time the butterfly unfurls. Television host Lloyd is on to tell us about the latest goings-on in Ottawa, Piroja is going over the family accounts, Pradeep is trying very hard to stay awake as he has just come off night shift the day before, and Sunila lies on her belly on the floor, her calves and feet twirling around as she scrawl words and notes on tiny scraps of paper.

"Whatever are you doing now?" asks Pradeep, trying to keep himself awake.

"Um," says Sunila, caught in her task, "just writing songs."

And music, I add.

"This band of yours?"

The foot-twirling Sunila nods vaguely.

"Do you have a name yet?" asks Pradeep, now actually interested.

"Well," says Sunila, "we thought of an animal name, you know, like the Byrds or the Beatles or the Monkees."

And then we thought of one-word leader-type names—the Presidents, or Monarch, or Rani.

"Or something leaderly. I liked Monarch," says Sunila. "Has both

417

leaders and animals, like butterflies. I thought Rani was just too—
too —"

Girly?

"Too girly."

"So?" asks Pradeep. "What do you call yourself?"

Piroja looks up from her bookkeeping and smiles. "The Dominion. She is calling the band the Dominion, because she was born on Dominion Day. Almost."

Exactly.

"It's quite perfect, don't you think, Daddy?"

"Hm," says Pradeep, pondering. "It doesn't sound too—harsh?"

"Harsh!" says Sunila. "It's so mild—you're soaking in it. Softens your hands as you do the dishes."

Pradeep looks perplexed. "I'm sorry?"

"Madge," says Sunila matter-of-factly, pointing to her left-hand fingernails. "Madge the manicurist. So mild you can soak your hands in it. That's the kind of band we have."

"I see," says Pradeep.

"It's a television advertisement," says Piroja.

"I see," repeats Pradeep, still not seeing.

"But," adds Sunila. "Mild and strong. Ha!" She cuts through the air with a karate chop. "Only one cavity!"

"Indeed," says Pradeep.

"The Dominions!" shouts Sunila, leaping to her feet. "The Dominions are the new sound."

"Dominion or Dominions?" asks Pradeep.

Either which way. Together, we are the Dominions. But each of us is a Dominion. I guess.

"Indeed. We are all dominions. In any case," adds Sunila, "you're soaking in it."

Consult, Panchayat style

"But what sort of life is it for a Parsi child, to be a musician?" Mr Godrej speaks this with the same querulous tone he uses when deriding fascist governments or complaining that his eggs are too soft. He lifts his shoulders from a hunch and turns his right hand so that it follows a 180 degree arc, a move that Pradeep thinks looks a little bit like screwing in a light bulb (and will gain notoriety and fashionability only many years later when the newest dance craze reaches Toronto from the villages of Punjab via London). "What sort, I ask you?"

"Well," says Piroja, "they said the same of nursing when I took it up. What does it matter?"

"Exactly," says Mr Godrej, screwing in another light bulb, this one apparently already hot to the touch for the hand spin is quicker and more acerbic, "nursing. We Parsis," he looks around the room knowingly, "we Parsis have to be careful how we present ourselves to the wider community."

There are eleven Parsis, one Hindu, and a Sikh crowded into Piroja and Pradeep's living room, invited for a social gathering, but, like all social gatherings at Piroja and Pradeep's, when the majority of guests are Parsis, it has turned into a mildly political squabble. Mr Godrej, whose first name is never disclosed though he uses the initials S.K. when signing documents, is there with his wife, Firozsha, whom everyone refers to as Fanny. Also present are the brothers Dhondy—Homi, Faroukh, and Dada—who sip their beer gingerly and in unison, contributing mostly in monosyllables. Staring out the window is Persis Sidwha, a sorrowful widower, and with him is his sullen daughter, Farah, whom no one has ever heard utter a word in social gatherings. Adi Khanga, a short and balding dastur, sits quietly with his hands folded on his lap and next to him his wife, Bapsi, a rotund woman who is constantly chewing on something and gesturing with one free hand, while with the other, feeding nuts into her mouth. Cyrus Metha is the tenth Parsi in the room, a professor of sociology with a specialization in religious thought who plays an active role in the community. Finally, there sits Gopal Singh, an ageless Sikh who has worked security at every large downtown bank and now operates his own security business, The Khalsa Group, whose trademark is a large, roaring lion's head.

"We have to be careful," repeats Mr Godrej, and Mrs Godrej nods emphatically, while the Dhondy brothers take a slow, then a fast sip, of the beers that Pradeep has provided for them, and Bapsi Khanga crunches on yet another handful of cashews.

"What about," asks Cyrus from the stool in the corner, "that conductor fellow in Montreal?"

"Conductor?" asks Persis, his attention brought back from outside.

"Yes-yes, the Mehta fellow. I think he left for the States."

"A conductor," says Mr Godrej, raising one finger and swinging it as a conductor might, "a conductor is not a musician. He is a leader. Yes, very fine and good."

"But," says Pradeep, "doesn't it matter if the music is well-respected?"

"Good point," says Homi Dhondy.

"Good point," adds Faroukh Dhondy.

"Excellent point," adds Dada Dhondy.

The brothers look at each other and smirk their agreement, then urgently take a large swig from their bottles.

"What he is saying," says Mrs Godrej, still nodding emphatically, "is that we Parsis have to watch our backs. We have to stand tall in the saddle. We have to be twice as good to earn half as much."

Bapsi Khanga stares at Mrs Godrej and throws three, then another four cashews into her mouth and crunches them excitedly.

"Well, yes," says the dastur mildly. "Mr and Mrs Godrej are correct, of course, and we have to be careful how we project ourselves."

And with that pronouncement, someone shifts a chair and someone else makes a brief note about the weather and then all of a sudden there are six different conversations happening, and the group seems not to mind at all that they have shifted from a one-person-at-a-time consulting circle to more of a party. Still, Piroja is bothered by all of this. Why is there such deferral to appearances? She shuffles off to the kitchen to fetch more snacks for the guests and stops to peer into Sunila's bedroom as she does so. Her daughter sits in front of her desk, writing furiously, and the way her head is bobbing up and down to an unheard sound, Piroja knows Sunila is composing yet another song to arrange. It has been two years since her daughter decided to form a band, and despite her relative youth, she has stuck with it, so that now, nearing her twelfth birthday, the small assortment of adolescents she auditioned and then asked to join her band are really quite good. The only concern, for Piroja, was how her daughter now seemed to talk entirely in advertising one-liners. If she or Pradeep were short of breath coming up the stairs, Sunila would tell them, "Put a tiger in your tank!" If her parents were discussing painting the bathroom eggshell white, "You'll wonder where the yellow went," is what Sunila would mutter. Sunila's clear favourite was, "You're soaking in it," which came to mean everything and nothing and soon was picked up not just by her parents but by her friends and some of her parents' friends. It was never, "You're up to your neck," or "He's buried in his work," or any such expression that signified similarly. Only, and always, *you're soaking in it*.

And, thinks Piroja, this is exactly what Sunila herself has done, immersed herself in the band and the music, soaking in it so much so that it was no surprise that their friends thought it was a bit over the top. Yet, when Sunila sat opposite to the twin that only she could see (although, she admitted, she could not *really* see), playing the cheap guitar her parents had bought her after that first year of playing makeshift instruments and tapping out rhythms on whatever percussive surface was handy, then, thinks Piroja, then everyone could see how music was indeed her daughter's calling. The lyrics of her home-made songs ranged from obtuse to simplistic, from profound to mundane, but when she sang, oh, when that girl sang, it was as if complementary voices filled up the tiny apartment. Then let anyone say anything about this music-schmusic thing being lowbrow, un-Parsi-like. Let them, thinks Piroja. Let them. And let her daughter sing for all she was worth. Piroja fetches more snacks from the kitchen cupboards and brings them to the living room, pausing once again to see Sunila's bobbing head keeping time to the scribbles on her notepad.

This ain't no disco

"But I don't know if we're ready for our first gig."

Of course we are. We have a drummer. And a bass.

"They seem a long way from ready."

Yeah, it seems. But we have to try.

"I don't know, Sunny. It's a stretch. We don't want to be soaking in it."

Hm. Yes, I see. But ...

Sunila is now fourteen and is, by all external perspectives, quite a song-writing and singing virtuoso. She goes to school by day and spends her afternoons in practice. For a while, Sunila got into a bit of junior-high-school sports, volleyball, basketball, even a bit of baseball, but her heart was not in it. She would hum to herself a few slogans from car commercials before (pointing and) serving, or try to compose lyrics to the rhythmic dribbling, or stand alone in left field anticipating the next crack of the bat as a staccato interruption into planned and sustained silence. Her teammates—for she was extremely popular, being all that girls of that age looked for: pretty, intelligent, kind, and independent—tried to loop her into further social activities, but Sunila would have none of that. She did once take a band class in Grade Seven, but who wanted to learn clarinet or flute and go through endless renditions of "Pomp and Circumstance" when, after all, she already had a band? So, much to the consternation of Piroja and Pradeep, she dropped band and took up shop instead, which proved eminently useful once they got beyond making tic-tac-toe boards and ashtrays and on to the finer points of welding and auto mechanics. (Beyond, too, the catcalls and critiques, the "What's a girl doing in shop anyway?" But after she arm-wrestled Jimmie Northrup and lost but then kicked his heels out from under him when he laughed at her for being a "wimpy girl," Sunila was more or less accepted, at first begrudgingly, then as one of the boys, at least by the other students if not Mr Blaine, who never could figure out what to do with a girl in his class).

And then there was the weekend busking.

Subway stations were best, though the Dominion would often play above-ground, too, if the weather was fine and the possibilities for gathering a crowd were there. Before beginning to play, they would look at each other and figure out which of the seven or eight current numbers to "put out to the people." Always, arm raised, hand outstretched, finger pointing to an imagined star in a invisible constellation somewhere behind the tiled tunnels, Sunila would start a cappella—her voice soft but strong and containing within it a wavering, captivating quality—for a line or two, at the most a verse, before the bass player, Jeremy Ess (his last name began with that initial but was far too multisyllabic and Eastern European for anyone to remember or pronounce), would duck in with either a resounding chord or an intimate note that would pick up on Sunila's voice, and off they would go. Percussionist Daisy Steward would pick up as the voice and guitar gathered speed and the band took flight.

The money they brought in through busking was good, surprisingly so, perhaps because it was the early 1970s and people did not know what else to do with their leftover change, or maybe it was because the sight of three teenaged kids led by a gorgeous brown girl singing in English (imagine that) strange and yet familiar versions of rock-and-roll hits (kudos for assimilation) was just too great a vision of multiculturalism to ignore. Coins dropped into a Panama hat. More notes, more lyrics, more subway stations, until one day, Sunila sits at a café on College Street, sipping cold drinks on a patio, the only customer not drinking strong coffee and gesturing wildly about politics.

I see. But, if we don't do this now, will we ever?

"Okay, okay, okay, so what do we do? What do we do with our bassist and drummer?"

We have to whip them into shape.

"But they're good. Daisy can bang a drum and Jeremy can follow a lead, so what's wrong with that?"

It's missing something. A lot. Someone has to play percussion, really play it, and we need some deep fourstring.

"Deep fourstring? What the hell does that mean?"

Hey, listen, just talk to them.

Sunila sits there and looks into where my eyes would be, across from her, if I were physical in the slightest. My hair would be a curious reflection of her own, which is finer and six inches longer (than my imaginary shag haircut) as it comes down to her shoulder blades. I would have fire in my eyes, sometimes, and this would be one such occasion.

"Okay," she says. "You have a point. I'll try."

Garage band

Sunila sits at the keyboard in the quiet and dark space that they have found as their "studio." When it is not their studio, a 1969 Ford Parklane sits in that space now occupied by a couple of music stands, a keyboard, and a drum set that has seen better days. Sunila runs a few keys idly with her right hand and hums a lyric to herself. Jeremy stands across from her and Daisy is seated at the trap set in the corner.

"The sound is just not right," Sunila finally says. "We need another voice."

"We should just do more covers," says Jeremy, his hand in front of his mouth, muffling his voice and hiding what he is certain are the most uneven teeth in the universe.

"We do enough covers," says Sunila, with a certainty that the band has become used to. "We need to do more of our own."

"Well, your own," peeps up Daisy from behind her drums. "You're the only one who writes for the Dominion."

Sunila looks over at her drummer. "Daisy? Do you want to write?"

Daisy blushes and looks down. "I—I like to write. Poetry mostly, though, I don't know how it would look as a song."

"Well, we are missing a sound. Maybe you should write for us. You too, Jeremy."

"Nah," says Jeremy, laughing. "I just play and back you up. I'm good with that."

"Then what will we do about the sound? We need—we *need*—another voice."

"Maybe we need another singer?" offers Daisy.

"No. No, that's not it. We need a different voice. And I have an idea."

Break free

Sunila sits in front of the bathroom mirror, inspects her face, experiments with various types of smiles and frowns, bats her eyelashes, and sees if she can see herself. No, she thinks. She cannot. If she had an anna coin, she might twirl it aimlessly between thumb and forefinger, might even scrutinize its scraped and worn surfaces, think about where the coin had been and through whose hands it had passed. But she would not toss such a coin, would not let her fate be decided by a sliver of silver, would not bet it all on one game of pitch and toss, and lose, and start again at her beginnings—none of that for her. She inspects her face, the smoothness of skin, the blemishes, the pores, and thinks that the choices are all hers, lying before her, hers for the taking. Hers and mine. Sunny's and Sunny's, and at this she smiles fully, showing her teeth, or my teeth, it all amounts to the same thing, to the same person. These, she thinks, are the best thoughts she can have, and when she sings, those will be the best words she can utter, and all that she does in the world, those will, indeed, be the best deeds. Sunila shakes her head so her hair, gloss-black and wavy, thick and full, takes on a life of its own, moving along her brow, her ears, her neck. Although she was always complimented on her eyes and face and form, her thick locks never failed to garner admirers. As a teenager, that cascade of long hair was still her most attractive physical attribute. The Girl with the Thick Black Tresses. So pretty, so fine, so beautiful.

Sunila lets her smile diminish to a straight-lipped visage, a perfect horizontal line formed by her lips. She raises her right hand and the mirror reflects the delicate but efficacious silver scissors. She does not look at them directly, only in the mirror. With her left hand she strokes and holds a few stray strands of hair that cross her forehead, and with her right hand she points at these solitary strands as if catching them in the crosshairs. With deliberate action, she embraces them between the fore and aft arms of the scissors, closes them together with a sharp snap, and the strands break free into her fingers. She gathers a larger section and snips. Then more. Soon she is cutting furiously, handfuls at a time, left side, right side, from the top, from everywhere. Cut, chop, snip—hair falling all around her now, tufts and chunks, wavy sections and straight portions, black as pitch, covering the sink, the floor, flowing over to the bathtub and clinging to the wall, hair everywhere. Sunila sees her face break free from the dark mass, expertly extricated, and the mirror shows only an inch of outcropping, magnificently and surprisingly even, as if professionally cut. When she is finished, she places the scissors into the sink so gingerly they don't make a sound, and Sunila inspects her face, her new face, unframed and bright, brilliant even, the smoothness radiant, the blemishes stunningly sharp. It is June 30, 1974, close to midnight, and tomorrow is a bank holiday, and Sunila will meet with Dominion in the early afternoon to tell them everything is about to change. Happy birthday, she says to herself and smiles a smile unfettered by feathers of blackness.

Happy birthday.

"Yes, it will be a happy one, won't it, Sunny?"

You look like me.

"Ha. In a manner of speaking! But I really look like me. Out from under."

You look like we.

"Hm. That is something I can live with. Looking like we. This time, I know it's for real."

You seem to be what you're not, I see.

"Too much pretending?"

Yes and no. Maybe too real.

"Time has come. We've got to go."

Where do we go from here?

"To the garage tomorrow afternoon. We have another voice."

My voice?

"In a manner of speaking, yet again. My voice."

Our voice?

"Hm. Let's call it *a* voice, a new voice."

And this time we know it's for real?

"Exactly. Everything new. Like the first time. Let me show you something."

Sunila moves away from the mirror, exits the bathroom leaving it exactly as it is, looking as if a mighty massacre of hairy animals has occurred, and goes to her room. She opens the small cupboard that serves as her wardrobe, a converted closet that somehow fits all that she owns. She reaches to the back, the furthest hanger from the door, and pulls out a bright yellow tunic, buttons down both sides, with ornate yet exquisitely underplayed sequins running the length of the top. It is vaguely militaristic, vaguely marching-band, vaguely religious. She slips it on easily, ties it firmly so that her breasts, modest to begin with, are strapped down. Not a masquerade, she says to Sunny and to herself, because the girl is still readily apparent, but the boy comes out too. Standing in front of the full-length mirror by her bedside, she dons mustard tights that complement and accentuate the tunic. Then she pulls out eyeliner, applying it to her lids in darker and deeper quantities that she has before, and she is the boy becoming the girl, or the girl becoming the boy becoming the girl. She flashes a grin to herself. Rhapsodic. All at once, she is everything, and this time it is for real. You're soaking in it, she says to herself, to me, and she hums it for the world to hear. You're soaking in all that is around you.

"Let's go make some music."
Let's get right out of here.

The band plays on

Jeremy and Daisy are sitting on the hood of the '69 Parklane inside the garage. Normally, Daisy's father would have moved it to let his daughter and friends have some space to make music. But today Daisy has told her father (for Sunila has told her) that they are only going to meet, not play, and talk about some ideas for the Dominion. So there they sit, legs dangling and heels lightly clicking back on the wheel hubs, waiting for Sunila.

"Did you try any writing?" Jeremy asks.

"Yeah, a bit. But it sounds so—sappy. Sunny won't like it."

"Me too. I can't seem to find the right words, you know? Far out."

Daisy smiles. Jeremy peppers his speech with what he thinks are cool phrases, but they never fully make sense to her or anyone else. Still, she humours him. "Far out," she agrees. "I wonder what Sunny wants to talk about anyway?"

"Got me. She did say that thing about another voice. Maybe she has another singer?"

"Nah. I don't think so. She's our singer. She's really the band, isn't she?"

"Yeah, groovy."

"Yeah. Groovy."

Daisy and Jeremy sit like that for a while, thinking idly, but not talking, so when Sunila finally does make her entrance, for just a moment, both Daisy and Jeremy think that they do have a new singer, but only for a moment. Despite the yellow tunic, the mustard pants, the short cropped hair, there is no denying this is their Sunila, the band leader. They both stop their swinging legs and sit upright.

"Wow," says Jeremy.

"Double wow," says Daisy.

"We have," says Sunila, "a new voice." And standing in front of them, she holds out a plastic baton that pretends to be a mic and begins to sing, as always, a cappella, but this time in a voice neither Daisy nor Jeremy, indeed no one, has ever heard before. It is almost baritone, wonderfully rich, exciting and full, everything a voice could be, can be, can ever be, and it fills that tiny garage and rappels down the sides of the Parklane, titillates the eardrums of the Dominion band members, lays into the undrywalled walls, circles the air like some predatory bird, scores the very cement floors. It carries upward an octave, then two, and drops back down three notes below from where it started, all within a single breath, and within that single breath are resonating thoughts turned words, flowing and floating in such tender and yet controlling ways that the sudden fistmaking and airgrabbing from the tiny brown hand seems perfect and delicious and performs the most delightful aria all on its own. This is a new voice, a new song, rambling between highs and lows and telling stories of operatic fantasy and love and folly, and it lasts, a cappella, for three incredibly long and fulfilling minutes, finishing with a high C that dribbles and drops down a full three octaves to gravel and groan into a deep recess of sadness, fading into silence, followed by further and lengthier silences as the two teenagers stare on, mesmerized.

"Holy shit."

"Double holy shit."

"That. That's the new voice. Sunny!" Jeremy does a cheekdance on the hood of the Parklane. "That's the New Voice. Totally cool!"

"But Sunny, where did it come from? Your voice was always ... versatile, but this, this is something else. This is ... incredible."

Sunila looks at her band members and points, slowly, at each of them. There is a time to be born and a time to die, she thinks to herself, a time to leave them all behind and face the truth. And this time I know it's for real.

Moving on

Nothing lasts forever. Things fall apart. And that goes for everything. I watch with what might seem to be sadness, but I am not so sure. I watch her sing. I watch the weeks and months of this new voice take on a new voice of its own. There are quibbles and troubles with the band, and although the Dominion still busks for a while in the subways, even does one high-school dance in the fall. But when there is newness, nothing can last. I can see that now, or maybe I always could. Oh, people try to make things work, try to make love stay, and all the rest of it, but after a steamy hot summer in Toronto and a fall full of arguments and some amount of spite, it is just before Christmas that they decide to call it quits. Or Jeremy and Daisy call it quits, intent on playing with each other, in more ways than one, and they just cannot abide this New Voice with which they cannot compete. It should not be a competition, this they know, but it feels like that, to them, to Sunila, to me. They know Sunila came up with the name, but they would like to keep it, they tell her. Sunila smiles. It's a name, she thinks, for a band, and they will make a band of it. Of course, she says, they can have the name. They can have their Dominion. And she—we—will have nothing but the Voice. That will be enough, though, more than enough. When Sunila gifts them with the name and walks out of the garage for the final time, there is no sadness for anyone, just a sense of moving on, resignedly, with choice and determination. The only impossible future, one that cannot be imagined.

Months turn to years. Sunila keeps her hair short, her makeup large, and her tunics rotating in colour, but always the same in their boldness. Her voice is always so pure and full it makes transit riders

435

miss their trains. Worrisome to her parents, of course, this strange sight of a girl, but their initial confusion has turned to something akin to fatigue. *Who is this child of ours?* they think. But Sunila is ever loving, ever caring, and ever theirs, and so oddness aside, shorn hair fading as an issue, gender still so complicated, Piroja and Pradeep acknowledge that these are changing times, and Sunny is a child of these times.

High school is over. Sunila turns nineteen and graduates with no shortage of beaus to take her to the prom; she happily, though not excitedly, chooses one who will be the least trouble, a kind slip of a boy, Nathan Everett, who desperately wants to kiss Sunila all night long but only manages the gumption to attempt this when he drops her off at midnight, and then it is an aborted attempt as he is already backing away from her on the sidewalk when his lips barely come in contact with her cheek. It's her first kiss, surprisingly, since so many wanted to, but none would dare. And she would have even kissed Nathan full on the lips if he had asked, but then, there he was, tripping on the sidewalk and running home.

"Waiting a year to go to college, that makes sense," says Piroja.

"Yes," agrees Pradeep. "But Sunny, you will go to college next year, will you not? Education … education is very important for us, you know."

Sunila takes this all in. "I cannot promise anything, Dad, Mum. But I can say that I agree, education is a good thing, so I won't write it off. For now, though, it has to be my music."

"Yes, yes, the music," sighs Pradeep. "Always the music. We know how important this is to you, yes. So the music it is."

"But," says Piroja, "where will you take this music? Still to the subway? "

Sunny laughs. "No, the subway was a training ground," she says. "Now it's going to be different. I don't have to go to school. And I've met some interesting people in the past few months, recording engineers, managers. Let's see where it goes from here."

Piroja and Pradeep look at each other haplessly, but not completely without hope. This is their daughter, and they will support her choices. On Sunila's birthday in 1979, they come to hear her play her first solo gig at a little club down on Yonge Street. The place is filled, the crowd is loud. And Sunny fills that place with a voice so pure and so complete that the room is blown away. The Voice has landed. Amazing. Hers, mine, ours; the voice is amazing and Piroja and Pradeep hold hands at the front table, and actually both begin to cry as they hear another voice that rises up from between the notes, a voice from long ago that once argued for medical school and a good Parsi marriage and husbandcide.

They feel Parvin float like a sonorous ghost between them, hovering over the table and singing in distinct disharmony with her granddaughter, and the voice grows hoarse with emotion and goes even further off-key, so that eardrums reverberate asynchronously. At that moment Parvin is there floating above the candle on the table shared by her daughter and son-in-law, smiling down, and her lyrics are choked into tears slipping down vaporous cheeks, coinciding with a temporary malfunction in the sprinkler unit directly above the table shared by Piroja and Pradeep, so the unit sweats out one orb, then another, each bulging and then slipping from the sprinkler to plummet to the faces below, one drop each, anointing husband and wife. The apologetic club manager will explain this as an unfortunate result of heat and humidity, but no explanations can explicate why only a single droplet touches the crown of each spouse, or why lysozyme and sodium, and not fluoride and water-treatment-plant calcium are present as precipitates when the drops evaporate. When they leave the club that night, while Sunny is talked up by her manager to her first record deal, Piroja and Pradeep walk home instead of taking the streetcar. They walk hand-in-hand and think to themselves how their job is done, and they even stop to kiss in the middle of the street, holding each other in the glare of city lights. And they are happy.

Voiceover

Yes, yes, yes, I want it all, and I want it now. Or I wanted it all, and I wanted it now. The best things in life are free, but they all come with a cost. Money can't buy love, but it can rent a bit of affection. And music can't buy a life. Travelling from Diu to Surat to Bombay to cities across oceans and across continents, we are always waiting, waiting, waiting, and always there is something else to wait for. Toto, you're not in Zanzibar anymore. I sit beside Sunila in a tiny office strangely wallpapered with a type of red velvet and adorned with three gold albums. This is downtown Los Angeles, and it is just before Christmas, 1980.

"But, baby, you can use this thing, what about a whistle or two, you know, beepbeep, that sort of thing, or one of those funky upside-down things, hey?"

"Mr Crow, that isn't really what I do. I'm more into the reaching out and touching someone, if you get my drift."

"Sunila, I totally know what you mean. My associate flew you down here because he heard your Toronto sound, yes he did, but, baby, he's more the find-the-sound guy, I'm the refine-the-sound guy, you know?"

"Um, where is Mr Devon?"

"Oh, poor guy, got himself laid up with some type of flu that turned into pneumonia, new-mo-sis-tis or some such thing. He wanted to be here, really he did."

"Look, Mr Crow, I would really like to work with your label, really I would. But the sound you're asking for is just—not mine."

"Suit yourself, baby, suit yourself."

"You know, I just don't want to wake up and find myself soaking in it."

"Uh, yeah, exactly, exactly."

Didn't exactly ring your bell?

"No, no bellringing."

Maybe we should go to London after all?

"Hm, might have to. Seems there's things happening there, at least, beside disco balls."

We are sitting in a somewhat dingy L.A. hotel room, another dismal day of record execs, and we have nowhere to go. Toronto is a day away, and then there are those execs in London who want to see us—that is, her. It has been a long slog, taking the voice to the people, and it will be a long road. Almost like waiting to be born. But all this can change with a phone call, which is what happens just now.

"Hello?"

"Sunila. It's Mummy."

"Hi, Mum! I was going to call you to let you know how things went. The execs here are looking for a sound that just isn't me, so I don't think I can do that. You know? Mum?"

"Sunila ..."

"Mum, what is it?"

"Sunila—it's your grandfather. He's—gone."

Revisitations

The trip "home" as Pradeep calls it, or the trip "back" as Piroja calls it, or the trip "there" as Sunila calls it, or the trip to "revisit" as I might say, is a flurry of rush and run. Sunila arrives back from L.A. and is greeted at the airport by her parents who have already packed and arranged for the three of them to catch their connecting flight from London on to Delhi. There is much hugging and crying at the departure lounge and more on the plane, and then it calms for the latter part of the flight, only to accentuate once they land and are greeted by relatives near and far. Just one night is spent in Delhi, then it's down to Bombay, where certain factions of the family have determined they should all gather for a large ceremony, even though Jamshed had spent so little time there in recent years. After the necessary fights and arguments, the three of them wend their way up to Delhi and down to Jhansi and decide to make a pilgrimage of sorts to Khajurao, even though it is well past Nowgong—because of family history, says Piroja—and then they are all there, all of us.

We make our way among the temples, admiring the friezes again, as we have done before at various times in our lives, stopping and fixating on the more obvious ones and speculating on the ones more discrete. Sunila reaches out to touch one of the figures, her hand opening and then clenching so that only a single finger points out, reaches out, touches and presses the hardness where there should be softness. I follow her lead and feel, of course, nothing, but then so follows Pradeep and his slender digits caress the figure most fondly, and then it is Piroja's turn, and she cups the body of rock with the palm of her hand, open and giving. I want to feel all this instead of only seeing.

I want to know all this. I want to explode in anger and curl up in pain, turn myself inside out and invent myself through fabricated fallopian tubes, taste the skin on the back of my hand and spit out bile, throw a punch that rounds back on my face and bloodies my nose, feel fear of dying and all the heart-thumping and breath-racing that goes with that. I want to smell the stale breath of the lover lying next to me and to look up into my mother's eyes—which are my child's eyes, which are my grandfather's eyes, which are my granddaughter's eyes—look up and enter into them, pair by pair, feel what it feels like to be them, looking out. I want to run in the afternoon heat and feel drenched by the evening rain, falter in speech and forget my own name as I grow old, feel the utter and intense hatred of a loved one who I've done wrong by and watch as hate turns to affection again when either I make amends or time lets them let go. This is what I want, this is what being born and living should be about; this is where I should be, instead of not-touching a golden body on a temple wall.

Is it so wrong to want it all, to be known for who I am, the elements kept hidden or revealed by the winds of time and change and mistake and misfortune, to feel blood go bad inside my veins and wonder how something so hot can grow so cold? Can I not be a man or a boy or a somebody, somebody who can be—yes, can be loved, is that so difficult to imagine? I have travelled the world over for an eternity, waiting, begging, pleading to be born, working things this way and that, over and under, and yes, I have loved well and loved fully, shown ways to love and learned from them. But in this form, this whisper that does not hint at body, the love cannot come back, cannot come near because there is no one here to bleed. Do I want it all? Right now, I just want my finger to feel a piece of rock made flesh. That is all I want. That is all.

Distilling returns

The little distillery in Nowgong looks exactly as it did the last time, thinks Piroja as she walks around the compound, the wall in slight but not overt disrepair, the gate's green paint letting only a bit of rust show through, the old house shedding a bit of plaster from its sides, but otherwise quite intact. The passion flower is in full bloom, even though it should have finished by now. A butterfly slips into her peripheral vision and then out again, a dog barks somewhere beyond the compound walls, and a high cumulus cloud drifts across the path of the sun bringing the haze down to a dusky glow. This is where she was born, she thinks, still contemplatively walking along the crooked line of bricks planted in the garden. This is where her father died. He had tried moving into Nowgong and set himself up as a semi-retired dastur, performing navjotes and other ceremonies when necessary, but that had made him feel too homeless. So he had moved back; the new distillery manager was only too glad to let out the upper floor to Jamshed. It was he who heard Jamshed coughing one night last week and asked him in the morning if all was fair. Jamshed told him his chest felt tired and his lungs weak, but he was otherwise quite well. The next night, the manager had heard that cough again, and in the morning, when Jamshed did not appear at his usual time or an hour later, he went to investigate.

"He was lying on his back, his eyes closed, a smile of peace on his face," the manager reported to Piroja solemnly. "He died like a saint, looking up and smiling."

Died like a saint. How, wonders Piroja, do saints die? And when, what choices do they make toward that end of life? Lineages and lines built out of bricks in the sand. Beginning and ending here. Right here.

"I can see you growing up here," says Sunila. She is standing a few feet in front of Piroja, who has not noticed her until she speaks.

"Yes. I imagine you could. You were here once yourself, you know."

"Hm, I remember. That is, I remember you telling me. Although it's strange, because I don't know if it's because you told me or if it is because I really remember, there is something familiar here."

"Familiar. Yes."

"Mum? I think I want to sing here."

"Sunila?"

"I think that's why I had to come here."

"Sunila, you came here for your grandfather's death."

"Yes. No. I mean, that's what brought me here. But I think I came here for a different reason."

"To sing."

"Yes. To sing."

"For your grandfather?"

"No, I think because of him, not for him. I think—I think I have to sing life into this place again."

Piroja looks around. The colour of sand permeates the compound. Really, apart from the passion flower blooms and the greenery in the upper branches of shade trees, it is all just the colour of sand. Piroja thinks of laughter as a child in this place. She thinks of tears as a young teenager in this place. She thinks of scorpions that do not kill and mango slices that she has never tasted and grandmothers that die so she might be born, and she thinks all of these things and none of them. She thinks of making dreams and forestalling dreams, of having futures cut off and pasts that irrevocably present themselves. Duty. Responsibility. What could have been could never have been.

"Sing? In this place?"

"No, Mum, not right here at the distillery. But here. India. Maybe Bombay. Somewhere that is … well, home."

"You see this as home?"

"No. Yes and no, but mostly not. I don't know. I just feel—"

"Like you're soaking in it?

"Uh-huh. That's it. Steeped like tea, more like it. Wondering where the yellow went. Putting tigers in my tank. That sort of thing."

"I see."

"Really?"

"No. Not really. But I think, yes, you should sing."

Sunila looks at this mother of hers who was so many things to her and to others and so little to herself. She vaguely remembers the boyish toys and outfits Piroja bought for her. She remembers how she heard a postman talking to a friend in a Halifax café, talking about the wondrous healing powers of this woman he delivered to, one Piroja Lal, enunciating every unfamiliar syllable as one does when used to reading names instead of speaking them aloud. She looks at her mother, who has brought good deeds about from her thoughts and words, but not really for herself. She opens her mouth to say thank you but burbles out a note an octave lower than she has ever uttered, followed by a note so high that not even those dogs who are supposed to hear everything can hear it. Piroja looks at her blankly. Sunila looks at her mother with the opposite of blankness. And this is what happens.

I watched the two of them that morning in the distillery compound, but later that day everything became quite a blur. Piroja called one of her friends, who called one of her friends in Bombay, and before you could say "Bollywood," the family was off to meet a music producer who had only to hear what erupted from Sunila's throat before signing her immediately. Within two months, Sunila had her first gig in Bombay, a sold-out affair, everyone wanting to come see the young Parsi girl ("But my, she is very boyish-foyish, no?") sing all the latest hits and then a number of songs even more fascinating, though no one had a notion of where they had been recorded. She played a room that sat fifty people the first night, 200 the next, and 350 illicitly packed in the next night, with a queue out the door and down the street another 200-people long. A week later, she played in a larger club. Before you could say "bhangra," there was a new sensation on the Bombay scene. The girl known only as Sunny had arrived. And, having started as a songstress playing nightclubs, she soon became a star performing in Delhi and Bahrain and Dubai and Cairo—an Eastern sensation. When jets were redirected to Cuba, there were one or two lost souls onboard who were dreaming of seeing young Sunny sing, and when a president was gunned down by her bodyguards, the hum in the aftersmoke would be replicating one of Sunny's renditions, and when populations grew into explosions and diesel went to CNG and bombs took apart northern playgrounds, there was the Voice, always, backing the scene.

Sunny sensation

Sunila sits in the middle seat of a middle row in the middle of the night, bound for Heathrow and then onward to Delhi and Bombay. She touches her torso and wonders where the sound within her comes from, how it hits the highs and lows she cannot herself make sense of. She experiments with a high-high note, so high that the elderly gentleman on her left and the young mother on her right cannot hear a thing, though the infant in his mother's arms does seem to register a response. Then she hits the lowest of low notes and if anyone were to hear it, they might confuse it with the rumbling jet engine as the 747 begins to follow a flight plan that will take it off the east coast of Canada and on to the United Kingdom.

What is that sound?

I sit beside Sunila, perhaps in the seat jacket in front of the elderly gentleman, perhaps tucked in between mother and child, speaking in dulcet tones to Sunila, telling her how things are going to be soaring now, just as we are, in the middle of the night, soaring from new worlds to seats of empire to colonized coasts. But Sunila appears not to be listening. She is quietly humming out of range and she does not hear me, even when I ask, *What is that sound?* I look at her eyebrows, deep and furrowed as she sings a song in her head and cannot hear the bluster around her. I look at her lips, so much like mine, if I were to have lips, that is, and I wonder why she has not kissed more with them, beautiful as they are, perched smartly below a Parsi nose and above a Hindu chin. I look at her finger as it taps on the seat tray and then points, idly at first, and then with more emphasis, at an imaginary star in an invisible constellation trapped just outside the wingtip. She still does not hear that sound, nor does anyone around her, or perhaps they simply carry on as if nothing really matters, confuse the chugging and clicking of things about to happen with the mechanical operation of a jet plane as it cuts through midnight North Atlantic air.

What is that sound?

I look at her shoulders, slightly hunched as she thinks of lyrics and arrangements and how to place her body just so as she hits a particular note on a particular night.

Sunila, can you hear me? I am right here. And what, what is that sound?

I look down at her breasts and wonder, would I have breasts like this or would they be deflated and flattened by a male physique or perhaps as imaginary as any other part of an imaginary body? And if Sunila slips out of earthly existence, what reminder to the world might there be that I existed at all, a wisp, a waif, a soul waiting to be born, a thought slipped and gone and thrown away? I look down at her belly and think that maybe I should or could be born from there, a different generation, generated differently, but that is not to be, not this time around the world. We have left Pearson and Mirabel far behind, and now we are headed for Heathrow, and from there—but what *is* that sound? I look down to Sunila's knees and wonder if mine would knock like hers or if they would be bulkier and more athletic, if only they were to be.

Sunila?

But she is lost to herself and to a world of bodies that I can only imagine or dream of, or perhaps I cannot even dream, but can just watch as if seeing a vision. I look down to her feet now, and I can hear her singing to me, singing so softly that the elderly gentleman and the young mother fall asleep as dawn approaches, the aircraft hurrying it along as it races the moon to sunrise, and the infant lolls its head from side to side in time to the music. But what is that

448

sound, the sound that comes from outside of Sunila's body, outside of my own sphere, outside coming inside?

The outside world is coming inside, from over 30,000 feet, where the air is one large, iced wind, and into the warm confines of this cylinder of humanity. It is time for me to leave, to wait for Sunila and her approach. I will not set this no-body down in London, or Delhi, or even Bombay. It is in Bombay, where Sunila is to play—the return of the Parsi girl—in two days' time. But I will not be there. I have other places to wait. I look down below Sunila's feet and see into the cavities of the plane, and still cannot understand that sound, though I have heard it all my life, waited for this moment to hear it for real. And for the first time, I feel tired, as if I must rest, but for how long, I cannot tell. I slip out of the porthole window of seat 46F, and I feel myself floating down in a summer dawn, down on to Irish coasts, feathering to the cold ocean, and I land, just another visitation and departure. It is cold, and I call out and back to Sunila, *What is that sound?* But now she does not answer because she cannot answer, and I am alone again.

Nowgong

I am sitting in a tree, high, high in the branches, overlooking the second floor of the manager's house. I start to hum a tune, a soft one, and if anyone hears it they will think it is the breeze rustling leaves, no more. But Sunila, of course, Sunila hears it and begins to hum along. She hums lower than I, and then higher, so that my hum keeps the centre point and she plays around it, though it sounds to all the world like one voice is humming a multiple-part harmony. I open my mouth to let loose a word or two, which will sound like a stronger breeze rushing around the window panes, and Sunila swallows and utters a most beautiful song, one that hits the high notes and sinks so low I think it will hit the ground. Singing softly together.

ACKNOWLEDGMENTS

This project began so long ago, and has undergone various incarnations, so it is both an imperative and endless task to acknowledge all who have been involved. My mother used to tell us stories of her early life which she later collected as a series of written memories that comprised a memoir of sorts. This text from Perin, and interviews I conducted with her, provided a perfect springboard for what would become an elaborate fiction based on kernels of history. *Reading A Zoroastrian Tapestry: Art, Religion, Culture*, edited by Pheroza J. Godrej and Firoza Punthakey Mistree, and *The Good Parsi: The Fate of a Colonial Elite in a Postcolonial Society*, by Tanya M. Luhrmann, helped enormously in contextualizing the social and cultural elements of the novel. Institutional support was also essential, and grants from the Canada Council for the Arts and the Social Sciences and Humanities Research Council gave me time and funds to research and write. I began this entire process while working for Emily Carr University, where administrative and collegial support was tremendous, and the opportunity to retreat to both the Leighton Studios and the "Babel, Babble, Rabble" thematic residency at the Banff Centre also provided much needed time for reflection and process. This support continued when I took employment at Thompson Rivers University, where I was able to work with writers, artists, and critical thinkers who participated in ongoing activities at the Centre for Innovation in Culture and the Arts in Canada (CiCAC). For all this institutional support, I am extremely grateful, and this becomes magnified when I think of all the wonderful friends and colleagues who have also been part of this process: Sita Kumar for her assistance with initial archival research; Hiromi Goto for her tireless editing of the first version of this manuscript; David Bateman for making such beautiful art in response to his many readings of many incarnations; Hank Bull, Makiko Hara, and the great people at Centre A and the Ottawa City Hall Gallery for staging the installation version of this project; and the folks at Arsenal, particularly Brian Lam and Robert Ballantyne, for their always strong vision, Susan Safyan for truly magnificent editing skills in the face of my often cantankerous resistance, and Shyla Seller for flexibility and exuberance in designing this book. In the final stages of research and revision, I so appreciated the company and inspiration of Ayumi Goto and my father, Parshottam Mathur, as we sought out and found the distillery site in Nowgong. The spirit of family and friends was always there, so to Anita Mathur, Glen Lowry, Roy Miki, Dina Khory, Sheriar Khory, Christine Kim, Yusuf Varachia, Roxanne Panchasi, Aruna Srivastava, Bill Hackborn, Louise Saldanha, Larissa Lai, Rita Wong, Sonia Smee, Shima Iuchi, David Chariandy, Sophie McCall, Bill Greene, Sharanpal Ruprai, Lisha Hassanali, Chris Bose, Will Garrett-Petts, Brendan Tang, Diyan Achjadi, Annette Hurtig, Jen Budney, Richard Swain, Sarita Srivastava, Shirley Bear, Peter Clair, all the others already mentioned, and so, so many others, my heart is open through your ongoing presence. Finally, and in full circle, to Perin Mathur (neé Panthaky), this always returns—thank you.

ASHOK MATHUR is the author of two previous novels, both published by Arsenal: *Once Upon an Elephant* and *The Short, Happy Life of Harry Kumar*. Born in Bhopal, India, he was raised in the Maritimes and has lived and worked in Calgary and Vancouver; currently, he is the Director for the Centre for Innovation in Culture and the Arts in Canada at Thompson Rivers University in Kamloops, BC.

An art show based on *A Little Distillery in Nowgong* appeared in Vancouver (Centre A) and Ottawa (City Hall Art Gallery) in 2009.